WITHDRAWN

No longer the property of the
Boston Public Library.
Sale of this material benefits the Library

Blood on Silk

AN AWAKENED BY BLOOD NOVEL

MARIE TREANOR

A SIGNET ECLIPSE BOOK

SIGNET ECLIPSE
Published by New American Library,
a division of Penguin Group (USA) Inc.,
375 Hudson Street, New York, New York 10014, USA
Penguin Group (Canada), 90 Eglinton Avenue East, Suite 700, Toronto,
Ontario M4P 2Y3, Canada (a division of Pearson Penguin Canada Inc.)
Penguin Books Ltd., 80 Strand, London WC2R 0RL, England
Penguin Ireland, 25 St. Stephen's Green, Dublin 2,
Ireland (a division of Penguin Books Ltd.)
Penguin Group (Australia), 250 Camberwell Road, Camberwell,
Victoria 3124, Australia (a division of Pearson Australia Group Pty. Ltd.)
Penguin Books India Pvt. Ltd., 11 Community Centre,
Panchsheel Park, New Delhi - 110 017, India
Penguin Group (NZ), 67 Apollo Drive, Rosedale, North Shore 0632,
New Zealand (a division of Pearson New Zealand Ltd.)
Penguin Books (South Africa) (Pty.) Ltd., 24 Sturdee Avenue,
Rosebank, Johannesburg 2196, South Africa

Penguin Books Ltd., Registered Offices:
80 Strand, London WC2R 0RL, England

First published by Signet Eclipse, an imprint of New American Library,
a division of Penguin Group (USA) Inc.

First Printing, September 2010
10 9 8 7 6 5 4 3 2 1

SIGNET ECLIPSE and logo are trademarks of Penguin Group (USA) Inc.

LIBRARY OF CONGRESS CATALOGING-IN-PUBLICATION DATA:

Treanor, Marie.
Blood on silk: an awakened by blood novel/Marie Treanor.
p. cm.
"A Signet Eclipse book."
ISBN 978-0-451-23156-7
1. Women college teachers—Fiction.   2. Vampires—Fiction.
3. Scots—Romania—Fiction.   I. Title.
PR6120.R325B58   2010
823'.92—dc21   2010019382

Set in Albertina • Designed by Elke Sigal

Printed in the United States of America

To Robert Gottlieb and Kerry Donovan,
who've made writing this book a pleasure
as well as a learning experience.

For Heather, MCDC,
who shares my longtime love of vampires.

And, as always, for my husband.

Blood on Silk

Chapter One

Saloman. Again.

"I'm beginning to hate that guy," Elizabeth muttered. "If he ever existed."

She spoke in English, so her informant, Maria, an almost entirely toothless old lady in black, merely grinned without a clue as to what she'd said.

"Thank you," Elizabeth said in Romanian, switching off the tape recorder on the table between them. "You've been very helpful." As she rose to her feet, Maria grinned again, adding to Elizabeth's suspicion that she'd just been fed a farrago of nonsense. It was as much for the locals' amusement as for her own—one of the challenges of her research was to pick out the "genuine" myths from the made-up ones, and it wasn't always easy.

The villagers who'd gathered curiously in the garden during the interview now fell back as Elizabeth stashed the recorder in her bag and turned to go.

"Thank you for the coffee," she added to the younger woman who'd brought it, and this time Maria's smile was genuine.

Elizabeth slung her bag over her shoulder and made her way along the shaded path toward the rickety garden gate. She'd get no further useful material here. The villagers would just vie with one another to impress her now—or fool her. It wasn't always clear which.

But although some of them stayed to chat with the old lady and her daughter, others walked toward the gate with her, as if eager to impart more nonsense. Elizabeth avoided eye contact, knowing she could be here for hours if she didn't. And she was tired. It had been a long day, and despite the weeks she'd spent here in the summer heat, she still found it grueling. She had never imagined she'd miss the cold and rain of a Scottish summer.

She liked this charming garden, though, full of fruit trees and vegetables as well as large, brightly colored roses and, most of all, the maze of paths lined with vines that had been trained to form an almost impenetrable roof. The shadowed tangled-lattice effect in the sunlight was pretty and, more important, cool.

"Miss Silk? What makes you think the vampire Saloman didn't exist?"

Damn. She'd met the speaker's gaze before she realized it, drawn by sheer surprise because he spoke excellent English. The other locals, as though accepting his victory, fell back and dispersed by other routes.

Elizabeth said, "Besides the word 'vampire,' you mean?"

The man smiled. She'd noticed him before, watching her a little too closely for comfort, while she talked to old Maria. Although she didn't doubt her ability to get rid of him—eventually— her internal alarm bell gave a warning tinkle. He was perhaps around forty years old and wore the traditional garb of most of the older villagers—long white shirt, belted in the middle, and dark trousers—and his dark, steady eyes were of the same nut-brown color as his sun-drenched skin. Only the mass of deeply etched lines around his eyes spoke of greater age, but then, the sun did that to people.

"If you want to hear about vampires, the villagers will tell you," he explained. "They always do."

She allowed herself a rueful smile. "I'm not the first to ask these questions around here, am I?"

"No. We've had people writing books, people making films, people who want to meet vampires, people who want to *be* vampires—"

"I'm a little more serious than that," Elizabeth interrupted. Her car was in sight, and she wanted nothing more than a cool bath and some dinner in her own room before a good night's sleep.

"Ah yes. You're writing your doctoral thesis." He held the gate open for her, and she cast him a quick glance as she passed, checking for any signs of mockery. The shading vines cast an intricate pattern of shadows across his face—an interesting, intelligent face, but not a comforting one. Something about him—something both attractive and repellent—bothered her. But then, she'd had that reaction to men before. Excessive interest might be flattering, but she didn't trust it.

"I heard you tell Maria," he added, obviously misunderstanding her suspicion. "What exactly are you writing about?"

She smiled and nodded a definite farewell as she passed through the gate. "Vampires, of course." Once she was away from the sheltering vines, the sun hit her like a wave.

He called after her. "So what's your problem with Saloman?"

Well, she could bore him with that till he shoved off. Then she could drive away, venting her frustration inside the car. She halted and frowned back over her shoulder. "That he keeps cropping up in too many eras," she all but snapped. "I have recorded stories of at least one Solomon before Christianity, several Salomans between the eleventh and the eighteenth centuries, and one Sal at the beginning of the twentieth. Oh, and Maria's Saloman in the nineteenth." She snorted. "And everyone claims they're the same man!"

"He's a vampire," her companion said reasonably. "He can exist for centuries."

Elizabeth cast him a withering stare and in spite of herself walked back to him as she dug in her bag for the car keys. "I'm writing a doctoral thesis, not a fairy tale. My interest is in the social conditions that inspired and fed the vampire superstitions, not in the gory details."

"And what were they?" the man inquired.

"What?" Distracted, Elizabeth fumbled the keys, dropping them into the recesses of her bag. She rummaged for them again.

"The social conditions," he said patiently.

Retrieving the keys, Elizabeth came up for air. She sighed. "Are you really interested in this?"

"Of course."

She shrugged. "My theory is that accusations of vampirism resemble accusations of witchcraft in western Europe, insofar as they were made against people who presented some kind of threat to their communities—either economic threats, such as the single, unsupported women who made up the bulk of so-called witches, or more physical ones. I believe accusations of vampirism were made after deaths to justify killings that would otherwise have been unlawful. There may be elements of guilt and other factors in there, too, but in basic terms, that's what vampire legends come down to—people who threatened villages by stealing, pillaging, excessive taxation, military levies. . . ." She trailed off. "Well, you get the idea. Anyway, generally it works. Most of the individual cases I've found support my theory. I can trace many such characters to legal documents and recordings of their deaths. But Saloman . . ."

She rattled the car keys against her palm in annoyance. "Saloman *keeps* cropping up, always as a vampire, and I can find no reason for the same personality to be inflicted on so many cases in so many different eras. Sometimes he's a hero, saving children from Turkish janissary recruiters, single-handedly repelling invaders or bandits; other times he's a villain destroying entire villages or tormenting individuals who've crossed him. But I can't find the remotest trace in folk memory, let alone in documentation, of his birth or anything that might corroborate his death. . . ."

"Oh, he died."

Elizabeth blinked. "I beg your pardon?"

"Saloman. He died. By a stake through the heart in 1697, to be precise, so I'm afraid Maria's nineteenth-century story was nonsense." He smiled. He had an engaging smile. "I'm sorry you wasted your time."

"Oh, I didn't," Elizabeth assured him. "I knew she was spinning me a yarn to keep me happy and entertain her friends."

It was his turn to blink in surprise, so she took pity on him. "What I find really interesting is that she picked that name. She could have called him Max or John or Count bloody Dracula, but

5

she didn't. She called him Saloman. Why? I hate the bastard because he doesn't fit into my theory and somehow I have to find out how to make him, or change my theory. But he is fascinating."

On impulse, she held out her hand. "Sorry. It's been good talking to you. Good-bye."

He took her hand with a shy smile. At least it looked shy in the shadows of the vines around the gateway. He might just have been baffled by her tirade. Despite the heat, his hand was cool and dry, its nails unexpectedly long and cared for.

"And to you. My name is Dmitriu. And if you like, I'll show you where to find Saloman's remains."

†

The village Dmitriu had shown her on the map wasn't far, although the roads were dreadful. Grasping the steering wheel tighter to control the beat-up old car as it bumped over a major pothole, she felt something sting her right palm.

As soon as she could, she took her right hand off the wheel, almost expecting to find a squashed bee, but there was nothing except a welling pinprick of blood. Frowning, with one eye still on the atrocious road through the mountains, she brought her hand to her mouth and licked the wound.

"Ouch," she muttered. Something was stuck in there. She waited until reaching a relatively smooth stretch of road, then laid both hands together on the wheel and tried to pick it out. It pulled free with a pain sharp enough to make her wince. A thorn—a large rose thorn. She must have picked it up at Maria's without noticing until she'd driven it farther into her hand by gripping the wheel so hard. Blood oozed from it sluggishly.

"All I need," she muttered, licking it again before deciding to ignore the sharp pain. A thorn would hardly kill her, and she wanted to press on. Although the sun was going down, she couldn't resist the opportunity of at last finding some sort of context for the wretched Saloman character. Dmitriu's unexpected information had given her a new lease on life, banishing the lethargy she'd felt at Maria's. Besides, this was it: Sighesciu....

It wasn't the prettiest village in these mountains. Despite the unspoiled natural scenery that surrounded it, Sighesciu itself looked run-down and poor. Leaning forward to peer farther up the hill, Elizabeth glimpsed a bulldozer and a mechanical digger. There were no signs of the ruined castle Dmitriu had spoken of, though. Taking the turn that appeared to lead up the hill toward the bulldozer, she let her mind linger on the enigmatic Dmitriu.

She'd been relieved that he hadn't suggested coming with her, had just sent her to the car for her map while he sat in the shade of Maria's vines to wait. There, he'd shown her the village and the hill and said that although he couldn't come right now, he might wander up there later to see how she got on.

Elizabeth wasn't quite sure how she felt about seeing him again. He was an intriguing character, apparently well educated despite his "peasant" style of dressing. She realized she'd no idea what he did for a living, although his manicured hands clearly showed that he wasn't a farmer. Insatiably curious, she wanted to know more about him—so long as it was all kept as platonic as their interaction that afternoon.

Her lips twisted into a smile and she laughed at herself. She was still harboring unrequited feelings for Richard, her PhD supervisor, who found her no more than an amusing curiosity. In any case, Elizabeth was smart enough to understand that half the attraction of Richard was his unattainability, if there was such a thing.

As she drew up to the top of the hill, she saw that the workmen were finishing for the day. Several cast her curious glances as they took off their hard hats and meandered past her battered old car. She'd bought it very cheaply in Budapest, but, although it didn't look like much, it had gotten her safely around many inaccessible and isolated villages in both Hungary and Romania, and she was almost growing fond of it.

Emerging into the gathering dusk, she wondered whether she'd left too late after all. She wouldn't be able to see so much if she had only a flashlight beam to work by. She might have to come back in the morning anyway. As it was, she had a bit of a drive ahead of her to the hotel at Bistriţa.

Casting that difficulty to one side, she looked around for someone to talk to. One man among those streaming back down the hill detached himself and called in Romanian, "Madam? Can I help you?"

"Thanks, I hope so! I was told there was a castle here."

The man took off his hard hat and gestured around him. Elizabeth took in the piles of stone and rubble scattered across the site.

"Ah."

"We leveled all that was left today, but there was nothing much to see anyway. Tomorrow we'll take away all the debris so we can begin building. Perhaps you've already reserved a house?"

"Oh, no. I don't live here. I'm just visiting."

The man laughed at that, as though the very idea of anyone looking like her—a pale-skinned northerner with untidy, strawberry blond hair; rather worn, old cropped jeans; a cheap sleeveless top; and a cotton hat dangling down her back from a string around her neck—could possibly be Romanian.

"These are holiday homes," he explained, "for foreigners who like our country."

"It's a very beautiful country," Elizabeth said with genuine appreciation. It was on the tip of her tongue to add that she couldn't afford luxury housing for foreigners, when it occurred to her that he might look on her request with more favor if he thought her a potential customer. After all, he appeared to be some kind of foreman or even manager.

She tried a smile and hoped it didn't look too guilty. "Would you mind if I stayed for a few minutes and looked around? Just to get a feel for the place and admire the views?"

He shrugged. "You're welcome. There are no gates to lock. Take as long as you like. Just be careful. We still have some old foundations to fill in, and some of them are pretty deep."

"I'll be careful," she assured him. "Thanks."

She made to pass on, but with obvious concern, he asked, "Are you hurt?"

She blinked, following his frowning gaze to the hem of her top, which now boasted a bright red, shapeless bloodstain. There was another smear across the leg of her jeans where she'd wiped her bleeding palm.

"Oh, no, it was just a rose thorn. I bleed easily, but it'll stop in a minute."

Satisfied, the man walked on, and Elizabeth began to pick her way over the rubble. Dmitriu had claimed there was a chapel here, and beneath it, a crypt. But neither was obvious at first glance.

Elizabeth rummaged in her bag until she found her flashlight. She was careful to hold it in her uninjured left hand, and shone the beam into the debris, looking for any carvings in the fallen stone, any lettering that might give her a clue. But if there had ever been anything, it had been obliterated by time and bulldozers.

She shivered as if someone had walked over her grave—instead of the other way around. But she couldn't quite laugh at herself. The hairs on the back of her neck stood up like hackles, and she spun around to see who was watching her.

No one. She was alone on the derelict site. Even the departing workmen had been more interested in their supper than in her.

What's the matter with you, Silk? she jeered at herself. *Vampires getting to you at last?*

Of course not. It was just that the sun seemed to set so quickly here, and this place did have an intriguing atmosphere. She *liked* atmospheres and had learned by experience that they could be useful guides. She preferred hard evidence, of course, but when that was lacking, sometimes you found something just by going with a hunch, a feeling.

Other times, you found nothing at all—like now.

Giving up, she spun around to head back to the car. Her foot slipped, and she flung out her right hand to save herself from falling. She winced as stones pressed into the thorn hole in her palm, and when she dragged herself upright, the flashlight flickered crazily across the tiny smears of blood on the stones. As another drip appeared, she brushed the dirt off her hand and thrust her palm at her mouth before following the beam of the flashlight to its end—a gap in the ground into which gravel and more rubble were already falling. That must have been where her foot slipped.

Elizabeth crouched down beside it, away from the bulk of the shifting ground, and shone her beam into the widening gap.

It was a room, like a crypt.

Excitement soared, drowning the last of her silly anxieties. She could make out rough carvings on the walls, perhaps angel figures. . . .

Elizabeth reached out with care and gave the rubble an encouraging push before leaping back to admire the effects. A little irresponsible, perhaps, but how else was she supposed to get in? She doubted her little avalanche was capable of damaging anything.

When the ground stilled, she edged forward. All seemed secure on this side of the wide hole. She knelt, trying to gauge the distance to the ground of the crypt. She was sure it was a crypt. It smelled musty and damp. If she were fanciful, she would have said it smelled of death, although any human remains would surely be long past the rotting stage. Maybe there were rats—not a nice thought. But she caught no scurrying creatures in the beam of her flashlight, and she thought she could lower herself down there without difficulty—"dreep," in the language of her childhood.

First, she rolled a fair-sized boulder to the gap and let it fall in. She might need it later to stand on to get herself out. Then, positioning herself, she gripped the side of the hole and let her feet slide through until she dangled. She let go and jumped the last foot or so to the ground.

It was an easy landing. Triumphant, she dragged the flashlight back out of her bag and shone it around the room. They *were* angels on the walls, worn with age but still remarkably fine for an out-of-the-way place like this. It made sense, she supposed. If this Saloman was important enough to have inspired so many legends, even after he'd been staked as a vampire, he would have been a rich, even princely, man.

The trouble was, there seemed to be no tomb—no markings

on the wall to denote he was buried behind them, no tomb on the floor. There were just angels carved into the wall and broken stone steps that had once led up to the gap she'd almost fallen down, where the chapel used to be. It was exactly as Dmitriu had described.

Except for the lack of a body or any kind of inscription.

Bugger. He must have made it up too, just as Maria had done. He couldn't have known about this hidden room—it had obviously been sealed for centuries, and there was no evidence whatsoever that a chapel had ever stood above it.

So Saloman's origins remained elusive. But at least the angels were pretty.

Elizabeth laid down her bag, pulled her camera out of it, and propped the flashlight on the bag to shine upward. Walking around the room, she photographed each angel in turn, changing the direction of the light as necessary. In the final corner, she stubbed her toe on something—rubble, she imagined, although her impatient glance could pick out nothing large enough. Ignoring it, she aimed the camera at the large angel above her head.

A shiver ran all the way up her spine to her neck, jerking the camera in her hand. She steadied it, irritated when a drop of blood from her hand distracted her.

"Whoever bled to death from a rose thorn?" she demanded, wiping her hand on her thigh again. Finally, she raised the camera and took the picture. And when she stepped back, she saw the sarcophagus right in front of her.

She blinked. "How the . . . ?" Perhaps her eyes had just gotten used to the particularly dark corner, but was the light really so poor that she'd missed *that*? Or was her observation so erratic? She must be *bloody* tired.

Grabbing up the flashlight, she shone it full on the stone sarcophagus. It was the size of a large man, its lid carved with a human figure in sharp relief, almost as if the corpse lay there looking at her.

As beautifully carved as the angels, it was a wonderful, detailed piece of art in its own right. She shone the flashlight from its booted legs upward over the long, open cloak, which revealed an ornate but empty sword belt. The emptiness might have been explained by the broken sword protruding from his stone chest; Gory, yet tastefully done. So *this* must be the basis of the vampire legends.

She'd need an expert to date the carvings, of course, but late seventeenth century seemed about right. That meant she'd have to look for differences between the legends before and after Dmitriu's date of 1697. There were a lot of those for so young a man. She'd also need to reanalyze those stories set before his likely birth date, perhaps around 1670.

In fact, she needed to speak to Dmitriu again, and soon. She'd never expected to find anything as beautiful as this. . . .

She took one hasty snap before dropping the camera back into her bag. Fascinated, she gazed down at the likeness of the man she now believed to be the legendary Saloman. The still, stone face appeared surprisingly youthful. With no martial beard or ridiculous mustache like Vlad the Impaler's, it was just a young, handsome countenance with deep-set, open eyes.

Why weren't his eyes closed? The irises and pupils of each were well delineated; they might even have been colored under the centuries of dust. Christ, he even had eyelashes, long and thick enough to be envied by most women.

But there was nothing else remotely feminine about this face.

Its nose was long, slightly hooked, giving an impression of arrogance and predatory inclinations. On either side were cheekbones to die for, high and hollowed, and beneath, a pair of perfect, sculpted lips, full enough to speak of sensuality, firm enough to denote power and determination, and a strong, pointed chin. Long, thick hair lay in stone waves about his cloaked shoulders, and again Elizabeth could almost imagine that the dust covered black paint.

The sculptor seemed to have imbued a lot of character into that dead stone face, as if he'd known him well and liked him; yet he'd also captured a look of ruthlessness, an uncomfortable hardness that sat oddly with the faint, dust-caked lines of humor around his eyes and mouth. Well, he wasn't the first or the last bastard to have a sense of humor.

And besides, if he was a likable man and the true hero of some of the legends she'd listened to, why had he been killed in such a way? Where had the stories of atrocity come from? His enemies? He was a mirror of Vlad the Impaler perhaps, except no one before Bram Stoker had made Dracula a vampire. The Saloman vampire stories were far older, and they came from natives.

There was a splash of discoloration beside his mouth. Frowning, she reached out and touched it. Wet—it was a drop of her blood.

"Oops."

But the carved face was so beautiful that she let her fingers linger, brushing against the cold, dusty, stone lips. Another drop of blood landed there, and she tried to scrub it off with her thumb. All that achieved was another drip and rather grotesquely red lips on the carving, so she yanked her guilty hand back and began to examine the rest of the sarcophagus.

It sat on a solid stone table, but it wasn't just the lid; it was the whole sarcophagus that was carved into the shape of a man, and she could find no hinges in the smooth stone. Perhaps the body was in the table underneath? Unless there were hinges or some kind of crack on the other side.

Leaning over the sarcophagus, she ran her fingers along its far side, but she felt only the detailed outlines of muscled arm and hip and thigh, so lovingly carved that just stroking them seemed intimate. She stretched farther so that her hair and jaw brushed against the cold stone of his face, and she felt along the table instead. It too appeared to be one solid piece of stone. So where the hell was the body?

Movement stirred her hair, almost like a lover's breath on her skin. Startled, she jerked up her head, but before she could leap away, or even see what was happening, something sharp pierced her neck and clamped down hard.

Chapter Two

She couldn't move, couldn't even cry out. Somewhere she knew she should be terrified, but in reality her brain was far too busy trying to work out what the hell had happened.

There was pain at the side of her neck where it seemed to be stuck to the face of the carved sarcophagus—a strange, cold pain that suddenly heated as whatever had gripped her began to suck.

Now the fear surged, deluging her. She felt the blood rushing through her veins, away from her heart, and she knew she was about to die. Worse than that, the cold thing clamped around her neck grew warm, moved on her skin, and the rushing of her blood became a stream of weird, sensual pleasure. Fire and ice flowed together in her veins as she was held captive. Everything seemed to tighten in her body—her muscles, her nipples, her clenching womanhood—until it came to her in a flash that this treacherous, paralyzing sexual response was killing her.

With a yell, as much for self-encouragement as fear, she tore herself free, falling off the sarcophagus into a heap on the floor and scrabbling backward, away from whatever had attacked her.

She knew, she'd always known, it came from the sarcophagus itself, and yet the sight of the carving rising from the table in a cloud of dust drew a long, low whine from her that she couldn't control. Her neck throbbed in agony; it felt slippery with her own blood under her questing, trembling fingers. Her heart hammered with the force of a pile driver, as the thing shook itself and emerged through the scattering dust toward her.

Not a beautiful stone carving but a beautiful, terrifying man, heart-churningly three dimensional as he yanked the broken sword from his chest and threw it to the ground. A sound seemed to hiss from between his teeth. It might have been pain, but right now, she didn't care.

In the spotlight of her fallen, wavering flashlight, he regarded her from burning, coal black eyes. His cloak, now streaked with black, fell around him in stiff, dust-laden folds as he walked forward with slow, deliberate strides. Beneath it, his clothing was torn across the chest, but no blood oozed from the sword wound. His pale lips parted.

"Silly girl." The deep, almost sepulchral voice vibrated through her entire body. "That's no way to break off a relationship like ours."

She scrabbled backward in a futile attempt to escape the horror, but inexorably, he kept coming.

"Is it?" he said, bending to take her numb hand and drag her to her feet. She stumbled and, appalled by the strength in his cold, flexible fingers, which didn't feel like stone at all, she yanked her hand free. Even then, she suspected he let her.

"Is it what?" she demanded. God knew she didn't care, but

some instinct always made her fight back in the wrong situations. She barely knew what she was saying.

"Is it sensible to break away from me like that?" he said with exaggerated patience. "Look what you've done to your throat."

He stretched out one long, pale hand toward the side of her neck; she flinched, staggering out of his reach. Even in the dim light she could see dust particles glistening on his skin, clinging in the creases of his knuckles.

"What *I* did?" she screeched in outrage. "I didn't bite my own throat like a ... like a ..." The whole impossible situation was collapsing in on her, burying her in a morass of ghastly confusion and questions.

His eyes gleamed. "Like a vampire?" he mocked, coming after her. There was nowhere to go but backward, until the wall ground into her shoulder blades and buttocks, and still he kept coming. Tall and broad-shouldered as he was, his very size threatened her. Most of his handsome face was in shadow, hiding any expression. She could make out only his eyes, blacker than the surrounding darkness, yet glistening with some deep, wild hunger it hurt to look at.

He lifted his hand once more to the wound in her throat. His fingertip was cold, yet seemed to burn her skin. She gasped, quivering, and when he bent his head toward her again, gazing at her bleeding injury, she began to fight, crashing her fists into his chest, pushing uselessly against his shoulders.

He smelled of earth and cold stone, and gave off no sense of human warmth. So why did her body begin to weaken its resistance? Her fists, her struggles, made no impression on him. He continued to lower his head to her wounded neck. At least she could no longer see those terrible eyes. . . .

At the first touch of his lips, she gave up; she could do nothing against him, and some dark, perverse part of her remembered the unique, agonizing thrill of his first bite.

But he didn't bite. He surrounded the wound with his lips and licked it once. She shuddered, helpless in the grip of fear and something she couldn't—or wouldn't—name. Then he lifted his head, and she stared at him, speechless, because the pain had gone.

The hunger hadn't left his eyes, but in the glimmer of her flashlight beam, she thought it was overlaid with mockery. The bastard was laughing at her.

"I'm saving the rest for later," he explained.

Her eyes widened. He was letting her live after all? At least for another minute. "L-later?" she stammered.

His fingers trailed across her throat, butterfly light, making her gasp. "Later. Your blood is strong and heady. I'm taking time to absorb it." He bent nearer her, inhaling, almost sniffing the air around her head and throat. The skin of his face looked so smooth, she had an insane urge to reach up and touch it. His sculpted lips moved faintly, as if a smile almost danced across them, never quite forming before it faded.

"Interesting," he observed, and his voice was different now, quiet, almost whispering, with just a hint of hoarseness. "I have to thank you for waking me. . . . What is your name?"

She swallowed. "Elizabeth. Elizabeth Silk."

The almost smile tugged at his lips and vanished. His cheek brushed against hers, barely touching; yet her stomach seemed to plunge. "Silk. How apt," he murmured. "Like your hair . . . and your skin, so soft and warm . . ."

His fingertips caressed her face, then slid down over her chin to her throat, and she gasped, jerking in panic. But the movement only brought her into contact with his body. He was hard and solid, and surely that stiff ridge against her stomach was his erection. . . . Vampires had erections? Unless that part of him was still made of stone?

Oh Jesus Christ and fuck!

She shrank, pressing her back into the wall once more. Shocked, she could feel wetness between her legs. *It's just fear, not lust; it can't be. . . .*

"And you are English," he said, changing to that language without warning.

"Scottish," she returned mechanically. *What the hell does that matter?*

He inclined his head, clearly humoring her. His body touched hers at breast and hips, hardening her nipples into aching peaks. Perhaps he felt them, for he said, "Do you know how long it has been since I have had a meal or a woman?"

Her stomach seemed to melt into her womb. Sweat had broken out on her palms and was trickling down between her breasts. But somehow she managed to do the math. "Three hundred and twelve years?"

His gaze dropped to her lips. "Don't ask me. After the first couple of centuries, those decades just fly by." He lifted his hand from her neck, tracing one tapered fingertip along her lower lip. She was afraid to move.

"Do they really?" she managed.

"No. But they let me work up some heady appetites."

"For what?" She sounded more suspicious than terrified. Was that good? Perhaps. The almost smile reappeared and vanished as his face leaned nearer hers.

"For dinner," he answered. "And dalliance."

His finger slid to the corner of her lips, pushing gently until she gasped, and when her mouth opened, he took it with his.

Heat consumed her, drowning her in some strange, welcome weakness. His cool lips moved across hers, sampling, parting them. He should have tasted of dust and death and corruption. At the very least he hadn't brushed his teeth in 312 years; yet what she inhaled in panic was something overwhelmingly seductive, an earthy sweetness, powerful and masculine, and, God help her, she wanted it. She wanted to give herself to his mouth, feel his kiss deepen and dominate while he pressed that large, hard body closer into her. She wanted to push herself against the hardness nudging her abdomen. She wanted it between her legs, pushing into her, because she'd never known a kiss as arousing as this, and the sex would be so . . .

Oh God!

Shuddering, she forced herself to be still, praying she'd given away none of her depravity. His lips released hers, and she glared into his shadowed face, summoning anger to hide the unexpected emotions that frightened her almost more than he did. But although she shoved his shoulder hard in an effort to barge past, he remained immovable in her path.

"You taste good enough to eat," he said hoarsely. His hand swept down from her cheek to her throat and breast, where it lingered, spreading a fire she couldn't control. Fresh moisture pooled in her panties. Again she had to fight not to lean into that hand—it seemed determined to tease rather than deliver. But he must have felt her pebbled nipple poking through her top, for his gaze followed his hand while his thumb traced a circle around her areola. "And beneath these very odd clothes, your luscious little body cries out to be fucked. You can take care of both my immediate needs."

She closed her eyes, as if that could remove the temptation as well as the terror. In a strange, strangled voice, she said, "What's wrong with the clothes?" If nothing else, it should distract him. She had to think about getting away from him, not about getting into his pants.

His hand brushed the curve of her hip. "Workman's trousers," he said with contempt, sweeping the caress upward until his hand lay just under her breast. "And a whore's bodice. Are you a whore, Elizabeth Silk from Scotland?"

"No!"

"Yet my coarse language doesn't offend you. You are an intriguing mix. And since you have awakened me, would you like me to awaken you?"

She pushed past him, hoping to fool him by the act of an offended woman—which, in fact, wasn't all act for some reason she hadn't quite grasped.

He let her go three steps, four. Her heart thumping, she worked out that if she got two more paces in, she could leap for the boulder, spring off it, and grasp the side of the hole to haul herself up into the open. He could follow, of course, but if she made it to the car . . .

One more step. She could feel his eyes boring into the back of her head. He had such bloody scary eyes—powerful, alien, opaque, and yet so deep you could drown in them. And hungry . . . *Don't think about them, don't even imagine what he could do. . . .*

Another step. She drew in her breath—and suddenly he was there in front of her. She cried out but had no time to run, for he took hold of her hips and drew her hard against him. At the same time, he gyrated his own hips just enough to make her bite back a moan of sudden, raging lust as the clothed ridge of his penis slid against her pubic bone.

"Don't pretend," he whispered. "I can smell your arousal at twenty paces. Whore or virgin, you're mine."

He lowered his head, and though she strained away from him, he buried his face in her neck. She grasped his broad shoulders through the dusty velvet cloak and tried in vain to push him off. His lips glided over her skin, finding the sensitive spot of her previous neck wound, which no longer hurt but tingled in treacherous welcome, even when his teeth grazed against it.

"It's sweet to satisfy both lusts together...." The words vibrated through her neck, shooting straight to her core. "For each of us." He sucked the skin of her throat into his mouth, and she couldn't keep still, instead jerking her head back. One of his hands tangled in her hair, holding her head. He bent her backward so that their lower bodies pressed closer together. His knee nudged her legs apart, and the column of his erection found the hot tenderness between.

Clutching his shoulders, she let out a moan that was half sob. His teeth teased her neck; his tongue flickered out in short, sensual licks. His whole mouth seemed to move on her skin, seducing her not just to compliance but to blind, desperate need. She wanted to feel his teeth bite into her flesh, to know again the strange icy pleasure as he drew her blood into his mouth, into his own body. And if he was inside her at the same time, giving her sweet, urgent sex . . .

How can I even think I want that? It's him, some dark, perverse magic. . . .

But would it really be so very bad to give in? To know this wicked thrill just once?

His hand roved over the curve of her bottom, drawing her harder into him, and it felt so good, so amazing. . . .

I shouldn't feel like this. I'm not this person!

"No," she gasped out.

Her fingers were gripping his shoulders so tightly that they hurt. She forced them to loosen. His lips stilled on her neck, then released her skin with one last teasing lick.

"No?" He lifted his head, regarding her with open mockery. "You like to deny yourself. Perhaps you're right. The pleasure is often heightened by postponement."

"You're full of shit," she said shakily. She didn't mean to say it; the words just came out. His eyes widened, giving her at least the satisfaction of having taken him by surprise. He stared at her for several seconds, while she wondered in desperation if that was anger, incomprehension, or simple lust boiling in his dark, menacing eyes.

None of those, it seemed.

The "vampire" threw back his head and laughed.

At the same time, he released her, and she backed away from him, listening to her own uneven breath rasping in her throat.

"Oh, decidedly, we will meet again," he promised. His eyes gleamed as he regarded her retreating person.

"No, we bloody won't."

"Have faith, my little thistle."

Stunned, she finally comprehended that he was letting her go. She turned, stumbling, then almost tripped over her bag before she grabbed it up and ran on shaky legs to the boulder. It was clumsy, but at least the fear lent her strength, for she took only one jump to grasp at the ground above and scrabble, climb, and haul herself through the gap into the blessed fresh air above.

Though there was no light out here, the velvet sky was clear, shining such welcome, beautiful starlight down upon her that she wanted to weep. Instead, she staggered to her feet and cast around for her car.

He'd said he wouldn't follow, but it seemed she couldn't stop running. She needed only seconds to reach the car, unlock it, and throw herself and her bag inside. A few more seconds saw the key thrust into the ignition, and then she was moving, driving hell-for-leather for the road, for Bistriţa, and for her hotel and blessed sanity.

But she was going too fast on the narrow, winding hill. When the figure loomed out of the darkness in front of her, she knew, even as she slammed on the brakes, that she couldn't avoid him. In the screech of tires, she had one glimpse, appallingly close up, of Dmitriu's dark, distinctive face, and then it vanished.

Before the car finished its final jolt, she threw herself out into the road. She ran all around the car, looked underneath it, and even searched the ditch at the side of the road on her hands and knees. But there was no sign of Dmitriu or anyone else.

She sat back on her heels, dragging one trembling hand through her hair. "I'm going mad," she whispered. "I'm truly going insane."

And then, since she could do nothing else, she stood up, climbed back into the car, and drove on with a last look around her. But this time, heeding whatever warning her disturbed brain had been trying to give her, she took it slowly and carefully.

✝

She'd gotten in. That much was clear from the gaping hole in the ground, and the wild, scrambled tracks surrounding it. What else she had done wasn't so obvious. After all, her white, drawn face as he'd glimpsed it through the car windshield might have mirrored no more than shock at almost running him over. And she lived.

Nevertheless, cautious by nature, Dmitriu stood well back from the entrance to the crypt and reached out with all his senses.

Vampire. There was certainly a vampire close by. He could hear the slow beating of the creature's heart and smell the recycled blood that powered his existence, but he couldn't identify him. He could be a strong vampire, masking his signature, or he could just be a weak fledgling. Either way, the creature was close. Below in the crypt, perhaps, or . . .

His spine prickled, and Dmitriu spun around, fists raised to defend himself.

The vampire sat on a boulder that had once formed part of the castle. His cloak stretched out behind him, barely stirring in the cool breeze of the night. Across his knees lay a broken sword, the top third of the blade apparently snapped off. His strong, handsome face was in profile, and he seemed to be gazing upward at the stars, but Dmitriu didn't let that fool him. The vampire knew exactly where he was and what stance he had taken.

Dmitriu let his hands fall to his sides. "Saloman."

The vampire smiled, almost as if the last three hundred years had never been. He rose to his feet in one quick, fluid movement, letting the broken sword fall to the ground, and Dmitriu saw that he wasn't masking. He was weak. It was mere willpower that gave him strength enough to move, to walk toward him.

Emotion threatened to choke him. It seemed after all that he, Dmitriu, was the weak one, for it was he who stumbled in, closing the distance between them.

"Dmitriu." Saloman embraced him, and he fell to his knees,

taking the cold white hand in his and pressing it to his lips. "You sent her."

Dmitriu nodded. A drop of blood had fallen from his eye onto Saloman's hand; embarrassed, he wiped both on his shirt before rising.

Saloman said, "How did you know?"

"I could smell her. She reeks of Tsigana. You let her go."

"For now. There's more to be had here than an instant of gratification." Saloman caught and held his gaze, and with massive relief, he realized at last that he was safe. Saloman had lost neither his memory nor his sanity in the frozen centuries. It didn't matter. Dmitriu would have done this, whatever the consequences. "I am grateful."

Dmitriu swallowed. "There's no need of thanks. I only wish I could have done it sooner."

"You didn't forget."

"I couldn't." A thousand questions choked him about how it had been for him and how much he remembered; yet he couldn't bring himself to ask. He didn't want to know. Distracting himself, he bent and picked up the fallen sword. It was surprisingly light, and the hilt wasn't Saloman's. In fact, it wasn't even a sword. Silver paint peeled and crumbled over a blade made of red-stained wood.

"So that's how they did it," he exclaimed. A stake disguised as a weapon that only threatened humans. "A contemptible ruse!"

"Several ruses," Saloman said without apparent interest. He'd had three hundred years to digest it, but Dmitriu wasn't fooled. He hadn't forgiven or forgotten.

Dmitriu lifted his gaze. "What will you do now?"

Saloman smiled. He stretched out his arms and turned as if

embracing the whole world from this hilltop. "Live," he said. "Feed. Fuck. Frolic." He came to a halt and stared into Dmitriu's eyes. "And take back what is mine."

Dmitriu smiled. For the first time in decades it felt good to be undead. "No 'f,'" he pointed out.

Saloman's lips quirked. "I'll think of one."

Dmitriu's heart pumped. He tipped his head to one side. "I can help with the feed. My blood is stronger than most these days."

"It should be," said Saloman, reaching for him. "It's mine."

Dmitriu's head jerked back as the other's fangs pierced his skin. He shuddered at the strength of Saloman's desperate pull, losing himself in the exquisite pleasure, not unmingled with fear. "Just don't bloody kill me."

Saloman lifted his head, blood trickling from the corner of his mouth. "No guarantees," he whispered, and plunged once again into Dmitriu's jugular, bending him back like a twig with the force of his hunger.

Chapter Three

$\mathcal{E}$lizabeth woke with a thud.

"Domnişoară?" Someone was rapping on her door. "Miss Silk?"

Elizabeth dragged her hand across her face and through her hair. She felt as if she'd just fallen asleep. "Hello?" she croaked.

"Can we come in?" asked a woman's voice, but it didn't sound like the chambermaid. Perhaps this was a different girl.

Elizabeth glanced at her travel clock—nine o'clock. She was normally up, breakfasted, and out researching by this time. But then, she hadn't gotten back until midnight.

"Domnişoară!"

"Coming," Elizabeth mumbled, sitting up and staggering out of bed in one clumsy movement. She grabbed some clean clothes from her open suitcase on her way to the door. Unlocking it, she opened the door a crack before heading back toward the bathroom. "Give me five minutes and I'll be out of your hair." That probably didn't make much sense in Romanian, judging by the girl's lack of response.

"Miss Silk? We're not hotel staff."

Elizabeth turned in surprise. Through her half-open bedroom door she could see one woman and two men, young and casually dressed, though not as casually as she was in the thin and ancient T-shirt she wore for sleeping. Clutching her clothes in front of her like a shield, she walked toward her visitors once more.

"What can I do for you?" she asked, puzzled.

"We need to talk to you," said one of the men. He was tall, fair, good-looking in a robust, square sort of a way. He was perhaps her own age, just shy of thirty. "About last night."

Her heart seemed to plunge to her toes. "Last night? Oh shit. Dmitriu?" They were the police. She really *had* run Dmitriu over and just hadn't seen the body.

"Dmitriu?" The three exchanged baffled glances, leaving Elizabeth to sway with relief.

"Sorry," she said. "It was a bad night. Er—who are you?"

"My name is Konrad," the fair man said. "This is Mihaela, and István. May we come in?"

"I'm not dressed."

"We'll wait outside," the girl, Mihaela, said.

Elizabeth, still half asleep and dizzy with relief at not having killed Dmitriu, shut the door on them and went into the bathroom for a quick shower.

As the cool water hit her, so did understanding.

By the time she'd pulled on her cotton skirt and top and was dragging the comb through her wet hair, she was sure she knew who her unexpected visitors were and why they were here.

It had taken her most of the drive back to Bistriţa before she'd realized the Saloman thing had been a trick. But she'd gotten there in the end, with a weird mixture of relief, guilty shame, and cringing humiliation for having fallen for it and been so damned scared, not to mention turned on. Who'd have thought staid, frigid Elizabeth Silk would have been so aroused by the idea of the undead she'd been studying so clinically for two years? Even now, the memory made her squirm. Thank God no one at St. Andrews would ever know.

But these people, her morning visitors, must have had something to do with last night. They must have been part of the trick. She wasn't quite sure what they'd done or how, but she knew it had gone too far. Probably they knew it too, which is why they were here.

She should have examined them with more care. One of them could be "Saloman." Involuntarily, she touched her throat, where she'd imagined the vampire bit her. A spooky atmosphere was a wonderful thing. She'd been so sure he'd pierced her skin, drunk her blood, when all he'd done was gum her a little. There was no wound, no pain, just a residual sensitivity. Even she had suffered more bruising before from a love bite. The dried blood that had spattered her neck and her top clearly hadn't come from there at all but from the annoying thorn wound in her palm, now healing at last—unless it was fake blood from the vampire trickery.

Oh well, she'd made a complete arse of herself and would have to live with it. Her one hope of retaining a smidgen of self-respect now was to accept their apology with dignity and good humor.

She threw down the comb and gazed doubtfully at her reflection in the mirror. She supposed she didn't look much like a serious academic. Like most of her clothes—old, and picked up from charity shops in Scotland—this Gypsy print skirt and loose cotton top, together with her long, damp, unstyled hair, made her appear younger than her true twenty-nine years. She had little gravitas and nothing, she suspected, in the way of presence. But this was all there had ever been, and it would have to do.

She crossed to the door to face her pranksters. At least she'd find out how they did it. She hoped it would prove stunningly clever, just so she didn't feel such a gullible fool.

Taking a deep breath, she opened the door.

They still stood there in the narrow passage, leaning against the walls, breaking off a whispered conversation to straighten up and gaze at her from serious, anxious eyes.

"Come in," Elizabeth said with resignation.

They filed inside, just a little self-consciously, and sat side by side on her hastily made bed, glancing at one another with what seemed to be nervousness.

Good. Serves you bloody right.

Refusing to make it easy for them, she stood there and waited. It was good practice for the next year when students would line up before her like this to make excuses for not handing in essays.

Glancing from the fair man to the dark one, she was sure neither of them had played the part of Saloman. She was glad of that. She never wanted to lay eyes on that character ever again. She did wonder how much of it they'd seen, although she'd been pretty sure at the time there had been no one else in the crypt.

Konrad took a deep breath and spoke. "Miss Silk, are you aware what you did last night?"

She let a cynical smile twist her lips. "I'm aware I was set up, if that's what you mean."

"Set up?" He frowned.

Perhaps she'd gotten the phrase wrong. Spelling it out, she

said, "Dmitriu sent me to Sighesciu. I'm presuming you three and your other friend set up the tomb and the dust to scare the pants off me. Congratulations—you succeeded. But I won't bear a grudge, especially if you give me a genuine lead this time to Saloman's death."

Glancing along the line of open mouths, she was sure they wouldn't be able to do that either. Saloman would remain a mystery, a side note in her thesis that this was one case that didn't fit, possibly because several different characters had become confused over the centuries.

Konrad said, "Dmitriu? The vampire Dmitriu sent you to Sighesciu?"

"Oh, for God's sake!" Elizabeth whirled around, pointing at the door. "Close it behind you, please, and don't bother coming back. The only reason I let you in this time was because I foolishly imagined you'd come to apologize."

"Apologize?" Mihaela sounded so baffled that Elizabeth itched to slap her.

"Don't push it," she snapped. "I admit you got me. You fooled me. You scared me shitless. Congratulations. But it's not dark anymore, and contrary to apparently popular belief, I'm not a *complete* moron. It's over. I know you tricked me. Now go. And if I ever set eyes on any of you again—or Dmitriu or your 'vampire' friend—I'll report your assault to the police. Good-bye."

She was rather pleased with that rant, but it didn't have quite the effect she'd hoped for. Instead of shuffling out with half-embarrassed giggles, they sat perfectly still behind her back, and when Konrad spoke, it was with an air of helplessness that ate at her cynicism.

"Miss Silk, please . . . We had nothing to do with hurting you.

33

We were nowhere near Sighesciu yesterday. But if you were assaulted, we need to know in what way."

"Guess." Elizabeth turned back to glare at him.

His gaze slid away, down to her throat, then back up to her face. "He bit you, he drank your blood, but he let you live—"

"Why did he let her live?" István, the darker man, interrupted.

"Perhaps he wasn't strong enough at the time?"

"Maybe he was grateful to her for waking him," Mihaela suggested.

Elizabeth said, "Would you like to make up your minds outside? I'm busy."

"Please, Miss Silk, you have to listen to us!"

"Um—no, I don't." Elizabeth picked up her bag, shoveled her notepad into it, and grabbed the car keys from the bedside table. If it came to it, she'd damned well leave them here and inform reception there were intruders in her room.

"Miss Silk, you have to understand that you are in terrible danger," Konrad said solemnly.

"So will you be when I get to the police station."

"I'm serious!"

"Oh, so am I." Elizabeth's eyes locked with Konrad's, and something like shock began to permeate her certainty. He didn't look like a prankster, but instead a cross between a serious academic and a determined athlete. If he had a sense of humor, he kept it well away from his face.

"Please sit down and listen to us. This isn't a joke or a trick or whatever you're imagining. We are serious—deadly serious. And you need to understand."

The last statement was certainly true.

Knowing she would regret it, Elizabeth lowered herself until she perched on the edge of the hard chair beside the bed. *You're weak*, she told herself. *You should have thrown them out. Now, you'll never be rid of them....*

Konrad said, "Will you tell us what happened to you last night?"

"No. *You* talk to *me*. Or go."

Konrad inclined his head. "All right. Last night, you went to Sighesciu and somehow discovered the tomb of the ancient vampire Saloman. Something you did wakened him after three centuries, and now he's loose in the world once more. My c—"

"How do you know?" Elizabeth interrupted.

Konrad blinked. "I beg your pardon?"

"If you were nowhere near Sighesciu yesterday, how do you know what I did or didn't do there?"

"Because we have a reliable—and petrified—informant who told us that Saloman walks again. He drained two fledgling vampires whom we know of and drank from several humans besides yourself. After three hundred years, he's starving and out of control. I can't begin to tell you how dangerous that makes him."

Elizabeth let her gaze flicker from him to the others. On her guard as she was, she saw no sign of deceit, no sliding eyes, no shifty movements or even deliberately steady stares. It occurred to her that these people believed what they were saying. How they knew of her interest in Saloman or her visit to Sighesciu she wasn't sure, but any of the people she'd been talking to over the past months could have talked to them too. The same lies could have been repeated to all. They weren't country people. In fact, she guessed that only the girl, Mihaela, was even Romanian. István was clearly Hungarian—although there were many ethnic Magyars in this part of Transylvania—and Konrad was probably of German extraction. But all of them had a sort of cosmopolitan, well-traveled air that sat very oddly with the nonsense they were spouting.

These were no wacky tricksters after all, but genuine, very serious nutters.

"I see," she said, carefully noncommittal. "And you are . . . ?"

Konrad's shoulders relaxed, as if the hardest part of his battle was won. "We are part of an international organization dedicated to eliminating vampires from the world. My colleagues and I are based in Budapest, but there is generally more work for us in the mountains of both Hungary and Romania."

"I see," Elizabeth repeated. "And your—informant—told you about me too?"

Konrad hesitated, exchanging glances with István. "Yes . . . But we knew about you already. We know about all the researchers who come here asking about vampire legends. It makes you a target for the vampires, and it's our duty to protect you."

Elizabeth closed her mouth. There was nothing to say to that.

Konrad continued. "The vampire Dmitriu already approached you and sent you to Sighesciu. It's not generally known that Sighesciu is—was—Saloman's resting place."

"Why not?" Elizabeth found herself asking.

"Other vampires, his enemies, could kill him for good, scatter his remains so far apart that he'd never walk again. His friends didn't want that. His enemies, who staked him in the first place, didn't want anyone finding him and waking him."

"How can he be awakened if he's been staked?" she asked, wondering wildly if she'd fallen into an old Hammer Horror script.

"Saloman is an Ancient," István said with careful emphasis.

"He is therefore very hard to stop at all. Staking him alone does not dispel his spirit; it merely holds him."

"Then why didn't his enemies scatter him at the time?"

"We don't really know that. There have been suggestions that they were too afraid of him, even staked. His power and his standing were awesome in those days, among both vampires and humans."

"How come?" Elizabeth demanded.

István shrugged. "Sheer strength, acquired through age and study. Plus, according to the sources we have, a formidable intelligence and force of personality. Perhaps his enemies were still influenced by these traits. But there is also evidence of a major battle, so it's possible they were disturbed or distracted before they could finish the job. On the other hand, if Saloman's friends won the battle, they were still too late to release him. He couldn't be freed without . . ." István broke off and glanced at Konrad.

"Without human blood," Konrad said. "I should tell you: I have been to Sighesciu myself and have never even seen his tomb. I was told it was hidden by magic from his friends and enemies alike, so I have no idea how you found it. Did Dmitriu attack you?"

"Of course not! He wasn't even there!" She frowned. She'd thought she'd seen him, afterward, even imagined she'd run him over.

"Then if Dmitriu didn't take your blood, how did it get on the tomb?"

"My hand was pricked by a rose thorn. . . ." *Oh hell, I'm talking as if I believe them. Lock me up quick.* "Does it matter?"

Konrad shrugged again. "Only as a curiosity. Perhaps it was drops of your blood that made the tomb visible to you. The point is, you wakened him, and you escaped before he could kill you. The blood of his Awakener is important to him. On top of that, word is out that *you* are responsible. Plenty of other vampires are pissed off at you for that, including Zoltán, the regional leader here. Seriously, you need to leave Romania and go as far from eastern Europe as you can get."

"I will," Elizabeth soothed.

"When?"

"Soon. I have to be back in Scotland in September."

"That's weeks away! You have to go now."

"I haven't finished here yet."

"Miss Silk, your life, your soul, are more important than any thesis!"

"Don't make me say my life *is* my thesis," she begged, although it was loweringly close to the truth.

"Please, come with us now. We'll look after you in Budapest until you can get on a flight home."

"Thank you. You're very kind, but I'll take my chances here for the next couple of weeks." She stood up. "And now, I really need to eat before I start work...."

"Miss Silk, please reconsider." Konrad stood up with her, as did the others. "At least let us teach you how to defend yourself. You really don't know what you're dealing with here. It's not safe for you to be out alone after sundown. Every vampire in the region wants you dead, and you must understand that Saloman was the most powerful vampire who ever lived. He's back, and he'll want your blood."

"Actually, I want his," Elizabeth said grimly. His and Dmitriu's. It looked as if they'd been taking advantage of people a lot more gullible than she. Vampire legends had gotten out of hand recently. She blamed Bram Stoker, Anne Rice, and Buffy the Vampire Slayer. "Um . . . Before you go . . . what *do* you know about Saloman's death?"

✝

Thanks to the delay caused by the "vampire hunters," whom she'd shaken off with extreme difficulty in the end, it was almost midday before she parked outside Maria's house once more. The village was quiet, most people having sought shelter from the worst of the sun's heat. But as she approached the familiar rickety gate, where only yesterday she'd paused to talk too long to Dmitriu, she saw Maria's daughter sweeping the garden path beneath the shade of the thick, tangled vines.

Catching sight of Elizabeth, she straightened and leaned on her brush. "*Domnişoară*," she called in greeting. It wasn't clear from her closed face if she was pleased, annoyed, or even embarrassed to see her.

Elizabeth returned the greeting, adding, "I'm looking for Dmitriu."

There was a pause, but the woman came no closer. "He isn't here," she said at last.

"Do you know where I can find him?"

She shook her head.

"Does he live in the village?"

The woman shrugged and returned to her sweeping. "He moves around a lot. I'd find someone else to talk to."

Yes, I'll bet you would, Elizabeth thought with a hint of bitterness. They'd all been in on it. Fool the crazy foreigner. Butter her up with Maria's nonsense, and then set Dmitriu on her as the more acceptable face of legend. Only, what was the point? Didn't it get boring after a while? She never paid anyone for talking to her—on the grounds that for one thing she couldn't afford to, and for another it would just encourage people to say what they imagined she wanted to hear.

She got back in the car and drove the now-familiar road through the hills to Sighesciu—not forgetting to check her rearview mirror for any vehicles following hers. She didn't put it past the "vampire hunters" to dog her footsteps until she left the country.

✝

The village looked different in the brightness of the afternoon sunshine; though still down-at-the-heels, it was less depressing. Parking her car in the shade of a parched tree in the empty market square, she found she could actually laugh at herself, and at the sight she must have presented last night, fleeing in panic from a "vampire" come to life from a stone sarcophagus. Her colleagues would laugh themselves silly if they ever found out—though she'd take damned good care they didn't.

And yet, despite everything, as she walked up the hill toward the castle ruins, she found her heart beating too hard and too fast. She knew she should feel as angry with Dmitriu as with his accomplice "Saloman," but the truth was, she needed to talk to Dmitriu again, to find out if any of what he'd said was true. The heat of her fury was reserved for "Saloman," who'd scared her, tormented her, and, worse than anything else, excited her out of her normal, reserved skin. For that, for him, she felt something approaching hatred.

She had no idea how she'd cope if she met him again. Would she yell at him, gibber like a fool, turn all tongue-tied like the shy schoolgirl she often still felt she was? Or would she still melt like butter under the heat of his hungry, mesmerizing eyes?

She curled her lip, knowing that in daylight, in the brightness of her returned common sense, he'd look no more than ordinary. No charisma, no magic would touch her or arouse her, which was a pity in some ways because she hadn't even known she *could* feel like that. It had been edgy, breathless, exciting. . . .

Hastily, she shut down that line of thought. It was the adrenaline, the fear, that had intensified and confused everything. That was all.

Diggers and workmen swarmed all over the hilltop. Keeping a low profile, she got quite close to the crypt corner before the foreman she'd spoken to last night spotted her. He yelled something to the driver of a large mechanical beast, who inched his charge forward out of her line of vision while the boss walked toward her.

Elizabeth gazed beyond him, at a completely flat piece of ground. The hole crumbling onto the crypt had been filled in. This entire part of the hilltop was smooth and even.

"You filled in the hole," she blurted before the foreman had even greeted her.

"What hole?"

"I found a hole in the ground last night—just there. There was a room underneath, like a crypt, with angels carved on the walls. Shouldn't you notify the authorities before building starts?"

The man smiled at her, a pitying smile, though why he pitied her wasn't clear. "There was no hole over there; nothing to fill in. We'd have seen such a thing, and if we hadn't, the surveyors who swarmed over the site last week would have. So, will you be buying a house?"

It was pointless. Either Dmitriu and "Saloman" had covered it up themselves, or the builders didn't want to wait for archeologists to grub about in the foundations before they started work, and so they would deny everything.

"No," Elizabeth said ruefully. "I couldn't live here now."

✝

Over a cup of coffee in the village square, she asked about Dmitriu, but no one seemed to have heard of him. She wasn't surprised. She'd been expecting to work without him. Her next stop was the churchyard.

However, there were three churches in Sighesciu: the Roman Catholic at one end of the main street, a Lutheran church at the other, and about halfway between, the Eastern Orthodox church. Each had its own graveyard. The "vampire hunters" had looked at her as if she'd grown horns when she asked them which religion Saloman had followed, although they'd all known he'd been staked in 1697.

"Did Dmitriu tell you that?" she'd asked suspiciously.

"I've never met Dmitriu," Konrad had answered with what seemed complete honesty. "The date is in our records."

Elizabeth began to think, having scoured all three graveyards in search of likely monuments, that she might have to ask to see these records, whatever they were. However batty, they might just contain the odd kernel of truth that would help her. After all, that's what she'd been doing in all her research so far, rummaging for pearls among the dross. Her reluctance to engage with the "vampire hunters" again was down to the simple fact that their very solemnity freaked her out.

Dropping onto a table stone facing the church building, she pulled out her water bottle and took a sizable swig as she cast her gaze around the cemetery in an accusatory way. Well, what had she expected? A nice, clear stone that read, *Here lies Saloman, a very ancient vampire, staked in 1697 by the following people?*

Perhaps he really had been buried under the castle chapel. If that was the case, his body and any inscriptions were lost for good—unless her photographs showed something?

Brightening, she shoved the bottle into her bag and held up her face to the sun, eyes closed. She'd head back to Bistriţa, get the photographs onto her computer, and see what she could see. And that would be the last time and effort she'd waste on Saloman. Tomorrow, she'd head south and pick up a few more legends.

A shadow fell across her face. Her eyes flew open and she sat up, shivering. No one stood over her; no vampire threatened to drink her blood; no one dressed up as a vampire threatened to drink her blood. It was just a tiny cloud passing across the sun; yet there'd been an instant, a tiny instant, when she could have sworn she smelled the cool earth and spice scent of the man who'd pretended to be Saloman.

†

She had some good pictures of the angels in the crypt. She even had one of the stone sarcophagus.

Sprawled on her hotel bed with the laptop on the pillow, she blew the sarcophagus picture up as far as she could and stared at it. It was as exquisite as she remembered, a beautiful piece of art with the handsome, expressive face, the lean yet muscular body very similar to that of the man who'd accosted her moments later. Her gaze lingered, taking in the empty scabbard on the carving.

She had a brief unbidden vision of "Saloman" rising from the stone table, then walking toward her in a cloud of dust while yanking the sword from his chest and throwing it on the ground. But it hadn't been a sword. There had been no metallic clank on the stone floor. The sound of it falling had been softer, blunter, like wood.

They'd fooled her with a clip-on wooden sword, and now that she thought through the stunned fear of that scene, she realized it had been too short for a real sword.

"Well, that's one trick explained," she murmured.

She refocused on the photograph, looking for more clues. The sarcophagus was undoubtedly stone, far too inert and dust covered to be the human male at this stage. And yet she'd been right—there was a gleam of black paint beneath the dust of his eyes and his hair and his cloak. It must have been old. No one could have rustled up something so wonderful just for a prank.

"So how did they do it?" she murmured. "Did they destroy it, hide it? And why is the dead man carved with a sword through his chest and an empty scabbard?" She sighed. "I wish I knew if you were really Saloman. . . ." She touched the computer screen with her fingertip, brushing the sarcophagus's face. "If I can't find Dmitriu, I'm going to have to speak to the vampire hunters, aren't I? And why am I talking to you anyway, computer image?"

Closing the lid, she pushed the computer aside and stood up. Her stomach rumbled, and she realized she'd forgotten dinner again. Well, she'd go out and get something from one of the stalls. She needed some fresh air before bedtime anyhow. And while she walked, she could decide whether to leave Bistriţa tomorrow as planned, or hang around to talk to the vampire hunters about bloody Saloman.

She grabbed a sweater for defense against the cool of the evening and went in search of food.

It was a clear, starry night, too late for there to be many people still around in the quiet streets near her hotel. But there was nothing threatening about this town. It was merely peaceful in the darkness, and by the time she approached home, munching her way through the warm pie from the corner stall, she'd made up her mind to spend one more day on the elusive Saloman. Though she was in danger of wasting too much time on one anomaly, another day couldn't hurt. And it would be worth it if she solved the mystery of his existence once and for all.

Emerging from the picturesque vaulted arches that covered the pavement in this part of the old town, she glanced up at the jeweled sky—and something hurtled down on top of her, rolling her to the ground.

Winded and shocked, she could do nothing for the first disoriented moment. Then she realized it was a man's heavy body pinning her to the ground, a man's brutal hand shoving her face to one side, and she reacted from pure instinct. Grabbing his hair in both her hands, she heaved with all her might. At the same time, she jerked her knee up between his legs and felt it connect with the softness of male genitalia.

He didn't scream, and the rising cry from her own throat got lost in shock as she stared into the red, glaring eyes of her attacker. His mouth gnashed like an animal's, revealing long, pointed incisors. He seemed to grin as he lunged once more toward her neck, paying no attention to the hair that came away in her hands as he pushed downward toward her bucking body.

She changed tactics and punched his face instead. Though it drew a grunt from him, it made little difference to his progress. In wild desperation, she tried another, thudding her left fist into his ribs at the same time. But still his slavering mouth found her neck—just as he was plucked off her and thrown several feet across the pavement.

Gasping for breath, Elizabeth glimpsed a tall figure with his back to her. He wore dark trousers and a white shirt, and long black hair streamed down over his broad shoulders. It couldn't be. . . .

An inarticulate whimper left her mouth at last, for her attacker

45

had picked himself up off the ground and was charging headlong at the man in front of her. The force of his crash should have knocked the other man off his feet, and yet he didn't even sway. The two men seemed to be inextricably tangled. Elizabeth heard a sound like a snarl, and then a snap, and her attacker simply disappeared.

For an instant, dust danced like stars where he'd been. The other man whirled around and strode toward her. Glare from the streetlight bounced off his pale, handsome face. It couldn't be, but it was—it was the man who'd played Saloman.

No residual dust now clogged his pores, his hair, or his clothes. No seventeenth-century cloak swung around him for added dramatic effect. Instead, a tall, fit man of the twenty-first century bore down upon her. His clean, black hair shone under the streetlight, stirring in the air as he moved. His strange eyes bored into her, twisting her stomach with unwanted memory.

Bending at the waist, just like last night's first encounter, he seized her, dragging her upright and into his arms. There was no denying they felt good around her, hard and strong and comforting after the violence of her attacker, but she couldn't forget what had just happened.

"Where is he?" she gasped, trying to peer past his broad shoulder. "What did you do to him?"

"I killed him for you." Even speaking such chilling words, his voice vibrated through her like an agitated flame. "Reward time." He lowered his head, bending her body into his. His silken hair fell across her shoulder, tickling her naked skin, and she felt his lips on her neck.

"Oh, don't start that again, you *stupid* bastard!" She slapped his head hard enough to sting her own hand. "What is *wrong* with you?"

His body stilled, then began to vibrate. He lifted his head, and his eyes gleamed so brightly she realized he was laughing at her. She struggled in vain to throw him off. Just like last night, he was too big, too strong—terrifyingly strong.

"I'm hungry," he explained, catching both her agitated hands and dragging them behind her back. "And you really don't believe in me, do you?"

"No," she spat. "I don't."

He regarded her, holding her breast to breast with him, his head tilted to one side. His arms felt like bands of steel. Treacherously, her nipples began to tighten at his nearness. It seemed that nothing, no trauma, fear, or anger, could prevent her body's excitement around him.

He said, "What do you think just happened here?"

Confused images struck her—of her attacker's snarling teeth, of her "savior" absorbing his furious charge, and the brief, flashing struggle that resulted in her attacker's disappearing in a cloud of dust—Saloman's specialty. He must carry bags of the stuff....

She stared up into his opaque black eyes. All she could see there was her own reflection. Slowly, he began to smile, revealing long, pointed canines. He was like a Halloween joke, only sexier.

"You're all insane," she whispered.

"You know, it's not going to be any fun dining on you if you don't accept me. It offends my sense of—appropriateness."

"Then fuck off," she snarled.

"Such foul language for a lady of learning." He bent closer to her ear and although she felt no breath, she shivered. One of his hands moved with deliberation over the curve of her hip and around to her waist, sliding upward and over her breast. She swallowed, forcing herself to remain still. His palm circled her nipple, forming an invisible line of pleasure to her aching loins.

"Think about it," he whispered. His lips brushed against her ear, as softly as a butterfly's wing, sending tingles all the way down her spine. "I won't allow other vampires to touch you. But I'm afraid I don't have time to convince you of that right now—or to enjoy my meal. We'll talk later."

His hand dropped, and his arms loosened, letting her walk away—again.

She did. This time, she held her head high and prayed he wouldn't see the shaking of her legs, of her whole body. Desperately, her brain tried to rationalize what she'd just seen and what she still felt.

She refused to look back, even when the hairs on the back of her neck danced with alarm. For some reason, his stillness scared her more than the brutality of her earlier attacker, and she didn't feel safe until she made it back to her hotel room and locked the door.

Chapter Four

*H*e made no sound. The air barely stirred as he walked between the trees, but Dmitriu knew he was there.

"You're late," Dmitriu observed, without taking his eyes off the run-down farmhouse.

"I was held up."

"By the girl. You reek of her. Did you kill her?"

"Not yet."

Dmitriu frowned and turned his head. Apparently untroubled, Saloman stood at his side, gazing through the trees at the ramshackle buildings across the field from their sheltering wood.

"Your return to full potency requires it. Both because she bears the blood of Tsigana, and because she revived you. Zoltán's in there, and without her blood, her life force, you're not strong enough to face him."

Saloman's lip quirked. In his understated clothes, he might have been a waiter or an old blue blood. Making the latter mistake might be excusable, but Dmitriu imagined few would make the former. "Zoltán doesn't know that. How many others are in there?"

"The three he brought with him—as bodyguards, presumably—and about ten local vampires, two of them weak. Zoltán is by far the strongest."

Zoltán's dangerous strength lay in his drive for power and his determination to hold it. There was a time when he'd feared Dmitriu as the older vampire, but these days he seemed to imagine Dmitriu's failure to seize power from him was due to weakness. It wasn't. It was due to inertia and boredom and a preference for a solitary life. Dmitriu had no desire to rule the mindless fools who sheltered under Zoltán's protection.

"There is a lot that Zoltán doesn't know," Saloman observed.

"Don't underestimate him," Dmitriu warned. "He is strong; he has massive support here and alliances with the vampire communes of most of Europe, America, and Africa. Also"—he drew in a breath and tore his gaze free—"he has dominion over zombies."

Saloman flexed his fingers. "Zombies? He raises the true dead? Even to me, that's an abomination."

"That's part of their value to him. He uses them as his army, his enforcers—instruments of terror, if you like. If they catch you, they'll scatter your limbs and your ashes so far apart that you'll be lost forever."

"I'll bear it in mind." Saloman stepped out of cover and began to walk across the field. No one else, living or undead, moved with that particular grace, almost gliding, yet visibly aware of every inch of his confident, beautiful body—which was about to get sent back to hell.

"Aren't you even going to mask your identity?" Dmitriu hissed after him. "At least until you get there?"

"No," said Saloman. "Let them—er—get the wind up."

He was enjoying modern language, Dmitriu thought resentfully. He was especially enjoying mixing English and American slang into Romanian. Nor did he care that Dmitriu didn't share his enthusiasm for provocation or for probable death.

Dmitriu's duty was done. He had brought about the awakening of his maker and onetime friend. He was quite at liberty to leave at this point and to return to the village and to Maria, who had once been his lover and still gave him shelter in her shady outbuildings, despite the protestations of her petrified family. He was accustomed to peace and solitude these days, and he wasn't going to get either around Saloman, even if he survived.

Dmitriu sighed, then followed him. He always had.

✝

Elizabeth sat on her bed, staring at the mobile phone she held in her shaking fingers. On her knee was the scrap of paper with Konrad's number. What scared her even more than the attack was the crumbling of her cynicism. She didn't, couldn't, believe all that nonsense, but neither could she come up with a reason for continuing any hoax this far. She needed clarification, and yet the last thing she wanted was to be sucked into the nutty world of the vampire hunters and lose all hold on reality.

She was an academic, a researcher. She wanted evidence. But all she had was a photograph of a stone sarcophagus and the dubious memory of the man who'd seemed to spring to life from it. She had a man with fangs attacking her and another man—also with fangs—claiming to have killed him. The evidence of her own traumatized eyes couldn't be trusted. It had been dark, the dim streetlight misleading, and it had all happened too fast to see properly, let alone take in.

If "Saloman" had really killed him, where was the body?

"Shit," she whispered, and keyed in Konrad's number.

She hoped he wouldn't answer. She wouldn't bother to leave a message, and then she'd switch her phone off in case he called back.

"Hello?"

Damn. Not only an answer, but a wide-awake tone.

"Hello?" he said again.

Elizabeth licked her lips. "Konrad. It's Elizabeth. Elizabeth Silk."

"Elizabeth! Are you all right?"

"Yes. That is, I don't know. I was attacked in the street."

His breath hitched. "Since you're calling me, it was not, I take it, a mugging?"

"I don't know. He was like an animal, trying to bite me...." She broke off, sucking her lower lip between her teeth as reaction threatened to overwhelm her.

"Did he succeed? Did he bite you? How did you get away?"

"Someone stopped him." She caught her breath, dragging her hand through her hair. "It was *him*. The man who pretended to be Saloman. He said he killed him."

"Look, I'll be right over."

"No, don't," she interrupted. "I'm fine. I just wanted to ask you—why would he save me from another vampire and then let me go?"

Everything in her screamed out against going along with this nonsense, but she had to make sense of it before she could decide the appropriate reaction.

"Why he would save you is easy. He doesn't want your blood 'wasted' on anyone else. Why he would let you go . . . I can't answer that. But he was a great player of games in his past. I suppose when you live for centuries, you have to work harder than most to entertain yourself."

"Cat and mouse," Elizabeth murmured ruefully. *Am I really buying this?* "Konrad? If the other 'vampire' was really dead, why wasn't his body there? Wouldn't it go rigid, like stone? Like 'Saloman'?"

"Oh no, most vampires just disperse into the air. Released from the borrowed blood that keeps them in existence, their bodies revert to dust."

"Saloman's didn't," she pointed out.

"Saloman is an Ancient. A pure-blooded vampire, the last of the original race. His kind lived for thousands of years until they chose to die, or went insane and were put out of their misery by one of their own. By the time Saloman was at the height of his power, there were hardly any others left, and he killed the last of them himself. Modern vampires are mere human hybrids. In any case, if Saloman's body felt like stone, it took centuries for it to get like that. Contemporary accounts make the point that lying there, staked through the heart, he looked only too alive. Listen, Mihaela will come and collect you. . . ."

"No, please, I'll be fine here." She gave a laugh that was both breathless and rueful. "After all, if Saloman's 'protecting' me, I couldn't be safer, could I?" *At least for tonight.*

"Actually, yes, you could be a lot safer. I've just had word from my informant that Zoltán is in Transylvania."

"Zoltán?"

"The regional leader of the vampires of Hungary, Romania, and Croatia. He's heard about Saloman, and about you. And he wants you both dead. The attack on you tonight might even have been instigated by him, or by someone trying to curry favor. He's summoned the local vampires to him. Elizabeth, it really is time you got out of here."

✝

Dmitriu wasn't stupid. When they made it unmolested to the farmhouse door, he obligingly kicked it open and stood aside for Saloman to enter first. So it was that as Saloman strolled inside, it was he rather than Dmitriu who bore the brunt of the attack.

What interested Dmitriu was that although perhaps fifteen vampires filled that bare kitchen, just one of them flew at Saloman's throat. Dmitriu saw no reason to intervene. Saloman barely needed two hands to catch the stupid creature, before sinking his fangs and draining him dry. The body fell at his feet and exploded into silver dust that danced in the light of the flaming torches on the wall.

"Thank you," said Saloman, as if grateful for the welcome, and walked forward into the room. Dmitriu elected to follow him.

The whole house reeked of human death. Zoltán was easy to spot, sprawled in the only armchair as if it were his throne. His foot rested on a pale, human body, which in death was bent into a grotesque shape.

In the corner behind him, two vampires had obviously been fighting over the last living creature in the room, a woman perhaps in her forties, whose eyes reflected madness and horror. Her family had been butchered by monsters in front of her eyes.

"My pleasure," drawled Zoltán.

He'd had time to prepare, to assume this position of careless power while Saloman and Dmitriu had openly crossed the field. He was a big, fair vampire, a lock of his untidy hair falling across his forehead. His face was not that of a thoughtful being, but it reflected a certain amount of intelligence and cunning as well as considerable self-confidence—and strength. He was stronger than Dmitriu remembered.

His gaze locked on Saloman's as the Ancient stepped over the bodies in his path. Zoltán smiled, lifted one hand, and snapped his fingers. "My guest is hungry. Since you can't agree, give her to him."

"You're too kind." Saloman didn't so much as glance at the outraged vampires or their traumatized victim.

"You need to gather your strength," Zoltán said with such obviously false consideration that Dmitriu had the urge to kick him. "Three hundred years is a long time to starve."

"Tell me about it," said Saloman. "I take it I need no introduction."

"I take it neither do I." His malevolent gaze flickered to Dmitriu in contempt. Dmitriu contented himself with a curl of the lip.

Saloman said, "Of course not. I can see at once that you are Zoltán, the great leader."

Zoltán's eyes narrowed with suspicion, but he'd learn nothing from Saloman's face. The two squabbling vampires, meanwhile, had dragged the terrified woman to the side of Zoltán's chair.

"That disobedient idiot was not my hospitality," Zoltán explained. "This is." He jerked his head, and with ill grace the two vampires pushed the woman at Saloman, who caught her before she fell. However, he didn't feed at once, but instead held her to his side. "He imagined that by killing you, he would become strong enough to usurp my place."

"Idiot indeed," Saloman agreed. The hand that held the woman slid up her shoulder to her throat and began to stroke idly.

"Obviously," Zoltán said, "I told them all you were not for the likes of them."

Dmitriu stiffened, recognizing a challenge when he heard one.

"Assuredly not." Saloman continued to stroke the woman's neck while regarding Zoltán. The woman turned her head and stared up at Saloman, confused, presumably, by his entirely misleading gentleness. She had a tired, overworked look mixed with the remnants of youthful beauty that reminded Dmitriu a little of Maria.

Refusing to be distracted, Dmitriu took another swift glance around the room, confirming everyone's position in his mind. If it weren't for Zoltán, he and Saloman could take the others easily. But Zoltán . . . Zoltán could be their undoing. He wanted to shake Saloman.

"The woman is not a bribe, by the way," Zoltán said. "Nor is she poisoned."

"I know. A great leader like you would not fear me enough to commit either offense."

Saloman's sarcasm was beginning to sound too much like flattery for Dmitriu's taste. He wondered when the hell they were going to leave, or at least do whatever they'd come here for.

"I don't," Zoltán said too quickly.

"And yet my blood is a draw. The blood of an Ancient is powerful."

"I could take it," Zoltán said. His hands, resting on the arms of his chair, convulsed, and Dmitriu tensed.

"My good sir," Saloman said, turning the woman in his arms, "I didn't come here to do anything so foolish as to fight with you."

The woman gazed up into his face, trustfully now—mistake.

Saloman spared her a quick glance, a half smile before he bent toward her neck. At the first touch of his lips on her skin, she gasped and threw back her head. The scratches on the faces of the quarreling vampires bore testament to her previous fights, but Saloman she didn't even try to resist. She welcomed him, as they all did.

Wouldn't make her any less dead.

Saloman drank. The woman clawed his shoulders in agony and ecstasy, and then gripped hard, as if holding him to her. The other vampires gawped, openmouthed.

Zoltán snapped, "Then why?"

Saloman lifted his head and licked a drop of blood from his lips. The woman moaned. "I would suggest an alliance," he said, and returned to her wounded throat. She sighed with satisfaction.

Dmitriu's grunt was anything but satisfied. *Alliance? What the . . . ?*

Zoltán laughed. "An alliance? Why would I need an alliance with you? I control all the vampires in three major countries. Those in three others would not dare to cross me. I have dominion over zombies and worldwide support. What do you have, apart from your bitch?"

He cast a contemptuous glance at Dmitriu who curled his lips once more and watched Saloman finish his meal. Her fingers no longer gripped him as she hung nearly lifeless in his arms. One more pull of his savoring lips, and he'd had it all.

Releasing her, he let her slide to the floor at his feet. Despite witnessing the unspeakable horror that had clearly unhinged her mind beyond any power of healing, she died happy in the end.

Saloman, unstained by as much as a droplet of blood, said,

"My—er—bitch has more strength in his little finger than you will ever possess. Without me. You need wisdom as well as brute force, my friend."

"To do what?" Zoltán jeered. "What more is there? Conquer America?"

He was a smug bastard, overly pleased with himself. Dmitriu began to wish he'd killed him after all, decades ago when no one would have minded.

"You think too small," Saloman chided. "You said it yourself— you rule the vampires of three major countries. How many beings is that, precisely? Even throwing a few mindless zombies into the calculation, not many. The majority of the population of those countries, as of all others, even America, is—er—human."

Zoltán frowned, still not getting it. Dmitriu got it, though— and was appalled. Saloman would turn the world upside down and regain the power that was his at the dawn of time. Humans would be his slaves once more, because they had betrayed him three hundred years ago.

Not just Elizabeth Silk, but the world would pay for Tsigana's actions.

If he succeeded. But either way, Dmitriu knew his peace was over.

†

More annoying than anything was Saloman's refusal to talk about it. As they watched the farmhouse burn, he wore a serious frown that repelled discussion. And then, appearing to throw off his somber mood, he strode back through the trees in the direction of Bistriţa with nothing more than the beauty of nature on his lips, whatever was in his head.

"You don't understand the modern world," Dmitriu burst out.

"It's not a few thousand people now, under the thumbs of a handful of the powerful. This is an age of democracy and superpowers and *money!*"

"It is fascinating," Saloman agreed, gazing upward at the moon. "Do you know, when I was first reborn, I almost hated the moon? I felt I would gladly shoot it out of the sky just for a ray of warm, soothing sunshine. And yet now, after staring so long at a stone ceiling, making pictures in my head from every crack, counting the strands of cobwebs and grains of dust . . . I truly value the beauty of the night sky."

Dmitriu glanced at him uncertainly. His words struck a chord as well as a memory, and it was the first reference he'd made to his three-hundred-year "sleep." On the other hand, Dmitriu refused to be manipulated away from his point.

"You're moving too fast—you can't take over the world when you can't even find your way up an escalator!"

"What's an escalator?"

"See? It's a moving staircase, powered by electricity. They're all over shopping centers and airports. . . . You don't know what they are either, do you?"

"Large indoor markets, and ports for airplanes. You explained airplanes on our journey here—noisy but effective vehicles, though bad for the environment."

Dmitriu's mouth fell open. In fact, he stopped in his tracks, and for a moment Saloman appeared to him as he would to any watching human—a patch of pale, glinting light flashing through the trees, almost like a sped-up film. He wouldn't know what that was either, would he?

He ran to catch up. "I suppose you know *how* airplanes are bad for the environment too?"

"I picked up bits and pieces." He spared Dmitriu a glance. "But you're right. My knowledge is sketchy. I've collected books—this age has a truly impressive number, even in such a backwater—and newspapers, but I think I really need a television. And Internet access." He smiled beatifically at Dmitriu's expression. "Yes, I do know what that is. Amazing age for fun, isn't it?"

They were entering the town now. Quiet, suburban streets flashed past. One couldn't even smell the smoke from the farmhouse here.

"Yes," Dmitriu snapped. "But you have to know what the hell you're doing! And you obviously don't! Allying with a mindless, untrustworthy thug like Zoltán? Can you really not see how far beneath you that is?"

Saloman slowed to normal walking speed, watching with apparent admiration as a car drove past. "These are amazing," he observed. "And so many of them, even here, and in the villages. How in Hades do they work?"

"Internal combustion engine. Do you have any intention of answering *my* questions?"

"Eventually." Saloman glanced up at the sky again. "So much paler in the town. The stars fade from view. Street lighting is a mixed blessing."

"You should see Budapest. It glows at night, almost like the sun."

"I will," Saloman promised. "I'm weak, Dmitriu."

It was so unexpected after the evasion of the last half hour that Dmitriu stumbled. Saloman smiled faintly. "But I can't be still anymore—I need to move forward, even while I'm learning, even while I'm gaining strength. I need time, and alliance with Zoltán buys it for me. He won't keep our agreement for long, and frankly, neither will I, but for now I have space to act without immediate threat."

Dmitriu swallowed. He couldn't remember Saloman's ever admitting vulnerability before. "Kill the Awakener," he pleaded. "Let me find Karl and Lajos for you, even if Maximilian is lost. . . ."

"I know where they are. I can sense them already."

"Then your strength *is* returning."

"Slowly . . . It's a delicate balance between the pleasure of vengeance and the strength I'd gain from it. As for the Awakener . . ." A smile flitted across his face. "She's like a fine wine I'm learning to appreciate."

They were in the brighter lights of central Bistriţa now, and the modest weekend crowds of locals and tourists filled the bars and cafés, spilling onto the pavement.

"All very well," Dmitriu observed. "But you'll have to drain the bottle eventually."

"Believe me, I'm looking forward to it." He frowned. "What is the matter with these people? They can't all be mad, clutching their heads and talking to themselves."

Dmitriu followed his gaze to the loud man outside the bar, to the two babbling women on the other side of the street, who seemed to be competing with each other for the most spoken words in a second, and began to laugh.

"They're talking into mobile phones—communication devices. Everyone has them now."

"Do you?"

Dmitriu took his from his pocket.

"Whom do you talk to?" Saloman asked curiously. "Do you call other vampires for a chat?"

Dmitriu flushed. "Hardly. Mostly services like taxi companies and laundry, and the odd trustworthy human to prepare for my return. One gets bored with sewers and cellars—and crypts."

"Unutterably," Saloman agreed. "What goes on in here?"

He'd stopped outside a hotel, from where the thump of relentless music beat through the pavement.

"They have a nightclub on weekends. Dancing. Loud music. Wine. Women."

"I have much to learn," Saloman observed, turning his feet toward the door. "Perhaps there will even be an escalator."

✝

In the light of day, the rotting supports of Elizabeth's skepticism revived. She didn't know how or why such a trick had been perpetrated on her, but what she did know was that vampires did not exist. Therefore, she would ignore the bizarre side of the vampire hunters and ask to see their documents on Saloman.

She'd arranged to meet them in a café, because it seemed impersonal and down-to-earth, and because a public place might stop them from talking about vampires as other than myths.

But after a poor night's sleep, she was early, and rather than wait half an hour in the café, she walked across the square to look at the fourteenth-century church. It had suffered a mysterious fire recently, but damage had been minimal.

Elizabeth liked churches. Not a deeply religious person, she nevertheless appreciated their beauty and the peace that often filled them. The door was open, so she walked inside. Vaguely surprised to find it empty of either worshippers or tourists, she walked the length of the aisle, gazing about her at the stained glass and carved stone, before sitting down on the end of a pew to soak up the atmosphere.

Atmosphere? That was what had gotten her into this mess in

the first place, although part of her strongly denied being in any mess. She was merely researching.

What an unexpected pleasure.

The voice made her leap up, glaring wildly around her. Worse, it seemed to plunge her heart straight down between her thighs where it continued to beat and throb, for the voice, deep and somber despite its note of mockery, was unmistakably that of last night's "Saloman."

Angry with herself for such a stupid reaction, she snapped, "I can't say the same. Where are you?"

He didn't answer.

Refusing to leap about searching for him, she sat back down on the wooden pew. "I see. Hiding again. Where this time? Something a little more mundane than a sarcophagus, perhaps?"

Why, no. I'm beginning to think it's not mundane at all. I'm in your head.

She froze, paralyzed, unable to think or speak. She knew it was true, even before he said it, not just because she couldn't see him, but because she could *feel* him. His low, powerful voice seemed to fill her mind from the inside. It didn't echo as it should have in the empty church. Panic surged, threatening to consume her as even last night's fear had not.

Relax, he mocked. *I'm only talking to you. Not raping your mind.*

How do I know that? she wondered in panic. *And how do you know that's what I fear most?*

I hear you went back to Sighescu. Were you looking for me?

"For Dmitriu," she whispered, "and for proof of your death."

Gone. Weren't you afraid to go back?

"No. Are you stalking me?"

Yes.

Oh shit. Oh Jesus, oh crap . . .

The maddeningly calm voice went on. *I'd be very interested to read your thesis when it's complete. Perhaps I can assist you with it.*

"For the price of a drink?" she retorted before she could help it, and his unexpectedly warm laugh brushed her mind.

Was that an offer? he mocked.

"No." With relief, she realized she was safe, that it was daylight, when he couldn't come out. *My God, I'm starting to believe it. And yet what else is there to do now? How do I blame this on trickery?*

Wherever he was, physically, it was far away from here. Unless . . . Her heart jolted. "Are you in the church?"

What, an unholy undead like me?

She swallowed. "Are you really?"

Am I really what?

"Unholy. Undead. Saloman."

And if I am?

"When and how did you die? Who killed you? Why?"

Again, his laughter echoed around her head and, dangerously, she felt herself drawn to it. *You're still researching your thesis. Very well, do you mean my first death or my staking?*

She swallowed. "Your—er—staking."

An alliance of hostile vampires and greedy humans killed me in the year 1697, in Sighesciu. By means of treachery. Why? Because I threatened them, which I understand fits your theory. However, unfortunately for you, I was already a vampire, and rather than using that as an excuse, they covered the whole incident up to the best of their poor ability.

"You've been talking to Dmitriu," she whispered. Where else would he have learned of her thesis, of her work?

Someone has to. Poor fellow gets lonely.

She gazed upward at the high, Gothic ceiling, wondering how

it was possible to sit in this holy place and talk so calmly with a mythical creature of darkness. "Is he a vampire too?"

Of course.

"But I saw him in the sun."

In the shade, perhaps.

But if that was all it took, was she really so safe from *him*? She hurried back into speech. "He did send me to you. He did set me up."

For dinner and dalliance, mocked the voice inside her head, and in spite of everything, her body heated.

Appalled, she stood so abruptly that she surprised herself. "But not today," she said with fierce triumph. "Not ever."

And that's when she saw him right in front of her, standing tall and erect in the shadowed aisle. Her breath vanished.

He wore plain dark trousers and an equally plain white shirt, open at the throat to reveal the strong, pale column of his neck. His long black hair stirred in a draft from the open door. In the night, half-covered in dust, he had been mesmerizing. In the light, even in dim church light, he was stunning.

Even the simplicity of his clothing looked both stylish and expensive.

His full, sensual lips tugged in the way she remembered, and she glimpsed those white, wicked teeth that had torn her flesh. She wanted to throw herself onto them; she wanted to drown in his shining black eyes, in the depths of his mouth.

Instead, she gasped out, "What do you want? What is the point?"

"Of existence?" He spoke normally now, leaving her head strangely empty. "It's an end in itself. What else is there?"

"An existence without blood!"

"Dull."

"I didn't *mean* to waken you," she burst out.

"I know."

"Then let me go."

"I'm not keeping you." As if to prove it, he lifted his arms to waist height and let them fall to his side. But perversely, given permission, she refused to take it.

"I'm told you'll do anything to take back the power you once had."

"Who can have told you such a thing?" he marveled.

"The vampire hunters."

He smiled, a rare, full smile that shot dangerous fire straight to her core. "Bless them," he said fondly. "Are they still about? Tell them I send greetings."

"Tell them yourself. I expect they're on their way."

He didn't look frightened. He didn't even look interested. He seemed more absorbed in holding a strand of her hair up to the light and letting it slip through his fingers. She wanted to step back out of his reach, but something, either the magnetism of his body or her own foolish pride, held her still. "What else do they say?" he murmured.

"That the other vampires will kill you. And me, because I woke you."

His lips quirked. "Then you'd better come with me so that I can protect you."

"But you'll kill me too."

"Poor Elizabeth," he said without noticeable pity. "Be easy. I won't kill you yet. You intrigue me too much."

"How?" she demanded with such scorn that he dropped her hair and met her gaze.

"Like that." Without warning, he took her chin between his long, pale fingers and tilted up her face. As she gasped, his fingers spread downward around her throat in a hold that was firm, neither threatening nor caressing and yet might have held something of both. "One day, you'll have to decide. Friend or foe?"

"Foe," she spat.

"I wasn't talking to you." His face swooped over hers, his mouth coming to rest a hairbreadth from her lips. There was no breath, nothing to stir or warm her skin, and yet she felt something potent and dangerous, drawing her ever nearer. "When I come to you next, we'll talk. And more. I hope you'll be waiting."

He released her and stepped around her. Without looking back, he strode up the aisle.

Elizabeth's eyes were riveted to his hips as he moved. When he disappeared through a door at the front of the church, she dragged in a shaken breath and started after him, from pure curiosity to see where he could possibly go. But without warning, the big outside door creaked farther open, and two chattering women came in. Had he heard them, sensed them before she had? Did he care that they would see him?

Caught in a moment of indecision, Elizabeth found herself feeling guilty, though for what she had no idea. When the women greeted her with politeness, she muttered a reply and left the church the way she'd come in.

Outside in the bright sunlight, there was no sign of him. But then, there wouldn't be.

✝

All three vampire hunters were waiting for her in the café, gazing anxiously at the same copy of a newspaper. She didn't even think of them in quotation marks now.

As Elizabeth sank into the vacant chair, they cast her distracted smiles.

"Look." Konrad pushed the paper toward her and pointed to the piece at the foot of the front page.

Elizabeth scanned the story about a whole family who had burned to death in a farmhouse just five miles outside Bistriţa. "That's awful. Even the children . . . tragic."

"It's worse than tragic. It's Saloman."

Her stomach twisted. She felt sick. "You're telling me he did this?"

"Not all of it. He set fire to the building, but they were all dead by then anyway."

"He killed all those people?" The man—the creature—who'd just spoken to her, teased her . . . Blood pounded in her ears, threatening to deprive her of consciousness. She fought it, trying to listen as Konrad spoke, almost with reluctance.

"Only one of them, I understand. A woman. Zoltán and the other vampires had already killed everyone else."

"It says nothing about that here," she said stupidly.

"Well, it wouldn't, would it?" said István. "There's not much left of their charred bodies that would show their blood had been drained. But we have an informant who was there."

Elizabeth stared. "An informant? Where the hell was he? Staring in the window?"

"Inside," Konrad said. "He's a vampire. But not a bad creature. In fact, he's helped us on many occasions, and thanks to him, we know exactly what Saloman is up to."

"What?" Dread filled her, threatening to overwhelm her.

"He won't be content with dominion over the vampire world.

He wants to rule humans as well, and expects Zoltán to help him achieve it."

"That's nuts," Elizabeth said, and when they all gazed at her in astonishment, she added, "Well, come on! Every stage and screen villain for the last hundred years has wanted to take over the world! No one ever manages it."

"This is real," Konrad scolded.

"Yes? Well, Hitler was real, and he couldn't manage it either."

"Are you defending Saloman?" Mihaela asked, curious, and to Elizabeth's shame, a flush spread upward from her toes, rushing up her neck and into her face.

"No," she muttered. "I'm just having a hard time believing any of this."

Chapter Five

"We can't afford the security of having a safe house here too," Mihaela explained as she turned on the computer. "We just rent this place, and we have a team in Budapest do all the research we need as it comes up."

It was a small but decent house in the modern suburbs of Bistriţa. The vampire hunters had driven Elizabeth here with alacrity when she'd expressed an interest in seeing their documents. Now, discovering that there weren't any at this location, Elizabeth suspected they'd used her interest as an excuse to get her here. She was going to have difficulty leaving.

"What do you want to know?" Mihaela asked, sitting in front of the screen and pulling over a chair for Elizabeth. Konrad hovered in the background while István went to make coffee.

"Everything," Elizabeth said, sinking into the chair beside her. "I want to know about vampires, how and when they came to be.

I want to know about Saloman and Dmitriu, and how much threat they really are to *me*. And I want to know about you guys."

"About us, you just need to ask," Mihaela said with a quick smile.

"Yes, but I mean the earlier vampire hunters."

Mihaela lifted her brows. "You're aware how long the organization has been around?"

"Since the seventeenth century anyway." She met Mihaela's gaze defiantly. "Saloman told me." For some reason, that was difficult to say. She needed to analyze things on her own first, and yet if Saloman was as dangerous as all that—and from the farmhouse incident she couldn't doubt it—the hunters needed to know what he'd said. For their own safety as well as her own.

I can't believe this. I still can't believe I'm buying all this. . . .

She drew in her breath and let it out. "I saw him this morning in the church, while I was waiting for you." Her gaze flickered to Konrad. His piercing eyes were steady, unsurprised. "He knew about you. He sent you . . . greetings."

Konrad rested his hip on the back of the sofa behind him. "There have been vampire hunters as long as there have been vampires—almost. Our records go back to the twelfth century."

"And yet you've never shared them? None of the universities have ever heard of you, or have even a sniff of the kind of rare documents you're talking about?"

"No. Our existence depends on secrecy. Who would believe in us anyway? You'd already met a vampire and still thought we were a bunch of crackpots."

Elizabeth flushed. "True," she admitted. "So . . . is your library online?" she asked hopefully.

"No," Konrad replied. "But you can ask anything, and our researchers will do their best to find the answers for you."

Elizabeth frowned. It wasn't the kind of research she was used to. She wanted the actual, primary source, not someone else's interpretation of it, and especially not that of someone she'd never met and knew nothing about, educationally or otherwise.

"I'd love to see your library," she said wistfully.

"Come to Budapest with us," Mihaela suggested.

"You're going back?" Elizabeth wasn't sure what she felt about that. Panic about being left to deal with all this crap on her own? Disappointment that they would so soon desert the sinking ship when all those vampires were in the same city?

"Tomorrow," said Konrad, catching Mihaela's glance. "Tonight we'll try and eliminate a few of the dispersing vampires."

"Including Zoltán and Dmitriu?" Elizabeth asked. *And Saloman?* The question lay unspoken between them, but it was so palpable, she was sure Konrad and Mihaela both heard it.

"Eliminating Zoltán is a tricky one," Konrad said as István came in with a tray of coffee cups. It was strong, Turkish-type coffee, and Elizabeth reached for hers with enthusiasm. It was just the blast she needed to wake her from this weird sense of unreality.

"How so?" she asked, and took a sip of the thick, sweet brew. *Wow!*

Konrad sighed. "Zoltán is strong and brutal, but his removal would create a power vacuum. And in the ensuing chaos, who knows how many people would die, as the vampires compete for power by displays of pure badness? Before Zoltán managed to seize power, it was horrific, believe me."

"When was that?" Elizabeth asked.

"A couple of hundred years ago. But it is a matter of record."

"Of course. So what is your aim, then? To keep the numbers of his underlings down to manageable levels?"

"Something like that," István acknowledged, sitting on the arm of the sofa. "Mostly, it's the fledglings who're the indiscriminate killers. The older vampires prefer a peaceful life, drinking from humans but rarely killing—apart from odd breakouts like last night at the farmhouse, which was something of a welcome party for Zoltán, I expect. And an opportunity for Zoltán to show the world—and Saloman in particular—what a badass he still is."

Elizabeth nodded. Worryingly, she could see the perverse logic.

Mihaela said, "On a more personal note, the bargain they struck last night stipulated that Zoltán leave you to Saloman. For that reason too, we need to terminate Saloman."

Terminate . . .

"The trouble is," Konrad went on, "Saloman has destabilized the whole thing. Vampires are breaking cover through fear and excitement, anticipating a war for the leadership. And to be honest, I can't work out whether or not that would be worse than the alliance that seems to have formed between them instead. Though they'll never be able to work together. They'll be jostling for position."

"Jostling?" Elizabeth queried.

"Well, yes."

"It's just . . . I can't imagine Saloman jostling." It sounded lame, even to her own mind.

"Possibly not," Konrad admitted. "I doubt it'll prove a long-lasting partnership, or a trustworthy one. But before we can find out, it's important we take Saloman out."

Why can't we take Zoltán out instead? Annoyed with her indignant thought, Elizabeth finished her coffee and replaced the cup on the tray.

"How will you do that?" she asked, as noncommittally as she could.

The three vampire hunters exchanged glances once more. "We need to talk to you about it," Konrad said. "How do you feel about being bait?"

✝

"Are you worried about this?" Mihaela asked. They were in her bedroom while they both changed. Mihaela's spare jeans didn't look particularly good on Elizabeth, but they were serviceable with the hem rolled up a couple of times. Elizabeth didn't care. She was sure she could run as fast in a dress as in trousers, but the others seemed to think it was the thing to do.

"I'm worried that I'm involved. But I don't think it's fear—yet."

"I'll be with you all the time," Mihaela said, raising her three sharpened wooden sticks before placing them in her capacious handbag. "And the others will be right behind, watching. Saloman is still weak after his awakening. Between us, we can take him. We have to, before he gets any stronger. Here," she added, passing another thick, pointed stick to Elizabeth. "Be prepared to use it. Aim straight for his heart or he'll simply pull it out again."

Elizabeth stared at the wooden stake. "I saw him do that already. Just awakened, he had no difficulty pulling it out. What's to stop his doing it again?"

"We are. Anyway, the awakening thing is different. He would feel something akin to an adrenaline rush that gave him false energy, false abilities that wouldn't have been there an hour later. Now he's just as vulnerable as a fledgling—probably."

"Probably," Elizabeth repeated, taking the stake and running one finger over the finely honed point.

"There hasn't been an Ancient awakened in centuries," Mihaela admitted. "Our only record is hearsay, and that's from a document dated in the fourteenth century, describing events several hundred years before that."

"Then you're guessing. It's doubtful evidence and uncorroborated."

Mihaela's flickering gaze acknowledged it. "We have to try—for the safety of the rest of the world. It's our job to protect people from vampires. I'm sorry—you didn't sign up for this, and we'll do our best to make sure you at least survive it."

Elizabeth, experimentally pushing the stake up the sleeve of her borrowed jacket, paused to glance at the other woman. "That's what you do all the time, isn't it? You risk your lives against . . . monsters so the rest of us don't have to believe in them."

Mihaela gave a lopsided smile. "Something like that."

"How come? How do you get to be a vampire hunter? Are you 'chosen' like Buffy the Vampire Slayer?"

Elizabeth knew she sounded too flippant, but fortunately Mihaela laughed. "Hardly," she replied. "We're just ordinary people who've come in contact with vampire evil one way or another and decided to do something about it. The rest is simple training—mostly."

The point of the stake dropped down into Elizabeth's palm, and she twisted her wrist to grasp the shaft and pull it out. Watching, Mihaela nodded with approval.

Elizabeth said, "I can't *not* admire that. It makes what the rest of us devote our lives to seem trivial."

"It's not trivial," Mihaela argued. "If it were, defending it would mean nothing either."

Elizabeth smiled. "You'd make a good academic."

Mihaela laughed, shouldering her bag. "Ready to go?"

Elizabeth nodded and followed her to the door. But there, she paused. "Mihaela? Does it ever feel like—murder?"

Mihaela's hand slid off her door handle, leaving the door closed. "No." She glanced back at Elizabeth, her perceptive eyes searching. "Elizabeth, he's not human. He's not a tame animal or a creature of instinct. He's a calculating, self-seeking monster who'd kill you as quickly and as easily as he did that woman at the farmhouse. Your blood is more, not less, necessary to him, and the fact that he hasn't taken it yet is not because he regards you as a friend—or anything else."

Rising blood seeped into Elizabeth's face. "He's playing with me. Amusing himself. I know that."

Mihaela hesitated, then said, "Vampires, particularly the older ones—and there are none older than Saloman—have a certain sexual magnetism. Even those who hate them or fear them the most are aware of it. No one is immune. It shouldn't shame you. But you mustn't give in to it either. He'd take your blood with your body."

Heat curled through her, reminding her unbearably of the few occasions she'd been close to him. Worse than anything was the surge of excitement at Mihaela's words, dampening her underwear and propelling her into movement because she couldn't be still.

"I know," she mumbled, fiddling with the stake in her sleeve as she brushed forward, reaching for other reasons behind her distress. "It's not that. It's just . . . I've never killed anything before. Not even spiders if I can avoid it."

Mihaela opened the door. "Don't worry," she soothed. "We'll do the killing."

✝

Elizabeth's sense of unreality intensified as the evening progressed. She and Mihaela spent time in the bars and cafés frequented by younger people—making sure they were seen—while Konrad and István took it in turns to drift in and out, to hang around the bar, or to sit over a bottle of beer and a newspaper.

Sitting at a pavement table just outside one of these modern, friendly establishments, Elizabeth found it hard to believe that any dark side to the city existed, and if it did, that any darkness would notice her here, let alone report it to Saloman.

And yet he'd found her in the church. He'd spoken inside her head. Though she wasn't quite sure why, she hadn't told the vampire hunters that part of the story and didn't think she would. But she wondered whether that was how he'd tracked her and whether he could be in her head now. The idea appalled and excited her at the same time. However, she could feel no trace of the tiny electrical buzz that she'd imagined in the church, so she doubted it.

Over one glass of wine and a cup of coffee, the twisting knot of tension inside her began to relax a little. The vampire hunters were wrong. Saloman would not be seduced into any trap. On the other hand, her hoped-for research at the vampire hunters' house had never come to anything, except in a very haphazard, need-to-know sort of a way, and right now she had Mihaela's brain to pick and a lot of questions that still needed answering.

Twisting the stem of her wineglass in her fingers, she said, "How come he was in the church? Could he be living there?"

"He might have been," Mihaela allowed. "But he isn't now. Konrad and István checked."

"How?" she asked at once.

"We have instruments that detect the presence of vampires."

Elizabeth's eyes widened. "Are you using them now?"

"Yes, mine's in my pocket. And Konrad in the car has a more powerful and reliable instrument."

"Can I see one of them?"

"Not here," Mihaela said, sounding shocked for the first time in their acquaintance.

"Later, then. When I've finished in Romania, I'd very much like to visit your library in Budapest too."

"You can't use our material in your thesis," Mihaela warned.

"Not directly," Elizabeth agreed. Dragging her mind away from speculation as to exactly how she could use their information, she came back to her original point. "It threw me," she admitted, "that he could be in a church. All the legends describe vampires' aversion to holy things and places."

"For the most part, that's true." Mihaela reached for her coffee. "Holy water, crucifixes, anything symbolic like that, will repel most vampires. Because when they died, they believed in those things, subconsciously or otherwise. But Saloman is an Ancient. He's been around longer than Christianity."

Elizabeth took a sip of wine and laid down her glass. She didn't know why it surprised her. After all, it explained some of the stories she'd heard. "So he's immune to the things that hurt ordinary vampires like Zoltán?"

"Exactly."

"And Dmitriu?"

"Dmitriu—probably. He was created in the fourteenth century, definitely in the Christian era. But he's also, probably, the last existing vampire to have been made by Saloman, so we're not quite sure. Dmitriu is a bit of an enigma, to be honest. He lies low, but he's always there. And he often has human protectors. A sort of quid pro quo, I expect. They protect one another."

"That doesn't sound so bad."

"If you don't mind being fed off like a slave—and can turn a blind eye to the rest of the evil perpetrated elsewhere."

"Of course," Elizabeth said at once, chastened. But she'd been right. Maria was in on "the trick" that had sent her to Sighesciu and Saloman. In fact, she was damned sure Dmitriu had somehow planted that thorn that had made her palm bleed so profusely. She moved on. "When we first met, you talked about revenge. Who exactly can Saloman take revenge on after three hundred years? Are the vampires who did it still around?"

"A couple of them still are. Karl and Lajos. Apparently, they didn't turn up at Zoltán's meeting. They'll know Saloman's after them, and they'll be keeping well away from Zoltán."

Elizabeth frowned. "Wouldn't they want Zoltán's protection?"

"They'll know Zoltán's days are numbered if Saloman's back. They don't want to be around Zoltán when Saloman strikes."

"Only he didn't, did he? He's using Zoltán as an ally."

"Saloman was always notoriously hard to predict," Mihaela said with a twisted smile.

"So . . . if you don't kill Saloman tonight, would you just let him kill those vampires for you?"

"Oh no. Vampire biology, for want of a better word, is complicated and based on completely different concepts. The blood of Saloman's 'killers' is especially valuable to him and will add immeasurably to his strength. We need to keep them apart. It's our best hope for stopping him before he regains all his former power. Fortunately, they're playing our game so far and are not, we believe, in Transylvania. And as for the third vampire killer, Maximilian, we have no idea where he is. He disappeared off the radar more than fifty years ago. He could have died of boredom—or shame. Some do."

Fascinated, Elizabeth asked, "Was he an Ancient too?"

"No. But after Saloman died, he emerged from the period of chaos as the vampire leader, which he remained until Zoltán challenged him and won nearly two hundred years ago. Rather than stay under Zoltán's rule, Maximilian left the region and wandered around Europe. He even turned up in America briefly. We don't know where he is now."

"Wow." Elizabeth sat back in her chair. "This is like a completely alternative history without any humans to add the boring bits."

Mihaela laughed. "It is fascinating," she agreed. "But humans *were* involved in Saloman's history, and he in theirs. In early times, he was often the power behind the throne, or the catalyst for change. But by the seventeenth century, he was more or less regarded as the evil monster he was in reality, if anyone of education believed in him at all. But some more obscure humans, hungry for power, still worked with him. We have records detailing his closest relationships with humans who ultimately turned against him—a nobleman called Ferenc; a priest called Janos. And Tsigana, of course. She was his lover."

Elizabeth's stomach twisted. "He had a human lover?"

"Oh yes, several over the years. But Tsigana had some hold over him. One description says she bewitched him. Certainly his behavior became erratic toward the end of his life. It's said he killed another Ancient over her, and it was his trust in her that led him into the trap at Sighesciu that allowed Maximilian and the other vampires to kill him in alliance with the humans Ferenc and Janos. It's said they all took it in turns to push the stake farther in, with Tsigana giving the final thrust."

"They betrayed him." Was that satisfaction or outrage curling up through her body? It certainly wasn't pity.

"Oh yes," Mihaela agreed. "And he's had three hundred years to brood on it. If he was insane then—as his enemies claimed as the reason for killing him—he'll be doubly mad now. And he won't give a damn about carnage, destruction, or secrecy as he takes his revenge. No vampire and no human with a drop of his killers' blood in their veins will be safe. Nor will anyone who gets in his way. He needs to be stopped."

Elizabeth nodded. She could see that. Had any of it been re-flected in his face on any of their three encounters? Those disturb-ing eyes held secrets older than Jesus Christ. But they gave none of them away. Did he have feelings? He must have felt something for Tsigana, surely quite a lot, unless it was his pride that got hurt. But those dark, profound eyes hadn't regarded her with anything more than amusement. He was more than two thousand years old, and she no more than one of a million drinks of blood that would make him stronger. . . .

She blinked, realizing Mihaela had stood up and was speaking. "Sorry?"

"Time to walk," Mihaela repeated. Elizabeth rose with alacrity. Mihaela's story had given her new understanding, but also new strength to add to the tension gripping her.

"All right," she said, this time with enough determination to make Mihaela smile with approval.

†

Bistriţa was pretty at night, the darkness hiding any decay, the streetlights adding an ambience that Elizabeth had always liked. But tonight, she saw threat in every shadowed building, every following footstep, every stranger who passed too close. Her nerves coiled as tightly as a drum, she couldn't help remembering the vampire who'd fallen on her as if from the sky, and she kept casting her gaze upward.

"It's all right," Mihaela murmured. "We'll have warning. My detector's on now. It will sense any vampire biological characteristics in its vicinity. And the others are close by."

"What if it's not Saloman?" Elizabeth whispered. "What if some random vampire just attacks me, like last night?"

"Unlikely. Zoltán and Saloman have both forbidden it. You're to be Saloman's." Mihaela grasped her hand and gave it a quick squeeze. "Trust me, that will be over my dead body—and Konrad's and István's."

"Oddly enough, that is not the comfort to me you seem to be imagining."

A breath of laughter came from Mihaela. "I must say, you're taking to all this madness very well."

"No, I'm not," Elizabeth said ruefully.

Mihaela tensed. Close enough to feel it, so did Elizabeth. "It's now. From the left. My side."

Oh shit, this is it. He's come to finish me, and they'll kill him. . . . Will they?

For an instant, she couldn't banish the tangle of thoughts chasing one another through her head, until the two shadows flew at Mihaela.

As instructed, Elizabeth leapt backward, shaking her right sleeve and grabbing the stake she'd been hiding there all evening. She had time to register that this was wrong, that they shouldn't be concentrating on Mihaela, that there shouldn't be two of them—unless Dmitriu was again helping him—and to raise her stake in panic, ready to spring forward and aid the belabored vampire hunter. But that was all before one shadow dissolved into dust. Mihaela spun, kicking out at the remaining vampire, who fell with a thud on his back. Mihaela jumped on him, stake raised. Her arm plunged, and the second vampire too exploded into dust.

Christ, you're fast. . . .

Already Mihaela was back on her feet, casting around for possible witnesses. But there was only one fair, careless stranger, perhaps the worse for drink, who wandered by, staring upward at the stars.

Mihaela started back toward her with a quick grin that froze before it started. Her free hand was in her pocket, presumably on the detector. "There's still something!" she hissed in alarm, just as the passing stranger's arm flashed out so fast it was a blur, and seized her by the throat, lifting her right off the ground.

And yet the stranger didn't even glance at her. His gleaming, greedy gaze was fixed on Elizabeth.

"Elizabeth Silk," he said in a grave, almost gloating voice. "The Awakener . . . Come to Zoltán."

Oh bloody, bloody hell! She'd seen the terrifying speed with which he moved, but perhaps this prepared her. At any rate, when his free arm snaked out, though she couldn't quite avoid his reach, she did manage to slash at it with her stake, viciously enough to draw blood.

"Go to hell," she snarled. The vampire hissed, presumably with pain—which was interesting because she hadn't known if they felt pain or not—but still dragged her closer by her hair. Elizabeth thrust wildly with her stake, jabbing his ribs, his shoulder. Chiefly, she was conscious of Mihaela hanging by the throat in the vampire's hand, unable even to cry out.

Zoltán grunted at every blow, but his lips drew back from his teeth to reveal the long, pointed canines that were becoming only too familiar to her. His eyes gleamed in triumph, and she knew she needed more space to get some real strength behind her thrusts. Resorting to more natural tactics, Elizabeth kicked at his shins, then brought her knee up between his legs.

What effect this would have had on its own, she never found out, for István seemed to materialize at Zoltán's back. Though she couldn't see it, she knew he held a stake against him, pointing at the region over his heart. The vampire's body went rigid.

From her left, Konrad said, "Let them go," and a long, pointed piece of wood slid in beside her body to cover Zoltán's chest.

Mihaela slumped to the ground, choking. Released, Elizabeth ran to her. "I'm all right," she whispered. "Watch him. . . ."

Of course, they wouldn't kill Zoltán. They'd explained that to her. But Zoltán had no such scruples. However, apart from dropping his victims, Zoltán hadn't moved, and neither had they.

"Hunters," the vampire growled. He sniffed the air around Konrad, reminding Elizabeth unbearably of Saloman's behavior on their first encounter. Zoltán laughed.

Konrad drew back. The vampire lifted his arms, and István stepped back too. Zoltán's muscles flexed, and a warning struggled from Elizabeth's dry throat.

Zoltán jumped. He seemed to fly upward, and then his shadow disappeared over the rooftops. As Elizabeth brought her stunned gaze back down, she imagined she saw another shadow move from the corner of her eye, but when she jerked her head back up, everything was still.

Chapter Six

"You can't stay here on your own," Konrad said adamantly. They were all gathered in Elizabeth's hotel bedroom. Mihaela was sitting on the bed, drinking bottled water. In between sips, Elizabeth rubbed arnica cream into her bruised throat. "Not since we failed to kill Saloman. Hell, we didn't even *entice* him!"

"Maybe he knew who you were," Elizabeth suggested, dropping the arnica back into her handbag and sinking onto the bed beside Mihaela to watch Konrad pacing the room like a caged tiger.

"How?" he snapped back. "He's been awake precisely three days. He knows of our existence, but not who we are—surely!"

"I never expected Zoltán to go back on his word so quickly either," István said. "But at least he knows now she's double protected—by Saloman and us—and should stay away. The other vampires won't risk attacking her, will they?"

Konrad stopped pacing to push his hand through his short

blond hair. "I don't know. By his action tonight, Zoltán might just have made her fair game again."

"Will it end the alliance between him and Saloman?" Elizabeth asked.

"I don't know that either. I suppose it depends how much Saloman needs him. What I do know is that you're not as safe as I'd hoped you'd be right now."

"I'm perfectly safe," Elizabeth argued, although her hands still shook. "None of them knows where I am. You checked yourself for vampires following us."

"Well . . ." His worried glance slid between the two women. "What if Mihaela stays here with you? Just to be on the safe side."

"Don't be ridiculous," Elizabeth objected. "Mihaela needs rest—and a doctor!"

"I'm fine," Mihaela croaked.

"See?" Elizabeth waved one indignant hand.

Konrad's gaze encompassed Mihaela and István. "What do you think?" he asked. And his doubts, the fact that he deferred to his colleagues, impressed Elizabeth as his previous commands had not. It showed he was shaken by the Zoltán incident, which he hadn't foreseen at all and which had clearly dented his habitual self-confidence.

A fresh twinge of unease spiraled up Elizabeth's spine, but she ignored it, because more than anything, she wanted, *needed* to be on her own. Though it might have been silly, this room felt like her haven of peace and sanity in a world gone nightmarishly insane. And the hunters, however much she was beginning to like and admire them, were definitely part of the insanity. She needed them out of here.

István started to say, "Perhaps—"

"Actually," Elizabeth interrupted, "it isn't up to them—or to you, Konrad. I appreciate—I really do!—your concern, but I *am* staying here. By myself." They all regarded her with surprised consternation. *Oh please, just hurry up and go. . . .*

"What," Mihaela whispered, "if we leave one of the detectors here? She'd have time to get out of the room and phone us."

She took something from her pocket and laid it on the bedside table—a small, square piece of plastic, perhaps three inches long, with a small rectangular display and an LED, neither lit.

Konrad frowned. "We can't leave equipment behind."

"Not normally," Mihaela agreed, touching her painful throat. "But I think we're in a special situation. We need to keep Elizabeth safe."

"That's why she should come with us!" Konrad was beginning to look harassed as well as frustrated.

"I'm not coming," Elizabeth declared. "Although I'll happily keep your device under my pillow and return it to you safely in the morning. Come on, guys, we all need some sleep."

Konrad drew in his breath. Mihaela stood, as if the matter were settled, and he gave a final, decisive nod. "Very well. Look, Elizabeth. Switch it on here and leave it on all night. It has enough charge to last beyond sunrise. The light comes on if there is any anomaly—vampire—in the vicinity. The display will show a rough distance and direction. The whole thing also vibrates when the light goes on, so by all means put it under your pillow."

"I understand," Elizabeth said, shepherding them to the door. It felt more like shooing, and she knew she should feel guilty about that. Probably she would in the morning, but right now, as she closed the door on them, she was aware only of massive relief.

It seemed that her habitual solitude, which sometimes depressed her with loneliness, had become necessary to her. Soon, she wouldn't be able to form any kind of relationship with anybody, let alone a live-in, lasting one of lifelong love and respect. Which she'd given up on anyhow after her last disastrous and ultimately humiliating romantic experience.

With a sour smile, Elizabeth went into the tiny bathroom and turned on the shower. It was a good way to empty her mind, to think only of the warmth and comfort of the water coursing over her skin and into her eyes and mouth. Not for the first time, she acknowledged what a sensual experience showering was, enjoying the gentle battering of water on her neck and shoulders and hardened nipples. As she soaped herself, her hands lingered there of their own volition before sweeping down her stomach to the soft, sensitive flesh between her legs.

Unbidden, she remembered Saloman's alluring touch, and the treacherous, perverse response of her body. And those responses began to repeat themselves. Her limbs felt languid and sexy; her hips moved under the water jet as the tingling heat spread downward from her stomach and upward from between her thighs, to merge at her core.

She lifted her arms, letting the water rush over her armpits and down her breasts, washing the soap away and leaving her skin clean and glowing and almost unbearably sensitive. Half-ashamed, she cried out silently for a man's touch, a man's caresses that would feel like his, that would make her feel . . .

"Oh, stop!" she whispered fiercely to herself.

She turned off the shower and stepped out. Grabbing a towel and her toothbrush, she brushed with unnecessary force, hoping the mundane frothing and spitting would calm the inconvenient yearnings of her body.

She'd long ago given up dreams of domestic bliss in favor of an academic career, and as she well knew, that career was a lot more successful to date than her few humiliating attempts at relationships. With a first-class honors degree, two years of challenging but acclaimed research into vampire superstitions that had earned her a teaching job at the university this year, and the beginnings of a strong thesis that should bring her a PhD by next year, she was justifiably proud. Even Richard was proud of her, although once or twice she'd have sacrificed the intellectual admiration in his eyes for the predatory glow she glimpsed in them as they rested on a nubile female student or the glamorous art history lecturer who was currently seen around town with him.

However, in her most honest moments, she acknowledged that romantic entanglement with Richard was pure fantasy. In fact, she suspected she used her attraction to him as a shield. If she was spoken for, even if only in her own mind, then she couldn't be flustered or seduced by other men—men who might actually get through her prickles and hurt her.

That all seemed rather pathetic now. Outside this room was a world she'd never even imagined, a world most people were entirely unaware of. And she, for once in her life, had a chance to make a real contribution. Admittedly, she'd done the world a disservice by awakening Saloman in the first place, but she could make that right.

She didn't know why he hadn't come for her tonight. But she knew it was just a matter of time. For some reason, he was amusing himself with her, toying with her, a little bit like Richard occasionally teased her; yet somehow she knew Saloman would deliver, and instead of romance, it would be death.

Death. And beyond that, the chaos he'd inflict on the world.

Padding across the bedroom, drying in the humid air, she dragged her worn old T-shirt from under the pillow and let it unfold. She frowned at it, then threw it onto the floor. Somehow, the act seemed symbolic.

Naked, she climbed into bed. As she reached for the lamp switch, her gaze caught Mihaela's detector, sitting dully on the table. She winked at it, stuffed it under her pillow and switched off the light.

Although she'd only accepted the detector to get rid of the hunters, she appreciated it now for adding to her sense of security in this room, her haven, where she'd finally grown up and acknowledged her responsibilities.

†

She woke in darkness, her heart thudding, her body tingling as if from some sexy dream. Her hand rested on coarser fabric than her sheets, and beneath the fabric was something both hard and supple—like human flesh.

It seemed she was still dreaming. Experimentally, she twitched her fingers and the flesh, whatever it was, moved under her hand in instant response—a slow, sensual ripple, like the reaction of a man to a woman's caress. It would be a good dream to continue . . . only . . .

Only it didn't feel like a dream—at least, no more than the whole previous day had done. Leaving her hand where it was, in case the flesh escaped her, she drew in her breath to scream and grabbed the lamp switch with her free hand.

Its energy-saving lightbulb flickered into a dim, easy-on-the-eyes glow.

Saloman sat on her bed, Mihaela's detector held between his long, elegant fingers.

Oh fuck, I'm dead.

She didn't even bother to scream. She didn't think she could in her current state. He looked right at her, not even blinking in the brightening light. Fear rose up and swallowed her.

"Good evening," he said, as if they'd met at some public soiree. His gaze dropped back to the detector. "What is this?"

Numb, still lying awkwardly, propped up on her elbow with her head against her shoulder, Elizabeth followed his attention. The device lay on his palm, the LED not even flickering. It did seem to be vibrating, but so slightly that it just gave occasional twitches. The display was as dead as it had ever been. *Piece of crap. Thank God I didn't rely on it.*

Hysteria rose up from nowhere. No, she'd relied on blind, stupid, ignorant faith, and now the bastard was actually sitting on her bed, playing with the hunters' secret weapon, which he had extracted from right under her pillow. One was as much use as the other.

"It's a vampire detector," she said defiantly, hoping to frighten him off with the potential arrival of the hunters—before she remembered that all that had kept her alive the other night had been her disbelief in him. "Or that's the nonsense they fed me."

"It doesn't work," he observed.

"That must be because you're not a vampire."

He cast her a quick, mocking glance, and her brief hope died. "Well, one of us is upsetting it. Interesting device." He slipped it into his shirt pocket.

"That's mine!" she exclaimed.

"No, it isn't. I'll return it to the hunters when we meet. I only want to see how it works."

So do I. The hysteria was back, catching at her breath until she swallowed it down. "How did you get in here? What do you want?"

"I came through the window."

"It's locked!"

His eyes glinted. "Give me some credit."

"Besides, I didn't invite you in," she added desperately.

"You've been reading Bram Stoker," he chided.

"So have you."

He smiled at that, not the swiftly vanishing half smile that had so intrigued her on their first encounter, but a proper, devastating smile of genuine amusement. "Of course. I'm not sure my friend Vlad would be impressed by this fresh assault upon his reputation. Though it might entertain him."

"Vlad the Impaler was your friend?" She didn't mean to say it. The words just spilled out with her involuntary excitement.

"For a time."

A tide of questions rose up, together with the realization that Saloman was a historian's dream. His gleaming eyes acknowledged it, forcing her to close her lips in silence. *What a waste. What I could learn from him . . .*

He's not a bloody teacher! He's a vampire!

"What do you want?" she snapped a second time, registering with vague surprise that her fear was getting lost in academic frustration.

"Your blood, of course."

Okay, so the fear hadn't gone. It had merely taken a brief— very brief—backseat. "Go to hell," she said shakily.

"You don't mean that," he mocked.

"Yes, I bloody do."

"Then don't hold my thigh so tightly."

Baffled, she followed his gaze to her right hand, which still rested on his black linen–encased leg, her fingers digging into his flesh. He moved his thigh suggestively, and with a gasp, she snatched her hand away.

"I was touched by your welcome," he said.

"I was asleep," she returned with what dignity she could muster.

"You must have pleasant dreams."

She flicked a glance at him, unsure. It was a mistake, for he caught her gaze and held it with frightening ease. She began to drown in the depths of his black eyes and clenched her fists on the sheet as if to grab hold of the last remnants of sense.

He said, "You're lonely." And oddly, it didn't sound like mockery, which she could have shrugged off. It sounded—surprised.

"I wish," she said bitterly. "Lately, I can't move for people in this room."

"You're far from home, alone in a strange country. . . . Do you have a husband, Elizabeth?"

Her name on his lips, in his deep, stirring voice, sent an unexpected shiver down her spine.

"No."

"A lover who pines for you?"

"No! Which is fortunate since you intend to kill me."

Somewhere she was still amazed by this bizarre conversation. But most of her could glare into his handsome, unfathomable face with anger and, she hoped, hatred.

"That's a point of view," he allowed. "A very selfless one." His hand lifted, and one long, tapered finger touched her shoulder—her naked shoulder.

Oh Jesus Christ, she'd gone to sleep in the nude. What in God's name had possessed her? *And why the hell should I care? I'll be dead in a minute.*

His finger traced a line of fire inward along her clavicle, heating her whole body beyond endurance. *I could lie here and be pawed and murdered. Or I could shift my perverse arse and get out of here.*

With a gasp of outrage, she slapped his hand aside and lunged for the other side of the bed.

She didn't make it. She didn't even come close. As if she'd never removed it, his hand pressed her back into the pillows and she couldn't budge. She felt as if she'd been winded. His hand over her heart was as unyielding as steel.

She aimed a vicious kick at him, but her leg tangled in the sheet and her blow lost all its strength. She could swing her fist, but with despair, she knew it would never reach him. He moved too fast, so she contented herself with a glare she was afraid looked more defiant than furious.

But her pathetic escape attempt didn't appear to anger him. She wondered if he'd even noticed. His hand on her chest relaxed its force. He spread his fingers across her skin, until two of them reached the upper swell of her naked breast. In this new position occasioned by her futile lunge, she was half sitting and terribly afraid that the sheet had slipped beyond all modesty, especially since his gaze appeared to be on his hand, as if admiring the effect of his skin on hers.

Her heart thundered. He would feel that too, thudding into his palm. His hand moved, subtly undulating and his fingers brushed against her skin.

"Silken," he murmured, "and rosy with warm, sweet blood . . . So—sacrificial."

"In your dreams," she gasped.

"Indeed. I thought I was dreaming when you first leaned over me, so beautiful and wondering, with that strong, stirring blood you were so obliging as to drip right on my lips."

She stared at him, mesmerized. "You saw that? You were awake then?"

"Oh yes. I was always awake in that sense. I could see you. I could hear you talking to yourself—*Whoever bled to death from a rose thorn?* I could even feel your tender, probing fingers all over my body. I just couldn't move. Not until you rubbed the blood into my lips—which, by the way, was an experience so sensual that I would almost be ready to die again to repeat it." His voice lowered to that husky tone she remembered, the one that both paralyzed and aroused. "Your blood and my lips . . . an enticing combination." She heard her own breath catch and quicken; she didn't know how to hide it. His hand, sliding lower, must have felt it all.

"Not from where I'm sitting," she spat. At least she wanted to spit. She was afraid she squeaked. His lips quirked, a smile dawning and dying as he leaned closer, inhaling her. His free hand came up and touched her throat, caressing, right over the old wound he'd created and healed. Unable to bear the sensitivity, she seized his wrist, but no amount of tugging made any difference.

"A meal to be savored," he murmured. "Served hot or cold. And yet"—his head bent nearer her throat, his voice softening until it was almost inaudible—"and yet I will regret the ending."

What the hell did he mean by that? That he didn't *want* to kill her? Could there be a way out of this? In just an instant, she'd feel again those soft lips on her skin, the prick of his teeth, and the long, ecstatic pull on her blood. Her body flamed, as eager to feel the pleasure as to avoid the resulting death. She felt the weight of his body pressing against her chest. A pool of sexual moisture broke from between her legs and trickled down into the sheet, spreading heat beneath her. She was sure his lips brushed the tiny hairs on her earlobes, on her neck. She jerked again on his wrist, but he only slid his hand around to her nape, holding her more firmly.

Whatever his regrets, they clearly weren't enough to stop him. She couldn't fight him physically. Her strength had always been her mind, and she cast around in it to find anything that might halt him or even slow him down.

"Zoltán!" she gasped out. "You've got more pressing concerns than this. Zoltán betrayed you! He attacked me!"

The vampire hunters wouldn't approve. He'd go and kill Zoltán, which was just what they didn't want. But right now that paled into insignificance beside the necessity of saving her own life.

In any case, it had an effect. Saloman went very still, and for a moment, she wondered if she'd won a breathing space at least. Then his lips closed on her throat, caressing and teasing her skin. She was sure he even flicked the vein with his tongue, tapping it like a nurse before inserting a needle.

She trembled, both yearning and dreading and unable to distinguish one from the other. Saloman relaxed the pressure of his body on hers, and the hand on her chest slipped lower between them and closed over her naked breast. She let out a tiny, inarticulate sound that might have been a sigh or a sob.

Saloman lifted his head. His black eyes burned into hers. "I know," he said, and dropped his gaze to her mouth, to her breasts. His palm moved, gliding over the aching peak of her nipple.

"Know what?" she demanded with desperation, having lost the thread.

"That Zoltán attacked you. He has no finesse."

"You were there," she blurted. "You were the other shadow...."

And yet she could have sworn she'd surprised him by her original revelation.

"The *other* shadow? I'm not sure I like that. It offends my sense of superiority."

A breath of laughter escaped her, as unbidden as it was appalling. "Are you for real?"

"Oh yes." His hand released her breast to draw the sheet farther down. "Don't I feel real?" His fingers touched her lips, parting them with a downward sweep that continued over her chin and throat and down between her breasts to her navel. She moved with the caress, arching under his hand because she couldn't help it. She felt like a musical instrument, played by his careless, talented fingers.

"I began this meal the night you wakened me," he whispered. "And I will finish it—all of it."

She swallowed, trying not to squirm under his devouring gaze. Jesus, no one had ever looked at her like that, with such greedy, urgent passion; but then, no one had ever regarded her as a meal before either.

His finger circled her belly button, dipping in and out.

She gasped, "What do you mean, *all of it*?" Was there a choice? Could she convince him to leave her alive?

The almost smile dawned and died on his lips.

"Sex," he said unexpectedly. She blinked, and his gaze moved up to her face, mocking, yet scalding in its intensity. "That's what you call it these days, isn't it? When you're being polite." He laid his whole hand flat on her stomach, then swept outward and downward to her thigh. "Let me say it in my own more familiar terms. Tonight, I will pleasure you. I will take every delight your sweet flesh can give me. And just before sunrise, I will finish the meal."

Could she negotiate for one without the other? Burning up

with his words, she wanted all of it. She remembered the staggering bliss of his killing mouth on her throat, was only too aware of
her helpless reaction to his touch right now.

*He could make me orgasm just by looking at me. . . . Oh shit, what is
the matter with me?*

"Well, that's novel," she managed, with what mockery she
could summon, forcing herself to be still under his idly caressing
hands. "Dalliance and dinner instead of the other way round."

His lips quirked. "I offered them both together, as I recall. I
believe I can still manage that. Afterward."

She squirmed, and he smiled, pleased and predatory.

Fighting herself at least as much as him, she tried for further
delay. "Why didn't you just do it, then? What's the point of all the
cat and mouse?"

"Fun," he replied, as though surprised. "And the fact that I
barely had the strength to stand, let alone fuck."

Her face flamed all over again, and his hand on her nape mas-
saged the muscles there, sending shivers all the way down her
spine. They felt more like bolts of lust.

He said, "I'm better now," and drew her forward by the nape
until her naked body rested against him. There was no time to
struggle, if she could have forced herself to it, before his mouth
closed on hers in the most sensual kiss she'd ever known. His lips
dominated, tasting, then sucking, while his tongue thrust in deliberate simulation of sex. She felt his teeth, those terrible fangs, and
without really meaning to, just unable to resist, she touched one
with her tongue.

A sound like a groan escaped him. She was swept closer into
his body, her breasts crushed against his hard, powerful chest
while the hand not caressing her nape splayed flat against her

naked back and began to play among her vertebrae, spreading wild, devastating lust straight between her legs.

He opened her mouth wider with his, deepening the kiss. She felt dizzy, as if she were falling, and realized he was pressing her back into the pillows, moving the rest of his body onto the bed with her.

This is it. He's really going to do it; have sex with me. Everything in her leapt toward that goal, that yearning that had become a need, a necessity. In just an instant, she'd feel the weight of his hard, muscular body. As he removed his clothes, she'd feel his naked skin on hers, his hardness pressing between her thighs. This amazing, beautiful being wanted to have sex with her.

And then he would kill her.

Her mouth opened wide under his. She didn't know if it was a sob of fury or a cry of desire. But at least it spurred her to jerk against him in a futile attempt to dislodge him—futile because she realized her hands were clinging to his long black hair and his shoulder, holding him to her at the same time as she was pushing him off.

And the bastard laughed inside her head. *Relax and enjoy it*, he said. She pulled his hair hard, just as she dragged her mouth free.

And something crashed and pounded on the bedroom door.

Chapter Seven

"Elizabeth!"

It was Konrad's voice, shouting through the door as he hammered on it. In fact there must have been at least two pairs of fists, judging by the racket. There would be complaints. She'd be asked to leave.

"Elizabeth, let us in. The detector won't work."

"Really?" said Saloman. And unforgivably, Elizabeth wanted to laugh. It wasn't funny. Saloman could bite her, drain her blood so fast she wouldn't even be aware of it, as he'd done with the vampire who'd attacked her the night before, and escape through the window before the vampire hunters could break their way in. Cornered as he was, and by those who could hurt him as she could not, she was sure it crossed his mind. Her blood was important to him, to bring him back to full strength, and he'd already said that the game, whatever it had been, would end before sunrise.

Something else crashed against the door. A shoulder? A foot?

"How disappointing," Saloman murmured, stroking her hair. He smiled. "I believe your knights in shining armor have come to rescue you—again."

She hated being so helpless. Worse, she hated that this situation was her own stupid, stubborn fault. One thing was certain. If she survived the night—which meant in effect the next two minutes—things would change.

"I love the way your eyes flash," Saloman said.

She opened her mouth to retort—something blistering, she was sure—but before she could say a word, the bedroom door flew open and Konrad and István tumbled in.

"Jesus Christ," István gasped, staring at the scene that met his eyes—Elizabeth in bed, naked in the arms of the vampire. He held a stake between his shaking fingers, but even as Elizabeth took that in, István's fingers gripped harder.

Konrad already held his like a spear, as if ready to throw. Would her life be worth it to rid the world of Saloman? In their eyes? Yes. They'd already used her as bait. In the grand scheme of things, the few puny lives of Elizabeth and the three hunters were all worth sacrificing for the safety of the rest of the world.

Saloman released her. In the draft of suddenly cold air, she seized the sheet and yanked it up over her body.

"Good evening," Saloman said, rising to his feet. Removing himself from her, he'd just made himself a more viable target. Was that deliberate? Chivalry?

No. He still wanted her blood for strength. He didn't want the hunters to kill her any more than he wanted Zoltán to do it.

He reached into his shirt pocket, and both men tensed. Saloman took out Mihaela's detector. "I believe this is yours," he said, tossing it in his palm. "It's—er—broken."

"No, it isn't," Konrad said. "It just doesn't recognize the body chemistry of an Ancient. Until now it hasn't needed to. Sorry," he added with a quick glance at Elizabeth. "We just found out. Did he bite you?"

She shook her head, unable to form even the simplest word.

"A vampire just can't get any privacy these days," Saloman complained. Without warning he threw the detector straight at István's head. István staggered, but before he fell, the stake had left Konrad's fingers, hurled in fury at Saloman's heart.

Elizabeth cried out, at which particular event she didn't know or care—at all of it, everything. At the same time, she watched the fast, true flight of the stake.

Die, you bastard! she thought, and wanted to weep.

The stake blurred. So did Saloman's arm. When her focus returned, Saloman held the stick in his hand.

"Thank you," he said, strolling across the room.

In spite of themselves, the hunters fell back. István was clutching his bleeding forehead while his right hand tried to aim his stake. Konrad, defenseless, cast wildly around until his gaze found Elizabeth's bag with the stake half fallen out on the floor. He took a step toward it.

Saloman didn't follow either of them, although Elizabeth knew he could have drained and killed them both—and still returned to have sex with her before dessert.

There were stirrings and whisperings in the passage outside as people came to investigate the noise. Konrad kicked the door shut and reached for Elizabeth's stake. Saloman didn't even glance at him, but from his position by the window, reached out and took hold of the curtain, leaving as he'd entered.

"Wait!"

Everyone glanced at her in surprise. Idiots. Partly, as guilt raged, she was giving the hunters time to kill him. And partly, away from the immediate threat of his dangerous and sensual presence, her brain could function again. She couldn't suppress a nagging doubt about him. He had been the friend of princes. However mad he'd been when they staked him, surely there had once been more to him than raging revenge and hunger for power?

"Is this what you really want?" she blurted. "Just revenge and meaningless power? While the world around you dies in chaos?"

His gaze, opaque, full only of darkness, connected with hers. "In this new, urban world of wealth and freedom, music and technology? Of course not." He smiled. "I want to have fun."

The curtain moved. But she didn't see him go. She didn't think she even blinked, but by the time he'd finished speaking, he was no longer there.

†

The hotel guests had been reassured; the staff pacified.

Elizabeth was pleased to see that her hands were steadier as she wrapped them around the cup of coffee István gave her. She'd never been so glad that she traveled everywhere with her little kettle and jar of instant coffee.

"Is your head all right?" she asked, glancing at the cut, now covered with a bandage.

"Fine," said István ruefully. "Though I can't say the same for the detector."

"Sorry about that," said Konrad, nursing the broken pieces of the useless instrument in his hand. "István was on watch and got the message from Budapest. We'd asked them for information on the physiology of Ancients, and it seems it was known that their body temperature was warmer than that of modern vampires. It's one of the things the detector picks up. We were afraid the biochemistry would be too different as well."

"It is," Elizabeth confirmed. "The thing barely acknowledged his existence." She took a sip of coffee and tried not to think how close she'd come to abject surrender. What she had to deal with was her behavior before he appeared. Ignoring the advice of the hunters, she'd assumed she knew best—she who'd wandered into this weirdness just three days ago, knowing absolutely nothing. What had seemed like sane, sensible, and healthy cynicism about the possibility of a vampire attack here in her room, was now shown to be crass, criminally negligent stupidity.

"I told him about Zoltán," she blurted. "I was trying to distract him, though it didn't work. He knows Zoltán broke their agreement by attacking me tonight."

"Don't worry," István soothed. "There's nothing we can do about that now."

"I think he might have known anyway . . . and I . . . I imagined I saw someone else up there. When Zoltán jumped onto the roof, I think it might have been him—Saloman."

"Why didn't you say that before?" Konrad asked, brooding over the broken detector.

"I thought I was imagining things," she said miserably. "My only excuse is that I've been having a hard job thinking of all this as anything other than imagination."

She took a deep breath and gazed at Konrad. "I'm sorry. I want to help. And I don't want ever to be caught out like that again—totally helpless, like a lamb to the slaughter. Will you teach me to fight? Like Mihaela?"

Konrad smiled. It lightened his anxious face, making him seem younger and more approachable. She wondered how old he was.

"Yes," he said warmly. "We'll teach you to fight like Mihaela. And we'll gladly accept your help if you accept ours. In fact, you may well be a valuable asset. As his Awakener, you might find you have strengths and skills you don't yet know about." He exchanged glances with István." I think it will take all of us together to defeat Saloman. But it can be done."

✝

Dmitriu found the underground network of sewers and cellars beneath Bistriţa distasteful. Though it was a convenient way of getting around the city during the hours of daylight, much of it was dirty and tended to stink. At least the rats understood the proper order of things and kept well out of his way. He was more likely to encounter a sewage worker or two, who, as Saloman had pointed out, could provide a decent meal.

Dmitriu thought it a pity that Saloman had had to move out of the church undercroft after so short a stay—the novelty of the "great evil one" living under such a holy place had appealed to Dmitriu, but after he'd shown himself to the Awakener, there hadn't been any choice. A home swarming with vampire hunters just wasn't comfortable, however many hunters one got to eat *en passant*.

Saloman's new "home," since yesterday, was a cellar complex beneath ruined and disused buildings on the edge of the town center—damp, but not too malodorous. He hadn't troubled to secure it with physical locks or with charm shields, a sign for any who cared to look that he was afraid of no one—or that he just couldn't be bothered when the residence was so temporary.

As Dmitriu entered the first cellar, he began to think that Saloman had already moved on. Silence rather than the normal greeting or cynical joke greeted his arrival. There was no scent of Saloman, and none at all of vampire.

Dmitriu moved farther in, searching for clues as to Saloman's whereabouts, until, in one of the back cellars, he found him seated at a battered old table by the glow of a single candle. An ancient television flickered silent pictures opposite. It didn't surprise him.

"There you are," said Dmitriu. Saloman's back was to him, and he didn't turn, seemingly engrossed.

Dmitriu would have understood that. Saloman was as fascinated by modern gadgets as by modern life. He'd taken to both with remarkable and admirable ease, his desire to learn as voracious as his ability to soak it all up. What Dmitriu didn't understand was why he chose to mask his presence. Nor did he lower his barriers when Dmitriu spoke. Alarm twinged.

"What are you doing?" Dmitriu asked.

"Counting my money," Saloman said, and spun around in his chair to face him. "Or at least what passes for money in these strange times. What was wrong with gold?"

Dmitriu's jaw dropped. On the table were piles and piles of bank notes. "Where the . . . ?"

"Here and there," Saloman said. "I had gold in lots of places. Some of it is even still there—and it seems some people still want it."

"What are you . . . ?"

"I'm bored with living in cellars. I've remembered I liked palaces much better."

"You did," Dmitriu agreed. He couldn't help smiling at the

memories, but Saloman made no response. "Do you want Maria to . . . ?"

"Oh no. Transylvania is a backwater. I'm going to Hungary."

Dmitriu walked forward and reached out to rifle through the money. "Already? You know that if this was stolen from banks, it's probably marked and you'll bring a heap of trouble down on yourself."

Saloman merely curled his sensual lips, giving nothing away. Irritated with Saloman's pointless secrecy, Dmitriu shrugged, as if he didn't care. "Will Zoltán go with you to Hungary? Incidentally, the hunters killed his bodyguards last night."

"I know. I was there."

"Don't trust him, Saloman," Dmitriu urged.

"Oh, I don't trust anyone. But this is a smoother transition of power. Everyone already knows Zoltán is number two. At the most."

"He'll go after the Awakener," Dmitriu warned.

"He already has. She's with the hunters."

Dmitriu frowned. "You should have fed on her when you had the chance."

"I'll feed on her when I like."

In normal circumstances, a derisive hoot would have been in order. Today, with Saloman in this strange mood, he said only, "How, when you're going away?"

"She'll know where to find me."

"How?" Dmitriu demanded.

Saloman smiled. "I told her."

Dmitriu threw down the bundle of money he'd been playing with. "I hear Lajos is in Budapest," he warned.

"Dear Lajos," said Saloman fondly.

"I'm sure you'll enjoy him," Dmitriu snapped. "Providing he doesn't unite with Karl and Maximilian—wherever that bastard is—to stake you again. And have you considered the threat those three would be to you if allied to Zoltán?"

"Why do you think *I* allied with Zoltán?" Saloman sounded amused, though there was a warning blackness in his eyes as he added, "My brain didn't atrophy as I slept."

Dmitriu sighed and thought with longing of Maria's pleasant, shady garden where he had the best of both worlds, no trouble, and pleasant scents in his nostrils. Budapest was large, grimy, and horribly noisy these days. He'd grown to hate it, though with Saloman it would be different, even exciting for the first time in decades. He said, "Do you want me to come with you?"

Saloman met his gaze. "No."

The word was like a kick in the teeth. His vague longing for peace melted to nothing beside Saloman's rejection. The Ancient stood up. "Your work is done. You sent me Elizabeth Silk."

He'd become boring, Dmitriu realized with a jolt. Shutting himself off from brutal vampire politics, retiring from both worlds to live in the half existence of Maria's comfort. What did he even get there? No sex, not anymore. Some thin old blood and a safe base from which to hunt younger, more nourishing prey. He'd been merely existing, much as Saloman had over the same period, except that Dmitriu didn't have the excuse of a stake through the heart.

He didn't want to think about that. In any case he was sure Saloman wouldn't answer the reluctant questions that gnawed at his heart whenever the thoughts sneaked in.

Instead, he tried for common sense. "You're moving too fast," he objected. "You need rest to improve your strength. God knows what you need to improve your mood."

Sex, probably. Despite all his "f" words on awakening, although he'd fed plenty, the frolicking had been pretty much in the way of business, apart from the nightclub visit, and Dmitriu was almost sure there hadn't been any fucking at all. It worried him. Either Saloman was weaker than he let on, or, even worse, he was still obsessed with Tsigana. After three hundred years? In this day and age he could have his pick with ease. Well, he always had in any age, vampire or human.

"Travel," Saloman replied. "Tantalizing new blood. And—er—tarts."

Dmitriu roused himself from the unaccustomed ache in his heart. "I never cared," he said, "for the letter 't.'"

✝

Saloman leapt across the rooftops of Bistriţa, reveling in the uplifting freedom of movement. To human observers, he would just be a blur against the blue-black sky.

Although he'd run like this from Sighesciu to Bistriţa, he'd been far weaker then, unable to enjoy it because of the massive aching of muscles he hadn't used in more than three hundred years. Even walking had been hard enough then. But in four days and nights of rigorous exercise, his body had begun to strengthen and rejoice. The old skills returned, and his senses grew increasingly sharp, which was how he knew where the traitor and murderer Karl was. And how he knew which house was occupied by his Awakener.

He couldn't resist pausing on the roof of the small, insignificant suburban house. The sound of her voice made his ears twitch and the blood flow faster in his veins. He jumped lightly to the ground, just beside the front window, but they'd closed the shutters and there was only a tiny crack to squint through. Sacrificing his dignity, he looked anyway.

They were all there. The girl whose throat Zoltán had damaged while trying to feed from the Awakener; the two men who'd interrupted his promise of passion last night; and Elizabeth Silk herself.

Just for an instant, he thought he was going to have to rescue his long-anticipated supper once again. Dressed in cut-down denim jeans that seemed to lengthen her already-alluring legs and a tiny top that looked more like an undergarment, she brandished a stick and circled the other similarly armed woman. Her normally rather unworldly face bore an expression of such fierce concentration that it fooled him for a moment, before he realized the fight wasn't real.

The sticks they held were blunt. The furniture had been carefully moved aside, not scattered in anger. And from the sidelines, the German issued instruction, encouragement, and praise.

Silently, Saloman began to laugh. They were teaching her to fight vampires. Did any of them seriously imagine such knowledge would protect her from *him*?

But then, perhaps she was joining the hunters, becoming one of them—and abandoning her research? Even if recent events had shown her plausible theories to be total bunkum, she still had a historian's insatiable curiosity. He hadn't missed the light in her eyes, the barely contained questions that sprang to her lips and remained unspoken only through pride when she'd realized all the things he could tell her—if she could trust his answers.

Christ, she even moved like Tsigana, graceful and sure. For

some reason, the recognition didn't please him. There was something too about the deceptively delicate structure of her face, which had thrown him on their first encounter. She looked and smelled too much like his old, treacherous lover. He preferred to look for differences—and found them. Her large, beautiful hazel eyes were very much her own, gentle and expressive—they only tried to be secretive—and her full, sweet lips, even now when they were clamped tight with the effort of her fight, spoke of a personal vulnerability that would have been quite alien to Tsigana. Beneath the disconcerting smell of their shared blood, Elizabeth had her own, subtle, alluring scent that called to all his senses, feeding his hunger for her body as much as for her blood.

And then it was good to see that she, Elizabeth, was faster as she flung herself aside to evade the Romanian's lunge, and spun on her heel only to stop and face her opponent once more, steady and watchful. Her quickened breathing was deep but even, lifting and dropping the soft, enticing breasts he'd caressed last night. A bead of sweat glistened between them, trickling down her skin and out of sight.

Peering through a crack in a shutter was not the correct position from which to appreciate Elizabeth Silk. She did the same things to his loins she'd always done, from the moment she'd first leaned over him in the crypt, her whole beautiful face alight with fascination. Her sensual touch exploring his body, on his lips, the first he'd known for centuries, had been almost unbearable. Lust was hard to deal with when one's body was frozen and couldn't react as normal. It was as if his very blood had ached, and yet he was sure it had stirred with excitement because of her beauty, and her blood, and her scent of Tsigana. Likewise, he had no time now to indulge such desires. He had to stop imagining those long, smooth legs wrapped around his hips in passion, and just appreciate their speed of movement.

As the Romanian closed with her and they fell onto the carpet, Elizabeth twisted in an effort not to be trapped beneath, as the brutish vampire had done to her the night before last.

She was learning already. It made him curious. He wanted to see her defend herself in reality, her red-blond hair flying out from her soft, delicate face, as she fought and defeated her enemies. Her small-boned body, which looked and felt as if it might snap under his hands, was in fact strong and flexible. But then she bore Tsigana's blood, and Tsigana was one of his "killers." Elizabeth had strengths she didn't yet dream of.

He knew an urge to tear down the shutters and crash into the room, to hold the others captive with one commanding point of his finger while he pressed Elizabeth's delectable little body into his.

She would fight it as she always did, but before he took her, he would make her respond with the passion he sensed that she needed. He was sure she wasn't a virgin—how refreshing of this age to disregard that "virtue" once more—but she was largely unawakened. Her unconscious responses, as well as her shock, told him that. It would make it all the sweeter to take her, to push inside her hot, welcoming depths and give her pleasure as he drained her blood.

He stepped back. He could no longer see into the room, watch her gaze at the German with trusting concentration, or observe the Hungarian boy staring at her with disguised lust of his own. She didn't see it. He suspected she saw none of it, lost in her academia as much as in her own faulty view of herself. She intrigued him, not just by her pale, refined beauty of which she seemed quite unaware, but by her contradictory characteristics: lonely and self-sufficient; unworldly and cynical; solemn and humorous; fearful and unexpectedly courageous; standoffish and passionate. . . .

Fuck. He could break in and end it now, take all the semimystical strength she had to offer, both as his Awakener and the descendant of his "killer." It would be useful in Budapest.

But on the whole, he preferred his original plan. He'd let her find him, buoyed up with hunter training. He would enjoy the fight all the more, and her end would be all the sweeter.

A man and woman passed in the street, a dog at their heels. The dog whimpered and cowered in at their legs, casting quick, furtive glances into the garden where he stood. Saloman didn't trouble to soothe the animal. He tensed his legs and soared into the air.

Feeling stronger with each leap, he ran west with ever-increasing speed into the Carpathian Mountains, following the sour stench of Karl's fear. He didn't trouble to mask his identity or his presence. There was nowhere left for Karl to hide, and it did his vengeful soul good to know the vampire was fleeing before him in panic.

Saloman's honed senses would have found him alone on any mountain peak. Karl clearly knew that. He sought refuge in a crowded village tavern. He may have imagined Saloman's senses wouldn't be able to distinguish him there. He may have imagined Saloman would choose not to kill him before human witnesses—though where such an absurd notion would have come from, Saloman couldn't imagine.

He halted at last in the street outside the tavern, once again merely a leather-clad man to any passing human—or perhaps not. An old woman sat on a stool by her gate across the road, enjoying the cool of the night. Most humans he'd encountered so suddenly since his awakening ignored him, assuming they just hadn't noticed his approach. This woman made the sign of the cross with one hand, and the sign against the evil eye with the other, and fled inside, abandoning her fallen stool as she hobbled away.

Saloman curled his lip. A place of old knowledge, it seemed; yet Karl had just arrived here—on this visit, at least.

Saloman strolled up to the door, nodding at the men he met in the doorway. They muttered polite greetings and stood aside for him to enter.

The place was noisy and smoky. Several men glanced at him as he entered, but Karl wasn't one of them.

The vampire sat at the back of the bar, sharing a table with several burly farmers who all but squashed him into the corner. Karl's face was turned toward one of them as if deep in some interesting conversation. He might have been. Karl was quite a charming fellow at one time. In fact, it offended Saloman to see him like this, pretending, cringing, masking with desperate futility, consumed by fear of the stronger being he had betrayed and joined with others to kill. There was no more fun to be had here. This was one to finish quickly.

Saloman looked neither to the left nor right, although he was aware of every gaze that followed him. He ignored them, walking straight toward Karl, staring at his face until everyone at the table looked up expectantly at Saloman, and at last Karl was forced to do the same.

Miserable worm. He lacked even the courage to face the consequences of his actions. Saloman halted and reached across the table. Karl jerked back as if to avoid him, moving fast enough to be a mere blur to the humans, but Saloman found his shoulder.

"Karl, my friend. At last." As he pulled Karl toward him, the men at the table made way. They couldn't see that Karl pulled back, resisting all the way, or that Saloman had to use considerable force. The struggle was secret, desperate, but the result of the encounter was never in doubt, at least not to Saloman, who pressed the vampire into his side and marched him from the tavern.

Across the road, curtains twitched. Saloman didn't care what the old woman saw. He lifted off into the air, taking Karl with him. He bounded across the village rooftops, coming to rest on the high, stout branch of an ancient willow tree.

Karl moaned, as if aware at last of the precise stage of Saloman's recovery. To him, Saloman was the same powerful being he'd been at his "death."

He wasn't, of course. But no one, let alone this worm, needed to discover that.

"You disappoint me," he said in a low voice. "I expected at least a fight, a chase. But you're barely worth the kill. The strength of your blood is outweighed by the meanness of your spirit."

"Then don't kill me," Karl almost squeaked. "I made a terrible mistake, but come on, Saloman, it's been three hundred years! Can't you forgive and forget?"

Saloman curled his lip, more at the use of his name than the wheedling that made him feel physically sick. At this rate, he'd have trouble keeping the bastard's blood down. He should have taken Elizabeth Silk with her strong, sweet blood and alluring body that would have trembled with desire as well as fear as she fought him. The puny, mortal woman had a spirit and courage way beyond this five-hundred-year-old vampire's. Karl would always be paltry.

Finish it. As the first blood of vengeance, it's pretty poor—but very necessary.

"I can't forget. And I never forgive." Saloman bent to his throat and, with the night world spread out below him, felt immeasurably better. Perhaps it helped that his victim began at least to scrabble at his hands, in a vain and feeble attempt to release himself. The willow branch swayed under them—another pleasing sensation.

The funny thing was, one serious blow would have damaged Saloman, but the idea never even crossed Karl's mind. Fear was a powerful weapon. He'd taught that knowledge to many human princes in the past.

Karl was still gibbering. "I never acquired the strength of the older vampires. I never sought it. Spare me and I'll give you Lajos, whose blood is far stronger than mine!"

Ignoring him, Saloman closed his mouth over Karl's throat and bared his fangs.

"I'll give you Maximilian!" Karl screamed.

Saloman paused. For the first time, possibly ever, Karl interested him. He lifted his head. "Maximilian," he repeated. "You really know where Maximilian is?"

Even Dmitriu didn't know that, and Saloman's senses couldn't reach him—yet. But the worm was babbling again. "I had it from Lajos, and you know how thick the two of them used to be. . . ."

"Speak," Saloman interrupted.

"Scotland," Karl blurted.

Saloman blinked. "Scotland? Why Scotland?" He laughed. "Surely not for the climate."

"But yes, for the mist," Karl babbled. "Lajos says he learned masking from an Ancient. That, combined with the mist, means even an Ancient could never find him. But I told you where to look!"

"So you did," Saloman said. "Thanks." And tore his throat out.

The blood was good.

Chapter Eight

"*T*his is amazing." Elizabeth gazed around in wonder. Although the building above was unexceptional, if old and spacious, the basement housed a huge library that seemed to stretch forever. The walls were lined with apparently infinite mahogany and glass bookcases. Tall filing cabinets were scattered among dark wood desks and tables, several of which supported computer terminals. Large and lavish Turkish rugs covered the floor, adding a bizarre air of opulence to the otherwise austere academic surroundings.

At the nearest computer, housed on a high, round table like an old-fashioned library-issue desk, stood a middle-aged man in spectacles, which gleamed at her benignly.

Konrad said, "This is our librarian, Miklós. Miklós, Elizabeth Silk from the UK. She's helping us with the Saloman problem."

Elizabeth had the grace to blush as she accepted Miklós's proffered hand. "I'm sorry. I'm afraid I *caused* the Saloman problem."

"These things happen," the librarian said, and a breath of

laughter escaped Elizabeth because he might have been excusing her for having damaged a book by leaving it in the rain instead of unleashing on the world the most powerful and evil vampire of all time.

Covering her inappropriate mirth, Elizabeth wandered over to the nearest bookcase, gazing in wonder at the ancient bindings. "All this is purely vampire related?"

"Directly, or indirectly," Miklós said. "We have the general reference books necessary to any decent library, plus several related to the paranormal, biographical, and historical areas. We have all the demonologies and supernatural works ever published, plus several that never saw the light of day. We had our own printing press for a while, so there are many learned texts published privately by our predecessors. Every document collected over the centuries pertaining to vampires or the supernatural world in general is kept here, indexed and catalogued. Diaries, letters, confessions, witness statements, even scraps of partially destroyed documents. We never throw anything away. We also have painstakingly compiled genealogies and biographies of all the known vampires born in eastern Europe or living here, which account for more than half of the world's vampire population."

Elizabeth's researcher's heart beat faster. What she could learn here . . . ! "And you maintain this huge collection all on your own?"

"Hardly," Konrad answered. "Miklós has a team of assistant librarians and researchers, all dedicated to getting us the information we need as fast as possible. We also have our own medical staff. Others are field operatives, like István and Mihaela and me."

Elizabeth frowned. "Are you government controlled? Funded?"

"Oh, no," Miklós replied. "Our funding is private and comes

from a variety of sources, all expertly and wisely invested: trusts and funds begun all over the world centuries ago; treasure confiscated from several wealthy vampires we've terminated over the years; donations of all sizes from many sources, including grateful would-be victims we've helped, as well as individual hunters."

Miklós smiled slightly at Elizabeth's obvious surprise. "Hunters are salaried, but their life tends to become their work, and much of it is given back to the organization at death, if not before. The same is true of the upper administrative staff such as me, and even the Grand Masters themselves."

Before Elizabeth, insatiably curious, could ask about the Grand Masters, Miklós hurried on. "As for government control, I'd say we are government-*tolerated*. But only a few at the very heart of government have ever known of our existence. The Communist regime ignored us almost completely, which was actually more comfortable than the occasional curious visitors from the present government. But secrecy is maintained. It has to be."

"Why?" Elizabeth asked. She could guess some of the reasoning, but she was eager to hear it all.

"Well, for one thing, the population would demand we be shut down as crackpots," Konrad said dryly. "For another, we don't want to be pestered by lunatics and attention seekers who'd waste our time. Nor do we want to advertise our location to vampires. This building is shielded and has never been breached. We need it to remain that way. And then, of course, there is the matter of human panic. Most people would not be happy in the knowledge that they share their planet with monsters from horror movies. We don't want to precipitate a full-scale war between the species. It's a war that humans, despite their overwhelming numbers, could only lose. So, for all these reasons, very few people are ever told of our existence."

"I feel incredibly—honored," Elizabeth murmured.

"You are," Konrad said with a twisted smile. He turned to Miklós. "Can you find Elizabeth everything we have on Saloman?"

"Everything?" For the first time, Miklós looked daunted.

"Everything," Konrad repeated. "But there's no rush. Elizabeth will be with us for some time."

"I can't stay indefinitely, though. I have to be back in Scotland in a couple of weeks. Three at the most," she amended, with a quick glance around the shelves. "Um—can we catch Saloman in that time?"

"Oh yes. We all need to do a bit more research, a bit more training. His awakening rather caught us off guard. But we have all we need here to get up to speed on him. And then we can return to Transylvania and nail the bastard."

Elizabeth looked at him, but he'd already turned away, ready to leave the library and continue the tour. She closed her mouth, keeping the churning excitement to herself for now. There would be other times to say she didn't believe they'd need to go back to Transylvania. Saloman had told her so. He was looking for "urban" fun. He'd come to the biggest city in the region, and he'd challenged her to follow.

✝

Emerging from Mihaela's spare bedroom, Elizabeth hesitated at the living room door. Mihaela was curled up in an armchair, nursing a glass of wine and reading a book spread open on her lap.

Elizabeth had gone along with the hunters' plans for her to stay with Mihaela in Budapest, but she felt unsure of her place here—lodger or guest?—and was reluctant to butt in any further.

This flat was clearly Mihaela's escape from work. Light and bright and modern, it contained no obvious reference to the supernatural world, which had to be a huge part of the hunter's life. Elizabeth felt like an intruder.

Mihaela twisted around to face her and gave a quick smile. "Glass of wine?"

The invitation seemed genuine. Gratefully, Elizabeth walked into the room and settled in the vacant armchair while Mihaela poured red wine into the empty glass already waiting for her on the low table.

"There's a casserole in the oven," Mihaela said. "It should be ready in half an hour."

"This is very good of you," Elizabeth said awkwardly, picking up the glass.

"Nonsense. All part of the service." With another grin, Mihaela raised her glass, and Elizabeth smiled back before leaning over to "clink" with her.

"You mean you often have to take in waifs and strays in the line of duty?" Elizabeth asked.

"Homeless victims usually stay at headquarters until they're ready to return to their lives. But you're not really a victim, are you? More of a temporary recruit."

"Do you have many of those?"

Mihaela sipped her wine. "Victims or recruits?"

"Both."

Mihaela shrugged. "Too many victims, not enough recruits. Ours is a rather specialized field of work."

Elizabeth regarded her curiously. Mihaela was an attractive woman, probably in her thirties. She wore no wedding ring. No photographs around the flat advertised the existence of children or other family. Elizabeth wondered what went on in the other woman's life; how much time she spent here in this cozy yet impersonal apartment. Not much, she guessed. Mihaela wasn't driven toward home-making,

"So how did you come into it?" Elizabeth asked. "Is vampire hunting a recognized career path in this part of the world?"

Mihaela gave a hiss of amusement. "Hardly. Most of us were witnesses of vampire attacks, or even victims, and were helped by the organization." Although she spoke lightly, matter-of-factly, a shadow seemed to pass across her dark eyes and vanish. "Like you."

Elizabeth didn't take the hint. "Which were you? Victim or witness?"

"Both, as it happens. Don't look so surprised."

"Sorry." Elizabeth took a quick mouthful of wine before setting down her glass. "The way you dealt with those vampires the other night, the way you just got up and got on with it after Zoltán's attack . . . It's hard to imagine you terrified and helpless." *Like me.* "You always seem so strong and capable and aware."

Mihaela's eyes dropped to her wine. "If I am, it's because I've learned to be."

"When did it happen?"

"When I was a kid." For a moment, Elizabeth thought she wouldn't say any more. Then she carried on almost abruptly. "My parents were killed at home by a fledgling vampire. I was rescued by hunters who arrived in time to kill it and save me. They were too late for my parents." Mihaela drained her glass in one quick, jerky movement. It was the only sign of distress she betrayed.

Elizabeth felt the blood drain from her face. There were worse, much worse experiences than her own. As Mihaela raised her dark, haunted eyes, Elizabeth glimpsed there the quiet, driven child who'd turned into this fearless, dedicated woman, determined never to be too late for anyone else.

"Mihaela," she said helplessly. How did you give sympathy for such a thing? What words could possibly make a difference to what Mihaela had suffered?

But the hunter clearly didn't want sympathy. The instant of vulnerability, if it had ever really been there, had vanished. Mihaela reached for the wine bottle. "Growing up, I spent a lot of time with vampire hunters. It seemed natural to follow them."

"You've been a hunter all of your adult life?" Elizabeth held out her glass to receive the offered top-up.

"Yes. Dull, isn't it? Cheers."

Elizabeth blinked. "*Dull?* Terrifying. Amazing. Entirely admirable. But surely not dull!"

Mihaela laughed. "You'd be surprised," she said, unwinding herself from the chair and standing up. "Mostly it's keeping track of and dispatching weak, fledgling vampires before they can cause any trouble. Hungry? I'll check on dinner."

†

Saloman almost missed the Angel Club. Its entrance was on an insignificant side street, close to the Danube in the old district of Buda. The faint echo of pounding rock music, picked up by his sensitive ears, could have come from any number of nearby clubs on either side of the river. Over the last few nights, he'd visited most of them, drawn by their sheer energy and the strange excitement of the unnecessarily loud, compelling music. He'd learned quickly to distinguish between the various types of modern music, and rejected jangly dance music in favor of live rock bands.

And so, hoping to follow the sound to its source, he nearly

walked past the Angel. It looked too insignificant, not just sleazy but boring. Even the angel carved into the stone above the door had no class. There was no doorman or sign. It might have been the entrance to a run-down apartment building or a cheap and nasty office block, except for the rather dull angel that drew his attention back again.

He stopped and gazed at it some more. In fact, it wasn't dull at all, but one of the finest architectural carvings he had ever seen. His lips twitched. "Enchanting," he murmured, and turning, he walked up the steps and pushed open the door.

Music rushed at him, the hard, heavy rock beat pounding behind the scream of electric guitars. He could smell humans, hear the rush of blood in their warm, excited veins. But more than that, his senses picked up several vampire presences, faint, almost fluttering through the second layer of general masking that surrounded the establishment.

It was a steep climb up the unappealing and none-too-clean stone stairs. Saloman didn't mind. He was intrigued. Since he kept his own far more powerful masking in place, the vampire in denim jeans and a black T-shirt who lurked outside the double doors at the top of the stairs barely blinked at him. He gave him a half-admiring up-and-down scan, which presumably approved his attire as suitable for the establishment—these were casual times, and Saloman rather liked the freedom to wear less—and then waved the Ancient through without even troubling to open the door for him.

The casual gatekeeper did follow him inside, though only to drop down at a table shared by two other vampires—females—and gaze with interest at the band occupying the stage opposite. They weren't bad, but Saloman found other aspects of his surroundings more interesting.

It was a large, open-plan area, and someone had achieved an extremely clever conversion while maintaining the original internal opulence of the eighteenth-century building. Paintings on the walls and on the curved, dome ceiling had been lovingly preserved and repaired, while the glass at the apex of the dome was retractable. It had been partially opened to let in the cool evening air. A modern bar occupied all of one wall, but table staff milled among the patrons seated at the many tables surrounding the dance floor, taking orders and delivering drinks. The area immediately in front of the stage was occupied by dancers and the more thorough appreciators of the band's particular brand of rock music.

The lighting was good too—warm and intimate without being so dark that one couldn't see the person sitting next to him. On the dance floor, it was dimmer, striving for a more exciting feel. Here, the lights moved, and occasionally settled, creating shadows and quick, alluring glimpses of the beautiful and transported individuals they selected.

Saloman, aware he had the full attention of the two waitstaff bearing down on him, and of several other occupants of the club, strolled to a vacant table of his own choosing in the shadows and ordered a bottle of vintage champagne. The world had not changed so much. People still jumped to obey the wishes of the obviously rich.

Saloman sat back and observed. Because he liked it, he let the relentless beat of the music insinuate itself into his consciousness, raising his awareness and his excitement on two levels. This, he thought, was a place where he might well have fun conducting business. It was certainly a good start. Judging by the number of vampires present, it was the place to come. This was intriguing in itself, since vampires tended to be solitary creatures, jealous of their own territory and power. Here, they mingled with the humans who came for the opulence, the comfortable coolness mixed with the only-just-sweaty-enough atmosphere of the dance floor. For them, it was something different too. And they no doubt provided meals for the vampire patrons. And all was accomplished with discretion, safe from prying or disapproving eyes.

Cleverness. Discretion. Organization. Artistic taste. None of them spoke of Zoltán. So who ran this establishment?

He scanned the room as the music urged his feet to follow the rhythm and his analytical brain processed information, faces, and possibilities.

You do. His gaze lingered on the beautiful woman who was watching him without embarrassment or apology from a high stool in front of the bar. She masked well, using a technique of the Ancients, which was interesting. She was definitely a vampire. She had stylish, short black hair, and a short, equally stylish black dress worn with elegant boots that emphasized the length of her long, alluring legs, which, under his blatant scrutiny, she uncrossed to stand.

Saloman smiled at her.

She spoke to the waitress who was just passing her with his bottle on her silver tray, and an instant later, it was the beautiful vampiress who bore his champagne. Saloman watched her approach. She walked briskly, neither seeking nor avoiding his gaze as she swerved among the patrons, greeting and speaking to those she clearly knew best. Saloman leaned his head against the velvet back of his sofa to look up at her as she deposited his bottle and his glass on the table, and then without fuss or explosion, removed the cork.

"Would you like to taste?" she inquired.

"Always. Will you join me?"

"There's only one glass."

"Not a problem for the owner of the establishment. Or even for me," he said, raising one finger to the nearest waiter who swerved toward him and then away again as he recognized the signaled order.

"You make assumptions," the vampiress observed.

"I make observations," he corrected, and indicated the seat beside him. This time, after a moment's hesitation, she sat.

"Welcome to the Angel," she said. "It's always a pleasure to see new patrons."

"I love the angel statue. Who taught you to enchant like that?"

Her eyes widened, the only sign of surprise or consternation. "What makes you think it isn't a gift?"

This close, she smelled of power, lightly worn but indisputable. He liked that. The paler, almost indistinguishable scent of Zoltán that clung to the edges was perhaps inevitable.

"All those layers of hidden beauty, masking layers of magical protection. Your angel makes a perfect base for a powerful disguising charm."

She glowed in his praise. Only the tiny, agitated movement of her thumb and forefinger rubbing together in her lap betrayed her unease. Clearly, no one before him had discovered how she protected the club and its vampire patrons. He smiled and, looking into her eyes, let a layer of veil fall from his mask.

She smiled back. "I thought so. But you mask like a master."

"Trust your observation," he said, and let another veil of protection slip away.

Her lips parted. "My God," she whispered. "You're *him*. Saloman..."

She wasn't the only one who'd picked up the signals. The vampire who'd let him in was staring. Several others were casting quick glances, intrigued or nervous, in his direction. They might not all have identified him, but they knew power when they were allowed to see it, and he was more than capable of hiding its current limitations.

"I am Saloman," he agreed. "And you are...?"

"Angyalka."

Saloman smiled. "The Angel. I like that. I like what you've done here. Does Zoltán?"

"Of course." Her shields were up, but he had no need to pry. He understood. She had worked at this, building her own little power base in Budapest while letting Zoltán believe it was for him. And she would pay lip service to his leadership.

"You are young for such an achievement," he said.

She shrugged. "Not so young. I died nearly two hundred years ago."

He let that one pass, merely accepting the glass from the waiter and pouring champagne. "To the Angel," he said, raising his glass to her.

"To your awakening," she returned. He could almost see her wondering what difference this would make to her here. If she was as smart as he thought, she'd know she needed his alliance, and yet her allegiance was already promised to Zoltán.

They sipped champagne. Saloman flexed his fingers. This was good. Wild music in his ears, drumbeat blasting up through his body from the floor, wine bubbles on his tongue, while he and this clever young vampiress hovered on the cusp of a new alliance.

After which, possibilities were endless. All he needed to make life perfect at this moment was for Elizabeth Silk to walk through the door.

He even cast a glance at it, but only an ordinary human couple came through, throwing themselves straight onto the dance floor. Angyalka was right. He did make assumptions. He'd assumed Elizabeth would follow; she would know where to look, if not to find. But he hadn't sensed her presence in the city so far. And he knew nothing about her, whether or not she liked, or was even aware of this kind of place, this kind of music. Perhaps she was *too* unworldly, *too* isolated in her ivory tower. Perhaps that was what drew him, why he wanted her to experience this newness with him. The excitement would thrum through her veins as they moved to the music, her soft, luscious body clamped to his, aroused and aware and ready. He remembered the taste of her blood, the scent of her skin, and his body stirred, demanding repetition and more. Elizabeth's end would be his beginning, but deep within her passionate, giving body, it would also be his joy—and hers.

Angyalka said, "I'm honored that you came to the Angel. There's no need to mask here. All we insi—ask—is discretion. Which means no fighting, no killing, no public feeding. Nothing must ever be traced back to the Angel."

"Sensible rules." He sat back in his chair and regarded her, banishing all thoughts of Elizabeth until he had opportunity to savor them. "Do you have plans for expansion?" he inquired.

✝

In Budapest, Elizabeth's life took on a new routine similar enough to the old to keep her feet on the ground. Staying with Mihaela, she rose shortly after dawn and drove through the still-quiet streets to the hunters' headquarters. There, in the specially constructed gymnasium, she worked out for an hour with a fitness specialist, and then, after a short break, spent another two hours learning combat—both unarmed and sword fencing.

"You're not serious," Elizabeth had quibbled when Konrad first mentioned swords.

"Deadly serious," Konrad reproved. "The older vampires still use swords against humans, especially in a large fight—which I hope you never have to witness, let alone take part in, but you have to be prepared. Remember with whom you're dealing."

She wasn't likely to forget it. He was rarely out of her thoughts, since every waking moment seemed to be devoted to learning about him and how to combat him.

Her muscles hurt with the unaccustomed exercise, though not so badly as she'd expected them to—or at least not yet. Instead, she found a new pleasure in the physical activity that stretched her body well beyond what she was used to. On top of that, she loved the speed of combat and was surprised by how quickly she learned and improved. So, it seemed, was her coach.

"Your reflexes are quick," he told her on the fourth day. "And you fight intelligently. You're a natural."

Elizabeth remembered to pick her jaw off the floor. "I never was before," she managed. "I was a poor athlete at school. I didn't exactly shine at netball, and I positively stank at hockey. Sports and I separated as soon as we could!"

The fit young man looked skeptical. "Then you never discovered the right sport. Until now."

Elizabeth laughed, then went off to shower, buoyed up by his praise. There was a time, she thought as she washed the sweat of exertion from her body, that such praise from—to say nothing of such close physical contact with—such a stunningly attractive

young man would have embarrassed her into a stuttering, clumsy
fool. Today, she was just glad to have pleased her teacher, who was
clearly an expert in his own field—not that she was immune to his
handsome face or his bulging biceps. Her eyes were not beyond
straying to his taut, sexy bum, but she felt only a kind of dispassionate appreciation. Although she didn't consider herself beneath
his notice, if he'd asked her out, she'd have said no—not through
fear because he was out of her league, but because they had nothing in common. And in fact, even his tanned, muscular body didn't
move her—not like Saloman's.

Saloman . . . She'd never even seen him with his shirt off; yet
one glance reduced her to butter, a useless, helpless blob of lust
who'd never even gotten as far as wondering whether she could
possibly please a being as sexually aware as he. . . .

She snapped off the shower and grabbed the towel. Well, that
was before—before she'd taken control and made her decision;
before she'd realized what the hell he was or what her own body
could do. When they met next time, it would be different. She'd
stake the bastard and enjoy it.

Well, no, she wouldn't enjoy it. In fact, she probably wouldn't
even do it. All the plans the hunters had discussed so far involved
using her as bait, with her being able to defend herself long enough
only to let the cavalry arrive and do the actual killing. Konrad, as
team leader, would put himself at the forefront, with István and
Mihaela as backup in case he was killed.

Weird how normal such thoughts had become.

Dried and dressed, she shouted good-bye to the coach, then
headed down to the library to continue her research into vampires
in general and Saloman in particular.

She had her own table now, near the front of the library, piled high with bound volumes and document folders. Just about over her awe of the age and rarity of the material, she was working her way through it, learning about the contribution of vampires—especially Saloman's—to the history of the region. So far as she could tell, the contemporary documents were genuine, and mostly supported by other sources, even if she'd never heard of those either. Miklós was happy enough to discuss sources with her, telling her the most trustworthy. But if only half the stuff she read about Saloman was true, he'd had just about as much influence on this part of the world as Jesus Christ. Military commander, governor, friend of princes and kings, diplomat, politician—it seemed there was nothing he hadn't done in the five hundred years of records covering his first life—or at least his second.

Frowning at the sudden thought, she glanced across at Miklós, who was fetching a large volume from the glass case nearest her. The only other occupant of the library she could see was a researcher, tapping away at one of the computers.

"Miklós? May I ask you something?"

"Of course." He came toward her, laying the book on the edge of her desk.

"How did the Ancients come about? From what I can gather, modern vampires—that is, all other existing vampires apart from Saloman—are some sort of hybrid of dead human and Ancient. What exactly are the Ancients?"

Miklós sank into the seat beside her and took off his spectacles. "Well, that's a difficult one. Their origins are lost in the mists of time. Most of the documents we have are only speculation, and the Ancients themselves were oddly reticent. I don't think they knew either. But look, there's something in here, a fragment, possibly from a letter, written by Saloman himself. . . ." Miklós rummaged among the document folder until he came up with a brittle piece of vellum.

Elizabeth, her mouth inexplicably dry, gazed down at it. A jumble of medieval Latin danced before her eyes. Miklós's finger pointed to the signature at the bottom, one word, Saloman, in bold, sloping letters. The "S" was large and ornamental, the upper loop covering half of the rest of his name. Her stomach twisted. *He* wrote this. Centuries before Vlad the Impaler. Before the Romanian principalities were even formed.

"It's undated," Miklós observed, as if reading her mind, "but that doesn't really matter for our purposes. He's defending the alliance of humans and vampires—possibly to a churchman or a prince; it's impossible to tell from this fragment—by stating that humans and vampires were once the same species, but that at some point, they diverged, like races within humanity. When some died, they died, their souls moving on. But others, it was possible to revive with the blood of others, and these so-called vampires were more or less immortal. They were given this gift, he says here, in order to protect their weaker, mortal cousins."

Elizabeth dragged her eyes away from it. "Is that true?"

He shrugged. "I don't know. I have no reason to doubt it. He sounds like an eminently sane and compassionate being, does he not? The contrast with the later Saloman in the seventeenth century is sharp and tragic. The collapse into insanity of the last Ancient, and with him, any real control of the far more bestial modern vampires."

Elizabeth swallowed. Compassion for Saloman—if that's what she felt—would not help her here. "What happened to the others?"

"Records are scarce. We believe some went similarly insane

and either ended their own lives or were executed like Saloman. Saloman himself is said to have killed the only other Ancient, barely two years before he was staked himself. Apparently they quarreled over a human woman, Tsigana, who is named as one of Saloman's killers."

This part of the story she knew. "Thanks, Miklós," she murmured. "You've made it much clearer."

"Any time." Miklós stood, hoisted his book once more, and took it to the researcher at the computer. Elizabeth returned to her own documents. Not for the first time, she wondered which of them she could get away with using in her thesis. Saloman had turned the whole premise of her thesis on its head. Was any of that stuff still valid?

Sighing, she tried to lose herself in the books. But despite the conducive surroundings, the peace, and the fantastic nature of the material, she could never quite do that here. Her nerves were too on edge. Her stomach twisted whenever she read Saloman's name. She imagined him whispering in her head, in her ear, stirring her skin without the faintest breath as he murmured hot words of lust.

She burned with shame, with unsatisfied need. And she hated Saloman for that, almost more than for the people he'd killed and would kill.

"What are you reading now?" Mihaela's hand on her shoulder some time later made her jump.

"How to kill the Ancients," she said with a quick grin. "You weren't kidding when you said it wasn't easy." Though as soft to the touch as anyone else's, their skin was believed to be largely impermeable, with an extra layer of hardness beneath the epidermis, which grew stronger with age. The first blow was vital. It had to be accurately over the heart, forceful, and performed with the sharpest possible wooden weapon. One source recommended the weight of several people behind the stake—which might explain why Saloman had so many slayers.

"You leave the killing to us," Mihaela soothed. "Are you ready to go back there now?"

Elizabeth blinked. "Back where?"

"Bistriţa. Transylvania. Saloman, remember?"

Elizabeth noted the page and closed the book. "Mihaela, I don't believe he's in Transylvania anymore. I think he's here, in Budapest." Saying it, like thinking it, sent a strange tension twisting through her body. It might have been dread, or hate, but it felt perilously close to excitement.

Mihaela's hand paused in midair, halfway to her hair. "You've seen him here?"

"No, no. It was just something he said about the new urban world and fun. I *know* he meant he was heading for the bright lights of a fun, modern city."

"It could be," Mihaela admitted. "We've heard nothing recently from our informant in Transylvania, so it's possible he's moved camp. On the other hand, it's been quiet here. And the vampire Lajos, one of the 'killers,' remains unmolested. He'd go for him first."

"Would he? Don't you think he likes playing cat and mouse, raising a bit of fear first? I'm sure that's part of his revenge."

Mihaela rested her hip on the edge of the desk, a frown furrowing her forehead as she regarded Elizabeth. "You think that's what he's doing to you?"

"I know that's what he's doing to me. Only I can't see why I'm due the punishment. I awakened him, didn't I?"

"Well, that may be the source of his ambiguous attitude. He's grateful to you, but he needs the blood of his Awakener to achieve full strength."

There was a slight catch in Elizabeth's laugh. "Well, that's a bloody stupid rule."

"It's a perverse and unnatural science," Mihaela agreed. "Though in this case, it serves the purpose of discouraging awakenings after executions. Isn't evolution marvelous?"

Unexpectedly, Elizabeth wanted to discuss vampire evolution with the vampire himself—the vampire who believed in the evolution of his own and her species several hundred years before Darwin. She stood, thrusting aside the unwelcome notion.

"We'll mention your theory to the others," Mihaela said, "but not tonight. You remember about the concert?"

"Looking forward to it," Elizabeth assured her.

✝

With the familiar distinctive sound of the orchestra tuning up, Elizabeth sat back in her seat and began to relax. She was so looking forward to this: a couple of hours to lose herself in music, in something that had nothing to do with all this scary crap, and yet everything to do with Hungary—a concert of Liszt and Bartók at the National Music Academy.

Perhaps it was because of the odd cloud of dread and excitement that she was living in, but on this, her third visit to Budapest, she'd begun to appreciate the city's beauty: the clean, classical lines of Pest spreading outward from the broad, curving Danube; the majestic bridges spanning the river to the ancient, picturesque city of Buda on the opposite bank, rising up the hill to the castle that had guarded it for centuries.

When she'd been walking with Mihaela along the river in the

gathering dusk, after their pleasant meal in a small, family-run restaurant, Elizabeth had found herself wondering if she'd only ever been half alive before. She'd registered that she liked the place, yet had taken no time to know it better, to soak up the ambience. She'd merely moved between her hotel and libraries, airport and railway stations. In the villages, it had been different, of course; she'd had to go out, mix with the local people to talk to them and ask her questions about vampire superstitions, but had she really appreciated her surroundings?

Perhaps everything simply looked sharper, more attractive, when the threat of death hung over one.

Or perhaps she just finally felt useful. Ever since awakening Salomon, she'd shared a clear purpose with the hunters.

Elizabeth gazed up at the ornate walls and ceilings—it was a beautiful hall, in a beautiful building, not too big, very art nouveau and, Mihaela assured her, boasted excellent acoustics. They had seats near the front of the stalls, and the balcony on three sides above, full of fellow music lovers, made her feel almost cozy. On top of that, she'd begun to value the quiet, no-nonsense company of Mihaela, an unexpected friend in the midst of her suddenly insane life.

The auditorium quieted, then erupted into polite applause for the conductor, before silence descended once more and the music began.

It worked. For a time, it really worked. She really did lose herself in the music and in her surroundings. The back of her neck didn't begin to prickle until halfway through the second piece. She covered it with her hand, casting a quick glance behind her at the rows of people who were paying her no attention at all.

Curling her lip at herself, she returned to the music. She

watched the pianist, enjoying the wild concentration on his young, intense face—a future international star, already producing exquisite music. Her gaze moved upward, along the line of violinists and cellists to the carving on the balcony above. As the music began to take her again, a shadowy movement caught the corner of her eye, and she jerked her gaze around to the balcony door. God, she was jumpy. She'd almost imagined a dark figure stood there, but the only people on the balcony were seated, and none of them looked remotely threatening. However, the balcony door was open a crack. She must have glimpsed one of the theater staff passing in the corridor beyond.

Was it always going to be like this? Living on the edge of her nerves, afraid of every shadow?

Only if you let it.

She took a deep breath and gazed determinedly at the pianist. By the interval, she'd regained her calm and her appreciation of the music.

"Drink?" Mihaela suggested. "We'll have to fight our way into the bar, but I know one of the waiters."

"Lead on," Elizabeth said with enthusiasm, and they joined the throng surging out of the auditorium. However, before they even reached the bar, Mihaela broke into smiles and began waving madly to a waiter who was easing through the crowd. He grinned back and gave her the universal thumbs-up sign.

"He'll hold them for us," Mihaela said with satisfaction, beginning to extricate herself from the crowd. "Which is good news, because I so need to go to the restroom."

"I'll wait for you," Elizabeth said, following her. It seemed preferable to fighting her way into the bar with everyone else.

Since there was a crowd at the ladies' room too, Elizabeth

strolled on to find a quieter spot to await Mihaela. As she went, she found herself admiring the whole interior of the building, particularly the beautiful murals, and as the stairs up to the balcony were deserted, she decided to have a quick look up there too.

The upper hall was empty and silent. As she walked, still examining the murals, her gaze slid ahead to the open balcony door. Mihaela was probably waiting for her by now. She should go back downstairs, yet she didn't. The shadow she'd imagined earlier slid back into her mind, almost drawing her on to prove it didn't exist—again.

Idiot.

She halted at the door, listening to the faint hum of conversation, and then glanced inside. A few idly chatting people still occupied their seats, although most were empty. With a vague idea of checking the view of the orchestra from up here, she stepped inside.

Her neck prickled. She spun around to face the door, and her heart jolted hard enough to make her dizzy. The blood rushed through her veins. She couldn't breathe.

Saloman stood just to one side of the door, leaning his shoulder against the wall, watching her impassively.

He wore black: black trousers, a black shirt, open at the collar, with no tie, and no jacket. His black hair gleamed against his pale skin, a lock falling across one side of his forehead. God, he was beautiful. He looked stylish, bohemian, and could be mistaken for a music student, perhaps a contemporary of the stunning pianist.

In this new, urban world of wealth and freedom, music and technology? I want to have fun. Somehow she'd never regarded this kind of concert as the fun he meant.

Was it possible he'd come here for the *music*, not for her . . . ?

He stood very still, as only he could, his dark, steady gaze on her face.

Convulsively, she grasped her bag, feeling through the soft leather the shape of the stake she always carried now. Her heart seemed to be beating in her ears. What the hell should she do? Warn everyone? Run for it? Try to stake him in front of all these people?

These people whose blood he must have come here to drink. Shit, he could have done so already. There could be a trail of undiscovered bodies all the way down some back staircase. . . .

His full lips curved, softening his hard eyes. He looked almost welcoming, not at all like a monster who'd just drained several music lovers of their blood.

"Did you?" The incomprehensible words spilled out without permission. He looked amused. Lifting one finger to his lips in mock disapproval, he took a step closer, and her breath caught in panic. But he stopped there, not touching her, yet close enough that she'd have felt his breath if he'd had any.

"A light snack, I believe is the modern term." It seemed he understood her after all.

"Are they dead?" Appalled by her own words, she cast a nervous glance around the scattering of people. A woman in the front row had twisted around to look toward the door, but otherwise no one was paying them any attention. It was as if she and Saloman were isolated in some private, intimate bubble.

Saloman said, "Of course not. I'm saving my main meal."

Bastard. "Me? Why don't you just kill me and be done? Why these cruel games all the time?"

His brows lifted. They were well defined, perfectly shaped,

distracting her by the texture of the short black hairs. "Cruel? Life
is to be valued. I've already let you live a week more than I could
have."

"I'm overcome with gratitude."

"No, you're not, but you should be. Don't tell me you haven't
appreciated this week more than any other in your life."

She stared at him, shaken to the core.

His lips quirked. "Are you enjoying the concert? You like this
music?"

"Yes . . ." Still too baffled to do more than give the bare truth,
she imagined the familiar mockery had vanished from his compelling eyes. They looked unexpectedly serious. "Do you?" she
asked, just as if they were genuine acquaintances who'd met by
accident.

"It's like court music, only with more musicians. Very different
from other modern music—although, of course, you won't regard
this as modern. Variety is good, but not at the expense of everything in the past."

She swallowed, parting her dry lips. "I could almost believe
you meant that."

He shrugged. "Nostalgia is the curse of the old. I love the energy of your rock music. I love the exquisite melody and technique
of *this*. And yet I miss the rough, untutored music that came before,
passed on through generations for hundreds of years. Even the
Gypsies no longer play it."

"Not here."

His eyebrows lifted again.

"In the villages," she blurted. "In the mountains, you still hear
it. Or something like I assume it might have been."

His eyes held hers. They seemed to flare until she imagined a flame dancing there, then blinked. He inclined his head. "Thank you."

"Don't mention it." Laughter was fighting its way up through her, hysterical and undignified. As if he recognized it, he smiled, and her loins melted. He might have been touching her, intimately, her lips, her breasts, the aching tenderness between her thighs. She was so glad he wasn't. She despaired because he wasn't. And yet, for the first time she recognized something else in his smile, what it was that made him trouble to converse with her, what shone and flamed in those otherwise dark, opaque eyes.

Reciprocation.

It stunned her, as if she weren't helpless enough already. Of course, she didn't doubt for a moment that Mihaela was right. He would take her blood with her body and slaughter her without compunction. But it wouldn't just be an act of excessive teasing, or stupid male domination or whatever else she'd been imagining. For whatever reason, he wanted her, *her*, and with a lust that burned as forcefully as everything else about him. The knowledge was elating, terrifying, huge. . . .

Laughter, oddly discordant, sounded in the corridor behind her. Someone brushed against her and apologized. She stepped aside as more people came in, separating her from Saloman.

Elizabeth backed out of the door. From the corridor, she glimpsed his tall figure towering over the jostling crowd.

Deliberately, he closed one eye. *Have fun*, he said inside her head. And then she turned and ran in search of Mihaela.

Chapter Nine

Convincing the others of Saloman's presence in Budapest turned out not to be so difficult, thanks to the encounter at the concert. Although Elizabeth didn't see him again and Mihaela hadn't seen him at all, they could both vouch for the way several patrons absently rubbed their throats throughout the second part of the performance.

"I might have directed him back to the villages," Elizabeth confessed. "But I'm sure he'll return here."

"You're right," Konrad agreed. "Lajos is here, as well as you. And the largest concentration of vampires, whom he'll need on his side before he can move any farther. So Plan A still stands. The location is merely altered, which makes it rather harder to find him."

"Konrad, he's finding us," Mihaela argued. "Or at least finding Elizabeth."

Was that true? Had he gone there in search of her? She was

sure now that he *had* seen her in the audience; he might even have drawn her to him by some supernatural power. But she still wasn't convinced that he'd come looking for her rather than the musical experience—and for fresh blood. The fun of the game for him now was for her to find him. And he must know she wouldn't come without the hunters at her back.

"Well, let's not wait until he breaks into your flat," Konrad said. "Let's start looking!"

"Where?" István demanded.

"Nightclubs," Elizabeth said, as she should have at the beginning.

"What?" They gawped at her.

"Nightclubs. He's been frozen for three hundred years. He wants action, and he likes rock music."

Mihaela began to laugh.

✝

Discovering the Angel was an accident brought about on the second day of searching by a chance encounter with a researcher who complained about his little sister frequenting dangerous, unlisted, and unregulated nightclubs.

Even so, provided with a vague address, they nearly missed it. But at the last moment, Mihaela noticed the uninspiring stone angel above the door.

Gazing up at it, Elizabeth felt her insides tighten. The more she looked, the more exquisite the carving appeared, its lines sharper and more expressive—and more familiar. "This is it," she said positively. "It's like the angels in his crypt."

Istvan frowned. "There shouldn't be a connection. This place must have been built well after Saloman was staked."

"Vampire artist?" Mihaela suggested.

146

"Let's find out." Konrad pushed open the door, and the detectors began to vibrate as one.

"Wow. They've masked it," Konrad said, peeking at the larger instrument inside his backpack, "but I'm getting loads of vampire readings. Two present right now."

"Remember, he doesn't show on the readings," István warned.

"Oh, I remember," Konrad said grimly. "Stakes ready. No killing without my say-so."

Mihaela opened her mouth, as if to object, but closed it again with an irritable little shrug. It struck Elizabeth that she'd ignore his orders if she thought it best, and didn't know whether or not to be comforted.

In contrast to the dingy staircase, sunlight flooded through the glass roof and the huge window that took up one entire wall of the club. Through it, Elizabeth could see the glistening Danube, and beyond it, the domed roof of the Parliament building and church spires of Pest.

"Human," Konrad breathed as a young woman approached them, smiling. "Are you open for coffee?" he inquired.

"Always. Please . . ." The girl indicated a table at the picture window, surrounded by large comfortable sofas.

A couple sat some yards away, ignoring everything but each other.

"Human," Konrad murmured again. "Bar staff the same. The vampire readings are farther away. Asleep, I suppose."

"Beautiful place," Mihaela observed when the waitress returned with the cups and coffeepot. "Is it new?"

"Oh no, been around for years," the girl replied.

"Have you worked here long?"

"Just over a year."

"Is it a good place to work?" Elizabeth asked, adding by way of an excuse, "I need to get a job."

"There are no vacancies just now, but yes, it's a good place to work. The management looks after you, pay's decent. I'll leave your name with Angyalka if you like."

"Angyalka?"

"The owner."

Konrad nudged Elizabeth's elbow, urging her on. "Could I speak to Angyalka?" she asked.

"She's asleep."

Vampire!

"I won't wake her. She's up all night at the club and clears up afterward too. Come back this evening. She doesn't bite."

Oh, I rather think she does.

"That's the place," Mihaela crowed when they again made it out on to the street. "Run by vampires, with ignorant human help. If he hasn't found it yet, he will."

Elizabeth's laugh was shaky. "Then let's bait the trap. Wire me up and send me in."

†

Saloman knew as soon as he entered the Angel that she'd been here. He could smell her and felt his loins stir with triumph and need. Well, they more than stirred, judging by the direction of Angyalka's gaze as she came toward him. She might misinterpret it, but he didn't mind that either. They'd been circling each other all week, revealing and hiding attractions that were at least partly genuine.

And once he'd had Elizabeth Silk, it was the sort of sophisticated and civilized liaison he might consider. Hell, he was considering it now, just to take the edge off his lust. And by the warm smile in her seductive eyes, she wouldn't be averse.

"You're early this evening," she purred.

"I couldn't wait."

"To see me?"

"To see Lajos," he corrected, indicating the uneasy figure who sat as if frozen in the corner. No one sat near him. Saloman smiled and the vampire looked away, picking up his beer. It was bravado that had brought him here, hearing no doubt that Saloman had become a regular visitor. It might have been bravado that motivated his rudeness now—or fear.

"Why don't you put him out of his misery?" Angyalka almost snapped. "I didn't peg you as small-minded enough for torture."

"Torture?" He glanced at her with sufficient force to drive the color from her dramatic face. "My dear, you don't know the meaning of the word. Let's talk about something else."

"Like the hunters who were here this afternoon?" Clearly, she hoped to surprise him. "Strong ones. Their energy shone like beacons."

"You needn't worry about them."

"Saloman, don't bring them down on my bar. I like it here."

"Don't think so small, Angyalka. It doesn't suit you, and you're capable of so much more. Let us talk instead of Maximilian." He settled into the sofa, gazing at her as she sat down on the edge of the cushion beside him.

"Maximilian? No one knows where he is."

"Nonsense. Someone always knows something. Karl did. Lajos does. And so do you."

"Don't be ridiculous. I didn't know the creature."

"Angyalka."

Her gaze flickered to him and away, but still she said nothing.

He sighed. "I, on the other hand, knew him very well. I recognized his signature on your enchanted Angel. You use Ancient techniques, taught to Maximilian by an Ancient. Namely me."

With an irritable click of the tongue, she threw herself back into the seat. "Damn it, I don't know where he is! He lost heart and went away. He wants to be left alone. I respect that. I respect *him*. Whatever he did to you isn't my quarrel. He was kind to me, and I won't repay him with betrayal. So bite me."

Saloman smiled. "You know, I might." He leaned closer, inhaling her cool yet seductive scent. "You are, after all, an ally worth having."

She'd bargained on it, of course, with her little loyalty rant, but nevertheless, her eyes half closed with involuntary relief. When she opened them fully, they contained blatant desire.

"I can be more than an ally." Her hands snaked out and around his neck. She was a tempting armful, even for someone not fighting three hundred years' worth of lust. He stroked her hair, knowing she was his for the taking. He could fuck her now. He could fuck her all night and still have Elizabeth Silk in the morning—Elizabeth, who loved music . . . and who knew what else? But his obsession with her was becoming dangerous, distracting him from more important aims. It was time to end it.

He pushed up Angyalka's chin with one knuckle. "Maybe one day," he said. "Right now, I have a problem sharing with Zoltán."

She pulled away, her color flaring once more. He'd never encountered a vampire who blushed so much.

Her voice shook. "You really are a bit of a bastard, aren't you, Saloman?"

"Oh no. I'm a complete and utter bastard. One can perfect these things over the millennia." He rose to his feet. "Time to chat to Lajos."

✝

Konrad parked the car with precision, then switched on the ceiling light and twisted round to face the backseat, where Elizabeth sat with a tense and silent Mihaela. István's long, serious face loomed out of the shadows from the other side.

"Okay." For some reason, probably nerves, Konrad looked at his wristwatch. "He's not in yet. We've had people watching the place since sunset. But don't take any chances. Be ready at all times, and remember, everyone you meet in there is a potential threat. There are likely to be so many vampires that a detector will be worse than useless. But you're not on your own. As soon as he arrives, we'll be there. Not just we three. We have reinforcements for this job—the best."

Elizabeth nodded. She wanted to sit there listening to Konrad all night. She wanted him to shut up so she could get on with it, get it over, have Saloman dead and get her life back.

"Just stay in the light, stay with the crowd. We think there must be some kind of no-killing rule, which the vampires have chosen—or been somehow compelled—to obey. There have been no reported killings or any other crimes on the premises, so you *should* be safe. Just remember, don't even attempt to kill him. That's our business."

Elizabeth nodded again.

"We'll buzz you as soon as we glimpse him," István assured her, "or anyone who might conceivably be Saloman. The best policy would be to make sure he sees you, but never quite reaches you. Seeing you alone, without us, should give him a false sense of security, and he should still be weak enough for us to take him. Vampires have few loyalties—the others are unlikely to intervene."

They'd discussed all this before. There seemed no point in doing more than nodding yet again. Hanging around here was making her feel more vulnerable than safe, perhaps because it suddenly seemed to be the hunters who didn't understand what they were dealing with here. *Vampires have few loyalties? Is that true? Make sure he sees you but never reaches you? Come on, guys, be real.* . . .

It was wishful thinking, of course. They hated letting her go in like that. They were still trying to protect her when what she needed now was to be active, to take back control of a life gone haywire. In truth, she just wanted to get the bastard once and for all.

Elizabeth reached for the door. "Got your buzzer?" Konrad demanded.

"In my bag."

"And a stake?" István pursued. "Just in case."

"Yes." She cast them a quick smile. "Good luck, guys."

"You too."

They'd come a long way in her mind from the pranksters and nutters she'd once thought them. She just hoped this wouldn't be the last time she saw any of them.

If I should die, think only this of me . . . What? That she died happy at last? That she was never sure whether she wanted to screw him more than kill him, and discovered the answer too late?

Oh no, that might have been true once. I'm stronger now. Because I know he wants me too. Hell, pass the shampoo; I'm worth it.

Squashing down the rising rush of hysteria, she became aware of Mihaela marching along at her side.

"You can't come with me," she warned. "He's seen you. He'll know it's a trap."

"Shit, Elizabeth, we both know he'll be well aware of that as soon as he sees you. It may be a deliberate blind spot with *them*"— she jerked her head back toward the car—"but you have to acknowledge it. . . ."

A muffled tinkle of ringtone Bach rent the air with all the effect of a bomb blast. Elizabeth and Mihaela stared at each other, wide-eyed for a tense microsecond. He'd been seen entering the club, coming toward the club; he'd really be there. . . .

Somehow, the phone was in her hand and at her ear, before she even saw the caller's number on the screen.

"Elizabeth? Richard. How's it going?"

Relief flooded her. *Not yet.* She still had time to get there, to dig in, to be prepared. "Fine. Richard, I can't talk now. I'll call you back. Bye."

She broke the connection and dropped the phone back in her bag with a quick, apologetic smile at Mihaela, who in her urgency didn't even acknowledge it.

"Listen, Elizabeth, I don't care what Konrad said—his control-freak stuff is seriously beginning to worry me. If you get close enough, you stake the bastard. Hard enough to hold him until we get there and finish the job. You have to. Since he'll spot the trap, he'll try to kill you quickly and get out."

No, he wants me—but how much am I really worth to him? Not as much as I want to be. He'll take my blood with my body. . . .

It was impossible to tell any of this to Mihaela—although she might have guessed. Elizabeth had dressed on her own, emerging from Mihaela's spare room with a long jacket closely wrapped around her. She hadn't bothered with makeup—afraid she'd botch it through unfamiliarity and clumsy hands that showed an alarming tendency to shake—but she'd tied up her hair in a much more elegant and fetching style, and beneath the jacket she was dressed to kill.

They came to the corner, around which the Angel's entrance would become visible. Elizabeth couldn't leave Mihaela with the same silent farewell she'd given the others. Mihaela was more than a protector. She was her most unlikely friend.

Elizabeth turned and hugged her once, hard. "Thank you," she whispered, and released her almost before she felt the returning pressure of Mihaela's arms. She bolted around the corner, aching to run for miles and miles until her body was too exhausted to feel this intensity of grief or hate or lust or anything more than duty, just as in the good old days before she revived Saloman.

And he expects me to be grateful?

She forced herself to slow down. It was no part of her plan to arrive at the club tousled, sweaty, and panting. She had the image she'd thought herself into in Mihaela's spare room, and she was bloody well going to stick to it until she stuck *him*—or someone else did. Either way, she'd be free.

For what? a little voice whispered in her mind. *To finish a thesis you already know is crap? To go home and pretend none of this really happened? That you don't feel—this?*

Yes. Oh fuck, yes.

Elizabeth entered the Angel as if she owned the place. It helped that she'd been before and knew where she was going, was prepared for the steep climb, and could sail past the man at the top of the stairs, who might have been a vampire, as if he were of no account. Certainly, he made no move to stop her, or even to search her bag, which was her one worry about the whole expedition. Even normal nightclubs were understandably fussy about weapons, and she could hardly complain about having a lethally sharpened stick confiscated. Defenseless, her one remaining option then would be to storm back out in rage, achieving nothing.

The hunters would have to hide behind cars and leap on him as he arrived. The image entertained her as she swanned into the club, entering the wall of noise with her head held high. Ignoring the cloakroom—God knew whom she might have encountered in there—she just shrugged her jacket off her shoulders and, feeling enough attention to make her skin prickle, she walked on toward the bar. Without looking, she registered that two insignificant men sat there, at opposite ends, and chose her place next to one. Hopefully, he'd buy her a drink before Saloman arrived. She sashayed over and leaned rather than sat on the high bar stool to take in her surroundings with unhurried interest.

It looked very different at night, the lights low and intimate, casting a deceptive air of privacy over each table and sofa, over each couple on the dance floor. The place was jumping, and the dance floor crowded as the rock band on stage gave it their all. They were very young, very serious, and not bad at all, although she saw no reason for them to be quite that loud. The bass vibrated through her stool and her hips, and despite everything, she felt an urge to tap and sway with the relentless beat. Compromising, she marked the rhythm with one wiggling foot.

Deep in the painted dome ceiling, the retractable glass window was fully open, letting the night air cool the fevered dancers below. She let her eyes move on, completing the circle of trendy, wealthy, and outrageous clientele until she came, finally, to the man sitting next to her.

Her heart, her whole world, seemed to plunge through the floor.

"Good evening," said Saloman.

He'd done it again. The bastard was here already. Somehow, he'd gotten past them.

✝

The hunters hadn't yet arrived to watch the club when Saloman had strolled through the predusk shadows in sunglasses in order to frighten Lajos and converse with Angyalka on the subjects of sex and alliances. He'd then entertained himself by helping the band set up their gear, taking note of what bits went where and how everything worked.

Angyalka had laughed at him, but Saloman was genuinely interested. The new age fascinated him, as did the new age people. He chose to watch the band from close to the stage, which is where he was when he "heard" her coming, and gave an involuntary smile. It might have been relief, or triumph. Certainly, it was pleasure.

With his superior Ancient senses, he found it simple to bypass Angyalka's shields. He not only knew as soon as Elizabeth entered the building, but well before, as she approached it on foot. He didn't even trouble to scan for the hunters. He knew they were there, though they were letting her come in alone.

He walked off the dance floor, ignoring the several silent but persuasive invitations to dance cast his way by both human and vampire females. He enjoyed the openness of modern women; yet it made Elizabeth's reticence all the more appealing. He elected to sit at the bar, from where he had an excellent view of the door. Tonight he wanted to appreciate her from first moment until last, even though she'd come to finish him, imagined she was baiting him.

Saloman was aware of the blood pounding in his heart, like a boy waiting for his first sweetheart instead of a three-thousand-year-old vampire preparing to kill his Awakener. He could laugh at himself for it, in a detached sort of way. But he'd existed as long as he had without descending into insanity only by living for the enjoyment of each moment. And he meant to enjoy each of tonight's very thoroughly.

The double doors swung open. Elizabeth walked through as if this were her second home. She was magnificent, stunning, sex on long, elegant legs that any man would yearn to have wrapped around him in passion.

Saloman wanted to laugh.

Though not because she didn't look gorgeous. In fact, the only reason she didn't take his breath away in that first glance was his lack of any to lose. It was just that she'd gone to so much trouble to look sexy in that red dress with the teasing neckline and the tiny, provocative straps—tying up her lovely strawberry blond hair in an artful disarray that displayed her nape and throat to perfection—when all she'd really needed to do was turn up in the old workman's trousers and whore's bodice he'd first met her in, with dust on her nose and cuts on her rough, dirty hands. Whatever she wore, however she styled her hair, she was beautiful and unique, and he wanted her with an intensity that consumed him.

And like this . . . Hell, yes, he'd play that game. She even walked differently, dressed like this, as if she finally knew how good she looked. If that was because one of those hunters had laid a hand on her, he'd take great pleasure in ripping his throat out—later; much later. He watched her sway across the floor without so much as glancing in his direction, and then shimmer onto the stool next to him. She looked like a sunset—or a sunrise. Whatever, she was just beginning to shine.

She took her time, still not even glancing at him; she couldn't feel the raging lust that strained at his trousers and clamored for gratification at last. Masking worked on humans too, made them less aware of a particular presence. And so it was all the sweeter when she'd completed her scan of the room, making sure no danger lurked in the shadows, before she allowed herself to glance at her nearest neighbor.

Her dark hazel eyes and her mouth both widened in shock, telling him all he needed to know. Neither she nor the hunters had been aware he was here. They were merely hoping he would arrive later, presumably on learning of her presence.

Careless—criminally careless—but their neglect was useful and really quite amusing.

"Good evening," he said as gravely as he could.

Chapter Ten

$\mathcal{T}$he buzzer, an attachment to her phone that would alert the hunters at once to her danger, was in her bag, along with the stake that just might save her life. The bag lay in her lap, so near and yet so far.

Well, there were plenty of innocent reasons to open one's bag in a bar.

So, from instinct, she pretended to be annoyed rather than completely thrown by his presence. "There's just no time off around here. Are you following me?"

"I was here first," he pointed out. "But broadly speaking, yes, of course I am."

"Well, don't let me interrupt your . . . drink." She waved her hand behind her at her fellow patrons, and was rewarded by a quirk of his sensual lips before she dragged her gaze from him to the young bartender who was hovering opposite her. He looked human. But then, so did Saloman, if you didn't pay too much attention to his eyes. "A glass of red wine, please. Something local."

The barman grabbed a bottle and poured a small amount into a large glass, which he passed to her to taste. Aware of Saloman's attention, she took her time, fighting the desire to throw it down her throat and hold the glass out for more. Alcohol did not steady the nerves. It numbed them, which might make the present more bearable but wouldn't help her stay alive.

"It's good," she pronounced, and the barman smiled as he filled her glass. Trying not to hold her breath, Elizabeth reached for the zip of her bag. She could press the buzzer while rummaging for her purse.

"I'll get that," Saloman said beside her. "We'll take the bottle."

"No, thank you," Elizabeth snapped, but it was too late. The barman had moved on, and Saloman was watching her with those knowing, mocking eyes while he poured wine into his own glass. Raising it in his long, elegant fingers, he saluted her.

There seemed to be nothing else to do but release the zip, raise her own glass, and sip. In a few moments, she could just take out her phone and pretend to check for messages or something.

Fascinated, she watched him draw the wine over his lips and into his mouth. He swallowed. She opened her mouth to ask what vampires could eat and drink—a subject on which her recent reading had been silent—before she remembered she was too angry with him to make conversation.

He said, "Would you like to dance?"

She set her glass on the bar. "No."

Saloman stood, and she glanced up at him in alarm. "What a pity," he said. "I've always wanted to dance with you. Another time—perhaps here, tomorrow."

Oh shit, now he was going to leave! What was she thinking? She was getting her roles all muddled. She'd come here to seduce him—or at least to appear to do so for long enough to let the hunters arrive in force, and here she was letting him walk out on her within five minutes! He'd walked past her. All she could see was his back.

"Saloman." Her desperate, helpless plea came out throatily enough to sound sexy. Unfortunately, she couldn't be sure he heard it over the music. She slid off her stool, reaching for his hand, when he turned and caught hers instead.

His eyes gleamed with laughter. She'd been had—again. But she'd learned her lesson. Stay in character. So she let her eyes and her lips smile back in rueful acknowledgment of his hit.

"Actually, I love to dance." After too many drinks in comfortable surroundings, but stone-cold sober in a dangerous vampire bar would have to do for tonight.

"I knew you would." His thumb stroked the edge of her palm, making her shiver, while his free hand closed over her bag. "You can't dance with this. Leave it here."

She tightened her grip in panic, before forcing herself to release it. She didn't think he would kill her here. There would be other opportunities. Even so, when he dropped it onto her vacated stool, she laid her hand on it, drumming her fingers as if still hesitating over whether or not to abandon it in such a public place. In reality, she hoped it would activate the buzzer.

Saloman's gaze lifted from the bag to her face, giving nothing away. Red lights from the dance floor flickered across his forehead and the strong line of his jaw. Part of his face always seemed to be in shadow, adding to his mystery and, for some reason, to his allure. She slid her hand off the bag and let him lead her with slow deliberation onto the dance floor.

Her heart drummed in her breast, seeming to vibrate her over-sensitive nipples as they pushed against the fine, thin fabric of her risqué dress. Anticipation thrummed through her, sensitizing every nerve ending in her body, because this time all the teasing and mockery he could summon didn't matter a jot. This time she had a job to do. She had to keep him here until the hunters arrived, and she had every confidence she could.

It felt good, swaying to the beat of the music, letting her body slide against his arm as she chose their spot, turned, and began to dance. The atmosphere was different here, dimmer, darker, full of flickering, shooting shadows and shafts of bright, mesmerizing light. It made her part of the heaving, jumping throng that hemmed her in, yet gave her the illusion of solitude in which to enjoy throwing off the inhibitions that were her reality. Her body was her weapon, gyrating, thrusting, and spinning to the music—provoking and enticing the beautiful, lethal being who danced so close to her.

Saloman moved with the grace of ballet, the freedom of modern dance, and all the energy of rock; yet he never strayed from the contained space that harbored both of them, never took his leaping, half-hidden gaze from her as he followed the movement of her throat and breasts and hips. Sometimes, she saw the brief gleam of his teeth and imagined the pointed canines that could rip her open for him to drain her blood in two beats of a song. But mostly, she watched his body mirroring the actions of hers, not dancing *at* her as most people did, but *with* her. For some reason, it was incredibly sexy, as if their circling, thrusting bodies were touching.

Between her thighs was a warning dampness, but the dance exhilarated her; his predatory attention urged her on. So long as he didn't touch her, she felt safe in her bubble of dangerous, reciprocated desire.

The driving music slammed through her. Saloman swayed closer, almost touching as he moved with her gyrating hips. When she thrust backward, he followed, weaving to either side with her, and back when she arched forward. It excited her, because it seemed so natural and she was still in control. She could see the bulge in his trousers as he danced, and God help her, she liked that too, so much so that when the shifting light flashed down his abdomen, revealing the full outline of his upright shaft, she flooded her panties with sexual moisture. She couldn't even pretend that was perspiration, and she didn't care, not so long as his gaze was riveted to her breasts.

She arched back, and again his hips followed hers. She thrust forward, and this time he didn't budge. With shock she came up against the hardness of his erection, and before she could slide free, his hands closed over her hips, guiding her to his lead.

Her whole body melted against the heat of him. Her abdomen burned and tingled to his touch. Her aching sex throbbed as her precious control began to ebb. The dance became his, not hers, their bodies melded together at the hips, thrusting in perfect harmony with the music and with each other.

In wonder, she gazed up at him, staring through the flickering shadows on his face to the warm, clouded lust he didn't trouble to hide. He leaned back, forcing his hardness closer into her. She gasped, swaying under his hands, leaning back as he did to intensify the pressure and the pleasure. It was blatant, but it felt so good.

When their upper bodies met again, her nipples seemed to cry out. His hands on her hips raised her up on her toes, his chest rubbed against her breasts, his erection slid lower, almost between her parted thighs, and still he danced—and she with him.

The music blasted her ears, the darkness cocooned her in wild, exciting lust. The vampire's eyes held hers with a promise she yearned for with every treacherous fiber of her existence.

Until the music came to a climactic close.

The dancers broke into a raucous, ragged cheer. Some began to move off the floor, or to change partners. Elizabeth and Saloman stood quite still, his hands on her hips, their bodies molded together as if actually joined.

Oh Jesus Christ, what would that be like?

The singer was talking, but she barely heard, never mind understood the words. Was it finished? Good, then she should pull away, get herself back together before . . .

A long, tragic chord sounded on the guitar. The music began again on a slower, more sensual beat. Saloman swayed, holding her with him until the music took her back, and she danced again too.

"Slower, and sweeter," he murmured in her ear. "Dalliance in dance . . ."

Dalliance and dinner, remember that? She swallowed. "You like alliteration." She could make out the texture of his neck, the tiny, perfect black hairs. Because she had a part to play, and because she wanted to, she gave in to her desire, and softly blew on them.

His head moved, twisting his neck in languorous response. "I like lots of things. I like this sexy side to you. I like your hot little body clamped into mine as if we're making love."

"We're not," she managed.

"We could be." His hand slid down her hip to her naked thigh. "I like your soft, silken skin." Something cool and moist touched her neck, forcing another gasp from her. "I like the way you dance." His lips brushed a vein, and in the panic induced as much by desire as fear, she grabbed at him. She found his hips, which slid and swayed in her hold, gratifying her on so many levels that she carried on dancing.

While his hardness rubbed against her pubic bone, slid between her parted thighs, his lips closed on her neck and kissed, teasing. Before she could panic again he raised his head to reveal burning eyes. For the first time she began to wonder how much control *he* had. But in this state of semibemused bliss, it didn't seem to matter.

"And as I recall," he whispered, "I like the way you kiss. . . ."

Her lips parted with shock and need. He lowered his head once more and, mesmerized, she watched the progress of his lips, parting, half smiling and straightening again as they approached.

Well, there's no one here to see. What harm in one kiss?

His mouth touched hers, brushed once, and closed.

All sorts of harm, if it was Saloman's kiss. She couldn't have forgotten its devastating effect on her. He tasted like no one else, strong and earthy and spicy, his mouth firm and commanding and yet moving so sensually on hers that the surrender was sweet. Her mouth almost fell open under his, admitting his tongue and his sharp, terrible teeth.

But with the flash of terror came the saving memory of her role. She was allowed to kiss him back. In fact, she had to, whatever the danger.

She slid her tongue along his, twisted around it, and sucked;

his mouth hardened in response, deepening the kiss. She fought him for it, nipping at his lips, thrusting her tongue into his mouth, and curling over his teeth as if to draw him nearer.

His hand stroked her naked thigh, then slid higher under her dress and over her bottom, kneading her into his erection. She flicked her tongue over his canines, felt their sharpness, and tasted a spot of her own salty blood before his tongue swiped over hers, stealing it. He sucked, and weirdly, she felt more pleasure at that than fear. For some reason it aroused her even more.

It was mad. She was dancing, practically grinding in public with a vampire who had his hand up her skirt and was sucking the blood from her tongue. And she liked it?

Hell, yes, it was the most amazingly sensual experience of her life. She lifted one leg, rubbing her thigh against his, parting her sex to increase the pleasure from his probing erection. The hand not on her bottom slid round to hold her leg, caress it, and raise it higher. And the kiss went on.

You can. You really can orgasm on a public dance floor.

Gasping, she dragged her mouth free and tried to lower her leg. She was almost disappointed that he let her.

"I need air," she said shakily.

He devoured her face with his eyes, sending all sorts of wicked shivers through her oversensitive body, and settled on her lips. He took another kiss, quick and sensual, and then stared at her gasping mouth wide-open with lust.

He smiled and threw one arm about her shoulders to guide her off the dance floor. Trembling, she closed her mouth with a snap. *Focus, Silk, focus. . . .*

But it was hard to concentrate with his steely arm around her, his fingers caressing her naked shoulder, playing along her clavicle. Only when she found herself sinking into one of the comfortable red sofas facing the large window, did she manage to say in panic, "My bag . . ."

Saloman crooked his finger to someone, made another quick hand signal, and sat down beside her, his thigh brushing hers. "They'll bring it." The familiar half smile dawned and vanished from his lips. "You're a constant revelation to me, Elizabeth Silk. I'm so glad you dance."

"You mean you'll miss me after you kill me?" She wasn't quite sure why she brought the subject up. Right now, it just seemed safer than the sex thing she'd been relying on for the last half hour.

"I will."

She cast him a lopsided smile. "Don't spare my feelings by pretending."

"It will be a good death, and a sweet one."

"Not for me," she disputed, wondering vaguely when she had learned to treat her own demise with such callousness.

"Oh yes. For you," he said as a waiter deposited her bag on the sofa beside her and a tray containing the wine bottle and glasses on the table in front of them. As the waiter hurried away, Saloman leaned forward, blocking her view, and trailed his finger down her chest and cleavage, where it lingered, brushing the swell of each breast in turn.

Elizabeth's body flamed all over again. She clutched the bag to her side like a lifeline.

"I promise," Saloman said huskily.

"Thanks. I'd rather keep my sour life."

"A life with mere academic thrills? Without wild, intense sex?"

She stared. "I can get wild, intense sex whenever I want to." It sounded so childish that she bit her lip as soon as the lying words were out. But Saloman frowned, as if displeased.

"Not like I can give you." He leaned even closer, hiding her from view with his body. His hand slipped under her dress to cover her naked breast. "Here and now, if you wish."

His hand was bliss and torture at once—on her aching breast, tweaking her nipple between his fingers. Almost with awe, she realized she had the advantage back, that he'd forgotten about her bag.

"I think," she managed, surreptitiously sliding open the zipper, "that you overrate the intensity caused by imminent death. On the contrary, I find it—er—a turn-off."

"Liar," he whispered, caressing her nipple between finger and thumb, over and over. Where in hell was that buzzer? She found it, pressed it, and as she slid her hand free, her knuckles brushed against the cold, hard shaft of the wooden stake.

If you get close enough, you stake the bastard, Mihaela had said. Well, she was close enough, but she wasn't stupid enough to imagine he'd let her do it. Nevertheless, she left her hand resting against the bag's opening. If the hunters didn't get here fast, the stake might be her only possible defense against certain death. How long did she have?

And how did you kill a man, a *being*, who was fondling your breast like a lover? At least when you liked it as much as she did. "Stop that," she begged.

To her perverse disappointment, he did stop, removing his hand in such a way as left her breast exposed to him, its rosy nipple stretching out in a silent plea for more attention. Gasping, she snatched up the strap of her dress, glaring at him.

"You have such beautiful breasts," he excused, and for some reason she melted all over again.

Struggling, she said, "Do you really have time to lavish such attention on all your victims?"

"My Awakener is special."

"Then perhaps you owe her more than a quick shag and murder."

His eyes darkened impossibly. "I never said anything about a *quick* shag."

Oh, God help me. . . . "I'm more concerned with the murder."

"You won't be."

Her fist tightened around her bag, ready to draw the stake if the opportunity arose. "You have no right . . . ," she raged.

"Actually, I have."

She stared at him. "Because of might? You're stronger than me, so you can take my blood and kill me?"

"I am and I can. But I meant right. You are only one human."

"I may be 'only' to you, but I'm pretty important to me."

"Kiss me," he whispered.

In spite of everything, her heart turned over. Grief and anguish rose up, but couldn't quell the anger that had been festering and building since this began. She jerked back to avoid his questing mouth.

As if unaware of her sudden reluctance, he followed, looming over her.

His mouth covered hers. He stroked her neck over the old, sensitive wound, and she gasped against his lips. Was it to be now? Her fingers twitched on her bag, before his hand covered them and held.

"Death comes after the sex," he murmured against her lips. "Otherwise, where's the fun in it?"

"You're twisted and weird," she whispered, and because she couldn't help it, brushed her mouth across his lower lip.

"And you want me."

"That's just the vampire thing. . . ."

His lips stretched into a smile while they kissed her. "That humans are drawn to evil vampire sex appeal? Equating sex with evil, you'll notice. I wasn't aware of your enjoying the attentions of the vampire I killed for you in Bistriţa, or falling for the charms of my good friend Zoltán. Perhaps Dmitriu was before me?"

"You're an idiot." She grasped his shoulders to push him off, and then, fascinated by the feel of the steely muscles under her fingers, let her fingers linger there instead.

"Elizabeth . . ." He laid his hand on her knee, caressed up the length of her thigh. "Nothing compels you but your own desire."

"Then I can walk out of here right now?"

"If you so desire."

She stared into the face so close to hers that the tiniest of movements would brush her forehead against his, her lips to his mouth. Her breath vanished. "I do desire."

Would his arms drop from her? Would he stand aside and just let her go, cold and frustrated and alive?

His hand slid back down to her knee. "But then I'd leave, and your friends just entering the building wouldn't find me."

Her breath returned in a rush. She gave an involuntary jerk of her head, trying to see if the hunters had indeed arrived to end this torture of agony and pleasure. But all she could see was his dark shoulder blocking her view.

She gazed into his pitiless, shadowed face. "Then it's over? Will you kill me now?"

His lips twitched. She didn't think he ever intended it as a smile. "No. But we still have time for the sex."

In a movement of bewildering speed, he rose, dragging her with him and spinning her onto the dance floor. He held her close into him. She found herself clinging to his shoulders, dizzy and disoriented.

"They've come to kill you, and you'll stay here for sex?"

"It's a game," he assured her. "Can you orgasm before they interfere and stop it?"

Though her hand itched to slap him, the rest of her body screamed out for the orgasm. Her mouth wouldn't work at all until he covered it with his. Seduced all over again, it began to move under his lips. He held her by the buttocks, one palm on each, his fingers digging and kneading, pressing her into the hardness of his erection. Her entire body flamed. It was as if the last dance had never been interrupted.

Except that, from the corner of her eye, she saw Mihaela enter the room, István and Konrad at her heels.

She dragged her mouth free. "Too late." As hard as it was to speak with triumph when the body yelled with fury and frustration, she did her best.

He laughed, a soft, melting sound that seemed to shoot straight to her womb. "Sweetheart, we have all the time in the world."

Other hunters entered too. She recognized some of them from the headquarters building. "No, we haven't."

His lips stirred against her ear, sending new, exciting shivers all the way down her neck and spine. "I could fuck you here. If anyone noticed, they wouldn't care."

Her fingers gripped his shoulders, half in warning, half in wicked longing. "I suppose it's a minor crime for a vampire."

"There is no crime in mutual pleasure."

She gave a small deliberate wriggle over his erection and with fierce triumph, saw his eyes gleam. As the watchful hunters moved around the dance floor, observed from the bar by a woman in black and the anxious young waiter, Elizabeth stood on tiptoe and whispered in Saloman's ear. "How does it feel to be trapped?" She dipped her tongue in his ear. "By your own lust?"

"Tell me," he invited.

She smiled, trailing her lips along his jaw to the corner of his mouth. "I'm freed. My friends are surrounding you, closing you in with your unfulfilled desires."

"Then you'd better pray I let you come quickly."

Christ, she was so sensitive, so aroused, that if she moved, just a little against his erection, she would come right now. With a superhuman effort, she held still. It was he who moved, deliberately gyrating.

"I can live without sex," she whispered. "I'm good at it."

He smiled. "No, you're not," he said, and kissed her mouth.

She couldn't resist closing her eyes. *Last kiss . . . oh God help me, help him. . . .*

His torturing hands caressed their way up her body to her throat. She opened her eyes. Konrad and Mihaela had seen them; were bearing down on them. The woman in black—Angyalka herself?—vaulted over the bar and ran toward the dance floor. At once, several people fell in behind her, presumably vampires.

Without warning, the music stopped. For an instant, the tableau seemed to freeze. Saloman, one hand almost caressing her throat, dropped the other around her waist and met Konrad's fierce gaze. The hunter, careless of being seen in this moment of emergency, held the inevitable wooden stake.

"Let her go," Konrad commanded.

Saloman laughed. "In the immortal words of our hostess— bite me."

He tensed, his legs flexed, and he leapt. Elizabeth felt as if she were flying. Her stomach rolled as she shot up through the air in Saloman's hold, impossibly high, impossibly fast over the faces of the stunned crowd. The velvet black sky with its myriad of sparkling stars seemed to rush down to meet her, dragging her through the open dome window into its cool, breezy grasp. But the powerful, only too solid arms that held her were Saloman's.

Chapter Eleven

At some point early on in the bizarre flight, her abject terror got lost in wonder. The world jolted as it sped by her eyes, in between long, soaring swings that felt more like the flying dreams of her childhood than anything with a basis in reality. Hanging on to his shoulder with one hand, the fabric of his shirt with the other, she registered the beauty of the city from this angle: the crowded rooftops of Buda against the blackness of the night sky. She even had odd glimpses of blurred people moving in the streets below.

"Are we flying?" she exclaimed. She dragged her fascinated gaze up to his face in time to see his gaze flicker to her in something like surprised approval.

"Alas, no." His gaze left her. She felt again the tensing of his muscles and the weird soaring through the air that made her want to clutch her stomach. "Merely jumping."

They landed with a soft thud, and almost before she realized it, he was running again—running far faster than was humanly possible across the rooftops and leaping over the spaces between.

Eventually, she remembered she should be angry, even if her fear had gotten temporarily lost. "Where are you taking me?"

"To my palace."

Palace. Not lair, or den, or crypt. "You have a palace in Buda," she repeated. Of course, his definition and hers would be different. He lived below the ground, in cellars and sewers—why didn't he smell bad?

"Oh no. I embrace the new city of Pest." He swerved, then jumped, and Elizabeth again saw the Danube spread out before her.

"You've been misleading them," she said in dismay. "Leaving a false trail."

"Just in case they had the forethought to watch, or have the ability to see."

They'd look like a blur to most people. He moved so fast, they'd just be a flash half glimpsed from the corner of somebody's eye. A blink to clear the blur and they'd be gone. No one could see and no one would know. Her bag with her phone and the alarm buzzer were back at the Angel. Now she was truly on her own. And in just a few minutes, if she survived that long, the fear would kick in with a vengeance. Right now, she could relish its absence, even wonder at herself for the crowing she couldn't resist.

"No roofs over the river! Even you can't jump that far! How will you cross to the other side?"

"Like this," Saloman said, and swooped. The air rushed through her hair, pulling at her skin while the ground leapt to meet her. This time she hid her eyes in his shoulder. But it seemed he had no intention of killing her in so pointless a manner. For an instant they landed on the cobblestones in front of the chain bridge. She opened her eyes, just as he leapt once more. Silenced, she could only gaze in fresh wonder as they bounded from the top of the first stone arch to the next, moving ever closer to the Parliament building on the other side. He even ran across that, apparently unnoticed.

There was nothing he couldn't do, no way she or the hunters could defeat him. And it was she who had awakened him. Not the sort of fame she'd ever imagined—a firm place in the secret texts of the vampire hunters. But he wouldn't be content with that either, would he? He wanted to rule the world, human as well as vampire.

Moving away from the river, they came to a series of well-planned streets and squares with large, classically built houses. Once the dwellings of the powerful aristocracy for whom they were built, they had long ago been divided into flats, or so she had been led to believe.

"Hold tight," Saloman said on the roof of one such building, just before he stepped off it.

If her bones were shattered, he could still drink her blood, and she wouldn't be in much of a position to fight back.

Her bones didn't shatter. He landed with bent knees, absorbing the force with the ease of obviously long practice, and let her slither down his body until her feet touched the ground. Numb and dizzy, she would have stumbled and fallen if he hadn't kept his arm around her waist as he moved along the side of the house to the imposing front door.

Humiliated, angry at her own helplessness, she snapped,

"There's no need to hold on so tightly. After that performance, there's not much point in my trying to run away, is there?"

"None," he agreed. He was unlocking the door, with a key. Not the cellar, then.

He opened the door, led her inside, and closed it. And Elizabeth's upsurge of anger vanished. After all, it was as pointless now as running.

She stood in a large, gracious hall, dimly lit by one retro wall lamp, but hung with large, opulent, Renaissance-style paintings. There wasn't much in the way of furniture—merely a tall, mahogany coat stand, with a black leather coat hanging from one hook.

She stared at the elegantly decorated cornice work of the ceiling as he urged her forward toward the massive curving staircase. It too was lit from strategically placed wall lights. She climbed. "You live here? In this house? Where are the owners?" Dead, of course; he'd eaten them.

"I'm the owner," he reproved, as if he'd read her thoughts—which she didn't put past him either, God help her. "I bought it. With the scraps of paper that pass for money in these very strange times. Come."

Through open double doors, he led her into a huge drawing room, hung with dark red velvet curtains and Eastern-patterned wallpaper. Leaving her at the door, Saloman moved around the dark room, lighting candles that gradually illuminated the contents: large rugs scattered on the floor; a chaise longue; innumerable Turkish cushions; a low, round table; and, bizarrely, a television.

Elizabeth's gaze moved on to Saloman, who stood watching her. She swallowed. This was her reality. She could no longer hide behind anger or lust or wonder, nor could she trust in others to save her. "You've brought me *here* to die?"

He walked toward her, lean and lithe as a large cat, unruffled by his recent race across the rooftops of Budapest. There had never been a creature more beautiful, or more lethal.

"I'm sorry." He took her hand. She looked at it, a rather pretty shade of golden brown from the sun, or from the warm lighting he'd achieved, lying inert and helpless in his large, pale fingers. His voice was soft, though not lustful or mocking. Instead, there seemed to be a hint of genuine apology. "I would never have done it in the club. I promised us both a night together. Not a furtive fuck on a public dance floor. I just couldn't resist playing your game. You looked so . . ."

Ridiculous.

"Desirable." His voice dropped lower, warm and husky, and in spite of everything, her body tingled in response. His gaze roved over her throat and shoulders and breasts, down over her stomach and hips to her legs, and back to her face.

"Why?" she whispered.

It wasn't a very clear question, but again he seemed to understand. "Perhaps because I owe my Awakener more than that." His fingers moved, stroking her palm, the soft, sensitive skin between her thumb and forefinger. A caress, covering a pause that went on too long; an uncharacteristic hesitation.

His free hand lifted and touched her cheek, cupping it in his palm. "And because your beauty haunts me. Not just this lovely face or even this delectable body, but you. I want to know you."

Elizabeth's muscles jerked, reacting to this strangest discovery of all. "You don't *want* to kill me. . . ."

"No," he admitted, "I don't."

"Nothing compels you," she quoted desperately.

"I wish that were true. But we are different species, you and I, and we think very differently. If I could choose, I would drain you of all the strength I could take without actually killing you. But then, the life force would remain yours, and if I don't take it, one of my enemies will. That is what I can't allow."

"Your enemies?" she burst out, annoyed by the soothing effect of his deep, reasonable voice speaking such monstrous words. "I didn't waken your enemies! What use am I to them?"

His eyes scanned hers, as if searching for an understanding she just didn't have. His lips quirked. "Come, sit down."

He led her across to the chaise longue and handed her into the seat with an old-fashioned gallantry that should have grated against his stated intention of killing her. And yet it didn't. It was as if she'd fully entered his insane world. Shit, was she actually forgiving him? That small layer of intense warmth she could feel growing around her heart, was that *pleasure* because she'd been right and he did feel something for her?

This amazing, beautiful, fascinating being cared for *her*. However mad he was, it meant something. She just couldn't work out what.

Dazed—was that any better than dazzled?—she watched him take a bottle and glasses from an antique cupboard in the corner, then bring them to the table in front of her.

"You like champagne?" he inquired, sitting beside her and reaching for the bottle.

"I've never been in a position to acquire the taste."

"I love it. I'm going to buy land here and plant vines to make my own. I understand it will never have the snob value of French champagne, but I'm hoping it will be at least as acceptable as the best Italian Prosecco."

She closed her mouth. "You really haven't let the grass grow under your feet, have you?"

The cork whizzed off with a pop, and he poured the bubbling wine into both glasses. "Just because you have lots of it doesn't mean you should waste it—time or wine. Cheers."

She took the glass from him. Live for the moment. And she would never have the chance to ask again. "So you eat and drink as well? Like normal people?"

His lip twitched. "Like normal people? No. I don't eat your food. I can drink since my body absorbs it. I can even get vilely drunk, but I won't. An inebriated vampire is not a pretty sight."

"Hey, I can take it. I've been in Glasgow on a Friday night." It was a thoughtless, throwaway remark she expected to pass him by. She wasn't prepared for the quick smile of appreciation, or her own foolish pleasure in inspiring it. In spite of everything she knew, it felt like a reward.

Like Stockholm syndrome . . .

"Is that your hometown?" he asked.

"Almost. We lived in a small town close by."

"We?"

"My parents and I."

He sipped his wine, regarding her with such intensity that she raised her own glass for protection. "You're a lady of learning," he observed. "An academic. What led you down that path?"

"I was good at it."

"Yet you only graduated at the age of twenty-eight. I understand that is old."

How in hell did he know that? Dmitriu. She'd given Maria, along with everyone else she interviewed, a brief biography with her qualifications to prove she wasn't just a time waster.

"I only took the standard four years. I was a mature student."

"Why? What did you do before?"

"I looked after my parents."

"Were they sick?"

She nodded. "My father had Alzheimer's." She cast a quick glance at him. "You know what that is?"

"A kind of dementia suffered mostly by the old?"

"Only mostly. My father contracted it when he was comparatively young, which meant he was in no fit state to look after my mother, who had Parkinson's disease." She took a mouthful of champagne. It felt weird to be talking about this stuff. She never mentioned it to anyone. Those who needed to already knew about it.

"When?" he asked. "How old were you?"

She shrugged. "Fifteen or thereabouts. When it got bad."

"Did you go to school?"

"When I could. I did all right, considering the absences."

He was frowning. "Did no one help you?"

"My aunt came twice a year and drank tea with my mum. My friends helped, covered for me . . . I coped. If I hadn't, the authorities would've done something, taken them into care of some kind. But my dad needed familiarity, not a new home, and my mum needed him there, even when he stopped knowing who the hell she was." She took a deep breath. "Oddly enough, when my mum eventually died, my dad followed within the year."

He nodded. "Somewhere, he still knew she was his roots, his hold on life. They needed each other as much as they needed you."

She'd never put it into words before, hating the schmaltzy sentimentality that could emerge from simple truth and sully it. She found herself watching him with something approaching gratitude.

Stockholm! Remember Stockholm?

Saloman stirred. "It happened like that with my people sometimes too. When the familiar things, the familiar friends—and enemies—all vanished, there was nothing left to make life bearable. It drove some insane."

As he spoke of his people—the Ancients—all of whom were now gone, she caught a glimpse, dark and unbearable, of a loneliness well beyond anything she'd ever known, even in her worst moments. It hurled her into speech. "They say *you're* insane."

His lips quirked again. "Who do? The vampire hunters?"

"There are documents," she said defensively.

"Of course there are. Written by whom?"

By those who were left when he'd "died."

As if he read the dawning comprehension in her eyes, he smiled. "There's a lot of truth in your thesis, Elizabeth Silk. Many things are said and claimed to justify acts that are otherwise unjustifiable."

She leaned forward to set down her glass. "They say you killed the only other Ancient still in existence. Over a woman."

"Tsigana." He watched her as he spoke the name. But she could see no trace of emotion.

"Did you?"

"Perhaps. Oh, I killed him. Perhaps it was insanity—certainly I can't justify it. And some of it was about Tsigana."

Elizabeth took a deep breath, but she had nothing to lose. "Is that why she betrayed you?"

His lips twisted. "No. She betrayed me because I wouldn't give her what she sought—eternal life."

"She wanted you to make her a vampire?"

"She loved power, poor Tsigana. It was what drew her to me. But when you can see power without touching it, it's no longer enough. She wanted more. I refused it, and Maximilian promised it. The rest was inevitable. Although it must be said the last laugh is mine. Maximilian never gave her the promised gift. She died a very old woman, I understand."

It might have given him satisfaction. It was hard to tell. He was gazing into his wine, the half smile not fading on his full, sensual lips.

"Didn't you know?" Elizabeth blurted. "Didn't you suspect they were betraying you?"

"I should have," he agreed. "I knew them both—knew them all—well enough. I suppose it must have been the insanity you spoke of." He lifted the glass to his lips and drank, as if that would hide the old, ugly wounds. But the softness of tragedy stayed in his black, not-so-expressionless eyes.

The knowledge rushed on her like a revelation, peculiarly devastating. Not insanity. Just simple love.

He lowered the glass and caught her staring. He laughed. "What's the matter? You think me incapable of love because I'm evil?"

"Are you?"

"Incapable of love? Come here and I'll show you."

"Evil," she said firmly.

"Like beauty, it's in the eye of the beholder."

It was so easy to drown in his eyes, in his darkness. To lose the fraying thread that bound her to reality—just.

"You really want to rule the world? Like some insane megalo-maniac from an old B movie?"

The gleam was back in his eyes—mockery or lust. Or both. "It's a long-term goal. Just now, all I want is to make love to you."

Her stomach lurched downward. "Oh no. I know what comes after that."

"It's a long time until sunrise."

They were bantering, flirting over her life. She should have been appalled. She should have been running like hell, whatever the futility. Was she so pathetic that she would just lie down and die for him?

Face it, Silk. It's not the dying you want. It's the loving.

Reaching out, he stroked her hair, brushing the tousled locks behind her bare shoulder. She might have been mistaken, but she imagined his hand shook. His touch on her skin was soft, sensual, unbearably tender. His compelling eyes burned.

He ached—as she did.

Her breath caught. The game wasn't over. She had one last throw, if she dared to take it.

She leaned into him and lifted her face closer to his. He inhaled her, not smiling now, but savoring. His lips parted, but still they didn't take hers. His only contact was the hand lying still and heavy on her shoulder.

God help me. . . .

Her heart pounded at the enormity of what she was about to do. She closed her eyes, gathering courage and strength, and brushed her lips across his. When they moved in instant response, she flicked her tongue along his upper lip, from corner to corner, then snaked inside his mouth, and fastened her whole mouth to his.

His arms came around her, not crushing but cradling, letting her kiss, letting her arms creep around his neck until her fingers could tangle in his long, soft hair. His mouth moved over hers, his tongue stroking hers without hurry. There was none of the hot urgency of the encounter at the Angel, and she was grateful, because right now she couldn't deal with that. This was a slow burn, though no less intense, no less pleasurable.

It was her hands that strayed first, stroking down the vertebrae of his back and under the waistband of his trousers. His skin was cool and soft, but he didn't stay still under her fingers. It was as if his body stroked them back. She wouldn't have been human if she hadn't pushed down further over the taut swell of his buttocks.

The movement of his body against her became more pronounced and far more suggestive, rubbing his chest against her breasts until the slow burn she'd been imagining suddenly ran away with her. When he slid his fingers under the thin straps of her dress and let them fall down her arms, her mouth opened wide in a gasp of need.

He seized the opportunity, plundering with insistent tongue and sensual lips, and sharp, wicked teeth that sent flames of desire curling through her with every graze and caress. The feel of them, the knowledge of what he was, should have doused her lust in abject terror. Instead, it released a flood of sexual moisture between her thighs, the danger urging her on to lick one of those fangs, to take it between her lips and suck.

She gave a small, inarticulate moan, and he caught her hair in his hand, drawing her back so that he could look at her. Her breasts heaved as if she'd won the hundred-meter sprint, causing her dress to fall lower with every frantic breath. Under his avid gaze, her body burned yet glowed, as if his eyes caressed her.

He reached out and tugged her dress by the neck, fully exposing her breasts at last. She didn't look. She knew her aching nipples stood out, begging. He looked for a long time, so long that she began to despair that he was changing his mind. He didn't breathe, let alone pant, to give her a clue as to his feelings. She had only his dark, devouring eyes. Tiny flames seemed to dance there, gold and amber . . . but it might have been the candlelight.

Saloman bent his head. At the same time, his hand in her hair drew her back against the cushion, and he took her nipple between his lips.

Her eyes closed as she tried to absorb the sensations that grew sharper, more intense with every pull of his sensual lips, every flicker of his tongue. His hand slid up her thigh, over the crumpled piece of fabric that was her dress, and settled on the breast not occupied by his mouth. He caressed it softly with his palm, cupped it, rolled the nipple between his thumb and forefinger. When a moan escaped her, he smiled around her breast and lifted his head to kiss her mouth instead while his hand continued its work.

Elizabeth was lost. Her upper body aflame with his attentions, the lower clamored for release. She arched her hips, seeking his touch, seeking comfort for the throbbing need of her sex. She found his hand. Firm and wicked, it pressed her down onto the sofa, making her whole body shriek with pleasure. His palm cupped her pubic bone, his fingers moved over the dampness of her panties, discovering her swollen clitoris with ease. He stroked it through the soaked cotton, and she gasped and whimpered, kissing him with hard, hot passion that was at least half a silent plea.

His fingers drew together, gathering the wisps of cotton into her sensitive folds until the panties began to slide down her hips and thighs and he could pull them off.

"I foresee a night of great pleasure," he whispered. "Come."

Straightening, he rose to his feet and took both her hands to help her follow. As she stood, conscious only of desire and need, the provocative dress fell the rest of the way to the floor, leaving her naked.

The vampire's clouded eyes stared. He lifted her hands to his lips in turn, almost like an act of worship that induced a new wonder in her. Then he began to walk, conducting her with peculiar, courtly grace to an inner door she hadn't noticed before. Mesmerized, she gazed at him as she walked naked beside him, through the doorway, into another large, luxurious room that contained first and foremost, a large, ornately carved four-poster bed, with heavy, partly drawn curtains that matched those at the windows of both rooms. Between them, she glimpsed pristine white sheets. They shone like silk.

Elizabeth heard her heart hammering. Fear rushed in on her at last, not because of what she was doing, but because of whom she was doing it with and because of how completely she had surrendered. There was no going back, but she so needed to keep herself together, to be aware of more than his beauty and her own lust. . . .

As if he felt her sudden tension, he halted beside the bed and kissed her mouth, melting her, drugging her with irresistible desire. He gathered her close into his arms, drawing the length of her naked body against his clothed one, and God, that was sexy too, from the buttons of his shirt pressing into her nipples, to the hard column of his straining erection grinding against her abdomen. She was falling again, losing herself again. Her stomach soared as he lifted her in his arms, still kissing.

And because she wanted to, she tugged at his shirt, pulling it free of his trousers with one hand, trying to unfasten his buttons with the other. It was a desperate bid for control—*her* desire, not his—but as he laid her on the bed and simply tore open his shirt, letting the buttons spill all over the floor, such trivia vanished. There was just one desire. And it had her reaching for him with both hands, desperate to feel that pale gold skin against her own.

He was magnificent, as she'd known he would be. Toned muscle rippled in his upper arms, across his broad shoulders. A dusting of black hair scattered across his powerful chest, narrowing to a fine line down his flat stomach, like an arrow pointing into the waistband of his trousers, which he began to unfasten.

From Elizabeth's admittedly limited experience, there should have been an undignified hopping and struggling to get them off, to get rid of his pants and socks. By rights, he should at least have sat on the bed to avoid it. But he didn't deprive her of the full sight of his gradually revealed body, even for a moment. Any underwear was pushed down with his trousers, letting his breathtaking erection spring free over his taut stomach.

Her attention glued to this stunning organ, she missed how he extracted himself from the trousers and shoes. She lifted her gaze only when he stepped forward and sank rather than climbed onto the bed.

She opened her mouth to speak, to say what she didn't know, and in any case it didn't matter, for he pressed her into the pillows and kissed her until the world was dark and swirling and beautiful. And that alabaster skin was under her hands, cool and smooth as she ran them up and down the length of his lean, gorgeous back, feeling the muscles undulate to her caresses.

Beneath her was the luxurious softness of silken sheets; above her, the electrifying hardness of his chest and hips and thighs as he loomed over her, covering her body. His tender mouth and hands melted her.

"In my life," he said, between kisses, "I have known many women, many loves."

Something close to jealousy twisted through her, not dousing but fanning her urgency. She writhed under him, tried to hold on to his mouth, desperate to silence him, to bury her upsurge of inadequacy in the intensity of his lust.

His hands were in her hair, holding her twisting head steady for his dark gaze to bore into her. "Each is different; each is sweet, whether it lasts a decade or an instant." His knee slid upward, parting her thighs farther, and she moaned aloud at the feel of his shaft sliding along her sex. "And if I have learned anything over the millennia, it is this: that in love, only the moment matters."

The head of his organ nudged her entrance. He kissed her mouth, long and sensually. "For this moment, this night, Elizabeth, I love you."

Her mouth opened wide in some soundless emotion, a sob that never came, for he entered her body in one firm, sliding push. Everything fled before the sensation, except the knowledge that she was now having sex with the most powerful vampire of all time. He let out a sound like a groan, which might have been a sigh in anyone else, and thrust farther in. Without conscious volition, she arched to meet him and gasped. Fully sheathed in her, he felt huge, filling and stretching her to her limit. And yet it was so good. No one else had ever felt like this inside her.

No one had ever moved inside her as he did either, slow and sensual, making love with his whole body, not just his cock. His back, his hips, undulated under her caressing hands, pushing into her as he bent to kiss her breasts. He reached deep inside her, finding places she hadn't been aware of possessing, places that glowed under his stroking and caught fire, filling her with wonder and desire for more. She met his rhythm, squeezed him, and cried out with the delight it brought. She wrapped her legs around his hips, drawing him closer and deeper.

"I'll pleasure you any and every way you want it," he whispered. "But the first time has to be like this, inside you."

"Why?"

"So that I can feel your joy at the source of mine. Because I find it sweetest. Because I want it. Because right now it feels as if I waited three hundred and twelve years and nine days for you, for this."

On the last word, he thrust hard and powerfully, and she cried out at the wild pleasure. Twisting under him, kneading the taut swell of his buttocks in her hands, she tried to make him do it again; she sensed the shadow of care and self-control he tried to keep and with her sudden, dangerous need to make him lose it, another game had begun. A game that was sweet and exciting and one she couldn't lose. At her urging, his strokes grew in strength and speed, shattering her with every thrust, building the fire that would consume her in seconds.

"You see?" he whispered, feeding the rising tide of her orgasm. "This is what you need, the thrill, the love. . . ." He kissed her mouth, driving into her, then dragged his lips across her jaw to her throat, and as the climax broke over her, he thrust again, intensifying it impossibly while sucking the skin of her throat into his mouth.

In that blinding instant, she knew that if she could survive by banishing this orgasm, she wouldn't do it.

He was right. This moment was worth everything. It was life.

Then all thought, coherent or otherwise, vanished into the massive, convulsive joy. Through it, as if from a great distance, she

heard his rising groan expand until it becam̶
rang in her ears and vibrated through her spasm̶
with his final, almost brutal thrusts that set it all off aga̶

His teeth scraped along her throat, seemed to tremble aga̶
her. She had a moment to anticipate the cold, numbing pleasure
she'd felt a lifetime ago when he drew her blood into his mouth, to
wonder with black, terrible excitement what added pleasure it
would give to her orgasming body. And then his mouth dragged
free. He reared up over her, taking his weight on his hands, his
howl becoming a shout of raw, primal triumph.

Elizabeth had never seen anything more beautiful than this
being's joy in her. The force of it shook him, contorted his body,
and added a powerful intensity to his handsome face, at once
focused and lost. That moment—a very long moment—of unexpected vulnerability totally disarmed her.

His arms collapsed, his weight crushed her, and his mouth
took hers again in a massive, devouring kiss. She clung to him as
the storm subsided. And the truth struggled up into her stunned
consciousness.

She'd won.

He'd taken her body, but left her blood.

She'd won.

✝

Saloman left her mouth at last, more to let her breathe than because he was finished with it. Blood still pounded through her, hot and sweet and alluring. Her heart and lungs pumped like pistons. But apart from her arms, which still clung around his neck, the rest of her body sagged, lethargic, almost limp under his weight. He let her bear it a little longer, because she could; because he liked it. After those days and nights of pursuit and teasing, of verbal struggles and all her determined efforts to kill him, it felt good to have her helpless and sated under him.

And in truth it felt good to gaze down at her soft, satisfied face, her eyes still closed, her swollen lips parted and glistening. Her delicate cheeks were rosy in the candlelight, flushed still with passion and exertion, her hair tumbling and tangled across the pillow.

Beauty moved Saloman. Watching Elizabeth slip from ecstasy to sleep made him ache. Perhaps it was release, after three centuries of enforced celibacy followed by nine agonizing days of self-imposed abstinence. And of course, anticipation always intensified the pleasure. Whatever the cause, this was one of those rare couplings that touched his soul.

Physical beauty, sexual skill, erotic surroundings—none of them counted beside this rarity. He was glad to have found it with her.

He eased his weight off her onto his elbows, and her eyes opened wide, dark hazel flecked with bewitching green, staring up at him. A dawning wonder began to cover the wild light of passion that had driven him on. He'd given her something new, and she liked it. He'd been right about that. There were unplumbed depths of sensuality in this woman, and he planned to release a few more of them before sunrise.

Without warning she smiled at him, dazzling him with her open happiness. And he smiled back, because against all the odds, he saw that she was his, that he had won.

He rolled over onto his back, to avoid crushing her to death, carrying her with him, still impaled. She lay on his chest and kissed his mouth before trailing her lips down his chest and fastening them to his nipple. He cupped her soft, pliant buttocks in his hands and squeezed before giving an experimental thrust that made her gasp.

"Isn't that meant to shrink?" she asked without noticeable dissatisfaction.

"No. Not when it's inside you." Smiling, he swept his hands up over the curve of her buttocks and her back and stroked her face. "I think it pleased you," he teased; yet he felt ridiculously like an inexperienced boy awaiting words of approval. It had been too long, much too long.

"*You* pleased me." The words seemed to spill from her without permission. As soon as they were spoken, her teeth closed over her lip, as if embarrassed, and to cover it, she kissed his mouth.

Saloman had no objection to that. He began to make love to her again, but very slowly, forcing himself to far greater passivity than was in his nature. Fascinated, he wanted to see what she would do—whether she would falter or wait in shyness for him to resume control, or take her pleasure with quick, wicked secrecy. She didn't.

She moved on him like a cat, slow and sensual, taking time for her hands and lips to learn his body, with a shy but obvious delight that aroused him all the more. But this woman he'd released no longer drew back in embarrassment from the sexual heat. She embraced it, craved his pleasure with her own, and set about achieving it with a wild determination that enchanted him.

In the end, Saloman reached up with his arms and held on to the bedpost, riding the whirlwind as she rode him, to a profound, devastating climax.

Smiling, he watched her come down once more. Since she sat astride him, and he felt far too comfortable as he was to move and kiss her, he contented himself with tracing the shape of her trembling lips with one finger. She caught his finger in her mouth and kissed it. She looked both decadent and angelic, almost like a Botticelli painting, as her pert, rosy-tipped breasts rose and fell among her tumbling, pale amber hair.

At last, she gave a breath of almost awed laughter. "You really don't get any smaller, do you?"

"I'm still inside you," he pointed out.

"What if I . . . ?" Teasing, she began to slide off, but he grabbed her hips to keep her in place.

"No," he said. "You're too desirable. And it's been a long time."

Her half smile paused with uncertainty. "A day or so?"

"Three hundred and twelve years, give or take a month or so. And nine days, of course."

Her eyes searched his. "You never struck me as a celibate being."

"I was never known for it," he confessed. "On the other hand, the three hundred and twelve years were not my choice."

"And the nine days?"

He moved at last, rolling her over and under him. "Not so much abstinence, as the desire to have you."

Her mouth opened, as if to say, "*Me?*" But she closed it again, clearly not sure whether to laugh in disbelief or accept it as a compliment.

He said, "Are you hungry?"

Bafflement flashed across her face. "Hungry? No. That is, maybe a little; I haven't been thinking of food."

"We can have sex with the leftovers."

Her body shook with laughter but also excitement. She clenched involuntarily around his cock, and he withdrew it slowly, to make her gasp—and to savor the sensation.

"You really have food?" she asked as he slid off the bed.

"Humans are always hungry."

She began to say something, then broke off, apparently distracted by watching him walk naked across the room. He liked that too, but he had no intention of inuring her to the sight. He picked up the black silk robe from the chair in the corner and went out.

The kitchen on the ground floor was not a place in which he spent a great deal of time. It had been cleaned with the rest of the house and never used. But the refrigerator—a useful invention for humans, he allowed—contained some excellent cheese and cold meats, salad, and fruit he'd ordered especially for his night with her. He began setting it out on a plate.

When he heard her soft footsteps on the stairs, it crossed his mind that she was escaping, running for the front door. It didn't matter. She wouldn't reach the street before he caught her again; yet when she didn't even pause there, but crossed the hall toward the kitchen, he smiled without meaning to.

Her shadow, and then her presence, filled the doorway. He glanced up to see her standing with her back to the wall. She wore his torn, discarded shirt, and the sight of it on her, of its parting across her beautiful breasts and of her shapely legs emerging from its hem, sent the blood racing through his veins once more.

But she looked serious, almost anxious. He wondered if, as the joy of sex faded, she'd come to plead for her life—or to ask for a cooked meal.

He placed some cherries on the plate and opened the cupboard door to find a glass.

She said, "The three hundred and twelve years. Were you conscious?"

He paused, his hand on the stem of the glass, then brought it down and filled it with the fruit juice from the fridge. "Mostly. I slept a lot too."

"I can't even . . ." She walked toward him with quick, agitated steps. "How did you survive the boredom?"

He glanced at her in surprise, because she'd unerringly found the hardest part. "Determination to survive. I thought a lot."

"About what, for God's sake? For three hundred years?"

"Everything. You understand I was already more than two thousand years old. I'm used to—er—passing the time."

"But you can't exactly have had many distractions!"

"Revenge is a good one. Ruling the world another. And, of course, there was the pain."

"Pain?" She sounded uncertain, as though imagining emotional turmoil.

He let the smile tug at his lips while he made a fist and thumped it against his heart.

Her eyes widened with shock. Her mouth fell open, and she grabbed the table as if to steady herself. "You felt that? For three hundred years?"

He shrugged. "The first few were the worst. One's body learns to cope and adapt. Sometimes, when I was just waking up, it seemed like my best friend. Almost a solid entity."

He said it to lighten her horror, to make her laugh. But she didn't, continuing instead to stare at him with a compassion that seemed to hurt more than his remembered agony.

He let his hands fall from the plate. "Elizabeth, I can take pain. I can take boredom and hunger. I can even take blinding, meaningless lust that I can't move to assuage. I can bear betrayal and the kind of fury that should make one's body explode. But not pity. Not from a woman I've just fucked."

He meant to shock her with his coarseness, but she didn't even blink, so he pulled her against him and kissed her, hard. And then, with her almost-naked body in his hold, he no longer knew which of them he was distracting. Although she responded with blind instinct, as if she could do nothing else, she began to ask more questions, unable to leave the subject until he thrust his hand under the shirt, between her thighs, and she gasped, staring into his face with a different kind of shock. She seemed to smolder. And so, predatory and triumphant, he laid her across the kitchen table and brought her to orgasm with his fingers while he rubbed cream cheese into her breasts and drizzled wine over her nipples; then, while she convulsed under him in helpless bliss, he licked it all off with slow, deliberate sensuality.

After which, he took her and the remaining food back to bed, to let her feast off him instead.

✝

It was a lifetime of experience crammed into one endless night. The excitement and tension of the Angel seduction, the astonishing flight across Budapest, the roller-coaster emotions that assaulted her throughout the night, swept her up, and threw her onward, learning about him and about herself.

To say nothing of the wild, intense, gloriously constant sex.

Elizabeth felt like a stranger in a strange world, yet she welcomed it with open arms. It seemed that this night, which had begun with the near certainty of death, was bringing her to life.

They talked a lot. He even talked during sex—not crude words designed only for self-arousal, but hot, moving ones that told her how beautiful she was and how much he wanted her, how much he adored what she was doing to him. Beside that, the novelty of their other conversations seemed far less, even snippets of events that had occurred hundreds of years ago. She found herself telling him bits and pieces of her own much duller life, the friends who were important to her, the few men she'd gone out with and trusted and lost. And she found she no longer thought of those men with the mixture of humiliation, self-pity, and self-deprecation that she was used to—it was why she avoided thinking about them as much as she could—but with dispassionate if rueful humor. They were experiences of life; that was all. And none of them came near this one, not even Richard, whom she also mentioned in passing. Richard, who'd never even kissed her, and now she was glad.

Once, as she sprawled on the floor, examining the horde of books she'd found in his bedroom, wearing only his silk shirt against the predawn chill, she said, "Is this how you caught up with the twenty-first century? How many of these have you read?"

He shrugged and sank naked into the chair beside her. He didn't feel the cold. "Bits of all of them. I read quickly. And television is wonderful. I have a laptop too—endless information at the touch of a few keys."

She smiled as he drew her back against his legs and glanced up at him. "You seem to take it all in your stride."

"Three hundred years seems longer to you than to me."

"You've been around since the world began...."

"Not quite," he said wryly. "I don't remember the dinosaurs. In fact, until this week I'd never even *heard* of dinosaurs."

"Are we really the same race?" It felt good to surprise him, to feel his stroking hand pause on her hair before carrying on.

"Where did you hear that?"

"I read it." She caught his questing hand sliding inside the shirt, not to prevent it, but to hold it against her breast. "You wrote it."

"I probably did, though with little idea of preaching to posterity. Where did you come across it?"

"In the hunters' library. It's extraordinary, the stuff they have there."

"I must take a look sometime."

She glanced at him with sudden unease, but all his attention appeared to be on his hand, which was now caressing her naked breast. His concentration, especially after all the sex they'd already enjoyed, was very gratifying as well as arousing. And God, he was beautiful, with the tangle of black locks falling across his pale cheek, his full, sensual lips parted, his large black eyes more warm now than opaque. She had learned to read some of the expressions there, the signs of lust as well as laughter, teasing, odd instances of sadness and anger.

He was thousands of years old. It would have been stranger if he *wasn't* a complex man. She'd always been prepared for that, and for her own curiosity about the history he'd touched. What she hadn't expected was the force of her desire to know *him*. And yet in a lifetime—her lifetime—even if she spent every waking moment with him, she'd never know it all.

She shied away from that thought. She was living in the moment, because she was still alive when she'd thought she would be dead. Because whatever he was and whatever he'd done or would do, he'd given her the most amazing night of her life—of anybody's life, surely.

There was no sign of dawn seeping through the heavy velvet curtains. She was glad, because sunrise would bring the rest of the world and the consequences of this night, whatever they were. Right now, the night stretched forever, and she was happy.

Happy . . . Had she ever been truly happy before?

She reached up to touch his cheek with wonder, and his hot eyes moved to hers. Most of his face was in shadow, dark and mysterious—and sexy. Her breath caught. "Were you always like this?"

He leaned closer, and she lifted her open mouth to receive his kiss. He took her hand, guiding it to the cool hardness of his erection. Heat flamed through her.

"Randy?" he inquired. "Oh yes."

"Undead," she reproved. "Or did you never die? Were you always immortal?"

"I died."

Fascinated enough to be distracted from the caresses of his hand, and the feel of his throbbing erection in hers, she asked, "When? Where? What were you in life?"

"You would call me a prince."

Of course. Anything less just wouldn't have been believable. "Here? In Hungary?"

"Not originally. East of here, Asia. I traveled here with my people when I was a very young man, and I died of the same illness that killed so many of them, including my father." His thumb flicked her nipple, over and over, spreading warmth and icy tingles of need. "My people preserved a balance in those days. Perhaps originally we sprang from the same race as humans, but by my time we were a distinct and separate race with certain powers over nature—you would call it magic—and over death itself. We could revive our dead. Our undead lived among our living, and we all existed beside humans, even the ones who made us ill."

"Why?"

"It was our duty. To care for them. A council of elders, including the king, decided which of the dead should be revived. Normally, undead were chosen only from alternate generations of each family, but my father's death happened too quickly, so they revived me instead."

"Did you want it?" she asked curiously.

His gaze lifted from her breast to her face, an arrested expression in his dark, once unreadable eyes. "I didn't want to die. Yes, I wanted it. I reached for it with both hands."

From his appearance, if that was any way to judge his race, he had been younger then than she was now. It was natural to hold on to life, to grab at it any way you could, only . . .

"A life without light?" she whispered. "A life sustained on the blood, on the death of others?"

"It's necessary. And there are compensations for living out of the sun."

"What, for God's sake?"

He cupped her breast and smiled, presumably by way of illustration. "Heightened senses. I can hear your heart beat from the next room, the blood rushing through your veins. I can feel and identify your presence in a city full of people. Every touch is intense, every pleasure, and ecstasy you can only dream of. Though perhaps I can help that dream along."

Her fist tightened on his shaft, and at the instantaneous flash of fire in his eyes, she squeezed and caressed until he lifted her in his arms and strode with her to the bed.

"Again?" she breathed.

"Oh yes."

"You will so need to change your bedding. . . . Do silk sheets wash well?"

"I don't know. I don't care. I like the feel of them. Like your skin, Mistress Silk." He laid her on the bed, kneeling, and took off her shirt before embracing her from behind, one hand over her breast while he turned up her face with the other and kissed her.

He knelt behind her, his long, muscular thighs holding her captive as he caressed and kissed. His erection nudged between her cheeks, nestled between her thighs and found its now-familiar way inside. Before tonight, she'd never cared much for penetrative sex. It had never measured up to her vague and possibly naïve romantic desires. Tonight, however, she'd discovered there was no greater joy than Saloman's shaft in her, working its magic inside while his hands and lips worked their own on the outside.

She pushed back against him, blissful as he thrust in long, slow strokes. As things grew more heated, his hand slipped down between her legs and she cried out. The sharp intensity of pleasure his fingers brought to her clitoris set her orgasm climbing.

"Take it all," he whispered into the skin of her neck, mingling the delight of his thrusts with the joy of his fingers. And God, she'd forgotten the sensitivity of her neck, the weird, cold pleasure of his teeth's grazing and caressing and biting. . . .

As the tide crashed over her, his teeth clamped down. Her hands, clinging to his thighs, opened wide with shock and pain. But she couldn't stop the ecstasy convulsing her; she couldn't stop the insidious rush of need as he pierced her skin. Then he began to suck, and the force of the new pleasure hit her like a blow, fierce, scary, and overwhelming. Pushing ecstasy into her below, he sucked the life from her veins into his cruel, tender mouth, took her blood with her body, and kept taking.

Helpless, lost in endless, mindless pleasure, reaching for it with both hands and her entire, greedy body, Elizabeth knew she'd discovered total joy at last. In death.

✝

Saloman gathered it all to him, her vulnerable body, convulsing on his cock, bringing him joy; her strong, sweet blood, spilling over his teeth and down his throat, strengthening his hungry veins with the power of the Awakener, with the potency of his killer, Tsigana. Two lovers, one bloodline.

Triumph flowed through him. He never wanted to stop taking Elizabeth, drinking Elizabeth. . . .

And it seemed she could take a lot of pleasure on her own account—more, far more than he'd expected. But then, she had the semimystical power Tsigana had taken from him by the act of killing. It was a cycle of power and pleasure, and he longed to keep it going forever. He wanted to feel Elizabeth's teeth in his throat, piercing the vein and feeding from him—at the instant of her death.

With a howl that sounded wolflike, even to his own ears, he dragged his mouth away from her and forced himself to be still, because she couldn't take any more. Her head lolled back against his shoulder, her glazed eyes staring up at him. Shaking like a man with ague, he bent and licked the wound in her throat. He couldn't help savoring the last taste of her blood as he did, regretting the loss as the punctures began at once to close and heal.

Her eyes were still open, huge in her white, exhausted, pleasure-blasted face.

"You drank from me," she whispered. "You did it after all. . . ." A single tear hovered at the corner of her eye, glistening. Fascinated, curiously stricken, he watched it tremble and fall. "Bastard," she said with surprising clarity, and collapsed.

Saloman laid her on the pillow, feeling for her sluggish pulse. He'd taken a lot of blood, but she wouldn't die. She wouldn't even need a transfusion since Tsigana's inherited blood cells would regenerate in her veins while she slept.

Saloman covered her with his silk sheet and sat back cross-legged to watch her sleep. She was beautiful, pale, lovely, and strong. A smile played about his lips. He was proud of her, and he rather thought she'd just changed all his plans.

He'd let her live, let her be the temptation to all who sought his downfall through killing her. But they wouldn't succeed, because she'd be with him, making him not weaker, but stronger.

Reaching out, he touched a scarlet spot on his white sheet.

"Blood on silk," he whispered, and began to laugh. "Elizabeth, you're mine."

†

He found Mihaela's flat without difficulty. It was easy to trace Elizabeth's residence now that her smell, her footsteps, her presence, filled his every sense. It was in a pleasant old house filled with unexpected light. No trace of her dark work littered the vampire hunter's home, just white walls and bright pictures and curtains that let in the early dawn light. He'd left it late. It was going to be hard to do all he meant to.

He broke in through the locked windows of the living room, carrying Elizabeth in his arms, wrapped only in his shirt and the cloak he'd worn for his three-century sleep. The flat was empty. Mihaela would be out with her colleagues, scouring the city for Elizabeth and for him. He hoped they hadn't wrecked the Angel; if they had, Angyalka would be spitting with rage.

He found the tiny spare room that was Elizabeth's temporary home. It was full of her stuff—the bags he remembered from Bistriţa, papers, tape recorder—all in a chaotic mess. Saloman laid her on the bed and opened the cloak as if it held a rare gift. For an instant, he gazed down at her. Then, with his fingertips, he touched her lips, the almost-vanished wound in her throat, and her steadily beating heart.

"I'll be back," he murmured, "after I've taken care of a few loose ends."

She didn't answer, but he was fairly sure she'd remember the words when she awoke. It didn't matter that much. She was his, and she'd come to him when he was ready. Until then, the vampire hunters would keep her safe.

From the open window of the living room, he saw a car draw up at the curb. It contained Mihaela and the Hungarian hunter. The woman got out, looking both defeated and angry. Well, at least she'd be happy when she got home. He'd left the bedroom door open, so she'd see at once that her friend was there.

"Sometimes," Saloman said to the breeze, "I surprise myself."

He leapt off the ledge into the wind. The two below glanced up in instinctive alarm, but all they would see were fading shadows fluttering over the rooftops toward the river, and Buda.

It was time to take care of Lajos—he'd made the rat squirm for long enough over exactly when the ax of vengeance would fall.

Chapter Thirteen

*E*lizabeth woke with a raging thirst and a sore head. When she opened her eyes, with no more profound hope than to discover a glass of water on the night table, she saw Mihaela sitting on the edge of the bed. And beyond her, arguing in low voices while Mihaela watched them, were Konrad and István.

"What . . . ?" she began, but had to break off because her voice came out as a feeble croak, and because as soon as it did, memory rushed on her with enough force to keep her silent for a very long time.

All three heads snapped around to her.

"Elizabeth," Mihaela said in obvious relief. "Are you all right?" Since she leaned forward as she spoke, helping Elizabeth to sit up before passing a glass of water into her grateful hands, there was time to let it all flood in, and to keep from answering by drinking. She felt weaker than a newborn kitten.

"You're alive," Konrad stated, with as much amazement as gratification. "He let you live."

Beyond the glass, which she still held to her lips, Elizabeth recognized the sleeve of the soft silk shirt she wore, and beneath the covering sheet, something made of black wool and, surely, fur. . . .

"Why did he do that?" István demanded. "Why didn't he kill you?"

Elizabeth lowered the glass with reluctance.

"Did he hurt you?" Mihaela asked urgently.

Stricken, Elizabeth looked at her and couldn't speak. What the hell could she say?

"Shit," Mihaela muttered. "What did he do to you?"

Hysteria arrived like an old friend, but at least she knew how to deal with that, swallowing it down before the laughter became more than a hiccup.

He took me to his palace and made love to me all night until I felt safe and warm and happy. And then he drank my blood. . . . He used words like "love," the meaning of which varies so much even among the truthful that it's hardly worth regarding. Except to note that a polite synonym of the verb "to fuck" is "to love." And trust me, in every sense, I've been fucked.

When she raised the glass to her lips once more, her hands shook. But at least her internal rant had remained internal.

She lowered the glass and held it in her lap with both hands under three pairs of anxious eyes.

"He drank my blood until I lost consciousness."

Mihaela turned her head up, searching for the wound. There might have been still a mark of some kind, for her breath hitched.

"How did you manage to get back here?" István demanded.

"I don't know." Elizabeth fingered the sleeve of her shirt. "But judging by my dress, he brought me."

"Why?" Konrad stepped closer. "Why would he bother? Why did he leave you alive when he needs your blood so much? Elizabeth, did he do anything else?"

For a moment, she wondered if he was referring to the sex. Not in her wildest, angriest dreams could she call it rape. Even stranger was her not wanting to pretend to herself. She wanted to remember her own desires, her own responses, her own pleasure. She just didn't want to feel so . . . betrayed.

"Did he make you drink his blood?" Konrad demanded.

"No," Elizabeth said, revolted, and watched the quick, relieved exchange of glances among the hunters. "Is that how it's done? Creating a new vampire? Like in *Dracula*?"

"Part of it," Mihaela admitted. "But it has to be done at the moment of death."

Elizabeth's stomach twisted. "Then I wouldn't know, would I? Perhaps he did kill me; perhaps he made me drink when I thought I was unconscious and I was actually dead—I wouldn't know."

Mihaela glanced up at the others. Konrad took his hand out of his pocket and threw something to Elizabeth. She caught it one handed, from instinct, and saw that it was a small detector. It was switched on and lay still on her palm, silent and dull.

"Is that conclusive?" she managed.

"On any but an Ancient, and we're working on that—" He broke off as a ringtone sounded, and fished his phone out of the other pocket.

"I think he'll be back," Mihaela said grimly. "He's still playing."

"He meant to kill me," Elizabeth blurted. "He told me so at the beginning, when we arrived in his house."

"You were in his house?" István jumped on it at once. "Where is it? Could you take us there?"

Could she? Even if her memory and her poor sense of direction came up to the mark, could she? The idea should *not* feel like betrayal. He'd fed from her, after everything that had gone before. . . .

She opened her mouth, but Konrad spoke first, snapping his phone shut and shoving it in his pocket. "The vampire Lajos is dead. Saloman killed him at dawn, along with a human who got in the way."

Water slopped from her glass, darkening a growing patch on the sheet. Blood sang in her ears. "Which human?" she whispered.

"Lajos's human protector—or slave, if you prefer. Nasty piece of work who's committed all sorts of foul crimes to please his master. We never had enough evidence to pin them on him. He was probably hoping to be 'turned.' The important point is, the Budapest vampires are falling over themselves to ally with Saloman now. As if they were just waiting to see how he handled his enemies. Zoltán has left Transylvania, presumably heading for a showdown with Saloman."

"He'll lose," István said with certainty.

"Will he?" Konrad sounded excited. "Think about it. Why did Saloman leave it so long to kill Lajos?"

"Games," Elizabeth muttered. "He likes to play cruel games."

Mihaela nodded. "Increases the fear."

"Perhaps," Konrad allowed. "Or perhaps he isn't as strong as everyone thinks he is. Whom has he taken out so far? Karl, the weakest of his vampire killers. He hasn't touched Zoltán, whom he might reasonably accuse of usurping his power. Perhaps he needed Elizabeth's blood even to be strong enough to take out Lajos."

"Then why didn't he finish her and get twice the power he did?" István demanded.

"God knows. He's an Ancient. He knows things that wouldn't even enter anyone else's head—vampire or hunter—as possibility. Perhaps he gets more by milking her, letting her recover, and going back. He's drunk from her twice now, after all, and she's still here."

Then why go to the trouble of seducing her? Just to pass the time? Just to amuse himself or scratch a sexual itch? A 312-year-old sexual itch. Excluding the nine days. No, there was more here. There was feeling for her; she could swear it. . . .

Who am I trying to fool? He's thousands of years old, fascinating, magnetic, dangerous, with all the added attraction that somehow implies. I'm a sexually inexperienced, socially inept nobody. What the hell could he feel for me except passing amusement?

Shite. Am I grateful even for that? What is wrong with me?

"You might be right," Mihaela said, "though I wouldn't like to bet my life on the weakness of the vampire I saw last night, flying through the Angel's roof with Elizabeth in one arm. The other point is, he's now a lot stronger. He has killed Lajos and drunk again from Elizabeth. Our time is running out, and we can't protect her. He knows she's here."

Konrad's face changed. For once, he said what Elizabeth was thinking. "He knows you're here too. Neither of you is safe. You need to move to headquarters until we get this sorted out."

✝

Dmitriu liked train travel. He liked the hypnotic sound it made, passing over rails, the pleasant sense of limbo, having departed one place, but not yet arrived in another. He didn't get that from walking or riding. And of course, there was often opportunity for a quick snack in a quiet, dark corridor. A little hypnosis as taught him by Saloman, and his victim didn't remember anything. The same hypnosis was useful when presenting the conductor with a piece of paper that was not a ticket, or the border police with an obviously fake passport.

This particular journey wasn't quite so pleasant. For one thing, he couldn't wander up and down the train in case he encountered Zoltán or one of his bodyguards. There was no point in total masking on a psychic level if one then walked physically into the person one was trying to avoid.

And so he sat alone and still, several carriages away from the other vampires, watching the darkness rush him rhythmically toward Budapest. At least there he'd get a decent meal—and the pleasure of Saloman's company.

On the other hand, he wasn't sure he was doing Saloman a real favor. The Ancient would know as soon as Zoltán set foot in the city. He didn't need Dmitriu to come and tell him. Dmitriu just couldn't shake the notion that Zoltán was up to something. Last night he'd visited a Romanian politician in her house and hadn't killed her. And then tonight he'd left in too much secrecy for a vampire who either had to confront or submit to his erstwhile ally.

In the meantime, the *puszta*—the great plain that spread eastward from Budapest—was dull. Even in darkness, Dmitriu preferred the hills and mountains of Transylvania. Still, it had been a long time since he'd experienced the crowds and the excitement of the city. And he admitted to profound curiosity as to what Saloman was up to.

As the train pulled at last into Budapest's Keleti station, he couldn't help the excitement that surged through him. It was almost light. He needed to find shelter fast, preferably with Saloman. He just hoped the bastard wasn't playing masking games. The word was that he was increasingly visible in Budapest, and that with Lajos dead—they'd all felt that loss, or at least all the vampires old enough to sense anything more than their own animal hunger—everyone was desperate to submit to the awakened Ancient. Dmitriu assumed this was what had dragged Zoltán away from his futile courtship of the scattered Transylvanian vampires and sent him rushing hotfoot to the city.

Watching from the window, Dmitriu waited for the other vampires to pass before he left the train. And there they were, Zoltán's two new bodyguards, looking like skinhead thugs as they swaggered through the crowd, which wisely gave them a wide berth.

However, where was Zoltán? Frowning, Dmitriu scanned the crowd both ahead and behind the bodyguards. There was no sign of him.

Alarm bells rang in Dmitriu's head. Time was passing. The bodyguards had gone, and still Zoltán remained on the train. He was masking, but with severe concentration, Dmitriu could see through it. Who the hell was he hiding from? Saloman? Saloman would find him in the blink of an eye, if he was looking. . . .

Get off the train, moron, before we end up in bloody Vienna. . . .

Vienna. That was the plan. Zoltán had never been going to Budapest. His bodyguards were a decoy. He was traveling on in secret, with no companions, and that scared the hell out of Dmitriu. Not for one moment did he imagine that Zoltán was running away, giving up the struggle with Saloman before it had properly begun.

What was there in Vienna?

Everything. It was the gateway to the rest of Europe.

Dmitriu groaned. More passengers were getting on the train,

loud in farewells and requests for help in finding their booked seats.

He could leap off and run to Saloman with this news that meant nothing, or he could stay aboard, arrive in Vienna in broad daylight, and find out where Zoltán was really going and why. While sheltering from the sun.

Why did he even send that girl to Saloman? Life was so much simpler when he slept.

And a hell of a lot duller.

The train roared back to life, and lumbered forward.

†

Elizabeth didn't sleep well at the hunters' headquarters. Not because her room wasn't pleasant; on the contrary, when she thought about it, she rather liked it, all faded splendor and solid comfort. Nor was she troubled by nightmares, although she woke often in the night with an odd impression of candles and blood and silk sheets, and the warm tingle of sexual arousal—or satisfied pleasure. It felt like both.

It wasn't so much her body as her brain that prevented her from sleeping. In particular, it was the simple question—*why?*

Why did he not kill her? He'd meant to, she could swear. The bizarre mixture of seduction and promise of death had been genuine. She could even pretend the death part had been what persuaded her not to fight the seduction—and there was some truth in that. There had been a time when she'd believed she was playing for her life. It had gotten lost with humiliating speed in the whirlwind of lust and sensual pleasure, and finally vanished when the first lovemaking had ended without biting.

I've won, she'd thought.

What in God's name had made her believe that? When had

he said, *One fuck, one bite, and you're dead?* Quite the opposite; he'd promised her a whole night of sex before killing her, and that was exactly what he'd given her. She had no reason to believe that he'd changed his mind, no evidence for her belief that she'd won.

And, of course, she hadn't. He'd bitten her, fed from her, just before dawn, adding that cold, insidious pleasure to all the rest that she'd absorbed and reached for so greedily. It was only when she'd begun to come down that the reality had penetrated her fog of stupid, sexual ecstasy with the awful realization that she hadn't won after all; that it had meant nothing to him.

And yet now, on her second night of tossing and turning in the large, soft old bed in the hunters' headquarters, her brain hung on to his words with tenacity.

For this moment, this night, Elizabeth, I love you.

She wanted to believe it. She needed to believe it. She couldn't bear the idea that she'd given herself to a monster without feelings.

Don't you always? Unkind. Her previous lovers hadn't been monsters. They'd just turned out to be somewhat—shallow. Besides, it had been her own loneliness, her own need and inexperience that had imagined those past relationships to be more than they were. She'd do the same with Richard, if he ever looked at her.

Was that the pattern? She needed to believe the men she slept with loved her?

For this moment, this night, Elizabeth, I love you.

He'd still meant to kill her at dawn. And he'd fed from her as he'd always intended. He needed her blood to be strong, her death to be stronger and to prevent his enemies from gaining that strength. But she was still alive. He'd brought her home. What did that mean?

That she was his milk cow, as the hunters believed?

Elizabeth sat up and switched on the light.

She avoided thinking about these things during the day. She trained hard, worked on getting her thesis evidence in order, and continued her research in the hunters' library.

"Waiting," she whispered into her fingers as she drew them across her dry lips. "I've just been waiting for his next move." She had a vague, confused memory that was little more than an impression, of his promise to return. But she couldn't pin it down to any reality. Somewhere, she *wanted* him to come to her, to show her that something had changed for him, that he hadn't killed her because he cared for her.

Is that likely, Silk?

It didn't matter. She wouldn't, she couldn't, wait any longer. She needed to know what he'd do next to help to counteract it. He'd killed Karl and Lajos now, two of the three vampires who'd staked him, to say nothing of any humans who got in his way. He'd be looking next for the strongest of the three, the mysterious and lost Maximilian.

While she recovered from her blood loss, the hunters had been wasting time, sharpening their sticks and watching the Angel, scouring the old city and the new for evidence of Saloman and Saloman's house as she'd described it. She herself had gotten lost in reading scraps of his documents, obsessed with drinking in every description, every history that involved him. She should have been pursuing Maximilian and determining from evidence that had to be there, exactly where he had gone. And when they found him, they had the weapon as well as the bait they needed.

Weapon? You'd really kill him now?

He fed from me, betrayed me.
He made love to you, let you live.
Why? Why? Why?

Elizabeth sprang out of bed. Another endless night of circling her brain did not appeal. The hunters' library was always
open, and if she found Maximilian, she would inevitably see *him*
again....

To dispel that unhelpful line of thought, she yanked on her
jeans with unnecessary force, grabbed a T-shirt, and strode to the
door, still pulling the top over her head.

Descending the stairs into the library was almost like entering
daylight and the real world, after too long in darkness and the hazy
fog of her undisciplined thoughts. Here, the electric lights dazzled,
computers hummed, and people worked.

Well, up to a point. Elizabeth closed her mouth on the greeting
she'd been about to aim at the assistant librarian, one of Miklós's
minions who manned the desk outside "office" hours. Her head
rested on her folded arms sprawling the breadth of her desk. From
her deep, even breathing, she was sound asleep.

Elizabeth shrugged and went to her own table. She'd wake the
woman if she needed her, but she might as well start with the
books she already had. Some of those were bound to trace Maximilian's movements after Zoltán's "coup."

But only minutes later, she stood up, dissatisfied. They stopped
too early, or were too vague. She needed the material filed under
"Maximilian," not "Saloman."

At her desk, the librarian still slumbered. Her arms only just
missed her computer keyboard. As it was, some of her hair trailed
over it.

It was a pity, Elizabeth thought, not for the first time, that only the librarian's computer contained the catalogue. She preferred to pursue her own research and trace all possible lines of it for herself rather than rely on what others thought. Inevitably, people—especially people who were not experts in the tiny area of knowledge that you were making your own—missed important bits and pieces.

She supposed that here it was not so much a matter of convenience, but a matter of discipline and keeping some kind of control over the knowledge each individual operative could amass. There was a lot of dangerous stuff here, and operatives were only human, with all humanity's failings and curiosities—like hers, except she wasn't bound by an operative's obedience.

Elizabeth walked around the side of the desk, altered the angle of the monitor, and eased the keyboard across the desk, careful not to tug the librarian's hair.

She typed in "Vampire Maximilian" and scanned the long list of items that came up. Grabbing a pencil from the top of the desk, she made quick notes of some locations, including one book she hadn't seen on Saloman's killers.

Next, she typed "Saloman's killers" into the search box, partly because it wasn't an angle she'd yet pursued in her study of him, and partly because it might provide clues as to Maximilian's character and places he might have been before he hit the limelight with his killing of the last Ancient.

Some more intriguing material came up, including something entitled *Saloman's Human Killers* and something else called *Tsigana*. Tsigana, the lover who'd betrayed him.

She hesitated over that one; she wanted to know too much, and it had nothing, if anything, to do with Maximilian. She scribbled it down anyway, then went to track down her new treasures. At the last minute, she grabbed the keys from the librarian's desk and walked into the deepest recesses of the library.

Elizabeth was used to libraries of all sorts. Although this one used a unique classification system, she'd already absorbed, almost unconsciously, how to follow it. It didn't take her long to find the books on her list. To save more time, she took them to the nearest table rather than dragging the books to her own. As she moved, another volume on a top shelf caught her eye. *Awakening the Ancients.* Since it might shed more light on her own role in all of this, she hastily laid down the other books on the desk and went back for it.

Because she couldn't resist, she flicked first through the pages of *Awakening the Ancients.* Among a lot of general hearsay and mythology, she found the story of the medieval Awakener she'd heard of before. Having awakened an Ancient he'd originally helped to kill, this Awakener had promptly fled, aware the vampire would necessarily kill him when he recovered his strength. Which the Ancient eventually did, though not before the Awakener had discovered extraordinary powers of speed and strength in himself—a bit like Elizabeth was doing now. But—and this was new information to her—her predecessor had gone a step farther, even claiming before witnesses that he was now capable of killing an Ancient by himself, without the help that would normally be necessary.

Elizabeth smiled wryly while she noted it down. The medieval Awakener had clearly believed himself invincible. It wasn't a mistake she intended to repeat.

Her stomach twisted. Would she even see him again? And as a lover or an enemy . . . ? *Shit.*

Anxious to relieve rather than add to her confusion, she

pushed *Awakening the Ancients* aside and reached for the first work on Saloman's killers.

After a while, she forgot to make notes. She was too appalled by the discovery that the blood of Saloman's human killers was at least as important as that of the vampires. No matter that they were dead. Their descendants carried their blood, and Saloman would want it. They were in danger, and the hunters either didn't know or hadn't mentioned it to her.

Feverishly now, she began to trace the descendants, all neatly mapped out through the generations. Previous hunters had watched and noted, because something else became clear too. Those descendants, the few who survived the original vampire attacks on them, carried some power of their own, a heightened awareness, a latent strength similar to that of Awakeners, that made them different, superior in many ways to their ordinary human brethren. Some of them became hunters, and were good at it.

This was a whole new area to Elizabeth, as fascinating as it was bizarre. Two weeks ago, even less, she would have dismissed it as fanciful nonsense. Now she knew better, and she couldn't stop digging.

She followed Tsigana's line of descendants, learning that they were regarded with particular respect by both vampires and hunters because they had possession of Saloman's sword.

Frowning, Elizabeth sat back in her chair. His scabbard had been empty when he awoke. She remembered it, and the proof was there in the photograph she'd taken of the sarcophogus. So Tsigana had taken the sword and passed it on to her descendants. Why? What use was it? It seemed to be regarded as more than a trophy. Was it some kind of enchanted object?

Elizabeth groaned to herself. Did she have to believe in magic now as well? She knew a brief longing for the comfortable skepticism she'd brought with her to this country, but acknowledged it was unlikely ever to return to her.

So who had this blasted sword now? Was it still extant?

Among Tsigana's descendants, only two diverging lines weren't closed off as having died out. The first led to one living man, Joshua Alexander, born 1972, resident in the United States. His name seemed vaguely familiar, but she didn't have time to rummage in her memory. She noted the name in a hasty scribble and turned to the other line, which had diverged from the Alexanders in the late nineteenth century.

Voices sounded in the distance, at the front of the library where the librarian no longer slept. Elizabeth paid them no attention. She'd traced Tsigana's last line to its end. And there she found a name she really did know well.

John Silk.

Her father. Not impossible that there were several John Silks born in the same year, even residing in Scotland. But not many at all would have one daughter, Elizabeth, born in 1979 and also residing in Scotland.

The librarian was being told off, presumably for sleeping. It was Miklós, taking over. Elizabeth didn't care. She couldn't move, could barely breathe, because at last she had discovered why.

Why Dmitriu had sent her of all the silly western researchers to Saloman. It wasn't any old blood that awakened him. It was the blood of his killers; Tsigana's blood that flowed in Elizabeth's veins, however diluted.

Why Zoltán had risked breaking his new alliance with Saloman to kill her. The blood of the Ancient's killers was as valuable to him as to Saloman. It would give him a greater strength that might even award him victory.

Why Saloman needed her blood so much.

And why he'd seduced her. He had been in total control, achieving her complete surrender. No wonder there had been triumph in fucking her desperately willing body. In seducing her, he'd seduced his beloved, treacherous Tsigana one last time, made her choose pleasure with Saloman over her own life. After that, he didn't care whether she lived or died. He'd had his revenge.

Revenge. She couldn't think about that, couldn't begin to analyze the awful, crumbling emotions rising up from her toes to consume her. So she did what she'd always done when life was unbearable. She studied.

And she found that Tsigana was not the only human killer who had descendants with familiar names. That answered a few more whys.

†

It was ten o'clock in the morning before they found her. They arrived in a panicked guddle, the affronted Miklós at the front, but Konrad, István, and Mihaela close on his heels.

"Miss Silk." Miklós's unprecedented formality as much as his frosty voice revealed his displeasure. "If you wish to continue with the privilege of using this library, you must respect the organization's rules!"

For a moment, Elizabeth didn't move. She remembered that she didn't like confrontations and avoided them wherever possible. She'd found what she needed to know. No confrontation was necessary.

But anger boiled very close to the surface, whipped up by a

deeper betrayal she couldn't afford to deal with. This was one she could handle, and she would.

"Rules," she repeated, throwing down the pencil she'd been unconsciously chewing as she read. Miklós watched it land on an open book and tutted. "The rules that allow you to use people as bait without allowing them the courtesy of the truth?"

"Elizabeth," Konrad said, shocked. "We've never lied to you!"

"No? But you certainly didn't tell me the whole truth, did you?"

"That does not give you the right . . . ," Miklós began, but Mihaela interrupted him without apology.

"What are you talking about, Elizabeth? We never kept anything from you, even at the beginning when we probably should have!"

Elizabeth couldn't look at her, because her betrayal had hurt the most. Instead, she kept her gaze on Konrad and laughed. "First rule of research: Never let anyone else interpret material for you. Always go to the source yourself. Too many people have their own ax to grind. They leave things out, by accident or design, or merely slant it their own way. I forgot that for too long. The subject is too new to me, and I was bowled over by your greater expertise."

Konrad met her gaze, his piercing blue eyes intense and challenging. For the first time she saw them also as intimidating. "To what, exactly, are you referring?" he asked with more than a shade of haughty contempt. That would be his aristocratic ancestor making his appearance.

"To your sending me into a lethal situation—namely into the Angel—without the full facts that might have made me more capable of dealing with it."

"Nothing was left out that could have helped you," Konrad insisted.

"You're wrong. So wrong." *I would have known it was revenge. I would have understood. It might have made no physical difference to what happened, but I wouldn't have fallen for it.*

"You're being melodramatic," Konrad said coldly. "And possibly transferring your own guilt. You've kept things from us. Such as what actually happened the night he took you from the Angel."

Elizabeth felt the blood drain to her toes. Was it really that obvious? "I have," she admitted, shakily. "I couldn't tell you because I couldn't handle it." She lifted her head. "And guess what? Now I don't need to tell you anything at all, because our association is at an end."

She stood up, facing all four astonished expressions.

"At an end?" Mihaela repeated. "But why? You can't leave now! It's not safe!"

"Yes, I can, and it is safer than you know. I can take care of myself for the same reason I was in danger in the first place. I didn't wake Saloman because I was the first person to stumble across his grave in three hundred years. I wakened him because I was one of the very few people who could. And he wanted my blood for the same reason. Tsigana was my ancestress."

István closed his mouth. Konrad and Miklós exchanged glances.

"Shit," Mihaela said. "That explains a lot."

"Doesn't it, though? As her descendant, I have the physical strength to survive on my own. I just need to cultivate it."

"You're an academic," Konrad retorted, "a mere bookworm! You need us."

"It's true I was never terribly athletic. I'm crap at sports. I had

no interest in any of them. But guess what? I'm a natural fighter."
She looked into Konrad's eyes. "Like you."

"If you're not our friend, you're our enemy. You have to go."
Konrad reached for her.

He hadn't watched any of her sessions with the combat coach.
Despite what she'd just said, he didn't realize how far she'd come.
She knocked up his arm so hard, he almost hit himself.

In shock, the others started between them, but somehow,
through them all, Konrad still met her furious gaze. "I'm not a
vampire, and I had no intention of hurting you."

"No, possibly not. Just keeping me quiet. But they have to
know."

"Know what?" Mihaela demanded. "Elizabeth, what the hell is
going on?"

Elizabeth held everyone's attention. She wondered if history
students would listen to her lectures with the same rapt concentration, and doubted it. She felt very tired.

She said, "I've read lots about the hunters now, right down to
you guys. Did you never wonder why Konrad is so much faster
than you in a fight, and yet never demonstrates to students? Why
two of his previous teams died while he alone survived? Why he is
so determined to be the one who takes out Saloman? He wants the
power that comes with killing an Ancient. Twice."

"Twice?" Mihaela was staring at her, eyes dilated. Konrad
himself was white-faced and rigid.

"Twice. He's descended from Ferenc, one of the human—"
Her phone chose that moment to burst into Bach. "Killers," she
finished as Mihaela picked it off the desk and wordlessly handed it
to her.

Miklós declared, "Mobile phones should be switched off in the library, or at least set to 'silent.'"

Elizabeth rejected the call without even glancing at the number and pocketed the phone before reaching down to collect her papers.

"Elizabeth, you're not really leaving because of this?" Konrad said. His voice was more controlled now, reasonable, almost cajoling.

"Yes. I really am. I can't trust you, and I've had enough." Perhaps she was being unfair. Mihaela and István had obviously been as much in the dark as she, but Konrad and even Miklós had known. And Mihaela, despite her obvious shock, was sticking by her colleagues. That seemed like a fresh betrayal.

Elizabeth was prepared to shoulder her way through them all. She felt bullish enough, but interestingly, they parted for her like the Red Sea.

"There's nowhere to run from this, Elizabeth," Konrad warned. "It'll follow you. He'll follow you."

No, he won't. He's taken all he needs from me.

"I'm not running. I'm just facing it, whatever it is, on my terms, my ground. I can't work on yours anymore." She glanced at Mihaela as she passed, and paused to let her gaze embrace them all.

They had warned her at the beginning, looked after her in their own way, and in spite of everything, there was a fondness, a closeness she'd seldom felt before. It wasn't their fault she'd discovered a complete aversion to all forms of betrayal.

"Though I won't forget you," she muttered, and walked through the stunned silence. It was a long way. Elizabeth wanted it to go on forever, because her next farewell would be even harder.

Chapter Fourteen

$\mathscr{P}$art of her hoped there wouldn't be time. And yet Konrad had been right. If she didn't see him, she would be running away.

So she cleared out of the hunters' headquarters, packed all her luggage into the old car she'd bought here several months ago, and drove to the airport. She managed to get a seat on a night flight to Glasgow, which left her several hours of inactivity.

After a strong cup of coffee, she left the airport and drove back into the city.

Why am I doing this? For my own peace of mind? Or because I can't stay away from him?

Because even shouting was better than the loneliness.

One night of false closeness had shown her what she wanted and had never found—that combination of exciting sexual ecstasy and companionship that had made her feel like a queen. And it wasn't even real. Gullible Elizabeth Silk, duped again, by a monster whom even she should have recognized for what he was.

It was easy to find the right area of Pest. On the first day of her recovery, the hunters had spent some time here, after Elizabeth had shown them the network of streets on a map, looking for him or his house without success. The day after, they'd tried to narrow it down by using the phone directory together with ownership and tenancy records. But it was a minefield of changing and multiple occupations, and despite frequent patrols, no one had seen him, or any other vampire, go in or out of any of the buildings.

Elizabeth parked the car and walked. She had no clear idea of where she was going. She was just sure she would know the house when she saw it. She would smell him—or something.

But it was a large area, and she walked for a long time. It had been dark that night, and she'd barely seen the outside of the house. They'd landed on a roof and jumped down to the side of the house before walking around to the front door. She couldn't even remember what color the door was. There were many buildings of a similar size and shape.

It was the curtains she recognized in the end. Thick, heavy velvet, and deep, dark red, they covered the two windows of his drawing room on the first floor, and two windows of his bedroom next to it.

Her heart beat hard. She knew this was it. She recognized the shape of the door now, the ornate, carved arch above it. The tall wrought-iron gates she hadn't noticed before. They were pad-locked, so, careless of passersby, she climbed over the wall.

She'd been wrong, though. She couldn't smell him. And as she approached the door, she even began to doubt this was the right place. She had a brief comic vision of barging in like a whirling dervish, brandishing her sharpened stake over a baffled family at the tea table.

As well she meant to ring the bell. What she had to say could be conveyed from the doorstep while he lurked in the shadows. It would be best that way. She wouldn't have to look at the bastard.

On the other hand, when she pressed the bell, she didn't hear any sound. She doubted it worked. It didn't matter. If she didn't smell him, he could certainly sense her, though he seemed to have no intention of answering the door. Interesting.

Unless he really wasn't in. Dmitriu had moved about in the daylight, keeping to the shaded paths of Maria's garden. She was sure Saloman had ways of doing the same in the city.

Well, damn it, she wouldn't walk away with her tail between her legs. Lifting her hand, she grasped the door handle, more to test the strength of the lock before she kicked it in than with any expectation of its turning.

It didn't need to turn. At her first touch, the door swung open.

Her breath caught. Had he gone already, sure she would tell the hunters about this house as she'd told them about the church in Bistriţa?

How many horror films had she seen like this? Stupid lone female walks helplessly into a place of obvious danger.

Well, she'd just have to hope she was right and he wouldn't kill her. After all, he'd had his revenge, which would, presumably, lose its sweetness if she was dead and unable to appreciate having been so utterly seduced.

And if she was wrong . . . *Just get it over with.*

She pushed open the door and stepped inside. From meanness, she left the door wide, allowing a shaft of sunlight to fall across the hall.

There were rooms downstairs that she hadn't been in. She

wondered what he did in them, what he kept in them and the rest of the house. If he wasn't home, she would look around, but she was damned if she'd lose her dignity by snooping in front of him. *What kind of weird dignity is that?*

She moved toward the staircase, schooling herself to walk with firm, even steps, although her mouth was so dry she doubted she could speak and her heart hammered in her breast like a piston.

She'd rounded the curve of the staircase before she saw him. Her stomach and her heart both seemed to flip, as if they'd swapped places. He stood in the upper hall, leaning one shoulder against the wall as he watched her approach.

His long, slender feet were bare. With fresh shock, she remembered the sensual feel of them caressing her legs, and forced the memory down. He wore his usual plain but stylish black trousers with a loose white shirt, unfastened. Or perhaps it was the one he'd torn the buttons off in his urgency to make love to her the first time.

Don't go there, for God's sake!

His raven hair fell in unruly tangles about his face and shoulders, completing the impression of a man disturbed too early before appropriate grooming could occur. The thought was stupidly arousing, and she had to squash that one too, because his eyes were far too bright and far too piercing to allow her to slip back into that haze of blind, depraved, wishful thinking.

"Elizabeth."

It was downright insulting that he should say her name like that. In a voice like that. It seemed to reach through her entire body and turn her outside in. But she was stronger now. Gathering the tatters of that strength around her, she imagined herself turning the right way out again.

"Saloman."

"I didn't expect to welcome you here again so soon."

"I'm sure you didn't." She came at last to the top of the stairs, and he straightened, bringing his body far too close to her.

"Please." Without taking his gaze from hers, he spread his hand toward the drawing room. Beyond the door, which stood ajar, open books and newspapers were strewn about the floor in a large, untidy circle with a bare patch of rug at the center, as if he'd been sitting there while studying in the semigloom. "Go in."

"I'm not staying," she said frigidly. "I'm leaving Hungary tonight. I just came to say that I know who I am and what my importance is. I know I can learn to fight you, and I will. Take what you have and leave the descendants alone. If you don't, I'll find a way to kill you."

His eyes searched hers. She thought the gleam had gone, but otherwise his face was expressionless. Had she really imagined she could read him the other night?

"You're a clever woman," he acknowledged. "You probably could, given time."

"Count on it."

"So they finally told you about Tsigana."

"They didn't need to. I'm a clever woman."

He inclined his head, apparently still unmoved. Because she had to, she said, "You've always known. Even Dmitriu knew. He sent me to you deliberately."

"He was a friend who remembered enough to act on it."

"He even planted a thorn to make me bleed."

"It's a simple matter for a vampire of his age to draw the blood from your veins without touching. He even followed you to make sure he kept the connection and the blood still flowed by the time you got to me."

"Then I did see him on the road!"

A faint flickering smile on his lips reminded her that she'd slipped out of character—and that she'd come to tell him she understood everything now. She curled her lip in a sneer. "I hope revenge was sweet for you."

"The sweetest," he said softly.

Blood surged through her, suffusing her face and neck. *You mean I was hotter than my great-great-great-great-grannie?* She swallowed the words before they spilled over her lips. There must have been a few more greats in there anyway.

Wildly, she reached for a safer rant. "You have to leave Konrad alone."

"Do I?"

Shit, she was just annoying him now, putting Konrad in danger.

"So," he said, "you're going home to Scotland. Why?"

"I have a job to go to, a thesis to write. A life."

His gaze had never left her face. "You're angry because they didn't tell you. No matter, you didn't belong with them. But you don't need to leave like this."

"Like what?" she snapped.

His lips twitched. "Angry. Hurt. What has made you like this?" His hand lifted, as if to touch her face.

She couldn't hit him. She wasn't that good or that fast. Not yet. But she could, and did, block his movement with her arm and step back.

"Elizabeth." Chiding, mocking, he closed the distance again. "You weren't so averse to my touch before."

"Before you drank my blood?" she snapped.

Flame flared in his eyes and burned, yet still he didn't move.

"I'm a vampire. Your blood was good, and I enjoyed it. So did you. Along with everything else."

"Arsehole!" Only unpalatable truth could have made her lose her composure, and she struggled desperately to bring it back. "I slept with you to save my life."

Through the fury, something hurt. Looking at him hurt. Without warning, his eyes dropped. For an instant, she wondered if she'd actually managed to inflict pain of her own. But of course, she hadn't. His gaze was on her hips, her breasts.

"Next time," he said, "it will be different."

But at least he'd swallowed it. Triumph spurred her on. "There won't be a next time. Good-bye, Saloman. I hope we never meet again. If we do, I'll kill you."

It was a good exit line. Unfortunately, she couldn't follow it up by spinning on her heel and sailing downstairs to the open front door. He stood too close, and even as she moved to make a less dramatic exit, he swayed with her, blocking her path.

His head lowered. Awareness flooded her, made her dizzy. And yet he didn't even touch her. There was no body heat to arouse her, just simple, overwhelming presence. He moved his head, inhaling her as he'd done several times in the past.

"I love a worthy opponent," he whispered. "Remember that, along with all the rest."

His throaty, husky voice seemed to vibrate inside her body. Before she obeyed him and allowed memory to flood to her, she threw dignity to the wind and edged past him. There was an instant of flaring contact, a brushing touch that had the effect of anyone else's most intimate caress, and then she was past him and rushing down the stairs.

This is me not running away. . . .

She half expected him to do one of his supernatural leaps and appear in front of the open door. When he didn't, she couldn't resist glancing over her shoulder as she crossed the hall.

Although she hadn't heard him move, he stood halfway down the stairs watching her. His face was serious, almost . . . lost.

But if he was sad, it was a deeper emotion than any she could inspire. Watching her go, he clearly thought of something else.

She would have liked to slam the door, but dignity—and spite—won the day. She left him to work out how to shut it while staying out of the sun.

She was still shaking by the time she found her car. But hell, she'd driven in worse conditions, namely after her first terrifying encounter with Saloman. She was stronger now, and more than capable of driving herself to the airport and the welcoming sanity of home.

She just couldn't work out why she still felt guilty, like a deserter. Or why the tears kept running down her cheeks.

✝

Saloman watched until her shadow had gone, and the sound of her quick, light footfalls had faded into the distance. Only then, when the sunlight had lost its charm, did he blow the door closed with the power of his mind and turn to walk back upstairs.

Considering it was the first time he'd been strong enough to use this trick since his awakening, he wasn't as pleased with it as he should have been, because he knew he'd made a mistake. He'd confused a certain empathy with knowledge and understanding of Elizabeth. He hadn't expected her to be so appalled by the blood drink; he hadn't expected her to leave. He'd meant her to stay in the protection of the hunters until he was ready.

He hadn't been awake two weeks. After three hundred years of total isolation, perhaps it wasn't surprising he'd lost a little reality in his dealings with humans. But to confuse her moment of love with trust was a basic error.

Saloman didn't like errors; nor did he care to be thwarted, or to lose the initiative in a moment of uncharacteristic hesitation. He could have made her stay. Whatever she was trying to pretend, she wasn't immune to him. Her body still trembled at his nearness, and it wasn't all fear. It wouldn't have taken long in his arms to reduce her to pliant surrender, or so he *thought*. But he'd made a mistake before; he still didn't know her and he'd hesitated. Because her body was no longer enough.

I slept with you to save my life.

It had never entered his head. He had never meant there to be a possibility of that. Her death was inevitable; he'd just wanted to make it sweet for her, to give her life before he took it. He'd never pretended anything else. God knew what had induced her to believe she could change his mind with sex.

Isn't that exactly what she did?

Saloman stepped across the muddle of books and papers in his drawing room and sat down cross-legged in the middle of it, where he'd been as he'd sensed her unexpected approach. The human woman who'd awakened him, touched him, and obsessed him was beginning to churn him up. He didn't like that either. He needed a clear head and less, not more, distraction. Why couldn't she just *accept* and *wait*?

They'd meet again, of course, whatever she imagined, and whatever game they were playing was far from over. It wasn't one she could win in the end. He rather admired her unexpected spunk in visiting him, just to tell him as she'd told the hunters, to go to hell. She was a complex creature, Elizabeth Silk. And he'd miss her presence.

Displeased, he picked up the nearest book and scanned the spread-out newspapers to regather his thoughts. He needed a human identity. Gone were the days when he could stand beside a throne and advise and influence the course of history. This was a hands-on era, like the good old days, and he thought he'd rather enjoy it.

He was most drawn toward the radical, socially active rock musician identity with enough clout to influence governments as well as ordinary people. Two Irishmen seemed to have rather cornered the market there, but they were looking a trifle craggy these days, and perhaps the world was ready for someone a little younger.

He gave a twisted smile. Younger looking.

The other, less self-indulgent idea—and one that probably had greater certainty of achievement—was politics. He rather liked the notion of being president of the United States of America, although the difficulties of achieving this for an eastern European immigrant with no documentation were not insubstantial! Perhaps some kind of adviser would be more sensible. After all, one only got to be president for four years, eight if one was lucky, and he had a lot more time to give.

Shifting countries and identities with the decades would not be easy in this new world, and even harder for anyone with a highly visible profile. But the more he discovered about modern life, the greater his excitement. There were possibilities here. He just needed to know more, much more.

The learning would distract him from his unpalatable emotions surrounding Elizabeth Silk, and would continue while he resumed control of the supernatural world and wreaked the last of his vengeance. He could take the hunter Konrad anytime, but before he could move on with his plans, Maximilian and the other human descendants of his "killers" had to be found.

Saloman. The voice in his head was faint, familiar, and filled him with pain. Another betrayal to avenge, another vengeance to savor, if he could.

What? he responded without obvious interest.

Zoltán has left the region.

I know.

A pause, then, *Do you also know that he's on visiting terms with a Romanian government minister? And dined with a Hungarian industrialist in Vienna?*

Saloman's smile was twisted. *Dined with, not on him? He's taking my idea of a human alliance seriously, then.*

And excluding you!

Yes, I got that bit, Saloman said patiently.

Another palpably disgusted pause. *Don't you want to know where he's going now?*

If the information's of any use to me. I'm busy.

Judge for yourself. . . .

✝

Elizabeth stared out of the airplane window as it climbed through the blackness of the night sky. She was too exhausted to feel relief at leaving this craziness behind, to look forward to seeing old friends and taking up the challenges of her new job. For three nights, she'd barely slept, except for the troubled, feverish sleep of the unconscious after he'd bitten her.

She closed her eyes. *Saloman. Saloman.*

Deep in her gut was a pain that wouldn't go away. She didn't know what it was; she didn't want to know. She wished it had a physical cause, so she could take some medicine and make it stop. Saloman was evil. He was a vampire who drank human blood to survive, and he'd survived a hell of a long time. He'd drunk hers, and she hated him for that as well as for what he was. The inconvenient lusts of her body, the sexual magnetism that tugged at her in his presence, were quite separate from that, as were the sensual pleasures of their night together.

Hatred. Fear. She was confused by a little lust because she was lonely, frustrated, and inexperienced with attractive men, let alone vampires.

A spurt of laughter surged in her throat, threatening to choke her if she didn't let it out. When she swallowed it down, it felt like tears.

I'm too tired to deal with this. . . .

She would always be too tired to deal with this because it went too deep. Hate, fear, lust—they were just words, and they had little to do with whatever it was she felt now. She couldn't and wouldn't name it, though she knew it would take time and effort to overcome it.

But I will. I will.

Chapter Fifteen

"Think about it," Elizabeth said. "Take down some notes, and we'll talk about it next week. Enjoy your lunch."

Thus dismissed, her first-year tutorial group grinned at her and began to depart in a flurry of scraping chairs and books and folders thrust into bags. Elizabeth made a grab for the coffee cups distributed around the table, which some of the students remembered to push toward her with quick words of thanks.

The more ebullient members of the group were already shouldering their way out of the door. Emma, who'd read today's essay, stood back to let them pass. Something about her shy, self-effacing manner reminded Elizabeth of herself in first year—isolated, morbidly unself-confident, and worried about her intellectual capacity to keep up. Of course, Elizabeth's experience was made worse by being older than her peers, but she had no intention of letting Emma suffer just because she was seventeen instead of twenty-four.

"Emma?"

The girl looked around apprehensively, clearly longing now to bolt out the door with the others.

"That was a good essay—possibly the best I've read from a first-year so far this term. Keep up the good work."

A lightening of the eyes, a quick flashing smile as she mumbled thanks and joined the squeeze, were reward enough.

Elizabeth gave a lopsided smile, dumping the mugs in her sink. As Emma made it through the doorway, Richard edged his way in to meet her gaze with a sardonic twist of the lips.

"*Is* she any good?"

"She could be. Handles the evidence well, has good ideas—she just needs the courage to state them."

"Like you then," he teased.

"No, I was always an opinionated cow. I was happy to state them on paper for posterity."

"And quiet as a mouse in tutorials. For a while we thought someone else was writing your essays."

Elizabeth laughed. She thought it was probably true. She turned back to the sink, giving each mug in turn a thorough rinse. "What can I do for you?"

"Two things. First, tell me how the teaching's going—in general terms. Any problems?"

"Not that I know of. Actually, it's going surprisingly well. I'm enjoying it. I suppose the proof will be in the exam results."

"I'm impressed." He eased his hip onto the corner of one of the three jammed-together tables around which she sat with her students. "To be honest, I didn't think you'd take to the teaching side of things half as well as you have."

She blinked at him, setting the last mug on the draining

board and reaching for the towel. "Then why did you give me the job?"

He tapped his head. "You've got it up here. And you need the experience. But plenty of the most respected university academics are crap teachers. I fully expected you to be another in this long and honored line."

"Thanks. And second?"

He smiled. "Want to go to Chris Harper's 'Not Halloween' party?"

"I haven't been invited. I don't know him," she added, just in case he imagined she felt slighted by the omission.

"I have and I do. I was hoping you'd come with me."

Her eyes widened as the significance sank in.

My God. Richard Kennoway, subject of my unrequited crush, has finally asked me on a date.

Now what the hell do I do?

Because unfortunately, since her return from Hungary six weeks ago, she just didn't feel the same. She liked Richard, got on well with him, but those butterflies that used to haunt her stomach whenever she was in the same room with him had flown away for good. In her more honest moments, she acknowledged that the only too real physical attraction to Saloman had made nonsense of her vague infatuation with Richard.

Richard, presumably staggered that she didn't jump at the chance, stood up, saying, "Let me know, Elizabeth. I have a lunch appointment in half an hour."

Still stunned, she watched him stroll out of the room. That would probably gratify him, if he noticed.

"Sorry!" said another voice in the corridor, presumably after colliding with Richard. It was Joanne, collecting Elizabeth for lunch. And Elizabeth remembered that she and Joanne were having dinner at her flat next Saturday—Halloween. She had a perfect excuse, if she chose to take it.

"What's wrong with *his* face?" Joanne asked, bustling inside. Some ten years older than Elizabeth, she was a plump, eccentric Glaswegian with spiky, partly purple hair, who accorded few people the respect they felt they deserved. She was also the deputy head of the department and a very distinguished academic and writer. Elizabeth liked her.

"I might have hurt his feelings," Elizabeth confided. "He asked me to a Halloween party, and I didn't exactly jump at it. You're risking my cooking that night. But he didn't wait to hear my reason."

"Your excuse?" she asked shrewdly.

"Not sure," Elizabeth confessed, reaching for the jacket on the back of her chair and slinging it round her shoulders.

Neither of them said any more until they'd left the department building and were walking down South Street. Then Joanne said, "You're not afraid of him, are you?"

"Afraid?" Fear was for vampires, for monsters who killed, and creatures who could make you feel what you knew you shouldn't, what wasn't real. "Why in the world would I be afraid of him?"

Joanne shrugged. "He's a womanizer. The whole university knows it. Never stops each woman he asks out thinking she's special and that she can be the one to change him. He does have a certain engaging charm, all that boyishness on top of that huge intellect. Irresistible."

Elizabeth glanced at her sideways. "Do you think?"

"If you can get past his ego."

Elizabeth laughed.

"And it sounds like you have," Joanne said approvingly. "A few weeks around him can work wonders for wearing the shine off a sex idol. On the other hand . . ."

Elizabeth stopped in alarm outside the ice cream shop until Joanne pulled her along. "On the other hand," Joanne continued, "he's actually quite a nice bloke. He won't marry you. He probably won't even call you for weeks. But if you don't expect any more than that, he can be fun."

Elizabeth didn't reply until they'd stopped to gaze out over the ruined cathedral. Then she said, "You sound as if you speak from experience."

"I've had fun with Richard Kennoway, and he didn't break my heart. Nor did I break his. You're probably ready for him now."

The wind blew her hair in front of her eyes, and she dragged it off with her fingers. "What do you mean?"

Joanne shrugged. "I mean I've known you since you were a shy first-year with a brain the size of a planet and less than no ability to show it. I've watched you grow as you graduated and began your thesis. I've seen you in his company often enough to see the signs of unhealthy infatuation."

Elizabeth smiled ruefully. "You think going out with him would be a kill or cure?"

"Oh no, I think you're cured already. If you'd gone out with him last year, it would have been disastrous. But this year . . . This year you don't blush when he speaks to you. You don't notice his teasing except to give back as good as you get. In fact, I think he began to look at you differently this summer. Seems to me that you've finally intrigued him when you've no real time for him."

"Really?" It was a little funny, a little pathetic. She was aware, even, of a little triumph. But it barely touched her. She liked her new life at St. Andrews. She liked teaching, and she liked her colleagues.

But beyond that, she felt emotionally numb, as if she'd lost it all in eastern Europe.

Be honest, you dumped it all in eastern Europe, where you found it in the first place....

Joanne cast her eyes upward at a threatening dark cloud. "You meet someone this summer?"

Elizabeth wanted to laugh. "Sort of."

"You going to see him again?"

"I sincerely hope not." It was the truth, and yet in spite of herself, even the thought made her heart jolt in her chest.

"I see."

She didn't, of course. She couldn't.

"Well, if you fancy a little no-strings romance on the rebound," Joanne said, moving back toward the ice cream shop where she had clearly determined to have lunch, "Richard's your man. I'll happily butt out for Halloween. You can feed me on Sunday instead—dinner as well as gory details."

Elizabeth regarded her as they walked, mulling it over. It was time she lived again, as intensely as in eastern Europe, just without all the scary vampire crap. She ruffled Joanna's spiky, surprisingly soft hair. "You've got quite a wise old head under that fluffy exterior."

"For the 'old,' you get to buy lunch."

✝

The attack came out of nowhere as she walked home late from the department that evening.

She'd taken the quiet route because it suited her mood and because St. Andrews had never seemed a threatening place, even at night. Her mind was not on danger, but on the complicated wording of one passage in her thesis, so she was taken completely by surprise.

Something prickled at the back of her neck, enough to make her head jerk up toward the high wall on her right, but it was already too late.

A shadow leapt at her, instantly gaining solidity as it crashed down on her. She twisted as she fell, just as she'd done in those mock fights with Mihaela as well as with the combat coach in Budapest, and heaved upward, so that almost before they landed on the ground, she was on top of her attacker. He snarled like a dog. Long, vicious fangs gleamed in the darkness.

There was no time to think. His hands grabbed at her, his mouth lunged, but already the stake from her coat pocket was in her hand and plunging downward. The vampire exploded into a cloud of silver dust, and Elizabeth, jolted by a fresh burst of energy, leapt to her feet, the stake still poised as she hastily scanned the road and the top of the wall, listening for any nearby movement.

That was when she began to shake, so it was fortunate the vampire was a lone attacker. She fumbled the stake back into her pocket and walked forward on trembling legs.

She'd killed a vampire. She, who couldn't even remember hitting anyone before, had committed murder without compunction, without any thought, acting completely, it seemed, on reflex. The whole incident had lasted seconds, and there was nothing left to show it had ever occurred.

Well, the training works.

And we have vampires here too. . . .

Oh shit, what if he followed me from Hungary?

She walked swiftly, trying to maintain her awareness and watchfulness while she came to terms with what she'd done, with what had been done to her, and with what it all meant.

She'd entered her flat and hung up her coat before she remembered what she'd felt at the moment of her first kill. It wasn't shame, or even triumph, but something physical, like an energy burst.

She sank onto the floor of the hall, oblivious to the draft whistling under the front door.

"It's true," she whispered. "Fuck, it's true. You do feel something; you do gain something from a kill."

It meant something else too. Her attacker hadn't been a fledgling. According to the mythology she'd read up in the hunters' library, fledgling kills gave you no extra power. But she felt different. She felt . . . strong.

That's just reaction. . . . You have more important things to worry about, such as where the bastard came from, why he picked on you, and if there are any more of them.

One thing was certain. She couldn't just hide here. She'd always known that. It was why she continued training in judo and fencing and always carried a stake in her pocket wherever she went. But in the six weeks since she'd come home, she had been lulled.

Tonight's attack was a timely reminder. It wasn't over yet.

✝

In a basement flat near Leith docks, in one of the old buildings untouched by modern redevelopment or the influx of wealthy young professionals, Dmitriu watched the daylight darken behind the thick but faded, dirty curtains of his hostess's living room.

Janine, the occupant of this hovel, was out working. She was a prostitute, too amiable or too strung out on drugs and alcohol to object to his staying with her. He'd had sex with her and fed from her the night he'd found her and come here. He'd even paid for it. Since then, although she appeared to remember very little about it, he hadn't touched her, sexually, a circumstance that appeared to

246

have raised him to the status of friend. He'd fed from her once or twice since, but it was more of an end-of-night treat than a proper meal—a quick way to get high. God alone knew what she abused her poor young body with.

But social work held no place in Dmitriu's plan. As soon as it was dark, he'd go over to the docks to wait for Saloman, who'd finally bestirred himself to deal with the Zoltán problem. He'd said he was coming on a cargo ship—down-market for Saloman—arriving tonight, and as always at the prospect of reunion, excitement simmered in Dmitriu's veins.

He drew back the dirty curtain. A band of dusky light showed across the top of the sunken window. He could go out now and hang around the docks. He should be able to find someone to feed off before Saloman arrived.

He remembered to pick up his stolen jacket from the mess on the floor. He didn't feel the cold, and the Scots were a hardy bunch—even on a cold, dank October night, there would be several of them heading for the pub in thin, sleeveless T-shirts. But Dmitriu looked and sounded foreign. He had no desire to draw attention to himself.

Halfway across the room, he paused. His ears tingled. So did the hairs on the back of his neck. He turned, gazing toward the source. Behind the bedroom door lurked an intruder.

Crime was rife in this neighborhood, but it was a bloody good burglar who could break into a vampire's lair unheard.

Dmitriu couldn't smell human. But he sensed presence—a masking vampire.

Zoltán.

Dmitriu had taken good care in the long stages of the journey to Scotland not to be observed. He masked continuously and shielded Janine's house. But Zoltán was a strong vampire, and he was looking for others. It wasn't beyond the bounds of possibility that he'd found Dmitriu, almost by accident.

Dmitriu crossed the room silently and speedily. He could take Zoltán, but it would be a hard fight, and he needed all the advantage he could gain from surprise. He flung open the door, fangs bared, fists and right foot at the ready as he swung to cover all angles.

He lowered his fists.

Saloman sprawled across Janine's unmade bed. He appeared to be reading her diary in the darkness. "What a tragic human being," he observed, "and she doesn't even realize it. Good evening, Dmitriu."

"Saloman. You're early."

"I've found it necessary to be one step ahead of my enemies—or one hour at the very least."

Dmitriu frowned. "Zoltán knows you're here?"

"Did you tell him?"

"Of course I didn't bloody tell him! I thought he'd tracked me down at last. I never thought of your sneaking in. Listen, I know what he's up to."

Saloman closed the diary, tossing it onto the floor where, presumably, he'd found it, but otherwise didn't move so much as an eyebrow in interrogation. He was going to pretend he knew already.

Dmitriu said, "He's courting powerful humans at home, whether to control them by mesmeric feeding or to turn them later, I'm not sure, but one way or another he plans to enslave them. That's set in motion, and then he travels here. Why? I thought at first he'd come for the Awakener. But he hasn't gone near her—yet. Nor has he been south to London where the people of greatest power in this country tend to congregate. I wondered if he was looking for support, raising a foreign vampire army with which to face you. If he looked powerful enough, he'd have a chance of attracting the old guard back to him. But that isn't it, either. He's only searching for one vampire."

He paused, looking Saloman in the eye for maximum effect. "Maximilian."

Saloman nodded, as if it was old news and he was waiting for more.

"Maximilian?" Dmitriu repeated. "Your enemy? The one who led your staking and usurped your power? And Saloman, I'm pretty sure Zoltán knows where he is. He's been raking up records of ownership and occupation of all the small western islands. And—he's hired a boat and crew. He's still in Edinburgh, but it's my belief he won't be much longer. He's going to meet Maximilian."

"Do you suppose Max will kill him?"

"He couldn't before. Or didn't bother. Don't you understand this, Saloman? These two have nothing in common except hatred of you! Maximilian knows you're bound to come after him. Even if just for a peaceful life, he's going to have to stake you again. Which he couldn't do then without some powerful allies, and he can't do now without Zoltán at the very least. It's my belief Maximilian's been hiding out on some island for decades, passively gathering the strength of increasing age. I doubt he's looking for trouble, but he'll be ready for it if anyone finds him. If Zoltán finds him. Together, they could bring you down, Saloman."

Saloman stirred at last, rising fluidly to his feet. "So you called me here, far away from my existing power base in Hungary and Romania, where I have the allegiance and the support of all vampires, to face this threat alone?"

Dmitriu blinked. "Forgive me. I thought you might like to find Maximilian for yourself."

Sarcasm was never lost on Saloman, but this didn't even alter his expression. "I know where he is—roughly. Lajos knew and told Karl, who told me. And if Karl told me, it was reasonable to suppose he'd blabber to anyone else he was remotely afraid of, including Zoltán."

Deflated, Dmitriu stared at him until unease as well as irritation spurred him into speech. "You mean I followed the damned thug all the way across Europe for nothing? I've been living in this hole, turning metaphorical somersaults to watch and elude Zoltán at the same time, all for nothing?"

"Oh, I doubt it was for nothing."

"What the hell do you mean by that? And why did you bother coming if you already know everything?"

"I came to deal with Maximilian—and you."

The bottom seemed to drop out of Dmitriu's stomach. He felt sick. Saloman's still figure was clear to him in the darkness. It was the occasional dim flashes from car headlights outside that made his face look sinister.

"Are the hunters here yet?" Saloman inquired.

Fuck and fuck and fuck. "How should I know?"

Dmitriu flew backward into the wall with enough force to blind him with pain. He didn't even know if Saloman had hurled him there with his mind, or if he had moved so quickly that Dmitriu hadn't even seen him. Either way, the Ancient's strength had increased a hundredfold since Bistriţa, and as his brutal fingers closed around Dmitriu's throat, death was a certainty.

"You betrayed me to the hunters," Saloman said, his voice husky enough to reveal his pain.

"I told them you'd been wakened," Dmitriu croaked. "They'd have found out soon enough anyway. I even told them I was petrified to scare them into inactivity. . . ."

"You can't play the informant around me, Dmitriu. There's only one side, and you didn't choose mine."

"I sent you the girl!" He wasn't pleading for his life now, but for understanding, to take away the blackness of his friend's hurt. Every other friend Saloman had had before the staking had betrayed him, and Dmitriu couldn't bear it. He couldn't endure the Ancient's terrible loneliness, even by proxy.

Rage blasted him from Saloman's eyes. "To awaken me for *this?*"

"Forgive me," Dmitriu whispered.

"I will never forgive you."

Dmitriu closed his eyes, not in fear, just to avoid the suffering fury in Saloman's.

"I curse you, with the last beat of your treacherous heart, which is imminent." Saloman's grip tightened. The air seemed to whoosh as the Ancient swooped for his throat. To drain him dry, break his neck, and turn his body and soul to dust. He was of no more account than the bestial fledgling who had tried to molest the Awakener. That hurt. More than death, that hurt. He didn't even care that Saloman would see the blood-tears squeezing from his eyes. They might comfort him in his loneliness.

But it was taking time. No teeth pierced his throat for several heartbeats, until he opened his eyes to the fierce contempt in Saloman's.

"You are nothing," Saloman whispered. "Exist with your pain." He pushed Dmitriu away from him. Dmitriu skidded along the wall and fell to the floor as Saloman strode to the door.

"How did you know?" The words broke from him without permission. He didn't even know if he'd said them aloud.

Saloman paused but didn't turn. "Elizabeth Silk told me. 'Zoltán betrayed you,' she said. Not 'Zoltán tried to kill me' or even 'Zoltán broke your alliance.' 'Betrayed' sounded like *your* understanding. And I'd wondered how the hunters found out about me so fast. Besides"—he curled his lip—"you have their numbers on your phone."

"It's the only way I speak to them," Dmitriu pleaded. "I've done it for years—fed them tidbits in return for a peaceful life. And for amusement, if I'm truthful. I wanted to tell you. . . ."

Saloman walked through the doorway. "Why didn't you?"

"Because I knew you'd kill me." Dmitriu struggled to his feet and followed Saloman into the messy living room. "Are you going?" he added, baffled.

"In this case," said Saloman, "I've decided life is a crueler punishment than death. Good-bye, Dmitriu. Make your own way to hell."

The front door shut noiselessly, leaving Dmitriu staring openmouthed across the dirty, straggling mess of the room. It seemed to mirror what was left of his existence.

Dmitriu wasn't stupid. He knew he'd been banished. A great yawning chasm of emptiness waited to swallow him. He wished Janine would come home so he could feed from her. He needed to get blind drunk.

✝

Striding along the dark, threatening streets of Leith, Saloman's whole body ached with unreleased fury. He wished he'd killed Dmitriu after all, lashed himself for letting the treacherous bastard go. It had been another on-the-spot decision, like not killing Elizabeth Silk. Instead, he'd left both alive to add to the threats surrounding him.

He hadn't expected the hurt to be so strong. Suppressing it for weeks, he thought it was under control, but it wasn't. And he'd wanted to kill Dmitriu so badly it hurt. Like when he'd killed his cousin Luk. That was what had scared him in the end. Decisions over life and death should not be made in the heat of hurt and fury when one couldn't see the consequences. That's what had saved Dmitriu in Bistriţa.

And again now, even though it had long been his plan to kill Dmitriu when they next met, his very rage had held him back, and then he just needed to get out. But the urge to kill was still strong, unquenchable.

When the local human thugs attacked, it was a gift to him. There were four of them, lean, mean wrecks of humans, obviously seeking money to buy the drugs to ruin what was left of their pitiful bodies and not fussy about who got hurt in the process. Hunting in packs, like curs. They rose out of the shadows before he paid them any attention, and jumped on him, knives flashing in the dim lamplight.

He broke the first man's neck and drained him as he died, while seizing another in front of him as a shield. There was a sharp pain where a knife bit, but it was easy to ignore it in the elation of drinking.

Dropping the first body, he bit into the second, spinning in a fast, whirling kick that knocked the remaining attackers to the ground. They should have fled when they had the chance, but something, amazement, curiosity, or sluggish reflexes, seemed to have paralyzed them. One crawled now and ran for it. Saloman let him go—he despised greed—but he caught the fourth man and drank him dry too. It made a sour dessert. And it would take all the power of his Ancient blood to combat whatever poisonous substances flowed in their veins. Nevertheless, it assuaged most of his ill humors at once.

Dropping the fourth man on top of his dead comrades, Saloman spared a glance at the carnage. His lip quirked. "Call it 'hello,' Zoltán," he murmured, "and do your worst."

Flexing his knees, he leapt onto the roof of the nearest building, from where he gazed out over the docks and the Firth of Forth. On the opposite shore stretched Fife, St. Andrews, and Elizabeth Silk.

✝

He had been here before, once, long ago, when it was still called Kilrymont. Macbeth had been king, and by the day's standards, the country had prospered in relative peace. Then he'd had to go south and been called back to Hungary, and affairs in blossoming Scotland went to hell in a handcart. He liked that phrase.

St. Andrews was very different now. Although there were many old buildings, little survived from those early days except the tall tower, which had once been part of the Celtic Culdees' little church and was now overshadowed by its massive neighbor, the rather beautiful cathedral lying in elegant ruins above the shore.

The town was full of young people walking in crowds, some carrying books and bags, some serious, some laughing, some heading homeward or into the many pubs scattered along the main streets.

She was here. He could feel her, like the warmth of the sun, and elation rose above the loneliness of losing Dmitriu. After all, he'd learned to live with the betrayal in Budapest. Dmitriu wasn't the first old friend to have been lost to him in this way. In time, others would become old friends too. Besides, he had no time to wallow. He had plans to make, to finish this, and clear his way to power. Tonight was an indulgence.

He found her on the beach, a wide, sweeping stretch of sand along which a few people strolled with their dogs. A young couple dawdled, arms around each other as they paused for frequent kisses.

Elizabeth stood out because she didn't stroll. She strode in a brisk, determined manner, as if, like him, she was working off excess energy. He halted on the grassy bank that divided the beach from the road, far enough away from her to make it impossible for her to make out more than a blur in the darkness, even if she looked right at him. But with the powerful eyes of a vampire, he could see her clearly, her fragile, beautiful face whipped into high color by the cold. Her loose, tangled hair streamed out behind her, and she held her head into the wind as she marched along. She wore jeans and a woolen jacket.

It was good to see her. He'd missed her presence. He wanted to leap down on the sand in front of her and take her warm little body into his arms, press her close, take her on the beach while the wind lashed them and the waves rushed nearer. It was very, very tempting.

I slept with you to save my life.

But not so tempting that he couldn't fight it. He knew she would side with the hunters in the coming fight. She had to, and he wouldn't make it harder for her. So, as she glanced over, as if sensing his silent, watchful presence, he moved back and, from the rooftops, watched her march up to the street.

Still at a smart pace, she walked along the road, greeting a few of the people she passed. Then she disappeared into one of the many pubs. Saloman perched on the roof and waited for her to emerge, listening for her voice in the throng of laughter and chatter and clinking glasses within.

She didn't say much, but she was at ease, talking with people who were obviously friends. He wondered what it would be like to talk to her under normal circumstances, without the threat of death or seduction hanging over her.

Perhaps normal was overrated.

She stayed for only half an hour before emerging with another woman to whom she said good-bye at the door before continuing her smart walk up the street. At the last building, she put her key in the lock and went inside.

He could look at her home, at her life. He could go inside and sit on her bed as she slept, just as he'd done before. He could drink her sweet blood again, make love to her as she began to wake up.

He could, except his indulgence hour was up. It was time now to find Maximilian before Zoltán did.

He could hire a boat, like Zoltán, to take round Scotland's opposite coast, sailing through the mists of the Western Isles until he found Maximilian's hiding place. If he was close enough, even Maximilian couldn't hide from his senses.

Or he could simply call him.

Maximilian, I'm back.

Chapter Sixteen

*E*lizabeth woke in darkness, her heart pounding. Her breath came in pants, and her whole body sweated. Heat pulsed between her legs.

It had become familiar since her return to Scotland, waking like this, agitated and aroused from the dreams. And this one had been more intense than ever—scarlet blood spilling over white sheets, and her body on fire from the caresses of the beautiful, merciless vampire who held her in thrall. In all the dreams, she knew it was wrong, but she surrendered anyway, because she wanted it, and it felt so good.

Waking was a different matter. With sweat and sexual moisture drying on her skin, it didn't take long for the cold fingers of loneliness and despair to close around her heart. Because she wanted and rejected at the same time, amid a swirl of confused emotions she couldn't fathom and didn't want to. They were already driving her to the verge of insanity.

She propped herself up on her elbow and switched on the bedside lamp. The familiar room sprang to life around her: her replica of a famous medieval tapestry hunting scene on the wall; her books in the secondhand bookcase she'd so lovingly restored; her parents smiling together in the photograph by her bed, taken in the happy days before illness had reared its ugly head.

But instead of comforting her as it usually did, something jolted inside her—a memory, a too-familiar image. This dream had been different from the others. His silk sheets had been there at the beginning, but before she woke, they'd been her plain cotton ones, along with this bed, this room, this flat she'd bought last year with the money inherited from her parents.

She dragged her shaking hand through her hair. Even here was sullied now with her lust and shame, with *him*. She had just about been able to cope with the flashback dreams. Why did she have to dream of his being here too?

There had been bodies on the bed, she remembered, fine trickles of blood dripping from puncture wounds in their throats. She'd been angry, grieving, remonstrating with him for his taking of life, although for some reason the corpses strewn across her bed had seemed a normal occurrence. None of it had mattered, though, when he'd touched her and laid her naked among the blood and the dead—wasn't he dead, anyway?—and made love to her.

She'd tried to remain angry, to keep the grief, but it had gotten lost in the storm of passion as he'd loomed over her, moving on her, in her, bringing her the wild, relentless joy she'd never found with anyone else and never would.

She'd wakened on the edge of orgasm, furious with fate for waking her, and now, in shame, she could only be glad.

But the obscene visions weren't dispelling as they should. The hot, steamy dreams had become familiar to her, welcomed in sleep, if rejected with revulsion when awake. Over the six weeks or so since her return, she'd learned to cope, to thrust them aside, and get on with sleeping and living. But this one lingered because the vision was here, not just in Budapest. No doubt that was inspired by the other night's nearby attack, but for this dream to be of her home was like an invasion, intolerable but insidiously exciting.

The hairs on the back of her neck stood up in the cold night air. She could almost feel Saloman's presence. He'd haunted her last evening as she'd walked on the beach, sat in the pub, prepared for bed. And he was still here, mocking her strength, her ability to fight him on any level.

She slid out of bed and walked to the window, pushing open the curtains. Below her, the street was quiet, with no traffic, no pedestrians, no vampires perched on the roofs.

She padded out of the room, across the square hall to the kitchen, and put the kettle on. It would be dawn soon. She could read in bed for a while, over coffee, then get up and let the day frighten away the nightmares of guilt and lust, loneliness and grief—the nightmares of wanting.

She drew in a ragged breath, gazing out over the sea while the kettle fought its way to a slow boil.

He could be here. Perhaps the vampire attack the other night was somehow related to his presence. A local vampire made suddenly aware of an Awakener in his neighborhood? Or an east European vampire who'd followed Saloman to find her? Were there others here too, just waiting for their moment to kill her? It wasn't beyond the bounds of possibility. And yet it didn't scare her as much as the idea of Saloman's watching her.

She had no way of telling if he regarded her farewell as final or as a challenge. He had no real reason to come here . . . and yet, not for the first time, she wished she'd kept in touch with the vampire hunters, just to be sure.

She'd overreacted there, spoiled some promising friendships. But the truth was, she couldn't live with all that crap over her head all the time. She took her hat off to Mihaela, Konrad, and István and to all the others who fought the shadows in secret without any thanks from the world. But such a life wasn't for her. She preferred books—and people without pointy sticks or fangs.

So live, Elizabeth.

Maybe Joanne was right. Existing in quiet and safety without love, lust, or excitement was mere half life. Being alive didn't mean fighting—or fucking—vampires. Or at least not all the time. It was time to move on, to be aware and watchful, yes, but also to experience life and maybe even love with an attractive man. She'd take Richard up on his invitation, go with him to the sociable Harpers' "Not Halloween" party, and see where it led.

In fact, her last tutorial finished at three o'clock. She had judo at three thirty, but after that, she could head into Edinburgh and buy a new outfit. It was Thursday, late-night opening at the shops.

Pleased at last with this decision, she took her coffee and a collection of second-year essays into her bedroom, and settled down to read.

✝

The skirt and top were a good choice. Since she'd no idea how formal the party was—just that it was to involve absolutely no reference to Halloween—it had been hard to find just the right thing, but in Jenners, she finally bit the bullet and spent far too much money on an outfit that was both casual and elegant.

Satisfied, she walked out into Princes Street and began to make her way through the late-night shopping throng toward the bus station. It was dark, and she felt pleasantly tired after her strenuous day. Judo had been hard work as usual, but exhilarating, even though she had to force her reactions to slow in class now, and practice the movements at home later. It was the same with the fencing lessons. She learned twice a week, and she practiced every day. If vampires ever came looking for her, whether Saloman or anyone else, she'd at least give them a fight.

As if she'd conjured him up with the thought, Zoltán walked past her.

It took a moment to register. She almost didn't realize who it was she'd seen. Then she stopped dead, causing people to bump into her. Apologizing with mechanical, meaningless words, she stared after him. It *was* Zoltán; she was sure of it, even from one glimpse. That shock of fair hair and that brutally handsome face with its annoying trace of smugness were unmistakable. He wore a biker-style leather jacket, but otherwise, he looked exactly as she remembered him when he'd grabbed Mihaela by the throat and reached for her. . . .

He was in a hell of a hurry too, scampering off around the corner in the direction of Leith Walk as if all the fiends of hell were after him. Perhaps that was why he hadn't noticed her.

Stunned, she let herself be swept forward by the crowd and turned up toward the bus station. While her brain was busy with possibilities—what the hell was he doing here, if he wasn't after her, and if he was here, was Saloman?—she went through the motions of checking her bus times and buying the evening newspaper to pass the waiting time.

That was when she began to understand Zoltán's agitation. Word was out.

The newspaper headline screamed, BIZARRE MULTIPLE MUR-

DERS IN LEITH. Three men had died with puncture wounds in the neck from which they had apparently bled to death. The police suspected some depraved, sadistic gangland killing.

Elizabeth suspected no such thing.

As her bus pulled out of the city and headed for the Forth Bridge, her mind began to claw its way out of numb horror.

Whatever the reason for the battle moving here, she had no doubt now that Saloman was involved somewhere, and that sooner or later she would be dragged in. Well, she wouldn't wait for that. She would act now. She was the key, something they both wanted. She could end their particular evil, along with the unendurable churning of her own soul, if she just stopped running and faced her responsibilities along with her demons.

✝

At least in her fury and hurt she hadn't deleted their numbers. As soon as she got home, despite the fierce rumbling of her neglected stomach, she threw off her jacket and sat on the comfortable old sofa, with her phone in her hand and scrolled down the contact list.

Since she'd no idea how any of them felt about her now, she went with Mihaela. Perhaps it would be best if she was transferred to voice mail, so they could get used to the idea of her again.

"Elizabeth?" Mihaela's anxious voice echoed in her ear, as if she were in the same room. "Are you all right? Where are you?"

"I'm fine, and I'm in St. Andrews."

"Listen, Saloman has disappeared from Hungary and Romania. So has Dmitriu—and Zoltán too. We're afraid they're in Scotland—and coming after you."

"I don't think so. A vampire did attack me the other night—I dealt with it—but Zoltán just walked past me on Princes Street and didn't turn a hair. I think he has other things on his mind."

"I think he has too. There've been open killings in Edinburgh, and the news got out before our UK people could cover it up."

"I know. Mihaela, where are you guys? I think you should come over here."

"We're on our way. Our plane leaves in an hour. We'll be with you by morning. Until then, I'll send you the number of our UK operatives. They're probably in St. Andrews already, watching out for you."

Unexpected warmth flooded her. She didn't ask why Mihaela hadn't called before. The answer was obvious. They doubted they'd be welcome. But they were coming, and in the meantime, they'd sent their colleagues to look after her.

"Mihaela?"

"Yes?"

"I *will* help you get him—get all of them. I even think I know how, if there are enough of us."

✝

Saloman approved of the invention of motorboats. Without it, he would have been forced to row through the rain and mist to Maximilian's bolt-hole, and that would have sacrificed some dignity. As it was, he drove the boat right up onto the sandy shore, doing little more than guiding it with one hand, in full view of the still, shadowy figure standing on the beach.

Saloman cut the engine and stepped off the boat. From there, he regarded Maximilian. He had no intention of speaking first.

Even in the darkness and the swirling mist, Maximilian looked pale and gaunt. On the other hand, he didn't look terrified.

He stirred at last. "Saloman, I knew you would come as soon as I felt your awakening."

"Thank you for inviting me."

"Did I? I remember only mentioning where I was. Foolhardy enough. Have you come to kill me?"

Saloman closed the distance between them. "Do you want me to?"

"To be honest, I don't much care."

"Ruling the unruly not as much fun as you expected?"

Maximilian sighed. "If you're anything like you used to be, you'll know every little detail of how I fouled it up and crowned my glory with defeat by a lesser being. I suppose we have that in common."

Saloman inclined his head at the compliment. It wasn't an apology. For what Maximilian had done, no apology was possible.

"You were too young, Max. Not ready." He began to walk along the beach, knowing Maximilian would soon fall into step beside him.

"So who awakened you in the end?" Maximilian asked. His voice sounded unused, awkward. Clearly, he didn't get many visitors.

"A descendant of Tsigana's."

Maximilian twisted his lips. "Power hungry and seductive?"

"Ignorant and naïve." Saloman paused. "And seductive." *And learned. Unexpectedly charming. And passionate . . . and clever enough to save her life.*

After a short silence, he said, "You're not looking well. Is that fear? Or bad diet?"

Maximilian shrugged. "I don't feed much. It doesn't matter. You'll still gain the strength from my blood. As for fear, I don't have any. I've always known you'd turn up in the end to kill me."

"I can be merciful."

"Tell that to Karl and Lajos."

"Weaklings, and unworthy allies for you. But I suppose they supplied the extra strength to hammer the stake right in."

"Don't." Maximilian's eyes closed. He too had had three hundred years to contemplate his act of treachery, and maybe, just maybe, something remained of the strong, just man he'd once been.

Saloman didn't bank on it.

He let the smile play around his lips. "Well. You do still have feelings, even if your ambition is dead. What do you feel about Zoltán?"

"Nothing."

"Don't you want to kill him?"

"I've no intention of going looking for him. But if he turned up here, I might."

"I suspect he will," Saloman murmured. "Turn up here."

Maximilian turned his gaze around to him. "To get me to ally against you?"

"I can see no other reason for him to be in Scotland, especially when he has a pet project at home to enslave humanity."

Maximilian's eyes widened. For a moment he looked as if he was about to say something passionate, but in the end he only shrugged. "That will not be good for humanity."

"No," Saloman agreed.

"I suppose you'll stop him."

"I suppose I will."

Maximilian gazed upward at the clouds and the mist. "He's looking for me. I can sense him. . . ."

"So what will you say, Max? When he comes with offers of whatever you want and the strength of an Ancient *again*?"

Maximilian stopped walking. "How about, 'Fuck off, I hate you both'?"

Saloman laughed.

†

"Elizabeth!"

Elizabeth glanced up in surprise. From the expression in Richard's voice, she gathered it wasn't the first time he'd spoken. She'd come into the department early, her mind and body buzzing with excitement that wouldn't let her concentrate on her work. Instead, sitting at her desk, she stared blindly at the computer screen and grappled with plans for killing vampires. The hunters were here, in the St. Andrews Hotel—she had a text that told her so—and she was meeting them there at lunchtime.

This time she would be bait without distraction. No dancing; no sex—just death and closure and an end to the unendurable emotions that wracked her whenever she thought of him, whenever she dreamed of him. Guilt because she'd awakened him and because she hadn't finished him. Shame for the influence sexual desire had had on her sense of right and wrong. She deserved to suffer as she did, but more than anything in the world, she wanted to be rid of that suffering and to do the right thing at last.

"Richard," she returned, dragging herself back into the real world. "Sorry, I was miles away."

"Lost in your thesis?"

"Sort of." Avoiding the question seemed safest.

"I read what you've done so far." Walking into the room, he dropped the familiar folder on her desk. "I've made a few notes, but on the whole, this is an excellent start. You have some fantastic new material there, and a very fine, if novel, interpretation. If you keep up to that standard, you'll have no difficulty getting the PhD."

There was a glow of pride at that. She greeted it with relief, glad her entire world hadn't become lost in vampire obsession.

"Thanks."

"I'll be interested to see how you resolve the issue of the Saloman legends. You'll have to be careful not to contradict yourself or ignore the evidence."

She swallowed. "I think his name became a symbol for whatever they wanted him to be. A Vlad the Impaler for all ages, if you like. Someone to give them hope, but also to justify, and to blame for, atrocity."

It was the best she could do. She couldn't leave him out. And babbling the truth would lose her any credibility. She wouldn't let him do that to her either.

Richard was nodding. He looked impressed. "Prove it."

"I'll do my best."

"Good girl. So, are you up for Chris's party next weekend?"

She hadn't even told him. She'd bought something to wear to it and hadn't even let him know she was coming. The knowledge brought a surge of deprecating laughter, making her smile brighter than normal, and she was rewarded with a dazzling one in return. A few months ago, it would have turned her knees to jelly and fed all her wildest hopes. Right now, she didn't know what she wanted.

Except for Saloman not to be here, tormenting her by his existence. Then she could live.

✝

A different country, a different hotel, but still the same problem—it felt too familiar, even though she was the one walking into their room, rather than the other way around.

It should have been awkward, considering the way she'd left them in Budapest. Elizabeth had looked forward to getting the first meeting over with for that reason. And certainly no one smiled as she walked through the door. But the three of them rose to their feet. Mihaela came first, solemnly embracing her, and afterward, István and even Konrad kissed her cheek. It was the normal custom of their countries, but it still brought a lump to Elizabeth's throat.

"I'm glad you came," she managed. "I shouldn't have left when I did. He's stronger now, isn't he?"

"He's bound to be," said Konrad. "On the other hand, this migration of so many of our powerful vampires is intriguing in itself. There is *something* here for them. Not descendants, apart from you—we've been tracing and warning as many as we could, but you're the only one in Britain. And for the record, Zoltán and Dmitriu had left Hungary before you did. We scoured the whole region for them, but found nothing until they turned up here."

"And now they're ignoring me."

Were they? A vampire had tried to kill her, after all. And what if Saloman had sent her the last dream, just as he sent his words into her head? What if he'd sent *all* of the dreams? Scary thought; yet . . . a part of her actually welcomed the idea.

"I doubt you'll be ignored for long," Konrad said. "They've obviously come here for something else of great value to all of them. . . ."

"I think I know what it is," Elizabeth blurted. "It's what I was

looking into by myself in the library that morning. I knew he—
Saloman—would look for Maximilian."

"Maximilian . . . ," Mihaela repeated, almost in awe.

"Here?" Konrad said, tugging at his lip.

"I never got as far as tracing his movements," Elizabeth muttered. "I got sidetracked. But why else would they both be here?
Paying *me* no attention."

Konrad gave a thin smile. "I'm sure they haven't forgotten your
value."

"Or yours," Elizabeth pointed out.

"Or mine," he allowed. "But I'm not the Awakener. Your blood
is still more important."

"I don't understand how all that works. Is it real? Or just in
their minds?" *And in mine . . . I believe I'm better and faster because I'm the
Awakener, Tsigana's descendant, and so I am?* It wasn't the first time this
possibility had entered her head. But that surge when she'd killed
the vampire had felt very definite.

"Real," István said with conviction. "We've analyzed blood from
vampires both before and after they've killed other vampires—or
even killed particular humans who've killed vampires, and it does
change. What particular quality provides the strength, we don't
know. We're still working on it. Unfortunately, we have no Ancient
blood to test. But we all undergo regular blood tests for the scientists
to try to understand how this phenomenon works."

It was the longest speech Elizabeth had heard him make. The
science of this, not the fight, was what fascinated István.

"So with every vampire you kill, you grow stronger?" she said
in amazement.

"Every vampire of strength," István amended. "Mihaela gained from killing Zoltán's bodyguards, but she'd have gained a lot more if she'd killed Zoltán himself. Fledglings are the easiest to combat, but their death brings little if any gain to the killer."

So she was right. Her attacker hadn't been a fledgling. "It's like some sick computer game."

"Coffee?" said Mihaela, bringing things back to earth.

Elizabeth took the cup and saucer presented to her and perched on the end of the nearest bed. "So it isn't just training," she mused. "All of you are faster and stronger than ordinary folk because of what you've done."

"So are you," said Konrad. "You have greater potential than any of us, even though you haven't yet killed."

Something twisted inside her. She didn't correct him. "Killed" was such an ugly word. And yet what else was there to do with vampires? *Vampires*, for God's sake! Not some daft eastern European legend, but a reality that killed young men on the streets of Leith, whole families in a Romanian farmhouse. Why had she never even asked him about that? She'd been too mesmerized by his beauty and her own perverse desires.

"Then maybe we have a chance," she murmured. "Our strength, the strength of your UK colleagues. I think I can make him come for me, if he thinks Zoltán is about to kill me." She gave a lopsided smile. "It does involve bringing Zoltán and me together. Can we capture him?"

"We have to find him first," Mihaela said. "We passed through Edinburgh on our way here, and even with the powerful detectors, there was no reading. Perhaps he's located Maximilian. We can get our researchers onto that at once."

Konrad, who'd been looking out of the window at the sea,

turned with decision. "There is also the fact that the four of us plus the UK operatives are unlikely to be strong enough now."

Elizabeth frowned. "Against one?"

"Maybe one. Maybe two. We don't know which way Dmitriu will jump. He's gone rogue, left the country without telling us—he was our informant in Transylvania—and now we don't know if he's joined Zoltán against his former friend. We need to find Zoltán, and then . . . we need to consider an alliance."

Elizabeth set her cup down in the saucer with a clank. "Alliance? Between us and *Zoltán*?"

From the shrugs and dropped eyes of the other hunters, it was clear this was something they'd discussed before and weren't happy about.

Mihaela said reluctantly, "It may be the only way. If Saloman is as strong as we think he is, and if he has Dmitriu on his side, then we need Zoltán and any vampires he's recruited in this country. You don't have many," she added with a quick smile at Elizabeth, "and they're not organized by our standards. But they're usually up for a brawl."

Elizabeth said, "He won't have Dmitriu. If he knows about you and Dmitriu, he'll regard it as betrayal." Yet another betrayal, but she wouldn't pity him. It was how his kind behaved. "Dmitriu may be dead."

Konrad opened his mouth as if about to refute it, then changed his mind. "You might be right. This is as much about avenging betrayal as gaining power. He wouldn't forgive Dmitriu. Even if Dmitriu sent you to him in the first place. In any case, we need Zoltán to hem him in, to let us get near him."

"After that," Mihaela said with a trace of anxiety, "the alliance is at an end. It is important that one of us—or all of us—kill Salo-man. If Zoltán does it, it's bad, because in the end, we need him as weak as possible."

Konrad sat down and recapped. "So we find Zoltán, bring him here as if he's threatening Elizabeth, and this will bring Saloman. We need to be prepared, to know Saloman's coming, so it will have to be organized at a location chosen by us. Preferably near a graveyard."

Elizabeth blinked. "To bury us quickly?"

Mihaela laughed.

"Zombies," said Konrad repressively. "Zoltán has the power to summon and control zombies—walking dead with no souls and no will except to obey him."

"It won't be a pretty sight," István warned her. "You'll have to ignore them and concentrate only on him, Saloman. The zombies will help herd him to us."

Elizabeth took in this mind-boggling addition too. They'd mentioned zombies before, way back at the beginning when she hadn't believed a word they said anyhow. They sounded nasty, in-appropriate, and downright dangerous. "Can you really trust Zoltán to that extent?"

"Until Saloman is dead."

"And then what about the damned zombies? Will they turn on us if he tells them to?"

"Yes," Konrad admitted. "But they are easy to neutralize, so long as they don't get a hold of you, and it's my belief Zoltán will lose interest in them once Saloman is dead. Even if we do the kill-ing, he has his enemy removed and the ability to take power back in eastern Europe."

"Wait a minute," Elizabeth pounced. "If zombies are so easy to neutralize, why would they be any use at all against Saloman?"

"Numbers. Also, we believe the Ancients regarded zombies as abominations—they may be the only things that frighten Saloman. They'll distract him from us and let us kill him."

Elizabeth shut her mouth. "It sounds a risky strategy."

"I don't see that we have any option. With or without any succession wars, Saloman is the biggest danger humanity has faced in centuries. If he reaches the height of his powers, all the hunters in the world won't be able to combat him and humanity will be doomed—slaves to murderous, bloodsucking fiends ruled by the whims of this insane Ancient." Konrad paused for his grim words to sink in.

He isn't insane, Elizabeth thought rebelliously. Or was he? Wouldn't that account for his erratic behavior? Where Saloman was concerned, appearances were oh so deceptive....

Konrad spoke again, his voice all the more impressive for being quiet and measured. "Saloman must die. After that, we'll just have to take care of peripheral problems."

†

It struck Elizabeth, as the days went by, that they were going to have to come up with a new plan. This one hinged on finding Zoltán, and so far they hadn't heard a peep from him. Nor had the researchers in Budapest come up with any helpful information about Maximilian's location. They could find no connection to Scotland.

The excitement that had buoyed Elizabeth up and spurred her into action faded over the weekend into a sense of frustration and anticlimax.

She found it difficult to concentrate in the daytime, either on teaching or on her thesis. While her nights were full of hot, disturbing dreams of Saloman—Saloman kissing her; Saloman biting her; Saloman caressing her naked body to blissful, trembling compliance; Saloman making love to her. And worse than her surrender were the dreams of her own seduction of Saloman and the wild triumph with which she rode him to roaring, howling orgasm.

She couldn't suppress the dreams any more than she could suppress her enjoyment of them. All she could do was sneer at herself on waking, and at him if he was sending them, and go back to sleep. She couldn't afford to be weak through lack of rest. It all made for an edgy, difficult life, but fed her now-unshakeable belief that she was doing the right thing at last. Saloman must die—not because of her wicked dreams, but because of who and what he was. And her role was pivotal.

But they couldn't find Zoltán. The UK hunters were scouring the country without success. The concentrated human energy of Elizabeth and Konrad in one small town *should* have drawn the attention of any self-respecting vampire.

On Tuesday evening, Elizabeth closed the lid of her laptop and sat back on the sofa, rubbing her eyes. The hunters were convinced they needed Zoltán to defeat Saloman. And if Saloman were here, near her, wouldn't Zoltán believe the Ancient was killing her at last, and come running? Perhaps they were even looking for each other and failing.

Perhaps, just perhaps she could move things on a little. Perhaps there was another way of summoning Saloman. Her heart beat too fast.

Why shouldn't it work? He spoke in her head; she heard him.

Because of Tsigana, because she'd awakened him, surely she had all sorts of latent abilities that she'd never tried to use, not just as a fighter.

She closed her eyes, tried to relax her body and empty her mind of anxious plans and stress, and thought of him. It wasn't difficult. He swam into her mind like a high-resolution photograph in all his dark, mysterious beauty, enhanced by his unquiet, mesmerizing black eyes. A smile even played about his lips, mocking, appreciative, curious. . . .

Saloman, she thought. *Saloman . . . can you hear me?*

Elizabeth.

The answer came back so quickly that she sat up, gasping, breaking the connection in terror—because it had worked, and because the very sound of his deep, rich voice overwhelmed her with so much unbearable emotion that she had to.

Now her heart thundered. She could do it!

He'd sounded just a little surprised, and *pleased.* God yes, he'd been pleased. Would he come now? Would that bring Zoltán hot on his tail?

Another thought hit her out of the blue like a battering ram.

What if he was here already? Just as he'd been in the Angel before she arrived. The hunters had no instruments that could detect him. Why had none of them considered the possibility before?

Because if he were here, he would have done something.

Someone had killed the three men in Leith—Saloman or Zoltán. Whichever was responsible, they'd been saying hello, come and get me, and circling until they found whatever it was they'd come to Scotland to find. Only then would they get to her, to their inevitable battle that *had* to be fought here.

She might have moved things along. She just hoped it wouldn't bring Saloman without Zoltán.

✝

She woke from the dream, sweating, disoriented, to the sound of her phone's ringing beside the bed. Grabbing it, she switched on the light, registering that it was Konrad.

"He's here."

Her heart, her whole stomach plunged. "Saloman?" she croaked.

"Zoltán."

✝

They'd cornered him among the ruins of St. Andrews castle where he had been feeding off a dazed and probably drunk student.

"He didn't kill him," Konrad said as she joined them. "He swears he didn't kill the three in Edinburgh either."

Hate spiraled and twisted through her. She hadn't wanted it to be Saloman. In spite of everything, part of her wanted him to be civilized, to be what he so palpably wasn't and, in all honesty, what he had never pretended to be.

Zoltán, sitting with deliberate casualness on a broken wall, curled his lip in her direction. "Ah, the Awakener."

"I thought you'd forgotten me."

He didn't get it, of course. He still had no idea that he'd walked past her on Princes Street.

"I must admit, it amuses me. The all-powerful hunters seeking my help."

"You can't deny it will be useful," Konrad said.

"It might be, but not necessary. I have another more powerful ally."

"Dmitriu?" Konrad guessed.

276

"Don't make me laugh. He may be old, but he's weak."

Konrad's lips twitched, as if he were about to contradict that view. But it was not part of his plan to gift Zoltán any information that would provide future advantage. "Who, then?"

Zoltán's deep blue eyes gleamed. "Maximilian."

She was right. The quick grins of the hunters acknowledged it. The vampires *were* here for Maximilian, the "lost" killer who'd taken power from Saloman and in turn had it taken from him by Zoltán. It was Maximilian who'd brought Saloman to Scotland, to complete his revenge, to drink the blood of his last vampire killer. Not Elizabeth—it had never been Elizabeth.

Konrad didn't dispute Zoltán's claim. He just said, "You prefer the alliance of a defeated enemy?"

Elizabeth stirred. "He only defeated Maximilian with a huge conspiracy against him. And Maximilian appeared to have already lost the will to continue." The others looked at her in surprise. She shrugged. It was one of the many things she'd learned in her unauthorized research into Saloman's killers.

It also helped her understand Zoltán's motives—an alliance with Maximilian to defeat Saloman and take back preeminence in eastern Europe. After which Maximilian, who had no interest in that kind of power anymore, would obligingly disappear again, leaving Zoltán in sole control.

"Maximilian was strong then," Zoltán said. "It was an honor to defeat him."

István pinched the bridge of his nose in a familiar gesture of deep thought. "And a vampire who can stay so completely hidden from his brethren for so long is still strong."

"He's not an Ancient," Zoltán allowed, "but he's the next best thing."

So why, if his new ally was so strong, was he hanging around here, still talking to the hunters instead of escaping, or at least baring his fangs?

"You've actually *met* Maximilian?" she asked.

Zoltán cast a contemptuous glance over her and curled his lip. "Of course."

Of course. But nevertheless, he didn't trust Maximilian. Why should he? It seemed unlikely that Maximilian would trust him, whatever the threat of Saloman's coming.

She glanced at the hunters. "A three-way alliance?"

"I have no objections," Konrad said, a little too grandly for the occasion, but Zoltán didn't seem to see anything over-the-top.

He stood, brushing imaginary grains of dirt from his hips. "Very well. You set the trap, and I'll bring you Saloman."

"How?"

Zoltán's smile looked more vicious than pleasant. "With me, Maximilian, and *her*"—he pointed at Elizabeth in an accusing sort of a way—"in the one place? He'll come."

"He'll sense a trap," Elizabeth warned.

"But not the scale of it. I can bring at least four local vampires of reasonable strength." He glanced at Elizabeth. "It would have been five, but apparently one branched out on his own and paid the price."

Grateful for the knowledge, Elizabeth gave a curt nod.

"And Maximilian," continued Zoltán, his smile still unpleasant, "along with my little army, of course."

His zombies. Elizabeth's stomach twisted. It might have been fear, but it felt a lot like distaste.

"And he won't expect us to be on the same side," Konrad said. "We'll have backup too. Local hunters." He was warning Zoltán against betrayal—which was bound to begin anyhow as soon as Saloman was dead. It was going to be hard to keep control of all these threads. . . .

"One thing," Mihaela said. "Like everyone here, I appreciate the need to eliminate Saloman, but we can't, we really can't have a full-scale battle in the middle of town, right under the noses of the inhabitants."

"Outside the town?" Konrad hazarded. "We can find a suitable place."

"Halloween," István blurted, and as they all stared at him in surprise, he added, "It's Halloween on Saturday. Don't you have some kind of celebration?"

"Of course." Elizabeth caught on. "Strange things happening among the ruins with strange beings will be put down to student parties. The locals will stay away, and we can repel the students themselves with some kind of cordon. If they see me, they'll think we're staff and keep their distance. It might work."

"Which ruins?" Konrad sounded quite excited now. "Here?"

"There." Zoltán pointed behind him, and Elizabeth understood.

The cathedral was one of her favorite places, and she was loath to sully it, but before she could object, Konrad said, "Good. It's surrounded by graveyards too."

"Saturday," Zoltán said. "From sundown. Don't be late. He won't be."

Elizabeth glanced over her shoulder, as if she expected him to be there already. But she found only sea and shadow, the distant beating wings of night birds, and the memory of his voice, rushing through the sound of the waves. *Elizabeth.*

✝

He should have killed her in Budapest.

He could kill her now. He had only to leap down from the castle roof and seize her, snap her delicate bones, and drain her in a heartbeat. He pushed his head back hard into the sloping wall behind him, digging his fingers into the stone in his effort to keep still.

He could barely think through this fury, this outrage he knew was ridiculous. His fragile, half-formed hopes lay in defeated ruin.

Saloman had returned to St. Andrews as soon as Zoltán's masked signature grew too close to Elizabeth's. Before he even heard her call, sweet and curiously familiar in his head; strong, yet a little wondering, hesitant, conjuring up her vital image in his mind. As if she missed him, as if she couldn't resist trying out a skill she'd never thought of before this moment; yet as soon as he answered, she vanished, leaving only the echo of her shocked gasp. That too had made him smile, because it was so Elizabeth—so unbelieving of her natural strength that she hadn't truly expected to reach him.

The whole tiny incident was over in a second, but now she could do it, she'd be back. The knowledge had pleased him— then.

He'd followed Zoltán to the ruined castle, which had been no more than a wooden edifice on his first stay here a thousand years ago, and watched him feed from a human male he had retained enough sense not to kill, at least not before the hunters arrived and made Zoltán let the boy go. And then Elizabeth came.

From his place on the castle roof, masked from vampire senses and hidden in the shadows from human sight, Saloman had heard everything, seen everything. He'd even been amused by the hunters' ruse of pretending an alliance in order to use Zoltán as bait for him.

Rejoicing in the sight of Elizabeth, Saloman had isolated the music of her voice among all the others and let it sweep him back into memories of their night together in Budapest, and forward into pleasurable imaginings of the future.

Yet when Zoltán departed, Saloman had been uneasy—no wonder. As Elizabeth and the hunters walked out of the castle grounds too, some of their words drifted up to his powerful ears. Unbelievably, they were taking this alliance with Zoltán seriously. It hadn't been a ruse.

Understanding had thudded into him like a powerful kick in the stomach. He even felt sick.

Fools! Didn't they know about Zoltán's human alliance plan? Were they really willing to risk such enslavement, murder, unimaginable horror, for their own people? Just for the chance to kill the last Ancient?

And whether Elizabeth was aware of Zoltán's plans or not, there was no excuse for her choice.

He couldn't stand the galloping emptiness, and so he'd let the anger in until he'd come to this ludicrous posture, trying to push himself into the wall behind him, just so he didn't drop down in front of her and tear out her throat there and then. He needed a stage for his victory, and this wasn't it.

But he couldn't be still. Releasing the cold stone, he threw himself off the roof in the opposite direction from Elizabeth. He landed on the rocks that dropped down to the beach, and ran. He ran so fast it made him dizzy, all but flying around the rocks before leaping into the town and bounding from rooftop to ruin in a pointless, necessary waste of energy. No one could have seen him, a mere blur of speed. But emotion interfered with his normally sure feet. He began to stumble, slowing, zigzagging, and veering at impossible angles as if drunk—drunk on bitterness, which made him uncharacteristically clumsy. The knowledge pulled him up and forced him to go to ground before he revealed his whereabouts to everyone, human and vampire.

Even so, it took him two attempts to jump through the broken loft window of a tall terraced house, though at least he landed in silence on the bare wooden floor. Blood oozed from glass cuts in his face and hands.

His legs buckled and he gave in, lying down in the corner to absorb his own anger. At least, he called it anger. It felt sour, rancid, and it burned like acid in his mouth, in his veins. Not like the righteous fury that had consumed him in the face of Dmitriu's treachery and had led him to spare the bastard in the end. This was different. It felt as if she were Tsigana all over again.

He lay still, letting emotion grasp him in a powerful, dizzying grip, knowing he had to go with it to release it, to think without passion.

Alliance with the hunters was natural for her. He'd always accepted that. And she'd promised to kill him if their paths ever crossed again. But her call to him earlier tonight had given him hope that she might yet come back to him without persuasion. Her voice had been soft and beautiful in his head, and all the more arousing for being so unexpected; yet it meant nothing, no more than his own upsurge of fierce possessiveness at her simply speaking his name.

The softness and the call, accidental or otherwise, were lies.

He was alone.

His hands opened wide in anguish on either side of his prone body.

He could bear it. He'd borne worse, much worse. He forced himself to relax until, slowly, his fingers lost their rigidity.

It didn't matter. He'd always been alone in reality, whatever the passing companionships of his long life. It had never stopped him, and it never would.

I slept with you only to save my life. Well, in the end, it wouldn't. He'd made too many mistakes already through the bonds of lust. Now she'd allied with another vampire against him—and such a vampire as Zoltán. That, finally, was unforgivable, and her death, inevitable. And this would be no loving death such as he would have given her in Budapest. It would be a killing.

And at the finish, she, along with the hunters and the whole vampire world, would learn that he could not be defeated.

Chapter Seventeen

"Penny for your thoughts," Mihaela said.

Elizabeth, gazing out of her living room window with one hand on her packed bag, jumped at the sound of the hunter's voice and jerked round.

Mihaela was sitting on the floor, sharpening her own and Elizabeth's swords.

Elizabeth said, "I was wondering how you got that thing through airport security."

"No, you weren't."

Elizabeth gave a lopsided smile. "No, I wasn't," she agreed. "I was thinking about the weird directions people's lives take. Two months ago I was a normal person, really enjoying my research challenges and yet vaguely dissatisfied with my uneventful life. And now I'd give anything to get back to that dissatisfying normality."

"That's normal too," Mihaela soothed, "in such circumstances."

"I thought I wanted excitement. . . ." She broke off, banishing the unwanted vision of Saloman from her mind as well as from the tip of her tongue. "I *hate* this turmoil," she muttered.

Mihaela glanced at her more closely. The brown, down-to-earth eyes were uncomfortably perceptive. "You speak of more than fear of tonight's battle."

She did. She had to keep banishing memories of her night in Saloman's arms, of all the feelings he'd aroused in her. She had to keep telling herself those feelings were merely sexual, to force her concentration back to the necessity of eliminating him from the world. And yet the whisper that he wasn't all evil, and the memory of her short-lived happiness, kept intruding, swirling and clawing at her stomach.

It was *so* time to finish this.

She gave a slightly shaky laugh. "I suppose I wonder what might have been." She watched Mihaela's steady hands, patiently honing the blade of her sword, then slowly lifted her eyes to the hunter's focused face. "Do you never imagine a different life from this? A 'normal' one with a steady office job, a husband, kids . . . ?"

"And an expensive car to wash on Sundays?" Mihaela interrupted with a faintly disparaging smile.

"That sort of thing. Don't you ever want them?"

"Doesn't matter. I'm not likely to get them."

"You could give up being a hunter."

"No, I couldn't," Mihaela said. For her, it wasn't even an option. Her voice was far too steadfast for her ever to consider the alternatives. And yet Elizabeth detected a note of sadness too, a hint that maybe, deep inside her—some similar place, perhaps, to the one where Elizabeth suppressed all her emotions about Saloman—Mihaela did crave that "normal" life. But it was a life the hunter would never have, because her work was more important.

With a twinge of guilt, Elizabeth rose restlessly, then walked toward Mihaela and the swords.

"Is it enough?" she asked abruptly. "Are we really strong enough?"

"I think so," Mihaela said calmly. "Zoltán, Maximilian, four medium-strength vampires, an army of zombies, six hunters—including Konrad—and you. Against him—and *possibly* Dmitriu, if he's still walking."

"I think he is. Zoltán would have gloated that he was dead. The older ones know when one of them dies."

Mihaela looked surprised that she knew such a thing—it was something that didn't impinge much on the hunters' daily, often brutal dealings with the undead. "Whatever. The odds are still in our favor. Saloman isn't infallible. He's been defeated before and at the height of his strength. Admittedly by people he trusted, but that's our lesson—be quick, sure, and unhesitating."

Elizabeth nodded. *Just focus on that. One more night, just a few more hours, and it will all be over.* . . . Picking up her own sword from its position beside Mihaela's leg, she touched the razor-sharp blade cautiously with one finger. She'd never be allowed to use it in the fencing club again.

Mihaela said, "He's coming to stop Zoltán's feeding from you. He won't expect an army."

"He'll know you're here, though. He'll sense Konrad as he senses me." They'd been over it before. She was going in circles. "But I know, he won't expect the rest. Still . . . Mihaela? I don't believe Maximilian will come. Zoltán may have found him, but I doubt he's tempted him from his retreat. If he had, he wouldn't have been so eager to accept our alliance."

"We have to take the chance. Can you fight like that?"

Elizabeth glanced down at her full skirt. She had two reasons for wearing the new outfit—to keep up the pretense of being Zoltán's victim; and to show Richard that she truly meant to come to the party later on. Having hesitated for so long as to whether or not going out with Richard was a good idea, she refused to go back on her final decision. There was no point in removing the obstacle to her living and loving, if she then blew it with a possible source of happiness.

"I can fight in anything," she said grimly.

"All right." Mihaela glanced out the window. It was almost dusk. "Five minutes, and then we should go."

"Let's go now—I need to call in on someone on the way."

†

"Elizabeth!" Surprised, Richard opened the door wide by way of invitation. He looked pleasingly rumpled in casual jeans and a T-shirt. Folk music was blaring inside, a musical taste she hadn't been aware of.

His gaze dropped, taking in her appearance, and a gleam of appreciation lit his eyes. It bolstered her confidence, her determination to move on with her life.

"I can't stop," Elizabeth babbled. "Something's come up, so I'll just meet you at the Harpers' as soon as I can."

"Oh." Clearly, it wasn't a situation that he encountered very often. He looked—deflated. "All right, then."

"Sorry to mess you around, Richard—see you later on." *I hope.* Impulsively, she reached up, gave him a quick kiss on the cheek, and ran back down the steps to the street before he could speak. She *would* make this up to him—and to herself. She needed to be rid of Saloman very badly.

"All right?" said Mihaela, trotting to catch up as Elizabeth passed her at a brisk walk.

"It will be. Let's get this over with."

Although the sun hadn't set yet, they'd all learned from the experience at the Angel, and the other hunters were already in the cathedral grounds—the three UK operatives as well as István and Konrad—all standing in a huddle by the east gable arch.

Elizabeth had always liked the ruins best by dusk. She could almost imagine the ghosts of monks gliding along the nave, heads bowed, praying. As the shadows lengthened and vanished into darkness, she could rebuild the walls and turrets in her head, think herself back six hundred years, and let the beauty and peace enfold her.

The hunters said its holiness didn't affect the vampires, because humans had abandoned the church, despoiled and neglected it as Reformation austerity took hold. They said it gave no advantage to good over evil, but Elizabeth thought they were wrong. She loved this place and knew now that it was the right, the only place in which to face him and finish this.

"They have keys," Mihaela murmured, jerking her head toward the British hunters—who seemed to be the proverbial Scotsman, Englishman, and Irishman of a million bad jokes. "Alarms and cameras are turned off, and we can shelter in the museum if we need to."

Elizabeth nodded. "Where is Zoltán?" she asked as Konrad came up.

"Here," said the vampire, so close behind her that she jumped. Zoltán laughed. He wore a real sword quite casually at his belt and on the other side, two sharpened wooden stakes like her own. "That should give him something to think about. I've been unmasked all day. He knows I'm here, with you."

"Then he'll know you want him here. . . ."

Zoltán shrugged. "It doesn't matter. He'll still come."

"And Maximilian?" Mihaela asked.

"Not here yet."

"Can't you sense him?" Konrad demanded.

"Of course not. He's a master of masking. One more thing. I have a condition of my alliance."

Konrad lifted his eyebrows, and Zoltán smiled. "*I* kill Saloman."

"No," said all the hunters together. It sounded like a football crowd.

Zoltán laughed again.

Konrad said, "Only if you meet our condition in return." And the others stared at him with as much outrage as anxiety. It was not, clearly, a condition he was allowed to agree to by all the rules and guidelines of their organization. But then, Elizabeth suspected he had no intention of keeping it anyhow.

"I'm listening," Zoltán said.

"Order your zombies to return to their graves as soon as he's dead."

Elizabeth's stomach twisted. It still seemed terribly wrong to countenance use of the dead in this way. And yet to stop Saloman, they needed every advantage they could find. They needed to be pragmatic. But she was well aware that if Zoltán did kill Saloman, the hunters would stake him straight afterward. No one imagined the mercenary vampires would hang around in loyal outrage.

Zoltán shrugged. "I'll make it part of my summons. We have company."

Four men were strolling through the cathedral from various directions, stepping through arches and climbing over a low, broken wall. They didn't speak to one another or to Zoltán, just nodded distantly, and stood around to await another vampire's enemy whose death they hoped would strengthen them. They were the first native vampires Elizabeth was aware of encountering, and the sight of them, the knowledge of them, sent an odd shiver up her back.

Elizabeth walked a little away from the others and sat down on a stone step, gazing up at St. Rule's ancient tower on her left. A thousand years old, it reached into the night sky like a stark but powerful symbol of stability. She scanned around the magnificent stone walls of the cathedral itself, watching the last of the light fade from its arched, upper windows, and moved on to the single tower and broken arch facing her. It was an iconic image for her, and she was damned if she'd lose it.

I will be strong. Directly or indirectly, I will kill you.

In the distance, she could hear loud hoots of laughter and voices calling. Local children were out "guising," dressed as vampires and ghouls and witches to sing their songs and tell their jokes in return for sweets, cakes, and apples and whatever loose change they could scrounge. And, of course, the students would be around, partying, teasing the kids they encountered, trying in vain to scare one another because at heart none of them believed it was real.

She knew better now.

Removing her backpack, she took out the pouch full of the pointed wooden stakes she'd made over the last couple of weeks, and the sword so efficiently sharpened by Mihaela. She tied the pouch around her waist and weighed the sword in her hand, preparing to commit murder—again.

Konrad sat beside her, gazing with her at the movements of the sword. She waited for him to speak, to clear the air before the battle when they would depend on each other for survival. *Am I really thinking like this? Elizabeth Silk, unworldly academic, avoider of confrontation . . .*

After a few moments, he said, "My secrecy wasn't meant to hurt you. It was to protect you."

"It doesn't matter. Whatever the reason, I overreacted." She lowered the sword and lifted her head higher into the cold air, trying to admire the stars and clear the air without emotion. "It was a difficult time for me. I felt betrayed by everyone. It was stupid, and I shouldn't have stomped off like that."

"No harm done. We have him now."

I hope so. I bloody hope so.

"So," she said, distracting herself, "did you always know about your descent? Is that why you became a hunter?"

He smiled faintly. "Yes, I suppose so. My mother always told me I was special, though I admit in my teenage years I rebelled and elected to believe she was mad. Until I witnessed an attack and was able to do something about it. Although I'd met one or two hunters before, that was my *real* introduction to them. I've been one ever since." She felt his gaze turn to her. "It's something you might consider. Even part-time."

"I was a part-time vampire hunter," she murmured. "I should write a book instead of a thesis, call it fiction. Only it would be rejected as too far-fetched."

She stood up, shivering, and drew her jacket more closely around her. Could she face more of this? She did find pleasure in being asked to join them. The sharpened stake hidden in her sleeve poked out as she bent her arm, and she flicked it back in a practiced sort of way.

"He's here," said Zoltán, and the tense knots in Elizabeth's stomach gave an immediate, violent twist. No, this wasn't for her. Tonight was all about getting rid of all the vampire stuff, fulfilling her responsibilities to eliminate the evil she'd unleashed on the world. And when it was over, when he was dead—for good—and she was free of the churning guilt and shame and lust, she never ever wanted to be reminded of him again.

Zoltán stood beside them, scanning the sky and the ruins, much as she did. "He's unmasked, letting me know—so he's come for a fight."

"Then let's give him one." Konrad signaled behind him to the other hunters before he too rose to his feet.

"Oh, I will. And when he dies, our alliance dies with it."

"You took the words out of my mouth," said Konrad.

Zoltán lifted his arms wide, forcing Elizabeth backward out of his way. He began to incant strange words, neither Hungarian nor Latin, yet containing something of each; he spun as he spoke them to encompass the entire cathedral—and the graveyard that surrounded it.

Oh shite . . .

A hand slipped into hers and gripped tightly. Mihaela. With gratitude, Elizabeth squeezed back and then let go in order to have both hands free when the horror began.

Smug and silent now, Zoltán dropped his arms to his sides. In the distance, someone shouted, and a burst of many-voiced laughter replied. The wind whipped Elizabeth's hair out of her face. The gravestones on her right seemed to tremble in the darkness, the earth to move and undulate. Ahead, under the west gable tower, something stirred beneath the arch, like the figure of a wraith-thin human.

Familiar hysteria surged up, trying to make her laugh at the ridiculous image springing into her mind, of St. Andrew's sacred bones carefully preserved in the museum in the cathedral undercroft—a bit of finger and knee bone, a shard of skull, whatever they were—rising up and trying to march out to Zoltán's command.

She sobered. It was obscene. He shouldn't be able to do this, not in this place. . . .

The back of her neck prickled.

"They're coming," Konrad warned. "But they're not coming for us. Hold firm. They're not our enemy."

A bat screeched, so close she jumped and spun around, staring in the direction of the noise. Something swooped through the darkness from the top of the right-hand tower, diving lower and lower until it seemed to grow into a huge shadow, the quickly solidifying shadow of a man in a long black leather coat. Before the open coat settled around him, she glimpsed the shape of a long sword and scabbard at his thigh.

"Jesus Christ," Mihaela whispered.

Saloman.

✝

Quite an alliance, Saloman thought on his way down. There might even be something for him to do.

Although his sudden movement had disturbed a nearby bat that screeched as he left the turret, only Zoltán picked up his presence at first, spinning to face him and forcing his way through the hunters and other vampires to get a better line of vision.

And Elizabeth, looking incongruously elegant and incredibly beautiful, her eyes huge in her pale, fragile face, stared at him as he landed. The sight of her, holding a modern sword in front of her just as if she knew what to do with it, struck at him, twisting through him like the piercing blow of a stake, but he would not, could not waver.

From all sides, Zoltán's zombie slaves marched inward, cutting off his escape by any route save upward. Skeletons draped in rags, and corpses in various stages of decomposition, complete with consuming parasites. Although he was prepared for it and had known Zoltán would invoke the power, fresh rage filled him that she could countenance this obscenity on top of the rest.

But breaking through the zombies' line, knocking one of them aside until it fell in a tangle of broken, twitching bones, strode another, faster figure—Dmitriu, armed to the teeth.

Ignoring the fresh pain, Saloman flexed his fingers. It would be easier in a battle.

But Dmitriu didn't join his gathering, watchful foes. He came straight to him with no sign of threat or fear and stood in silence beside him.

"What are you doing here?" Saloman inquired, leaving most of his attention still on the zombies and on Zoltán and his cohorts.

"I've come to fight at your side. As I always have."

He could hide the sudden warmth, the pleasure of having a friend to stand beside him—this friend. He could even hide his forgiveness. Foolishness, after all, was not betrayal. "If they don't kill you, I might."

"I know. But I bargain on any ally being better than none. We're alone against too many."

Saloman smiled and drew his sword with a long, satisfying scrape. "You're never alone on All Hallows' Eve."

✝

"His bitch is back," Zoltán sneered.

"Are you planning to fight him or just insult him?" Konrad snapped.

"I plan on letting my zombies exhaust him first."

"What will they do to him?" Elizabeth whispered, staring at

the approaching horror with mingled revulsion, outrage, and pity. One tripped over a stone, fell, and rose with part of its arm missing. It just stomped on toward Saloman.

"Normally, they eat the flesh of the living," Mihaela said dispassionately. "Or try to. In this case, since Saloman is not technically alive, I imagine they'll just hold him. The thing about a zombie's grip is, once it's got a hold, it doesn't let go. And if Zoltán bids them, they'll carry Saloman's limbs and organs so far apart, he really will be dead."

"They give me the willies," said the English hunter. "Thank God they're not coming for us...."

"Do we *know* that?" Elizabeth hissed.

"Oh yes. Zombies can follow only one command at a time, and they're definitely after Saloman."

"Ouch!" Konrad yelped without warning. "What the fu...?"

He kicked one leg in the air, shaking it, and something fell off, a small figure that bounced back up and grinned. It was no more than a foot tall, but it had a lot of teeth.

"It bit me!" Konrad said in disbelief.

"Bloody hell," said the Scottish hunter in awe. "Is that a goblin?"

Before anyone could answer, something rushed through the air at them, insubstantial but roaring fire from its huge mouth.

Someone screamed in Elizabeth's ear. It might have been Elizabeth.

"Defend yourselves!" Konrad roared. "Kill anything you don't immediately recognize as a friend!"

"What the fuck's going on?" István demanded, swiping at some wispy spirit.

"Saloman! The one night of the year when all supernatural

beings have access to this world, and he's bloody using it! They're on his side!"

Something, perhaps another goblin, flew at her face. From sheer instinct, she brought up her fist, and the thing fell like a stone. She could have sworn it groaned before a swarm of others enveloped them, and she had to wrench up her sword, jerk the stake from her sleeve, and use all her speed and all her newly learned skills to survive the vicious creatures who seemed determined to terrorize as well as kill.

It was a weird fight against impossible beings, many of whom just disappeared when hit or stabbed. How did you kill disembodied heads and wisps of smoke and air? Some only roared in her face; others burned or scratched or bit. While she fought them, she was aware of Saloman and Dmitriu pushing and hacking their way through the closing zombie army, drawing inexorably nearer. And even in the middle of that carnage she found herself admiring the way Saloman moved, sure and graceful and brutal. *I'm totally unhinged....*

With every minute, the creatures surrounding them seemed to grow in strength as well as size, while others appeared behind Saloman and Dmitriu. The whole cathedral site swarmed with zombies, vampires, goblins, winged demons, ghosts.... Surely these really were the ghosts of monks charging them now? Fighting monks with insubstantial swords growing more solid by the second...

"Quickly!" Mihaela raged. "We have to do it quickly, remember?"

It was too late for that. The element of surprise went to him.

With a howl, Zoltán leapt high into the air, hacking through a goblin as he rose with the sword he held in his left hand. In his right was the stake he meant to plunge into Saloman's heart. "Charge!" he yelled, and the Scottish vampires all ran or leapt after him. Joining the push forward, the hunters surged with them. One of the Scottish vampires ran fastest, throwing himself at Saloman. In a blur, the attacking vampire flew backward through the air, landing on the ground with a clearly broken neck. He roared in pain, and then lay still. A stake protruded from his heart. As the vampire turned to dust, Zoltán lifted that stake too and ran at Saloman.

But Dmitriu parried him, and then Elizabeth was lost in her own battle, fighting her way through a cloud of creatures and bizarre, solidified ghosts wielding golf clubs, in order to get to Saloman. At some level, she appreciated that she could fight almost without thought, kicking, spinning, punching, stabbing, her movements instinctive and sure. She took blows, but they didn't hold her back. In the novelty of this chaos and horror, her recent training became part of her.

✝

For Saloman, there was no respite. Although he never doubted his ability to win, especially since Dmitriu had joined him, he had hoped for a few moments of peace, an interval, however short, when he could send the zombies back. But there was never an instant from the opening of the fight when either he or Dmitriu wasn't beset by zombies or vampires or hunters—or any combination thereof. And now they all attacked at once.

He may have made a mistake. Perhaps he should have sent them back as soon as they were summoned, but that would have lacked the impact, the opportunity to show his enemies whom they were dealing with—and to create another legend.

Then, abruptly, another presence broke into his occupied senses—behind him.

Do it, Maximilian said, with more anger than he'd said anything on their previous encounter. *Do it now*.

Saloman smiled, then bowed out of the fray, allowing Maximilian to step smoothly in.

✝

Having "killed" or disarmed the already long-dead golfers, Elizabeth tried to catch her breath while scouring the site for Saloman. To her surprise, he had stepped back from the fight. Another vampire fought side by side with Dmitriu, working to split up the hunters, while Saloman himself stood perfectly still, the wind just stirring the hem of his coat and blowing a lock of hair across his cheek as he threw his head back and began to speak.

His strange, incomprehensible words echoed around the walls of the cathedral, bouncing back on her ears, chilling her even as something like awe rose up to choke her. He sounded not just sepulchral but all-powerful, like she'd imagined God would sound when she was a child—like her father, only much louder. The sound reached through every nerve in her body, filling her.

Then she realized the zombies were no longer stomping over their fallen brethren. Their movements sped up to a blur. Running forward or backward, they all traveled outward from the fight like an explosion, blasting out of the cathedral. The fallen bones lifted into the air and rushed with them, whooshing through the night air and disappearing into the shuddering earth.

"We've lost the zombies," Konrad shouted.

"I didn't know he could do that," Zoltán yelled in frustration. "I didn't know *anyone* could do that!"

Saloman laughed. The sound chilled Elizabeth to the bone, filling her with anguish as well as fury. "Ignore everything else!" she cried. "Even Dmitriu! Throw everything at *him*!"

He didn't hold back any longer, running into the fray with a speed no one expected after his recent physical inactivity. A Scottish vampire exploded in a cloud of dust. Saloman seized another as she fought through the cloud of spirits and goblins and sharp-toothed winged creatures to get at him.

István and Mihaela were fighting Dmitriu, trying in vain to disengage in order to fulfill the primary mission to kill Saloman. Protecting the Ancient, Dmitriu kept them occupied, but that still left Zoltán, four hunters, and Elizabeth to surround Saloman.

Another vampire disintegrated. Zoltán and Saloman circled each other in a blur of blows, kicks, and sways like *The Matrix* gone crazy. Konrad and the English hunter ran at Saloman's back.

It's almost over....

The rushing emotion stopped dead as Konrad flew across the ground, felled by Saloman's back heel. Zoltán leapt forward. The English hunter slammed downward with his raised stake and fell like a stone to another, unexpected sword.

Saloman whirled, knocking Zoltán over as he turned to face his rescuer—the tall vampire Elizabeth had first seen before the zombies disappeared.

"Maximilian," Konrad croaked from the ground, picking himself up.

Maximilian. How the hell had that happened? Not only was he *not* with Zoltán, but he was *with* Saloman, whom he'd previously betrayed and staked. What was this? Reparation? Whatever, she had a bad, bad feeling....

For an instant, as if everyone else was held in shock too, the tableau remained unchanged, with Zoltán, half risen, staring upward at the two facing vampires. Then, Saloman inclined his head.

"Don't mention it," said Maximilian, and staked the last Scottish vampire almost casually before turning and walking away.

"Bastard!" Zoltán yelled, staggering to his feet, and Saloman laughed, a great, booming sound that followed him as he seemed to fly through the air at Zoltán. Elizabeth seized a fresh stake from her pouch. She and Konrad both lunged forward to Saloman, but the two vampires were swaying together as if locked in an embrace.

Saloman's head swooped downward. Elizabeth was close enough to see Zoltán's hands squeeze on Saloman's throat before they sprang open as abruptly as a trap. And Zoltán, leader of the Hungarian vampires, turned to dust.

Saloman smiled, redness dripping from his fangs, and with his freed hands, he reached for Konrad.

"No!" Elizabeth yelled, dropping her sword with a clank. "Oh God, no!"

Close enough at last, she plunged the stake, aiming at the middle of Saloman's back. He twisted, deflecting the blow on his turned elbow, but he didn't so much as loosen his grip while he drank Konrad's blood. With a roar of rage, Elizabeth launched herself onto his leather-clad back, clinging there while she thudded the stake between his shoulder blades, tearing the protective leather of his coat, yet never seeming to penetrate his skin.

Of course, she needed help. It had taken three vampires and three humans to push the stake home three centuries ago. Alone, she could achieve no more than mere annoyance. But at least she'd managed that, for with a muttered expletive, he dropped Konrad and spun on his heel to dislodge her.

She fell to the ground. Konrad lay beside her. Fury and anguish such as she'd never known propelled her to her feet once more. But

Saloman was speeding away from her, toward where Mihaela and István still battled Dmitriu. The remaining British vampire hunters fell back before him, running to Konrad. Elizabeth sprinted after Saloman, shouting for the others to follow. There was one more chance. If she could stake him from the front, where the leather coat couldn't interfere, if she got a good angle and used every ounce of force she had, if the others would come and add their weight to hers . . .

But there would be only one chance; of that she was sure.

"Retreat!" Mihaela yelled through her pleas. "Just go, get the hell out! Elizabeth—run! We're done here!"

"I'm not!" She spoke too quietly for anyone but Saloman to hear. She grabbed his arm, tugging with enough strength to have spun most grown men around to face her. Saloman chose to let her, turning on her with a snarl that bared his fangs in the splash of moonlight.

For an instant, his sheer fury held her captive. Time seemed to stop, like a paused video. She'd seen him mocking. She'd seen him kill more casually than most people cracked nuts. But the anger was new to her, and it stunned her because it mirrored her own.

The hunters, obviously assuming she was with them, ran in hectic disorder for the road, carrying the prostrate Englishman and Konrad with them. Dmitriu stood still, gazing toward her and Saloman, and then turned and walked off in the wake of the hunters. Even the ghouls and goblins seemed to know the fight was over, for they were disappearing into the distance, dissolving and fading into the air around her. She paid them no attention.

"You killed him," she raged, the words spilling out with all her guilt and anguish. "You killed Konrad. . . ."

"I wish I had. You were annoying me, like a gnat."

In spite of everything, a tiny ray of light fought its way through her anger. People and vampires had died, the night was lost, but if Konrad lived, then there was still hope. From nowhere she remembered the dusty tome in the hunters' library, *Awakening the Ancients,* and her medieval predecessor who'd believed he had the power to kill an Ancient without any help. He hadn't achieved it, and yet . . . What if he was right? What if it wasn't his power but his execution that had failed?

Her heart beating fast with new excitement, new possibility, Elizabeth faced the Ancient with no leather between them now— his coat still gaped open at the front—and a sharp stake in her right hand. She could do this.

His hands closed around her throat with terrifying strength. She had one chance before he lunged at the speed of light and pierced her vein with his fangs. There would be no added weight to push the stake fully into his heart. But she was the Awakener; the blood of Tsigana flowed in her veins; and she *believed.* One sure blow and her conviction, her sheer hatred, would do the rest. And he'd know why.

Accusations struggled for supremacy, to find a voice to match her fury, for she couldn't go quietly, or let him.

"You betrayed me!" she shouted. *Shit, not that one! Evil, bloodsucking bastard destroying the world for vengeance, that's the one you want. . . .*

His lips curled with ferocious contempt as he jerked her nearer to him. His fingers poised to snap her neck, either before or after he drank from her. "You betrayed me."

One chance. She gathered the power and felt it collect and focus like a rushing stream of water into a bucket. Almost euphoric, she snapped back her arm and thrust the stake with all her strength and hate and belief.

She even stared into his cold, violent black eyes that mirrored his evil soul. She was moving too fast to think, and yet abruptly she wasn't fighting him but her memory of those eyes alight with laughter and passion, with depths she never had and never would plumb.

She cried out in loss and fury—a sound of total desolation that echoed among the ruins—even as her fist flew open, and she let the stake fall harmlessly to the ground. "I *hate* you!"

His eyes narrowed, then widened, never leaving her face. His fingers moved on her throat, whether in a threat or a caress, impossible to tell. "I hate you."

"Bastard." Tears coursed down her face, rose up her throat to choke her. Because all that apparent hate—confused by inconvenient lust, all that churning fear, and all those other unnamable emotions that swamped her—had resolved into one terrible, unwanted truth. She was drowning in it, and still she couldn't even go quietly.

"I slept with you to save my life," she gasped out. "I did!" She squeezed her eyes shut, as if that would hide her tears or her agony. "At first. Partly, maybe. But God help me, I always wanted you, and you made me see . . . you gave me . . . you made me . . ."

She wrenched her eyes open, helpless to make him understand the feelings that tore her apart; yet she needed to say it, just once. His fingers lay still on her throat. He stared down at her, his dark eyes wide and blazing, a frown hovering between what might have denoted disgust or triumph, but looked almost—fearful, as if he was actually afraid of what she would say next—or of what she wouldn't say.

With another gasp, she hurled herself into him, seizing his face between her hands, and stretched up through his suddenly passive fingers to thrust her mouth onto his.

"I love you," she whispered brokenly against his still, stunned lips. "I love you."

And then his fingers were not passive at all. They were all over her neck, and his other hand was tangling in her hair, holding her head steady for the onslaught of his mouth.

She stumbled backward under the force of his kiss, but he followed, sweeping her closer into his arms as passion flared. Mouths and bodies fused, they moved as they kissed, as if dancing, until she felt the cold of stone at her back and opened her eyes.

They stood under the arch between the towers of the east gable, which stood out, stark and beautiful against the moonlit sky. In the distance, students were singing some questionable song; a scream was followed by a burst of childish laughter; and a rush of footsteps ran along the street outside the darkness of the cathedral grounds. Life went on as if none of this had ever been, never was....

"You love me," he whispered. His head lifted. His eyes were still wild, still furious, yet the violence in them had altered with the intentions of his body. He'd been prepared to kill her—again. But he still wanted her. "You love me."

She tried to speak, to explain how impossible it was and how it made no difference, but he silenced her with the force of his mouth, grazing his fangs along her tongue and lips. "There's a time for words and a time for silence. You love me, so love me here."

Since he had her pressed into the stone, his hands sweeping up her thighs under her skirt, his meaning was obvious. She should have been appalled, and yet everything in her leapt to meet his command—everything but her voice, which alone seemed to cling to sanity.

"I can't. Not here, not ever. It breaks my heart. It breaks *me*, Saloman. Saloman...," she whispered as he kissed her again, devastating her. There was no planned seduction about his actions this time. They were spontaneous, like her kiss, and that was totally intoxicating.

Her pouch full of unused wooden stakes fell to the ground.

"You think too much," he said between kisses, fumbling between their bodies for the fastening of his trousers. "Live for the moment."

"Then how do I live for the rest of my life?"

He paused, staring deep into her eyes. She slid her hands down his face to his mouth, caressing along his lips with her fingertips. "Saloman... Saloman..."

"There is no life without love."

"Then I'm dead," she whispered.

"No. Tonight is a gift, as unexpected as it is sweet. Take it, and live."

"And tomorrow?" In anguish and joy, she was kissing him back, because she could do nothing else.

"Tomorrow, I'll go, if you bid me."

She gasped as he pulled aside her panties and his naked erection slid between her thighs, unerringly finding its way to her entrance where it stilled. Impossible choices, impossible emotions. Fury rose again. Almost with frustration, she impaled herself on him.

Her cry was lost in his groan. There was no time to adjust to the size or the urgency of him deep within her, stretching her. He was already moving, thrusting, pushing her hard against the wall. She clung to him, helplessly, as everything in her welcomed him. After the first few stunned moments, she met him halfway, at least as urgent as he, writhing, twisting, reaching with wild determination for the fulfillment she'd craved since Budapest.

"Will you drink my blood?" she gasped.

"If you want me to."

"Will you kill me?"

"I'll never kill you."

"Saloman," she choked.

"Take it," he said harshly. "Take it." And with one more thrust she did, spinning with him into the darkness, where the joy no longer seemed wicked, and only the senses mattered.

Chapter Eighteen

*H*er heart in her mouth, she opened the front door of her flat and let him in. It felt more symbolic than her first kiss, more important than the hot, urgent consummation in the cathedral, because this small place represented all that was Elizabeth Silk— her private self.

As if he knew, he took time to look around him as he stepped inside and brushed past her. There wasn't much to see except a mess in the small, square hall, just a clutter of coats and gloves and shoes, most of which had missed the hall stand.

She walked into the living room, and he followed, scanning the pictures on her walls, the wild seascape, the peaceful garden, the atmospheric antique print of a well-known Scottish castle, and the fun, crooked drawing of a St. Andrews street, done by an artist friend.

He smiled. "Facets of Elizabeth Silk." Confused, she thought ruefully. Like the piles of essays on the sofa and the beginnings of her thesis on the old table among two used coffee cups, a women's magazine, a broken wooden stake, and a chocolate wrapper—and the books that littered the house from obscure historical monographs to the trashiest novels. She was a woman without a clear identity. . . .

"Constantly changing, open to everything. I like that."

She flushed at his flattering interpretation. He walked to the window, looking out over the dark North Sea. She said, "I wanted you to like this house. I don't know why."

He turned. "Thank you." His voice was low and husky, and when he touched her, she melted into his embrace.

She'd texted Mihaela already, to say she was home and would contact her in the morning. She knew that Konrad was weak but alive. Her phone was switched off. The world was shut out. This was her stolen time now, and the theft was incredibly sweet.

Her awkwardness and fearfulness had vanished. While she showered, she heard him putting on music, trying and discarding many disks with the speed of familiarity, until he found a mood to please him—Billie Holiday; loving and poignant. She thought she might cry.

His shadow darkened the shower curtain, and her pulses began to race all over again. Opening it with one stroke, he took her hand and helped her out and into his arms. In silence, he wrapped a towel around her, drying her hair and her body, taking extra-tender care of the bruises and lacerations that littered her flesh from the night's weird battle.

"Don't you have any?" she asked.

"I heal too fast."

She glanced up at his concentrated face and realized she didn't want to blot it all out and forget it. She wanted to understand it, to understand him. "How did you compel Maximilian to fight for you? Or at least," she amended, "to turn up for you?"

"I didn't. I told him my thoughts and Zoltán's, and I let him choose."

"I thought you would kill him."

"I contemplated it. But the thing about Maximilian is, he thinks for himself—always did. He was ambitious and thought he could rule better than I. And of course, he wanted Tsigana. But the reality turned his ambition to ashes. He would have seen very quickly that Tsigana was not worthy of immortality. I think he wished fairly quickly too for a return to my rule. Of course, factions emerged; Zoltán emerged. The desire for newness, for change that had allowed me to be ousted, worked against him too. Zoltán was the face of the new vampirism, brutal, thoughtless, selfish, and Maximilian couldn't stomach it."

Saloman smiled. "When I sensed him, I thought he had come to kill Zoltán. He owed him that, after all."

"He might have come to kill *you* when you were so beleaguered."

"He might have, but he didn't. He came for a look and, perhaps, to make sure I had a chance." Saloman's lip quirked. "Paying a debt, he said."

One of his hands had come to rest under the towel on her naked breast. The other caressed her throat, just over the place where he'd bitten her in Budapest and in Sighesciu.

She glanced up at him. "He was your friend, wasn't he?" That was how they'd trapped him. His lover and his friend.

"Yes. He was my friend. One of only two vampires I've made over the millennia. The other is Dmitriu."

She touched his face, unwilling to add to the pain he didn't reveal but which she sensed anyway. Maximilian and Dmitriu were like his sons. Both had betrayed him in different ways; yet they stood beside him tonight in battle. "Dmitriu tells the hunters things."

"I know."

"I thought if you knew, you'd kill him."

"I nearly did. I nearly killed you too. The trouble with death is"—his lips twisted—"it's so final."

"It wasn't for you."

"It will be one day. But not yet." His mouth closed over hers, and she pressed up into him. He lifted her, carrying her to the bedroom, laying her among the clothes she'd tried and rejected this evening before returning to the skirt and top she'd bought for her date with Richard.

Shit!

Oh well, I'll apologize tomorrow. This is the only time I have for Saloman, for us. . . .

Saloman lay beside her, naked, kissing her breasts with strong, sensual pulls that drove her wild. His mouth glided upward to the hammering pulse at the base of her throat and around to the side of her neck. He sucked the skin into his mouth, and she arched upward, throwing her head back with peculiar bliss and need. His teeth, razor sharp and caressing, grazed her vein.

A little drink, he murmured inside her head. *To have you inside me as I'm inside you . . .*

The words were arousing, covering the pain of his piercing teeth. His heavy thigh moved over her, pinning her down. His hand took hold of her between the legs, and she felt the slow, cold pull of his mouth, heating to burning, relentless pleasure. She clutched him and came as he drank from her.

Somewhere in the torrent of bliss, she was aware of Billie Holiday. *"Hush now, don't explain, you're my joy and pain."* And she wanted to weep, except there was no time, for he loomed over her, entering her body as he licked the pain from her wound, and it all began again.

✝

At some point during the storm of shuddering climax, their mouths had come together, for he separated them slowly afterward, licking along the length of her quivering upper lip.

She swallowed. Desolation trembled on the edge of her fragile, very temporary happiness. "Was that revenge too?"

"It was never about revenge. I wanted Tsigana's blood. And then I wanted you."

"Saloman, go before I break. . . ."

She pushed at his chest, but he remained immovable, inside her and out. "You gave me tonight," he reminded her, "and I want it all."

She gave up and wound her arms around his neck. "So do I," she whispered. "Oh, so do I."

A little later, she rose from the bed and went to the window, parting the closed curtain a chink to see out onto the quiet street. She was in limbo, between the last battle and the next, whatever that would be. Glancing over her shoulder, to where he lay on the bed, his powerful arm across his chest as he watched her, she caught a glimpse of blood on the sheet. She stared at the tiny drop as memory flooded back.

"It's like the dream I had. . . ." There were no corpses, except for the ghosts and horrors in her mind from the recent fight, but Saloman and blood were on her sheets. "Did you send the dreams?"

"No. But they don't surprise me. We had unfinished business, you and I."

As he rose and came to stand beside her, his muscles rippling in his beautiful, pale body, Elizabeth ached. "It's not clear-cut, is it? Good and evil. That's what you meant when you said evil was in the eye of the beholder. We all see it differently." She leaned into his shoulder. "I truly meant to kill you tonight, because it was right. And now . . ." She closed her eyes. "I wonder if it was more than love that stopped me."

As his arm came around her, she opened her eyes and glanced upward into his face. "Are you evil?" she whispered. "Would you really enslave humanity?"

"Enslave is not a nice word."

"It's not a nice action."

"Some forms of slavery are clear and incontrovertible. Like the foulness of raising the soulless, will-less dead. Others are more a matter of perception."

It was so weird to be having this conversation naked in her bedroom, his arm around her waist. But this was their stolen night. Letting her head drop against his shoulder, she inhaled his distinctive yet elusive scent and tried to absorb him through her skin.

"You're playing with words, Saloman. What is it you intend to do?"

"I don't know yet—exactly. But you must admit, the world has gone drastically wrong without me. In the last century alone, two world wars that killed millions, a society gone amok with hatred . . ."

"That's over with," she argued.

"You still have famine and greed. Your world is torn with religious bigotry and hatred, violence, murder, dishonesty; yet you despise vampires for the same acts. . . ."

"No one denies we've made mistakes," Elizabeth retorted, "or pretends the world is perfect. We'll make more mistakes, but they have to be ours."

"Why?"

She lifted her head to stare up at him. "Why what?"

"The earth belongs to me as well as to you. Why should you make all the mistakes when I could make things better?"

"Better for whom? Vampires?"

He inclined his head. "In the short term, yes."

"Vampires kill people. *You* kill people...."

"Rarely. When it is right."

"But *how* can it be right, Saloman? You told me you think differently from us. So why should you judge which of us deserves to live or die?"

"Because I can."

She gripped his shoulder and shook it, but before she could speak, he said, "I see more than humans *or* vampires. You kill each other, both believing you're doing the right thing. You're making judgments too, based on little more than prejudice and misunderstanding. Zoltán would have enslaved as many humans as he could—after I gave him the idea. That *would* have been slavery, rooted in his own violent, bloodthirsty hedonism—an unimaginable nightmare for your people. I can bring justice."

"It's not justice without consent!"

"Consent will come with knowledge."

She didn't know whether to be more fascinated or appalled. It didn't sound like the insane carnage and destruction prophesied by the hunters and no doubt promised by Zoltán, and yet... "You really do want to rule the world, don't you?" There was a catch in her voice.

"I'm good at it."

313

"I won't let you, Saloman."

"I know."

She slid both arms around his waist and laid her head on his chest. She closed her eyes against the pain. "Then after tonight, we're enemies again. It will be over." Ugly words, ugly emotions among this sweetness that she should never have allowed, yet couldn't regret. She felt his lips in her hair, and her throat constricted. If she wept, he'd feel the tears on his chest.

"Make the most of what we have," he said in her ear, and she could have sworn his voice ached as hers did. "There are many hours until morning. But Elizabeth . . ."

She gave in to the insistence of his fingers and lifted her head. His beauty was blurred, but she held on to the tears. He kissed her, his mouth moving over her lips like breath as his words sounded inside her head.

It will never be over.

Epilogue

$\mathscr{I}$ n his New York penthouse apartment, Josh Alexander laid the heavy sword on his living room floor and unwrapped it.

Beside him, his visitor let out a gasp. Josh wasn't surprised. He'd lived with it all his life, and it still got him that way. The sword gleamed, almost glowing in the lamplight. Gold and silver intertwined in the elaborately carved hilt. The blade, unmarked by any signs of deterioration, shone like new—clean, sharp, and lethal. The whole weapon seemed to draw all the apartment's expensively designed lighting to itself, brilliant against the dull, mundane old coat on which it lay.

Sometimes, like now, when he hadn't seen it for a long time, Josh *almost* understood why his father had imagined the sword contained so much power. It was beautiful, stunning, an exquisite, deadly piece of timeless craftsmanship. Age only lent it greater majesty.

Yet tonight, for the first time ever, Josh had to force himself to touch it. It looked strangely . . . alive.

With a deprecating smile, Josh closed his fingers around the cold, carved metal, as he'd done countless times before. The pain hit him instantly, like a jolt of electricity blasting him backward, even as he dropped the sword with a cry of astonished agony.

Dizzy, he fell to his knees, clasping one burned, throbbing hand in the other while his head swirled with horrific visions of the sword—swinging, lunging, hacking, its shining blade dripping with scarlet blood. The hand holding it wasn't his own. Ungloved, it was pale, strong, and sinewy. Blood trickled in elegant rivulets over its knuckles and long, tapered fingers. An unknown man's dark face swam into his vision, young and hard and handsome, with terrible, blazing black eyes and ruthless, unsmiling lips. His thunderous voice echoed in Josh's head, paralyzing him with awe and dread.

I am Saloman. Give me my sword.

Turn the page for a sneak peek at
the next thrilling romance in

MARIE TREANOR's

Awakened by Blood Series,

BLOOD SIN

Available in April 2011

"Seriously," Josh murmured. "Dante's parties are always fun. None of the other stuff really matters. Everyone will be nice."

Which might have been his way of saying that however much Jerri hated her presence, she wouldn't get too nasty. Elizabeth didn't really care. She'd met much nastier creatures than bitchy movie stars. Squaring her shoulders, she concentrated on getting through the evening as pleasantly as possible, and hoped for a few opportunities for friendly tête-à-têtes with Josh. By the time the party ended, she was determined to have convinced him of the danger he faced, and to make him aware of the option of hunter protection.

As they entered the big, impressive drawing room where pre-dinner drinks were being served, Elizabeth's first thought was that it wasn't as bad as she'd expected when Josh first invited her.

There weren't as many people as she'd feared—maybe around twenty. The men all wore formal evening clothes, some traditional black tie, some a bit more individualistic. The women wore formal dresses too, of all lengths and levels of daring. Elizabeth allowed herself a quick sigh of relief that her own gown did indeed suit the occasion. Then she noticed that despite the formality of the attire, the guests themselves didn't seem to be stuffy in the least. Several looked over and smiled. Some actually waved, and one man called out, "Hey, Josh!" from the other side of the room.

And then Dante, standing just inside the doorway with a group of traditionally garbed men, welcomed them with a big smile. An instant later a waiter was before them with a tray of drinks. Elizabeth took a glass of champagne as Dante introduced the men around him. Their names passed right over her, although she smiled and shook hands with each.

"These guys are all expert antiquarians," he explained. "I was telling them about your sword, Josh, and how you'd be glad for them to take a look."

"Sounds like a most interesting piece," one of the men said. "How long has it been in your family?"

"Hundreds of years, so I'm told." Josh sipped his champagne. "I'll show you it after dinner if you like. Just don't let the senator convince you I'm prepared to sell it, because I'm not!"

"Whatever the price?" one of the men joked.

"Whatever the price," Josh confirmed.

If it really was Saloman's missing sword, the price was probably higher than they knew. Elizabeth said lightly, "May I see this amazing sword too?"

"Of course," Josh agreed at once. Then he said to the others, "Elizabeth's a historian, so she might well have some valuable knowledge."

"How come you've never tried to find out about it before?" Elizabeth asked, curious.

Josh shrugged. "Never really thought about it because it was always around when I was growing up. Just recently, I've become more . . . intrigued by it. No doubt because of the senator's interest!"

Dante laughed and toasted Josh with his champagne. Over the top of his glass, his piercing blue eyes twinkled, yet Elizabeth caught a hint of hardness there that might have been acquisitiveness or distrust. Possibly the latter, because for the first time since she'd met him, she had the uncomfortable feeling that Josh wasn't telling the entire truth. She began to wonder whether there wasn't more to his relationship with Dante than he'd let on.

Elizabeth let her gaze wander away from the antiquarians and around to the other guests, who all looked to be in good spirits. She spotted Jerri Cusack, stunningly glamorous in a risqué white dress, laughing up at a tall black-haired man—with his back to Elizabeth—whose arm Jerri playfully shook. The woman on his other side didn't seem very pleased, judging by her rigid body language, although she kept smiling

"Actually," one of the antiquarians was saying, "my interest began with the paranormal and paranormal artifacts, and it was from there that I moved on to more general antiques."

Elizabeth's attention swung back to the speaker, whose name she thought was Bill.

"What in the world," she asked, "are paranormal artifacts? Sharpened sticks for staking vampires?" Or a cloak that had once belonged to the most powerful vampire ever to have walked the earth—or the sword belonging to that same vampire.

What a coincidence, she thought with a sudden chill, that one of Dante's antiquarians was interested in the paranormal. If Josh's sword really was Saloman's, would Bill recognize it for what it was?

Although a ripple of laughter had greeted her words, Bill's response was immediate. "Hardly! Merely objects imbued with supernatural powers," he stated.

"*Are* there such things?" That was Josh, taking the words out of her mouth.

Dante laughed. "The star of two *Psychics* movies needs to ask that?"

"You know perfectly well *Psychics* is complete bunkum," Josh said dryly. "However much fun it is."

"But certainly there are such things," Bill said. He smiled thinly. "I *have* come across one or two objects with magical properties."

"Yes, but what did they *do*?" Elizabeth asked, keen to get to the point.

"Well—"

"Josh! Darling!" interrupted a gushing voice. An instant later Jerri Cusack embraced Josh and everyone fell back to give her room. Her movements were all quick and dramatic, and she seemed to have released him almost before she'd grabbed him, reaching behind her in high excitement to exclaim, "I've just *got* to introduce you to Adam Simon!"

The name alone would have made Elizabeth turn in the direction of Jerri's grasping hand, but the speed of Josh's spin to meet the man interested her far more. She stepped aside to get a better view, and almost dropped her glass.

The man walked toward Elizabeth, his black hair flowing loose over his shoulders. Alone of the men present, he wore no dinner jacket, just a black shirt that might have been velvet or crushed silk, with a matching tie that looked more like a cravat. He moved with all the grace and threat of a panther.

All this she absorbed in the first instant before his beauty blinded her, as it had always done. Yet it never entered her head to doubt her own sanity, or even to wonder whether her recognition was faulty. His mask had fallen.

He gazed only at her. She took a step toward him without meaning to and he smiled, the rare, full smile that haunted her dreams. Shock overwhelmed the emotions struggling for release.

Then joy broke through like a tide, propelling her forward and into his arms, her face already raised for his kiss. Amber flames danced in his black eyes, burning her with love and need. His mouth no longer smiled as it covered hers.

Elizabeth, he said telepathically. *Elizabeth*.

Saloman.

It was an instant, a very small instant of bliss. The powerful arms she'd never thought to feel again closed around her while his mouth—his incredible, wonderful mouth—moved over hers with tenderness, accepting all her need and all the uncomplicated happiness of her kiss.

But it wasn't uncomplicated. And they weren't alone. A fact which Saloman, clearly, had never lost sight of for a moment. Even as she gasped into his mouth, trying to force herself to draw back, to ask questions that had only half formed in her brain, he was already releasing her. Her stunned lips felt cold, her body rebellious as his arms fell away. The tips of his fingers trailed over her naked back and lingered, though, so she stood in the circle of his arm, being inexorably turned as if to be shown off to friends.

She shivered, desperately reaching for what dignity or even

sense she could muster. They were being watched by several people with varying degrees of surprise, interest, and disapproval.

As if from very far away, Josh's voice said, "I didn't realize you two were acquainted."

"Neither did I!" Elizabeth hoped she didn't sound as hysterical as she felt.

"We met in Eastern Europe," Saloman said, and, God yes, his voice still sounded the same. A little more modern in its intonation, perhaps, but it still reached right inside her, turning her outside in. "I expect Elizabeth remembers the Hungarian form of my name."

"Oh, yes," Elizabeth agreed, fighting the urge to laugh.

"What would that be?" Jerri asked eagerly.

"You couldn't pronounce it," Saloman said blandly.

Elizabeth, who, incredibly enough, was still clutching her champagne glass, hoped she'd spilled some of its contents over his mocking, arrogant person. Lifting it to her lips with fingers she prayed didn't shake too visibly, she took a sizable gulp and tried to think.

What the hell was he doing here? And why was he posing as Adam Simon? Shit, what had he done with the real businessman? Was he after Dante?

No, you blind, blithering fool! He's after Josh! Josh, whom you came here to protect, remember? To warn him against this very vampire? Well, Silk, now's your moment!

ABOUT THE AUTHOR

Marie Treanor lives in Scotland with her husband and three children. She has been writing stories since childhood and considers herself very privileged to continue writing as a professional career. She has published more than two dozen e-books, including *Killing Joe*, an e-book bestseller. In *Blood on Silk* she is delighted to be able to bring together her long-standing loves of vampire stories, romance, and gothic fantasy. To find out more, please visit www.MarieTreanor.com.